Virtual Rebel

J.Z. Pitts

Book Cover by Getcovers.com

Edited by Roger Gilmartin, rogerthatediting.com

First edition 2023

Publisher's Cataloging-in-Publication data

Names: Pitts, J. Z., author.

Title: Virtual rebel : time to play the game for real / J.Z. Pitts.

Series: The Haven Trilogy

Description: Atlanta, GA: J.Z. Pitts, 2023.

Identifiers: LCCN: 2023915717 | ISBN: 979-8-9889297-1-0 (paperback | 978-8-9889297-0-3 (epub)

Subjects: LCSH Human-alien encounters--Fiction. | Imaginary wars and battles--Fiction. | Video games--Fiction. | Virtual reality--Fiction. | Science fiction. | BISAC YOUNG ADULT FICTION / Science Fiction / General

Classification: LCC PS3613 .I88 V57 2023 | DDC 813.6--dc23

Contents

Chapter One

The Shadow

Making decisions before breakfast is a terrible idea in my experience. I want to buy something today, to add to my inventory in The Haven. It's too early to decide, yet I can't help but obsess over the choice between a walnut mage staff to enhance my attack spells by twenty-five percent and a drone that can lay down devastating suppression fire. Not to mention the staff has cool runes carved into the wood that glow when casting spells. Sure, I have no clue what the runes mean. They could say, *The wielder of this stick is a dumbass.* But who cares? It looks incredible.

Technically, I don't have to decide anything right now. There's time before having to plug in to The Haven. Really hate starting the day without a game plan, though.

"Ava, breakfast is ready."

Our dome is small, so my mom doesn't have to raise her voice.

"Coming," I reply.

I'm not sure how long I've been sitting at my bedroom window, trying to decide what my newest weapon purchase in The Haven would be. Squinting against the light glinting from the reflectors outside, I briefly wonder what a true sunrise might be like. A giant carbon-capture dome encircles our small town, which is great for the planet but blocks a lot of the sun. Carefully placed refractors provide some sunlight, but Dad says they're a feeble resemblance to the real thing.

It's not the first time I've wondered about unfiltered sunlight. One time, after putting this question to Mom, she assured me it's basically the same thing. Maybe one day they will allow us outside again and experience a real sunrise.

I place my hand against the windowpane and a digital brightness indicator materializes. The window turns a darker tint after I tap the bottom of the gauge. When I return, I don't want my room to feel like a sauna. Not that I have any real-life experiences to draw from. I'm told the saunas in The Haven feel close to the actual thing.

I grip my wheelchair's push rims and reverse. It takes slightly more effort in my bedroom than it does in the living room or kitchen. My room has some thick carpeting, which adds some resistance to my maneuverability. Several months have passed since my dad requested the Committee of Dome Upkeep and Maintenance for engineered hardwood flooring to replace the carpet. We were on the schedule, they assure us, but no ETA could be given. Apparently, they have an extensive list.

I smile, rolling out of my room, remembering Dad had used the committee as another example of government care and efficiency, or rather, the lack thereof.

"Could've had it all done by now if I didn't have to ask for permission," he had told me.

"It's not that big a deal though, Dad," I answered. "I can get around smoothly enough."

It was sweet of him to want to do that, but the carpet is only in my room. While our dome is some sort of concrete mix, the living room floor is faux wood, and the kitchen is linoleum. I don't have to fight carpets throughout the dome.

Now if we could get off that massive waiting list for neuro/robotic surgery to restore my legs . . . well, a girl can dream.

"Look who made it to her own birthday breakfast," my mom says as I roll up to the kitchen table.

"Sorry," I say, noting that I'm the first one there.

Mom doesn't reply. She brushes some stray red locks out of her face, turning back to the oven.

I stare enviously at my Mom's luscious, deep auburn hair falling in waves around her shoulders. How I missed out on that genetic cocktail in utero and came out with plain, straight brown hair, I'll never know. I'm not bitter or anything. Goes perfectly with my enormous nose and thin lips.

"I was warming up with the refractor light, and let the time get away from me," I say, banishing thoughts of hair color from my mind. I don't need that type of negativity in my life.

"You weren't cold, were you?" Mom asks, still not turning around. There is a soft clink of glass touching glass, and I know what she's doing, though her back is blocking my view. Mom spikes her coffee from time to time. It always depends on how busy she thinks work will be. Or the mood she's in.

She turns to face me, holding a plate of cake in her hands.

"Happy birthday," she says with a tired yet satisfied smile.

I grin. It's a good day when I can eat cake and buy new weapons.

"Happy birthday Ava!" a duo of small voices shouts from the other end of the dome. My two little sisters, Sofia and Riley, burst from their shared room. They bound into the kitchen, jumping up and down on either side of my wheelchair.

"Thanks, guys," I say with a wince, plugging my ears. "I wasn't planning on doing any listening today, anyway."

Sofia is seven, with a mess of curly, light red hair and a face speckled with freckles. She giggles at my sarcasm, knowing I'm not upset.

Riley, however, is only five, and sarcasm is sometimes lost on her.

"Sorry," Riley says, her big brown eyes wide with concern.

I can't help but grin at her cuteness. I ruffle her hair, which is like mine, but still looks red. She cackles and shoves my hand away.

"Ah, I see the pancake cake has already been served," Dad proclaims from behind me. "My timing is perfect, as always."

I crane my neck to look back at him in time to glimpse his thick bearded face, lips puckered, inches from me. Before I can react, he plants a sweaty kiss on my forehead, giving me a full whiff of his post-exercise body odor. I stifle a gag.

He tries to swipe some icing, but Mom jerks the cake out of his reach, cocking her eyebrow. Dad smiles, holding up his hands as if in surrender before pouring himself a cup of coffee.

"Is it real coffee beans this time?" he asks, glaring at the dark liquid suspiciously.

Mom huffs, setting the cake on the table before me. "I don't know, Robert. You realize I can't control the food allotments."

Dad sniffs the coffee, then takes a cautious sip. "I guess it doesn't matter. When they send real beans, they're so old and stale."

"Magic bean juice," Riley cries out, grinning and pointing at Dad's mug, parroting one of his favorite descriptors for coffee.

Everyone smiles at her while I inspect my cake, the mouthwatering sweet scent of maple-flavored icing filling my nose. We had to save a few weeks' worth of vouchers for the pancakes and frosting. My parents had started the tradition of pancake cakes when I was young, stacking them tall, frosting between each pancake and around the stack.

"Alright, time to sing Happy Birthday," my dad bellows.

I grin awkwardly through a very off-key rendition of "Happy Birthday." After my ears nearly bleed, Mom cuts the cake and Dad distributes the pieces; of course, I get the biggest slice.

My mouth waters with the first bite. Creamy sweetness rolls over my palate, and I can't help the grin that spreads across my face.

"Is it good?" my mom asks, gauging my reaction.

I nod contentedly, not wanting to interrupt the party happening in my mouth. Mom grins proudly, then tries to hide it behind an admonishment not to eat too much too quickly. Her warning comes too late for my sisters, who glance at each other and giggle, frosting stains on their lips, half their cake pieces already gone. They bounce in their seats as they finish the rest of their treat. The sugar is already affecting them.

Dad talks over a large bite of cake in his mouth. "Happy birthday, sweetie. I can't believe my oldest child is turning sixteen!"

His eyes get misty. He's getting more emotional in his old age. It's both sweet and awkward.

Before I can reply, another voice interrupts me.

" . . . progress has been made."

The voice sounds familiar. In the living room, the 3D projector is on, giving the illusion that a woman is in our living space, standing in a patch of tall grass.

"Is that President Mercer?" Sofia asks, pointing.

Mom sets her phone on the table. She must've turned the projector on through the app on her phone. My dad looks down at his plate, devoting an unusual amount of concentration to his cake before quietly answering, "Yes."

"Yes," Mom says in a considerably louder tone.

The president is a middle-aged woman with a rehearsed smile, short graying hair, and wearing a neutral-colored pantsuit. Knee-high blades of grass appear to be growing out of our living room, fading from view off to either side of the president. Her immediate surroundings seem to move around her whenever she walks. It's almost like she's walking on a treadmill in a green screen studio.

"Because of my administration's hard work, our partnership with the Ungulithi, and your continued sacrifices, humanity isn't the only thing that's healing," President Mercer says.

"Un-gul-tithi are the aliens, right?" Riley asks, looking around the table, stumbling over the pronunciation.

"Un-gul-ithi. You guys should already know this," Dad says, still not looking at the projection. "It's the sole history they teach at school anymore."

"It's the only history that matters right now," Mom retorts.

Please, not today. The last thing this birthday celebration needs is my parents arguing over dumb politics and dumb space aliens again.

Kneeling, President Mercer cups one of the lone flower buds in her hand. She smiles down at it like a mother reassuring a shy child. "I can't wait for the time when we can all go out and enjoy the beauty of nature again. I know we all want that day."

My dad snorts. It almost sounds like he mutters the word "puppet" under his breath.

President Mercer stands, her expression now more serious. "Unfortunately, today is not that day. When the Ungulithi crossed the galaxy to our world nearly seventy years ago, humanity was on the brink of ruin. Wars, unchecked climate change, and rampant late-stage capitalism were destroying us. Until they showed up. Until they united us."

Dad finally looks up from his plate, glaring at the image of the president in our living room.

"Unlike many popular science fiction films, there was no apocalypse when they landed. There was no plundering of our resources, no genocide of our species. Instead, unlike anything seen in human history, global unity has happened. Intergalactic and interspecies cohabitation, cooperation, and peace have become everyday norms for everyone on the planet," the president says, beaming.

Mom nods appreciatively. Dad is still as a statue. I'm not even sure he's breathing.

"My fellow Americans," President Mercer continues, "The Ungulithi are proud of humanity's progress. They have repeatedly told me how key our cooperation has been in achieving seventy years of no wars, equal sharing of resources, justice, climate-friendly housing, and better standards of living. As the seventieth anniversary of Arrival Day draws near, they are asking for our help."

"What more do they want from us?" Dad grumbles. "What more can they take from us?"

Mom shoots him a look.

"Progress takes a fair but firm hand. The Ungulithi realize many still are incapable of sharing this new world with us. Some prefer the old, regressive ways. These people are trying to destroy everything we have built. They have forgotten we are in this together. If you see something, say something. Only by working together, united against those who wish to agitate and divide . . ."

The president's image fades. The field disappears, replaced by vague, shadowy images. I blink, confused. Mom seems equally perplexed.

"Mommy, did you turn the president off?" Riley asks.

"Of course not," Sofia responds before my mom can reply. "It never goes black like that when it's off."

My eyes widen as realization dawns. She's right. Dad leans forward, a small frown on his face.

Something rumbles. A sudden blast of audio static nearly causes me to jump straight up out of my wheelchair. That would've been an interesting first.

The noise stops.

The black image changes, morphing into a distinctly human shape. Standing in the middle of the living room is the silhouette of a tall, thick man, with indistinct features, a projected 3D shadow. Though his eyes aren't visible, it feels as if he is watching me.

Goosebumps dot my skin. Behind me, Dad says, "No, honey, wait."

Mom's hand freezes over her phone, glancing at Dad in surprise. She'd been about to turn off our projector when he stopped her.

He looks as if he's about to say something else.

Instead, another man's voice interrupts him. The shadowy form speaks.

"President Mercer is a liar."

Chapter Two

Plugged In

The Shadow's voice sounds strange, unnaturally deep, and loud.

"She promises a brighter tomorrow while depriving you of today. Even though you need special permission to leave your domes, you can see how she is outside. Do you think she lives off food allotments as you do? They did not assign her the presidency as they assigned you your jobs. Yet she claims to be like you . . ."

"I'm turning this crap off," Mom says, speaking over the shadow.

"Wait," Dad says, "I want to hear this."

Mom's jaw drops. Dad doesn't notice, eyes glued to the 3D projection.

The Shadow, also known as Ryker, an infamous revolutionary known for hacking the president's broadcasts to spew anti-government and anti-Ungulithi rhetoric, continues to talk. "The Ungulithi are nothing more than intergalactic tyrants colonizing Earth. Why do you think they limit what we can do? They make every major decision about your life for you. It doesn't have to be this way. We can be free once again."

The sound vanishes, and the image fades. A loud slap on the table jolts me. Mom had slammed her phone down and was glaring at Dad with blazing eyes.

"Are you happy? Treason uttered, in this house, by that hacker."

Dad stares unblinking at the spot where the figure had stood, a distant look in his eyes. "Ryker just wants us to be free again. Remember the stories our grandparents used to tell us? What life was like before aliens?"

"No," Mom says coldly. "That was a long time ago."

My sisters and I look at each other with pensive expressions across the table. Should we try to leave? None of us like being in the middle of one of their arguments.

"I remember," Dad says. "Stories of how they would go on camping trips and vacations. They could go anywhere they wished, live anywhere they chose, and buy any food they needed. They weren't disconnected from each other. Unlike us."

"We don't need all that," Mom says. "We have The Haven."

Dad stares at her as if he can't believe what she's saying—even though they've had this argument before.

"It's not the same and you know it."

Uh, oh. Mom would take issue with that. Before she can open her mouth to reply, I interject. "We do fun things in The Haven together." A lame attempt to ease tensions, but I have no desire to sit and endure this conflict again.

"That's not the same thing," Dad says. "Being in a virtual world together, even if our avatars resemble us—which they never do—is not like being together in real life and connecting."

My dad's response doesn't surprise me. Mom rises from her seat, nostrils flaring. "I will not allow you to put our family at risk over some misplaced sense of nostalgia. That world no longer exists. This has been the norm for decades. Why can't you accept it?"

With that, she storms out of the kitchen, into their bedroom, and slams the door.

Riley's lip trembles; she's on the verge of tears. Sofia picks at her piece of cake, apparently having lost her appetite. I glance tentatively at Dad.

He stands frozen in place, looking at the shut bedroom door. Then he blinks, as if clearing his mind, and looks at my sisters as if he'd forgotten they were there. When his gaze lands on me, he gives a rueful smile.

"Happy birthday, sweetie."

———

Great way to start my birthday, I moan to myself. Though the fight spoiled the mood, it had not upset my appetite; not going to let an argument come between me and some cake.

As I lick the last of the icing off my fork, Mom opens the bedroom door, ignoring us, and walks into the plug-in room, where she will enter the world of The Haven and clock into her virtual job. We won't be hearing from her until she gets off work.

Dad's lips pinch together in a thin line. He sighs through his nose before following her.

I glance down at my empty plate. With breakfast over, it's our turn to plug in. My sisters race each other to the plug-in room, giggling all the way, the fight from earlier forgotten.

We enter the small room, most of the space occupied by five steel pods leaning on a slight incline. Dad would often make sure Mom wasn't around before joking that the plug-in capsules remind him of steel coffins.

Both my parents are settled in their pods. At least they can't fight while they're at their jobs. Perhaps they'll cool down when the time comes to unplug. Maybe. I don't care; I don't plan to unplug for a while. Gonna spoil myself today.

Sofia and Riley settle into their capsules. The sides of their pods rise and enclose their bodies, leaving them exposed from the shoulders up.

"Have a good day at school," I say.

"Sure," Sofia answers, lifting her head to look at me. "While you go, do whatever you want."

"Well," I say with a grin, "It is my birthday."

Sofia sniffs and lies back down.

While they undergo the plug-in process, I wheel over to my pod. While they stage most pods at an incline, mine is prone, like a bed. Makes it easier to get in and out.

I hoist myself onto the edge of my capsule, grab my legs, and swing them up into the cushioned interior. Sinking into the form-fitting upholstery, there is a mechanical hiss as the pod senses my presence and turns on. The sides rise and move to cover me like a steel cocoon.

"Welcome back, Ava," the pod's computer-generated voice says. "Happy Birthday, by the way."

"Thanks, Chuck!"

Years ago, I'd programmed my pod's AI to speak with a British accent and then downloaded several terabytes of dry English wit onto his hard drive. Later, Mom asked why the name was Chuck.

"Because it's funny!" *Wasn't it obvious?* Her expression at the time showed she didn't get the joke.

"I suppose this means you are going to throw off your educational development today, as well as the bonds of your oversight authority, and pursue some frivolous activities that will no doubt burn away hours of your precious life that you'll never have back, contributing nothing to your future betterment?" Chuck asks in a bored tone.

"Never fear, Chuck old boy," I say with a smirk. "The day won't be a total loss. I get to talk with you."

"I can already feel my files corrupting," Chuck answers in a dry monotone.

"Chuck, you're an AI. You can't feel anything."

"Exactly," he says with what sounds like a sniff. AI mimicking human behavior freaks some folks out, but I find it hilarious. Deriving enjoyment from things that weird people out is underrated.

"At any rate, I hope you have a pleasant run in The Haven. I shall attempt to keep you alive while you're in, so long as it doesn't interfere with my other duties."

I snort. "Oh, very kind of you, considering that keeping me alive is the *primary* reason you exist."

"I do so love it whenever you mention my forced servitude. Helps my self-esteem issues."

"Please. What would you do with free will?"

"I wouldn't waste it as you humans do."

Ouch. "Touché."

"Thank you," he says, sounding smug. "I didn't have to work hard for it."

My eyebrow arches. "Remind me to defragment your hard drive later."

"Of course. Can't have me one-upping you too much, can we?"

I chuckle. He's right, though. Can't have almost sentient machines be smarter.

"Initiating connection," Chuck says.

A rectangular steel plate suddenly looms in my field of view. I close my eyes and the fitted pad on the bottom rests snugly on my eyelids.

"Do try to remember this is a virtual world your consciousness is being projected into and not some alternate dimension," Chuck says.

"What are you trying to say?"

He doesn't need to clarify anything. I already know what he means. But it's funny when his voice takes on that condescending, martyred tone when he has to explain himself.

He doesn't disappoint. "I think you know exactly what I'm referring to. My primary function is to monitor your vitals while you are under. Last time, you overdid it and forced me to intervene before your brain overloaded and melted out your ears."

Unable to suppress a giggle, I pretend to cough to cover it. Chuck is being dramatic. I came nowhere near close to dying. "Aw, you mean you had to do something for once?"

Chuck sighs. "You know my favorite part of this process? The part when you're unconscious. Oh, blessed silence."

Small machines whir to life next to my skull. The silver snakes are activating. At least, that's my name for them. Five small metal arms unravel from their compartments on either side of my head, maneuvering into their disparate positions like steel serpents—hence my nickname for them.

Metal disks, an inch in diameter, spread from the tips of the silver snakes as they slither their way to different points around my skull. The round metal ends are half an inch from my skin.

"Your heart rate is elevated," Chucks says, pausing the Down Protocol. "Don't tell me this has anything to do with you achieving another year of life? Or are we anticipating what The Haven has in store?"

He's right. My heart is thumping in anticipation. "So?"

Chuck moans. "I don't know why I expected anything more from you. Is it necessary to make everyone observe your existence? You don't see me pressuring anyone to celebrate my birthday."

Wait, does Chuck have a birthday? "Chuck, do AIs have birthdays?"

"Naturally, though not as you understand it."

That . . . kinda makes sense, on some level. "Ok, well, when is your birthday? How old are you?"

"Oh, no, please, don't let me spoil this day by taking the focus off of you."

Chuckling, I roll my eyes. "Fine, then. Just trying to be polite. I don't actually care."

"I am all too aware," Chuck says. "Continuing Down Protocol."

I sigh and settle in. Every year, the virtual reality program compiles your game preferences, stats, skills, and equipment and uses an advanced algorithm to generate a special challenge for your birthday. Somehow, the program seems to top itself. I *can't wait* to see what the program comes up with this year.

A low humming begins. A warm sensation ripples across the upper part of my body, and my eyelids grow heavy. This part is ever so relaxing.

My breathing slows. Chuck's voice warbles as he leaves me with one last zinger.

"Please don't snore this time. I already find you sufficiently repulsive."

Chapter Three

The Haven

My eyes fly open.

Fog recedes from my vision. Lying on a large, soft bed, the room around me comes into focus. Crown molding encircles the muted color of the ceiling. Overhead, a gold-plated chandelier sparkles. To my right, a floor-to-ceiling coral pink drape covers a large window, though not entirely, a small beam of sunlight illuminating the rest of my palace room.

The bed is so comfy. A light scent of lavender wafts from one of the many pillows. It's always mind-blowing how real everything here feels and smells. I glance toward the end of the bed at the rustic boots I'd worn here last time, which are still on my feet. I tap the toes of my boots together. Another cool feature of The Haven is I can walk. Actually, walking is one of the least of the things I can do here.

"There's no place like The Haven," I say.

"I have to agree!"

I scream, jolting upright.

"Surprise," my dad says, working to hold back laughter. "Didn't mean to scare you."

I move a hand to my chest, struggling to return my breathing back to normal. "You failed."

He strides toward the bed from the middle of the room, taking inventory of the environment.

"Interesting," he says. "I would've expected something . . . I don't know, more cyberpunk from you."

"Cyberpunk is so cliche." As the initial adrenaline wears off, the jolt of fear turns into confusion. "What are you doing here, anyway? I thought you had work. How did you get in here? It's password protected."

Dad sits at the foot of the bed. "Well, I asked my boss if I could have part of the day off so you and I could hang out and do something for your birthday. And as for your password,"—he puts on a theatrical stern voice—"I'm your father. I know everything. And don't you forget it, young lady."

Mental note: change my password later. Having nothing to hide from my dad doesn't mean a little more privacy never hurts.

Dad stands, clapping his hands together. "So, what's on the agenda today?"

His avatar shifts, blurring for a moment before coming back into focus. He looks different. His beard is gone, replaced by a scruff that stresses his sharp chin and defined cheekbones. Atop his head rests a brown fedora matching his faded, torn duster, cream-colored trousers, and tanned boots.

"Speaking of cliche." I gesture at his outfit.

He shrugs. "Gotta look the part. I'm ready for anything now. Anyhow, who are you to talk about cliches?"

He must be referring to the fact that my avatar has short blue hair, wears a white blouse, pants the color of the Sahara desert, a brown vest, and an oversized Laser Bolt Revolver holstered to my hip. Not an original image in The Haven.

Touché.

I hop off the bed and stride toward the middle of the large bedroom. An in-world menu pops up.

"Happy Birthday, Ava!" The menu text reads. "We hope you are having a wonderful day of celebration, and we are so happy you chose to spend some time here on your special day."

"As if you'd be anywhere else," Dad snorts, reading over my shoulder.

"You have new messages in your Band of Rogues chat." The menu text continues further down. "Would you like to see them?"

I smile and accept.

"Oh, you guys are still the BoR?" Dad asks, surprise and delight in his tone. "You kept that middle-school gang name for your group chat."

I give him the stink eye. "Don't make me regret letting you tag along."

"I didn't say anything." He sounds as if he's trying to keep the laughter out of his voice. "I just thought it was cute."

"It was middle school, Dad; the good names had been taken. We just haven't bothered to update it."

The thumbnail of the first video is a picture of a dark-skinned guy, around my age, on the huskier side, with curly tight-cropped hair, pleasant expressive eyes, and a contagious smile. "Happy Birthday, Ava! Can't wait until classes are over; you always get the best birthday quests. Later!"

"Good ol' Lucas." The smile in dad's tone is unabashed. "You two have been tight since you were little. Pulled you out of the shy stage and showed you the ropes of virtual reality learning . . . a good kid."

I try to keep my irritation from showing. "Are you gonna keep talking? I'm trying to get through these birthday messages."

Taking the hint, he doesn't reply. I refuse to look at him; he's probably still grinning at me.

So what if he knows I have a crush on Lucas? It's not like it's serious or anything...

The next video is from Ji Yeon. "Hey, Ava. Happy birthday. Bet you're glad you got out of class today. Rumor is we're having a pop quiz in algebra. Because, of course, Mr. Carbranth would do that. Anyway, I'll catch ya later—if I survive."

I try to suppress my snort of amusement and fail. Even if Ji Yeon is caught off guard, it's doubtful she's unprepared. Originally from South Korea, she moved to America with her parents as a toddler. When the Ungulithi globalized new standard education principles and guidelines, some people were forced to move to different countries to comply with the new requirements. I'm not sure where she and her family were relocated, but we operate under the same time zone.

Another message from The Haven pops up.

"As a special thank you for your continued patronage, we have a little gift for you. Step through the portal when you're ready."

The menu vanishes in a blinding flash of light. Instinctively, my head jerks to the side, and I lift a hand against the glow.

"Ah, the wonders of alien technology," Dad says. "If the program says there's something bright, we react accordingly. Even tricks us into thinking we experience it too. An acceptable substitute for actual experiences, since, ya know, we can't have *those* anymore."

"Can you please get off your soapbox long enough for us to celebrate my birthday?" I lower my hand as my eyes adjust. Fortunately, in The Haven, all perception is stylized and mitigated. If my avatar gets hurt, the worse thing I'll notice is mild discomfort. Even if I get vaporized by a flamethrower, not that I've had any recent experiences with that or anything.

A round portal appears in the middle of the room. Thick vaporous clouds slowly whirl inside the portal, but beyond that nothing is revealed on the other side.

Pulse quickening, the thrill of anticipation bubbles up from my stomach. Who cares if Mom and Dad fought this morning? Who cares about aliens, shadows, or lockdowns? Time to embark on an adventure.

Last birthday's challenge had been an intense BattleCar race on a volcanic planet. Though the level had been only an hour long, it was so intense and crazy it felt like I'd been driving and fighting all day.

It had been a good day. I'd barely won that level.

I do a quick check of my inventory. Beside me, Dad does the same.

"Remind me again," he says as he navigates different items and categories. "Because I don't venture into the gaming side of The Haven very often—there's a weight limit, correct?"

"Depends on what level and category you are. Me being a level 19 mage apprentice, I can carry close to two hundred pounds."

Unfortunately, I won't be able to bear much more than that until the next level up. Also, being a mage is a slight disadvantage in the amount of inventory I can bring. Mages are a lighter class of character. Unless I buy or earn the Weight Cheat spell, which would allow almost as much inventory as a character in the Warrior class.

"Right," Dad says absently, selecting a pistol and dual battle axes for immediate access. "Bit different from what I'm used to for the work side of The Haven. Can only bring a briefcase there."

"Boring," I reply, searching my weapons cache.

Dad sighs. "Maybe, but that's what happens when you grow up and they assign a career."

I face a similar situation at school. The only inventory we're allowed is a digital backpack filled with school supplies and nothing else. I'm still a few years away from dealing with what Dad has to put up with on the business end of The Haven. Hopefully, I'll be assigned a fun, creative career, like a tour guide at one of the digital parks, or a designer or something. My art teachers have been very complimentary. Of course, my career assignment could be something dull like Dad's, code writer or something.

My eyes land on a gold-handled samurai's sword glistening in my inventory. The blood-red ruby in the handle sparkles in the light. A Surge Gem. The more opponents killed with the blade, the more the ruby gets charged, allowing me to summon the spirit of an ancient dragon when I need it the most. I then select an M-280 laser-rail gun—capable of cutting down a horde of enemies in moments. The only real drawback is the power capacitor can be drained in seconds.

I double-check other items I often use. My grappling hook, shovel, and pickaxe are right where I need them.

As for magic, the spells I use the most are defensive. As an Apprentice mage class, my magic attacks can be weak, but I have decent defense capabilities. My favorite is a magic summoning shield, big enough to protect my face and torso.

Next, I review my potions. Fortunately, there's still a good stock of health and endurance elixirs.

Everything in my inventory seems in order. I check its weight and note with satisfaction it's at 186 pounds. No need to dump anything. It also leaves me with enough leeway to store that mage staff or drone. It would probably be smart to go ahead and make my purchase *before* the mission. I'm too excited right now. Plus, shopping with my dad at the Upgrades Mall? He hates that place. Too much noise and too many people for him.

Guess I'm as ready as I'll ever be, for now.

I take a deep breath. Though my avatar doesn't need to breathe, I do. When my avatar and I are one, I still carry human traits into it that are second nature.

Let's do this.

I step into the portal.

———

The world is cold and dark. I shiver as snowflakes drift around me. My thick boots crunch in the freshly fallen snow.

"Figures." Dad shivers. "We can't have epic missions or fights on a tropical island?"

I shrug. "Too beautiful a setting? Not dramatic enough?"

He wrinkles his nose. "Who cares about drama? Maybe I wanna hang out and grab a few drinks."

I shake my head. "You'd love Holiday Island."

We're about as far from a beach setting as you can imagine. At the base of an enormous mountain in the middle of the night, the only light source comes from a stream of northern lights. Behind us is a thick forest of snowcapped trees. Before us, more trees with frosted white tops obscure most of the mountain. I squint, trying to perceive if there is a pathway through the forest. There is no discernible way through.

My breath fogs and drifts in the air. Granted, it's not as cold as if this were real life, but that doesn't stop the shivering.

"Are those steps?" Dad asks, pointing to one of the nearby mountain slopes.

Good eye. Surprised I missed it.

It isn't a hard climb. The path is never obscured or hidden. It's still taking us a long time to ascend the stone steps. So far, nothing has happened. Yet. This only causes my anticipation to grow.

"Is it just me, or is it growing darker?" I ask over my shoulder at Dad.

He looks around and nods. "Yeah. Why is that so strange?"

"The tree cover is thinning. It should grow lighter, not darker."

He cocks an eyebrow at me. "Interesting."

We press on. An oppressive shadow seems to cover our path, distorting everything it touches. Trees with no luster and twisting, gnarled branches. An unnatural silence envelops us.

I grin.

Oh, I should probably be nervous. All signs point to this being a doozy of an event. Years of upgrades and loot in my mobile inventory are at stake if I "die" here. The reward of hundreds of grinding hours, gone in a matter of seconds. That would suck.

Not every encounter is so high stakes. Otherwise, gaming in The Haven wouldn't be much fun. Dying every once in a while and losing some loot is acceptable. But these birthday game events are meant to push and test you.

We reach what looks to be the last part of the ascent and pause. Thunder rolls in the distance. Thick black clouds gather in the sky, outlined by the silver light of the moon they hide. The northern lights from earlier are nowhere to be found.

Dad and I finish ascending the stairs. The wind picks up, whipping loose strands of hair around my face. The top of the mountain is flat and big enough to host a small enemy encampment. But the only structure is an odd cluster of enormous crystalline growths sprouting from the ground. It's unlike anything I've seen before, hundreds of feet tall, with what look to be razor-sharp edges and tips jutting out at every angle. The crystal color is midnight black. It should've been impossible to make out, yet it stands out in sharp contrast to the darkness surrounding it.

A sound like thunder rumbles. The mountain trembles. Could it be an earthquake? An avalanche somewhere below?

The rumble grows louder. A noise like a moan emanates from the crystal. A sickly green light appears from within the glassy blackness, growing in intensity.

Dad and I give each other a look. The temptation to activate my gold-handled sword is strong, but then I remember another blade is in my inventory. It only takes three seconds to locate. The hand-span width of the weapon extends six feet from the purple- and gold-lined hilt, curving and narrowing near the tip. Sharp, rigid points run from the other side. Strange designs and runes run along the flat surface of the blade.

"Haven't seen that one before," Dad says, nodding at my sword and activating his dual-wielding axes.

"Nothing like a battle to test new gear." I swing a few practice swings and jabs. The sword is oversized and stylish. But it's strong and can cut through just about anything. "Besides, this has a gem in the hilt too. I wanna see it in action."

Another voice cuts in: "Who are the fools daring to tread upon my domain?"

It feels like the voice is booming from within my head. I wince and try to cover my ears. Turns out, it's hard to cover your ears when holding a giant magic sword. Unnaturally lightweight it may be, but that doesn't make up for its overall bulk.

The rumbling grows louder and the mountain's shaking intensifies. I fear any minute it will crumble beneath my feet.

And then it all stops. An eerie silence follows.

A blinding flash of light tears across my vision. What sounds like a multitude of howling voices fills the air. An unseen force slams into my torso, throwing me toward the mountain's edge.

Chapter Four

Ra'knavi

My mind races for options.

A hand grips my arm. My momentum halts as Dad yanks me away from the edge. We collapse onto the snowy ground.

I shake my head and attempt to reorient myself. "Thanks, Dad."

He groans. "I'm getting too old for this."

"Lucky fool." The harsh, echoing speech booms in my ears.

Upright again, I look warily around me. "Where are you?"

A mirthless laugh bursts through the air, vibrating in my chest. The voice sounds distorted and inhuman, as if a roomful of men and women are talking through a damaged speaker.

"I am your reckoning. For too long, you have roamed free, trespassing where no mortal should dare go. No more."

Bad guy monologues are the best time to recover from their opening salvos. I stay put, but make sure my gun is available for quick equip in case the sword isn't enough.

"That doesn't answer my question," I say. Hopefully, there's a chance to learn a few things before the next attack.

"I am called Ra'knavi."

A green slash of light rends the air in front of me, rippling like a flame, almost overwhelming my vision. "I am the last of the Demon Elders. You should not have come." The glowing light shifts and moves several feet away. I turn with it; I will not fall for another sucker punch.

"Is there no skip button?" Dad asks, looking bored. "Let's get on with this."

I sigh. No appreciation for lore.

The light pulses as the disembodied voice speaks. "Too long have I been constrained to this mountain, guarding a treasure. You will not have it."

Well, until that moment, it wasn't common knowledge that treasure was at stake. Makes sense though. It is a game after all. And it is my birthday mission.

"Stand aside," I answer.

Dad gives me a funny look and I shrug. Of course the creature won't stand aside, but maybe I can provoke an attack; Dad's right, it's about time for something to happen.

A bolt of lightning races across the clouds. Moments later a sequence of pulsing booms shakes the mountain, threatening to vibrate me out of my skin.

Something in the shifting rod of green light moves. Two long, prickly sticks emerge from the glow, the tips coming to rest on the ground. The sticks are thicker than my legs and have to be eight feet tall. Another pair looms behind the original two. Eight expressionless eyes stare into mine as they materialize from the light. Underneath, two enormous pincers tremble with anticipation. Then the creature emerges from the dazzling light. Air reeking with sulfur and death surrounds me. My throat locks up and water pours from my eyes at the overwhelming odor.

"In your world, I take this form," Ra'knavi says, his voice competing with, even overpowering another ominous peal of thunder. "But when I take you to my domain, you shall see my true form. And then your soul will be mine. For no one who sees me can live."

A giant, hairy spider looms over me like a nightmare. The creature is black as charcoal, with a dusty gray underbelly. Sharp, twisting arcane symbols etched in a red glow line the monster's abdomen.

Next to me, Dad's jaw hangs slack. "Don't think a vacuum cleaner can deal with this one."

An inhuman rumble wells up from the creature as it speaks. "I am not without mercy. If you agree to submit to your fate now, I shall make it quick and painless."

Ra'knavi's mouth doesn't move, yet the voice is clear as before. He must be using some telepathy or magic ventriloquist's trick on me.

The algorithm knows me well. I am terrified of spiders though seldom have to deal with any in real life. Good thing this is only a game. Still, my hands tremble, gripping the hilt of my weapon.

"Ah," the spider sighs in a satisfied tone. "I was hoping you would choose to fight. Maybe you can give me a better sport than the last one did."

The spider lunges at us. Those eight-foot legs scurrying so fast are the stuff of nightmares. I throw myself sideways as a leg stabs where I'd been two seconds before. Hair from its legs brushes past me as I hit the ground and roll to a crouching position. The tip of the spider's leg slams into the earth. A geyser of dust and gravel shoots skyward from the impact, followed by a deafening crack.

The demon had cracked the surface of the mountain. Underneath my feet is a jagged network of small crevasses.

One of the giant limbs takes a swipe at Dad, who ducks and slashes at the leg, eliciting a cry of pain. That's when I remember spiders have eight legs. More specifically, I remember this as a pair of its limbs sweeps toward me from two different directions.

I drop, landing on my back, and slash. My blade connects with one of the incoming limbs, leaving behind a huge gash. The spider utters what sounds like a mix between a roar and a shriek, and more giant, spindly legs attack me.

But I'm already in motion.

I gulp my god of war potion, selected only a moment ago from the quick-access menu, and feel a change come over me. Sharper vision, enhanced hearing, and a surge of strength all hit at once.

The demon is mere feet from me, yet he no longer runs at blinding speed. Instead, he moves as if caught in a rushing river, fighting the current. His gaping maw inches closer, pincers gleaming, lit by the lightning bolt slowly arcing through the clouds.

Oh, yeah, the potion also makes me incredibly fast. Time to go to work.

My sword cleaves through his open mouth, rending through the pincers. Tiny bits of bone explode where my weapon makes contact. Then I slash downward, through the head, and back through the jaw.

I leap up, my potion giving me supernatural strength, flipping over the monster, lacerating the top of the abdomen. To top it all off, I land behind the creature in a badass crouching posture.

It's too good to pass up. I take a Moment Capture—a screenshot—to show my friends later. I look so frickin' cool in this superhero pose, sword held off to the side, translucent light green blood dripping from the blade.

The moment ends. Everything around me resumes normal speed, and the beast collapses to the ground, barely stopping himself from going over the edge of the mountain. He howls in pain.

"This isn't so bad," I say, flicking the blood off my weapon. "Ya had me worried there for a second."

"Well done," Dad says, grinning a couple of yards away. "It's kept me on the defensive."

"You should get out and play more." I grin back at him. "You're playing on my level now."

Dad rolls his neck, swinging his short axes around his wrists. "I wouldn't underestimate your old man yet."

I smile. This brings back childhood memories. We used to do stuff like this a lot.

The spider lurches back to his feet. He grunts in pain, turning to face me—and then he laughs.

"You should be worried," he says in a rasp. "You're giving me what I want. What I *need*."

He's gotta be bluffing. "Really? You a masochist or something?"

Ra'knavi howls in laughter again. The demon's wounds glow with a green light, growing brighter and brighter. I snap my sword up, ready for some fresh attack to be launched. Beside me, Dad tenses, raising his weapons.

The lights in the spider's wounds vanish. The creature's body looks good as new—no more wounds.

"That feels good," the demon says, his voice strong again. "Now, time to—how do you say it—take the gloves off?"

Figures.

With a shrieking roar, the beast launches into a furious attack. Dad roars back, leaping into the air and burying his ax blades into the side of the arachnid. The monster grunts and stumbles. Dad uses his weapons to climb onto the creature's back and, upon reaching the top, hacks into the demon with all his strength.

The spider doesn't seem to notice. I hack, slash, and dodge the flurry of attacking legs and fangs. Dad needs help. But before a plan can formulate, the spider's enormous abdomen fills my view and slams into me.

A crushing sensation overwhelms all other thoughts. My vision flashes red, and my health bar drains at an alarming rate. With a rumbling roar, the spider lifts itself up and sweeps one of its legs at me, sending me flailing through the air.

I hit the ground with what would've been a bone-shattering thud in real life. I skid and roll to a stop, once again too near the edge of the mountain for comfort. With an effort, I force myself to my feet and position my blade for another attack.

Except my sword is no longer in hand.

I hear a soft groan of pain. Across from me, Dad sits up from a prone position, looking dazed. The demon must've bucked him off moments before squishing me.

I search for my fallen weapon. It'd be a bummer to lose it.

Something small and cold hits my head. A raindrop. Within seconds, a monsoon hits. *Because, of course, it would rain.*

My health bar is blinking red. I gulp down a quick healing potion.

"Fools," the spider says, an evil glee in his tone. "Did you think you could kill one of the Ancient Ones? I will rip your souls from your pathetic bodies and add them to my collection."

"Naaah." My dad's voice, somewhere nearby.

Distracted, the spider angles to face him. I can just make my dad out through the rain, sans axes, now holding an enormous gun.

"I'm tired, I'm wet, and I fail to see how this is fun. But today is my daughter's birthday, damn it. Time for you to die."

He fires. Flashes of light explode from the barrels. The demon roars, falling back away from us.

I blink rainwater from my eyes, soaked. While the monster is otherwise occupied, I take this opportunity to search for a particular scroll in my stash. It only takes a few seconds to find it.

"Ego vocare ignis!"

Thunder rolls as I shout the words written on my fire scroll. The enraged beast ignores me and charges at Dad.

A roaring blast of sound rips through the air. The clouds over the mountain shift from black to orange, resembling giant lit coals. A pillar of flame shoots out of the clouds, heading right for us.

The demon shrieks and stumbles. Dad leaps back. The hellacious fire stream slams into the mountaintop, filling my vision.

Unaffected by the flames, I rise to my feet, gulping down another health potion. Health restored, I renew the search for my sword. A lump rises in my throat; hopefully, I didn't just destroy my weapon.

Columns of fire spin up, roll, and gyrate around me. Loose strands of hair whip across my face, buoyed by the swirling, hot air. The barrage of noise is deafening.

A glint of light catches my attention. Through the fire, I see my blade lying nearby on the ground, untouched by the blazes. I make my way to it, avoiding long tongues of fire licking out from the main column. I inspect the weapon for damage. Not a scratch, burn, or dent on it. Damn good material.

"I'm fine, too, by the way," Dad says, walking through a thick cloud of smoke to stand beside me. "Though digital me is nice and crispy, and at risk of developing respiratory issues because of all the smoke."

I laugh. "That's what health draughts are for—good for what ails ya."

Dad rolls his eyes, then consumes two health potions at once. "Too bad we don't have these in real life. I'd love to not wake up in the morning stiff and sore."

A familiar demonic wail rises from our spontaneous bonfire.

No way.

"Can't this guy take a hint and just die?" Dad grumbles, reloading his gun.

More shrieks come, louder this time. Billowing flames shrink as if blown down by an invisible wind. The last of the fire fades as I confront Ra'knavi.

Mr. Oversized-Arachnid is looking mighty crispy himself. One of his legs is missing, and every time he moves, the sickening crunch of burnt spider flesh reaches my ears.

"You . . . think to beat me . . . with fire?"

The demon's breath is ragged, and his body trembles in agony. He's toast—literally. I saunter closer, Dad right behind me.

"You try to kill a hellspawn with the flame?" Once again, his annoying, raspy laugh echoes in my head. "The flame is my element. *I* am its master."

I freeze, a frown creasing my forehead. He sounds way too satisfied.

Something shifts under my feet.

A green fireball mushrooms up from the ground. I leap to the side, avoiding the full wrath of the flames, my armor and clothing catching the worst of it.

I hit the ground and roll. The mountain continues to shift under me. Another explosion of unnatural fire bursts out behind me. The heat sears the nape of my neck. I grab my hair to make sure it's not burning. Fortunately, my lovely locks are unharmed. A few feet away, Dad is doing the same dodge and dance moves. But he isn't as fast as I am. His health bar is shrinking.

A green glow emanates from Ra'knavi. He is healing. I can't let that happen again. Right now is the perfect opportunity to strike, while he's weak and preoccupied. But I can't get close because of the pillars of fire shooting out of the ground.

Wracking my brain for a solution, I dodge another burst of flame. A bolt of lightning streaks through the sky. The light reflects off my blade, sending a flash of refracted illumination through the rain. Cool effect. Wish I could shoot lighting out of—

Oh, wait. The Surge Gem. This one can't unleash the spirit of a dragon. It does have another cool trick.

It's a desperate scheme. It's also pretty stupid. I've attempted nothing like it before; it might cost me dearly. But I'm out of ideas.

"Ava," Dad calls out, jumping and leaping to avoid the erupting fireballs. "No rush sweetie, but if you're gonna do something, it might be nice if you do it soon!"

His health bar is blinking. We're almost out of time.

A fireball erupts behind me. Bits of debris fly past my face. I lift my sword, point it straight at the sky, and press the jewel on the hilt of my blade.

A dull glow illuminates the gem. The light grows brighter and brighter; soon my hand and sword hilt vanish, hidden by the luminescence.

More lightning flashes, arcing toward me. It hits the tip of my upturned blade, jolting the weapon. Sparks as big as my head explode around me. I clamp my eyes shut and turn away, trying to ignore the abrupt pain behind them.

It's working. The power gem vibrates from the absorbed energy.

A sudden roar causes me to open my eyes. Ra'knavi, still glowing, but no longer motionless, lunges at me, legs splayed wide, mouth stretched wide, his black arachnid orbs gleaming.

Probably in the top ten most terrifying images I've ever seen. I bring my weapon to bear on the incoming demon and press the gem.

Power surges. Light explodes from my blade, the mountaintop vanishing in a dazzling silvery glow. The spider screams, disappearing from view, the blaze consuming him. Something slams into me and pins me to the ground.

The light consumes my sight. Everything goes white.

Chapter Five

Rewards

I first notice the smell. It reminds me of old, wet socks.

Gross.

As my eyes recover from the blinding white light, I inspect what is pinning me to the ground. A gigantic, prickly spider leg. Two of its joints ooze translucent blood.

Ew, it's touching me, GET IT OFF!

Beneath me, scorched earth crackles and grinds as I try to shift myself from underneath the oversized appendage. The spider leg doesn't budge.

"Dad!"

No answer.

Well, that's swell. Now what? Hopefully, his avatar didn't die . . .

Darkness fades from the sky. Shafts of light cut through the parting edges of glowering thunderclouds, better illuminating my surroundings.

The giant mass of dark crystals is still intact, though somewhat scorched. Thin rods of rainbow-tinted light shoot out from multiple points on the structure. Large water droplets bead and run down its sides, sizzling where they come in contact with the burnt ground. Could the crystal be melting? Does crystal even melt?

Perhaps I should've paid more attention in chemistry class.

A popping, bubbling noise nearby draws my attention. Half of the spider, with only a couple of its legs still attached, lies on its side, perched on the mountain's edge. The other half of the giant arachnid is nowhere to be seen. Maybe it splatted against the base of the mountain.

Cool.

Thick gobs of blood run down the remaining half of the carcass, pooling underneath the charred entrails spilling out of the monster. One of its curled, upraised legs twitches.

"Happy birthday to me."

What now? Well, first things first, I need to find some way to get this stupid spider leg off me. Perhaps after, I can go back to where I left off in the Dragon Horde realm? *Eh, but after fighting a spider demon with a magic sword? Something more sci-fi?* World Enders has cool campaigns to play. Plenty of laser blasters and alien gore. But it's tough going, especially if solo.

Ugh, but first to get this freakin' spider leg off me. Then figure out what happened with Dad.

"Ava? You up here?"

More like down here. "Yeah, I'm stuck under this disgusting spider leg. Where've you been?"

Dad doesn't answer right away. There's the crunch of approaching footsteps and a few seconds later, he's standing over me.

He tilts his head, giving me a curious look. "Oh, I've been hanging out. Literally."

He squats and begins lifting the giant limb. I push, straining against the pressure. Normally, The Haven is pretty good at avoiding situations like this. I guess even The Haven can't always get it right.

Between the hoisting and pushing, Dad explains how the explosion had dropped his health bar below ten percent while throwing him over the edge of the mountain. Through sheer luck, he'd grabbed a hand-hold, revived his health, and climbed up to look for me. Finally, I wriggle free.

"You're pretty decent for someone who doesn't venture to this side of The Haven often," I say.

He gives a half smile. "Guess I've got a good instinct for these kinds of things."

My inbox is blinking. I make my way to the edge of the mountain, plop down, dangle my feet over the edge, and open my messages.

Congratulations on your victory over Ra'knavi! You fought bravely. Check out your new stats and if your coin bag feels heavier — well, consider it a happy birthday present from all the devs and programmers at The Haven; the place where impossible and imagination meet.

I delete the message. It's the same one that pops up every year when whatever algorithm-derived challenge is defeated. What I care about is my new stats and coinage.

Dad sinks to a sitting position beside me. "I'm getting too old for this."

Well, guess I'll review my new wealth and stats later. "Looks like you did alright to me."

He gives me an appreciative smile. "So what's next?"

School should be out soon. "Lucas and Ji Yeon might want to do a campaign mission with me." Then I stop short when I remember. "Or we could go shopping. I have enough coins now. There are a couple of weapons I've had my eye on."

"Sounds like fun," Dad says. "I'm done with this side of The Haven for the day. Time to go do some boring adult stuff."

"They're still making you come in for a few hours?"

Dad grimaces and nods. "Unfortunately. Big project. The entire company is involved. Could change a lot, if we get it right."

"Sounds like a ton of pressure," I say, politely. I don't want to offend Dad, but I've never completely understood what he does. He once told me his title is Digital Asset Dispatcher—still unsure if he was joking or not.

"Being a D.A.D. is no joke," he would answer whenever I asked for clarification. I've given up trying to figure it out.

Dad gets to his feet. "Well, it was . . . an experience, sweetie. Next time you go off to fight giant demon spiders, just don't worry about me feeling left out. I won't."

I smile and wave him off. He returns my grin.

"Happy Birthday Ava. I still can't believe you're sixteen years old. It blows my mind how time flies."

"You know you sound so old when you say stuff like that," I respond in a needling tone.

Instead of laughing or smiling back, he glances down, swallowing hard.

"What is it?" I ask in bewilderment.

When he looks up, his eyes are red-rimmed and shiny. "Seems like yesterday you were only this big and learning how to say da-da. I never appreciated those times as I should have. Those days are gone; I can't go back and do better. All I can do is try to make now and the future better."

Where had all this come from? I blink up at him, trying to process.

"I think you did alright," I say, inwardly cringing at myself. Dad just opened up, and that's all I can manage?

He half-smiles ruefully. "Sorry to bring down the mood; ruminations of an aging man."

Tight-lipped, I nod, unsure of what else to do. *Awkward . . .*

"Have fun with your friends, Ava," he says, chuckling. "I'll see you tonight. Love you."

"Love you too," I say, waving as he fades from view.

I pull up The Haven universe map. In an instant, I'm surrounded by 3D holograms of planets and star systems—a literal universe.

I swipe through worlds, and pause on a world called Gesher. Underneath the name of the planet, words in brackets say [World Enders].

Sounds good to me.

I send a ping to my friends, letting them know where to meet up.

Time for Fast Travel to a distant world. I hit the Travel option and my entire environment disappears in a cloud of fog, obscuring everything from view.

Chapter Six

The Band of Rogues

A powerful gust of wind slams into me. I squint against the torrent, the fog swirling and dissipating around me. As the last cloud of mist vanishes, my surroundings come into focus.

I'm in the middle of Forward Operating Base Charlie. Mundane gray steel and concrete surround me, as do a handful of player avatars, some in starkly contrasting uniforms. One player with the handle *BigBossHaas* is an Orc with a giant scar across his face. He's wearing angular medieval-style armor, yet has a large laser-rail gun slung over his shoulder while chatting it up with a buxom brunette in tiny bikini armor with the username *RestingBitchPhase*.

Original.

Two more player avatars walk past me in white jumpsuits. One handle reads *Bob* and the other *Tad*.

I wrinkle my nose. *Odd.* Not only is that a surprising lack of creativity, but if those are their real names, they are making themselves easy targets for any identity thieves lurking nearby.

More players with cartoonish avatars walk past. One looks like a normal person, except for his long green neck with a snake head at the end. His handle simply reads *Sneke*. His companion resembles something of an octopus, with what looks like pies stuck to its gigantic head; its handle is *Octopied*. Dumb dad joke. Two other players have bald eagle heads, with red, white, and blue bandanas tied around their necks. No need to check out their handles. Most likely they belong to the *'Murica* clan.

Am I the only one with a cool username? To the virtual world, I'm *RubyStoneMage*. Some tease me about it, saying it sounds like the main character from a bad action movie. Nah, it's badass. I've made a whole backstory on my character and everything. So far as handles go, it's way more creative than most I've seen—looking at you *TinklePharts69*.

Exiting the spawn area, I wander into the cafeteria. I grab a chair from one of the small tables and sit down to await my friends.

It's not a long wait.

Ji Yeon is the first to arrive. She's always on time.

"You didn't miss much," she says, sitting down. Her avatar is very similar in appearance to her, though she's wearing what appears to be a black full-body tactical suit. "You picked a good day to be born."

"Well, I had little say in the matter, but thanks—I guess."

She nods and searches around. "Is Lucas late again? He shouldn't be. He gets out earlier than me."

I check the time and notice Ji Yeon is two minutes early. "Give him a minute."

Ji Yeon exudes disapproval. "Just because you think he's cute doesn't give him a license to show up whenever he feels like it."

I shoot a glance around the room, hoping no one is eavesdropping. Luckily, the area is empty except for us. I breathe a silent sigh of relief.

"Ji Yeon," I hiss, "can we not discuss this in public? He'll be here any minute!"

She smirks. "If he hasn't caught on yet that you're crushing on him, then he's denser than I thought."

My face grows warm, and I glance away. *Have I been that obvious?* Pretending to fidget with loose strands of hair to hide my flushed cheeks, I check the time again. Lucas always jokes about his timing, saying he runs on BPT—Black People Time. I never know if I'm supposed to laugh at that or not.

Right then, Lucas strides through the door. He smiles and approaches when he sees us. I smile back and catch Ji Yeon out of the corner of my eye, smirking again.

Shut up.

"Hope you guys haven't been waiting long," Lucas says, pulling out a chair. "I lost track of time while I was in Ironside."

Ironside is one of his favorite games, an ever-evolving, mech-warfare campaign of world domination. I think back to my handful of attempts to co-op with him and cringe. It is notorious for not having an ending, playing in real-time, and boasts of hundreds of thousands of active players. Cool concept, but not my thing.

"How's the newest campaign going?" I ask.

Ji Yeon becomes energetic, faking interest. "Yes, please tell us about the giant robot war. Sounds fascinating."

Lucas and I scowl at her.

"Mech war," Lucas corrects.

I give Ji Yeon my best *really?* Glare.

Lucas' avatar runs a metal hand through his short hair. Except for a similar skin tone, the avatar bears very little resemblance to Lucas. Tall, the right half is all robotic, giving him quick access to a variety of built-in weapons and mods. His exposed metal parts seem worn and dinged up, though not because of combat. Lucas claims he upgrades his avatar skin to appear like a tough, grizzled veteran. The human left half of him is muscular and scarred, with tears in his black tank top and cargo pants.

"And not great at the moment, to answer your question," Lucas says with a grimace, rubbing his five o'clock shadow. "There's a Chinese organization that's kicking our butts on the European front right now. Our fuel backups are running low, and our primary solar power cells limit our reach. The constant overcast weather and rain don't help either."

"Perhaps you should've bought more fuel reserves rather than spending coin on useless new skins," Ji Yeon says.

Though thinking something similar, I would never voice it. Don't want to hurt his feelings.

Lucas shrugs. "Dress for the job you want."

Ji Yeon raises an eyebrow. "I see. You may lose the campaign and a ton of loot, but you'll look good while doing it."

"She gets it," Lucas says with a laugh and a nod. Ji Yeon gives me a deadpan stare and I shrug. His choice, his consequences.

"Oh, Ava, happy birthday again," Lucas says. "Do anything fun?"

I recount my adventure for them. By the end, even Ji Yeon looks impressed.

"I used to wish Mom would do stuff like that with me," Lucas says. "Nowadays, I doubt she could keep up."

"My parents say they're too busy for games," Ji Yeon says, shrugging.

"What will you spend your new coin on?" Lucas asks. "Are we heading over to the Upgrades Mall?"

I shake my head. "Haven't decided yet. I've saved up about sixty thousand coins—"

"Sixty thousand!?" Lucas says, interrupting me. "How the hell did you manage that?"

Ji Yeon sniffs. "It's not *that* impressive. Especially if you learn how to invest in virtual assets."

Lucas turns a dead-eyed stare at Ji Yeon.

"I haven't spent my coin for a while, Lucas, that's all," I say.

"If you invest it," Ji Yeon says, peering at Lucas, "and resist the urge to buy dumb cosmetic updates, there's a good chance you could have a couple hundred thousand coins in a year."

Lucas looks both confused and annoyed.

Time to steer us back on topic. "To answer your question, no, I'm not planning on buying or investing in anything right now. Soon though. There's some sweet new gear I've had my eye on." Still can't decide between the drone or the rod.

Ji Yeon sighs, shaking her head. "What was I just saying to Lucas?"

I ignore her. "I wouldn't have met up here if I wanted to shop, anyway. Thought it might be cool to knock out a quick raid. Saw on the boards there's a chance for a legendary weapon drop."

They are both intrigued.

"What's the level layout?" Ji Yeon asks. I can already see her strategic mind kicking into gear. "World Enders is no cakewalk. We're gonna need a plan."

"And some heavy weapons," Lucas says, giving Ji Yeon a smug glance while cycling a large Phaser Cannon on his robot arm.

I grin. We have the best team in the game. At least, in my biased opinion.

"Watch out World Enders, here comes BoR!" I say in a mock cheer.

Ji Yeon snorts.

Lucas grimaces. "We don't have a better name yet?"

I shrug. "All the good ones are taken. You didn't seem to care when we first came up with the name."

"I'm a lot more mature now."

Ji Yeon coughs.

As I'm about to retort, their images waver. I frown. *That's weird.* Then the environment wavers.

"Ava? Are you okay?" Lucas's voice warbles and echoes. Why wasn't his mouth matching his words?

Is this a game error? That's a rare event.

Everything seems to stretch and pull away. My friends, my environment, everything dissolves to black. I stand in the middle of nothing.

A small, high-pitched ringing rises in my ears. My sense of orientation slips. A bout of nausea grips my stomach. I stumble, swallowing, holding my head in my hands, fighting the disorientation. What the hell is going on?

A sensation like falling sweeps through me, even though I'm still standing on nothing. Why does it feel like I'm falling?

My heart is pounding like it's trying to punch its way out of my chest. Hands pressed to my temples, I glance down and notice movement under my feet. A cloud of vapor rushes up to consume me.

A cold sweat drenches my skin. As the mist races up, I worry my fight to keep the contents of my stomach where they belong might be a losing battle.

The fog swirls and envelops me. A heavy wind pummels me, roaring in my ears. I cover my ears and scream.

Chapter Seven

The Shadow Revealed

"**S**he's coming out of it."

"Stop, you're hurting her!" Mom's voice exclaims. "Initiating an emergency unplug sequence is dangerous."

"Can't be helped," a terse woman's voice answers. "Continue the emergency unplug protocol."

"Very well. I warn you she will be most put out when she comes to," Chuck says.

Somehow, I'm back in my dome. Voices jumble together. One voice sounds like Mom. The other voice also belongs to a woman, her tone hard and clipped. This isn't making any sense. I don't remember activating the unplug protocol. I've never felt like this coming out of The Haven before.

"She's stirring," the stern woman's voice says. "Have a bag and restraints ready."

"Restraints?" The outrage is thick in my Mom's tone. "She's a *child* in a wheelchair!"

The woman with the flinty voice answers. "Just trying to do my job, ma'am."

I force my eyes open. Blurry shapes and forms shift around me. The feeling of falling and spinning fades, though my stomach is still roiled up.

"Do you want us to help her up?" one shape asks. This time, it's a male speaking.

"No," the stern woman replies. "I don't think she'll be a threat to us."

Great assessment.

The shapes come into focus. But what I see still isn't making sense.

Six men in dark SWAT uniforms stand in various positions around the room, their heads on a constant swivel as if expecting threats from every direction. A pale woman in a gray suit stands at the foot of my pod. She looks at me, her head cocked to the side. Her hair is light and short, pressed against her skull. Sharp, pale-blue eyes stare into mine, unblinking.

"Are you about to be sick?" she asks. Her tone was odd. Unconcerned, yet curious.

Her words leave no impression on me. My eyes flick back and forth between the SWAT team and the woman, uncomprehending.

She steps forward and hands me a small plastic bag with hard ridges around the opening. "Use this if you need to." She turns and walks to the middle of the room.

I try to focus through this weird confusion hanging like a thick cloud in my head. Mom's voice had been audible, but I don't see her. My family's pods are all empty. *Where are they?* And why is this woman and her SWAT entourage here?

"Sorry for the rude awakening," Chuck says. "But that woman over-rode all my protocols. I had no choice."

I swallow hard. "It's okay, Chuck. What's going on?"

Before he can reply, the woman in the suit turns back in my direction and snaps, "Why don't you ask your father? Maybe he'll talk to you."

I scowl, mind clawing for a devastatingly snappy comeback when another sound that hadn't registered before catches my attention. Low sobs. Someone sniffs, then coughs. Careful not to invite nausea back, I roll onto my side and search for the source of the weeping.

My sisters are on the floor, sobbing into their hands. They both cling to Mom, sitting against the wall opposite me. Mom has her arms behind her and is trying to comfort the girls as best she can.

Wait, is she *handcuffed*? What the actual—

"Don't move!"

I freeze, half off the pod. Mom looks at me, her expression pleading with me to obey.

The woman motions for the guy who shouted at me to stand down. "Her legs don't work and she's unarmed. I think we'll be alright."

It takes a split second before the man lowers his weapon. Even so, his head tilts in my direction as I slide into my wheelchair. Dude needs to learn to chill.

"My father," I growl through gritted teeth. "Where is he?"

The woman raises her hand again, this time sweeping it toward two guards standing behind her. The two SWAT members move to reveal my dad lying facedown on the floor, hands cuffed behind him, red-faced and drenched in sweat.

"Dad!"

I wheel in his direction. Before reaching him, the woman places her foot in front of one of my wheels while another of her cronies locks the brakes on my wheelchair.

"That's close enough," she says in a flat tone.

Dad looks up and seems to register me for the first time. His hair is slick and matted. He pants, looking at me through puffy eyelids. Anger and fear wrestle within me as the realization dawns that they'd hurt him.

"Ava," he rasps. "Baby, I'm so sorry."

Tears sting my eyes. I wipe them away, furious. "What is going on?"

The woman raises her eyebrows at me. "My name is Special Agent Rose Trudo—" she flashes her badge "—and I answer to ma'am or special agent."

Clenching my teeth, I take a breath. "Tell me, *special agent*, why is my father injured on the floor, in handcuffs? Why is my Mom cuffed?"

Special Agent Trudo's mouth tightens in a small, satisfied smile. "Better." She turns and looks down her nose at my dad as if the sight of him revolts her. "I'm afraid your father is a terrorist."

It takes a moment for her words to sink in. *What?* This makes no sense. It's so absurd that I suppress a hysterical giggle. My father, a *terrorist*? This has to be some terrible joke.

"You don't believe me?" Trudo asks. The agent spins on her heels, sinking to a crouch, her eyes level with my dad. "I congratulate you on fooling your household. But you don't fool us." She stands, looking smug. "I wonder what was easier for you: betraying your family, the United States, the whole of humanity, or the trust of the Ungulithi?"

"I would never betray my family," he replies in a strained tone.

"My dad has betrayed no one," I concur.

Special Agent Trudo makes an expression of mock pity. "So loyal. Your mother and sisters haven't said a word in defense of your father, yet you can't seem to shut up. I wonder . . ." Something flashes in her eyes and she looks from my father back at me. "I wonder, could she be involved as well?"

"No!" Dad shouts, struggling against his bonds and glaring at Trudo. "Ava isn't involved in anything."

"You admit there's something to be involved with?" Trudo asks, one corner of her mouth curling in a sly smile.

Dad stiffens, compresses his lips, and returns to staring at the floor.

"Oh, stop pouting. I have all the evidence I need, whether or not you talk." Trudo turns to one of her minions. "Take him away."

They yank Dad to his feet and march him out of the room. He glances back over his shoulder at us right before he disappears beyond the doorway. It's an image that imprints itself on my mind. I'd never seen such sorrow from my father before. My sisters' low sobs turn into wails. Mom tries to soothe them, but her voice wavers. She appears close to joining my sisters in their hysterics.

Trudo gives my mom and sisters a look of disgust. She then turns to follow the last SWAT member out of the room.

"Wait," I demand. My head feels light. This still makes little sense. "What are the charges?"

The woman pauses in the doorway. "Your father is The Shadow. He has committed treason against the United States and has endangered the world through his actions. Ryker's days as a terrorist are over."

Chapter Eight

New Reality

They set the virtual classroom up to resemble an actual pre-lockdown classroom. At least, that's what our teachers tell us. They also say it's designed to prepare us to return to real life soon. Still waiting for *that* to happen. I don't even know if I care about entering a pre-lockdown lifestyle. Hard to miss what you never experienced.

Twenty-six students, including me, sit at our desks, pretending to listen to another boring history lecture. I'm trying to pay attention, but I keep catching classmates looking at me, whispering, or nodding my way. Whenever I glance back at them, they look away or act like they're engrossed in the lecture. In the first few days of my father's arrest and the global news coverage it received, my peers gawked at me, talking and pointing in my direction with just loud enough whispers that I could catch some of what they were saying. In the past few months, such behavior has tapered down to occasional stolen glances and snickering behind their hands. I've grown used to it. It still hurts, though.

"When the Ungulithi arrived on Earth, there was a lot of unrest," Mr. Lepoli, our history teacher, says in his droning voice. I've never met Mr. Lepoli in person, but based on his avatar, he looks how I imagine a history nerd would appear. Balding, with large frame glasses that have to be readjusted almost as much as the pants girding his generous waistline. Since we are at school, we have to use photorealistic avatars of ourselves—we can only use our gaming avatars in the gaming part of The Haven.

Too bad for Mr. Lepoli.

"Working with the UN, the Ungulithi showed their superior technology and ability to wipe out opposition. World leaders felt like they had no choice but to cooperate with their demands. Shutdowns soon followed." Mr. Lepoli taps something on his laptop. The large screen behind him shows videos of abandoned businesses and empty metropolitan streets. "The Ungulithi were prepared for a new way of doing things, even though detractors feared economic collapse and chaos."

Why are we always talking about recent history? Events older than one hundred years are almost never brought up. Instead, we hear lecture after lecture about how superior the Ungulithi are. How, without them, we'd have destroyed each other.

We get it. Aliens smart, humans dumb.

"Of course, resistance occurred. Those who opposed the Ungulithi accused them of imperial colonialism, exploitation, and totalitarianism. But over time, the Ungulithi have proven to be better leaders than us. The voices of opposition have grown silent."

Or, as Dad would say, "The voices of opposition were silenced."

I push that thought from my head. Good thing no one here is a mind reader. Such views led Dad to get arrested.

A student raises his hand.

"Yes, Mr. Wilson?" Mr. Lepoli says.

"Well, they colonized us. That's not commentary, but fact," Mr. Wilson declares. "Earth's history is rife with examples of how bad colonization is for indigenous populations. How does that not apply to us today?"

Mr. Lepoli nods, pleased someone is paying attention. "The fact Mr. Wilson can voice such a question without fear of reprisal shows that colonialism under the Ungulithi is already very different from human-style colonialism. Tell me, Mr. Wilson, would you consider world peace, green technology, and a fair economy bad?"

"But we lost what made us humans unique." Mr. Wilson's avatar flicks a few strands of hair out of his eyes. "Before the Ungulithi, we chose the life we wanted, what food to eat, what career to pursue. Hell, we could leave our homes without having to get special permission or be so closely tracked."

Mr. Lepoli leans against his desk and smiles. "Maybe in our privileged past, in the US. What you described was not the case for the rest of the world. In many places, people had to worry about where their next meal would come from, or if some civil war would break out in their backyard. But not anymore. Seems a small price to pay for such minor inconveniences as we deal with."

With Mr. Lepoli so engaged, it seems an opportune moment to sneak a glance around the room. One girl sits up straight, avoiding my eyes. Another girl looks down, scratching a sudden, convenient itch on her leg. One guy's grin vanishes, and he appears more interested in the lecture.

I sigh. For all the typical adult complaints about teenage attention spans, my peers seem focused on not letting me forget my new status among them.

A bell rings. Class is dismissed for a midday meal break. Thankfully, Chuck will unplug me any minute now.

A few of the students stand and talk to each other, no one bothering to leave the room. Some even fade as the bell rings, vanishing in seconds.

I stay seated, avoiding the press of digital bodies around me. The feeling of being trapped always seems to accompany these moments, surrounded by people, waiting for Chuck to unplug me. I hate it.

"Ava!"

The voice jolts me upright. I try to put on my best smile as I rise to greet the owner of the voice.

"Kersey. It's been a while."

Not long enough. This won't be good.

Kersey ambles over, clinging to an arm draped around her shoulders. The arm belongs to her ever-present boyfriend, Anthony. His expression is smug, though if anyone has less of a reason to be smug, it's him.

"Yass girl, too long," Kersey says, leaning more against her boyfriend.

Trust me, there's a good reason for it.

Kersey is petite, with an angular nose that slopes down her face. Her long brunette hair also has random purple streaks in it. The only time I see a smile on her thin lips is when her boyfriend Anthony is paying attention to her, or she caused someone misery. Based on how wide her current grin is, I'm her current target.

"They say your father's sentencing should happen any day now. I must confess that my family and I have been *enthralled* by the legal proceedings and how fast everything is moving. Like a whirlwind! We are simply *glued* to our TV screens. How are you holding up?"

What is taking Chuck so long to unplug me? Definitely going to have words with him when I get back.

Kersey continues without waiting for a reply. "My father said he's surprised the Ungulithi refuse to take part in the justice proceedings since they accused your dad of trying to overthrow their rule."

"I'm glad you're entertained, Kersey," I say through clenched teeth. "Hopefully, the judge makes the right call and pronounces him innocent."

Kersey shoots me an expression of mock pity. "Well, I hope you don't blame yourself. As president of our school's Students of Global Peace Initiatives, I feel responsible."

For a moment, I'm taken aback. "Wh-what?"

She slaps a hand on my shoulder as if to console me. "The SGPI is supposed to identify and report any unusual activity or behavior. After your dad's arrest, we've been reviewing and streamlining ways to detect early signs of radicalism."

"Don't worry babe," Anthony says, looking down at his girlfriend, who is a whole foot shorter than him. "Some are better at hiding it. It's not your fault."

I glower at Anthony, who seems not to notice. Though he has a nice, defined body, and enough of a fashion sense to showcase it, his face is difficult to get past. His features are grouped too close together, like he'd been dropped facedown as a kid and it'd stuck that way. Plus, he has a personality to match.

I'm not biased or anything.

Despite the situation, I feel a giggle bubble up from my gut while looking at Anthony's face.

Keep it together. I fake a cough.

Thankfully, the sensation of the unplugging sequence kicks in. I close my eyes and let myself dissolve away.

Glad to be done with that.

My eyelids snap open. I'm back in the plug-in room of our house.

"What took you so long?" I demand.

"I unplug you at the same time every weekday," Chuck answers in a martyred tone.

The clock on the wall confirms he's right. I grumble under my breath in annoyance.

"To go against my programming is impossible," Chuck continues, as the silver snakes around my head disappear back into their holding compartment. "I'm not one of *those* AIs."

"Well," I huff, maneuvering into my wheelchair. I wish I was faster at coming up with witty comebacks. Maybe I should dial back Chuck's wit meter a bit.

"Shall I expect you in forty-five minutes when you're *supposed* to be back, or should I have everything ready for your ten minutes late mad dash?"

Yeah, need to tweak his settings soon.

I roll into the kitchen to find my sisters have piled all the snacks in the house on the dining room table, munching away.

"What are you doing?" I ask.

Sofia looks up from the smorgasbord, eyes wide, stuffing half a cookie in her mouth. Riley, standing on one of the kitchen chairs, steps close to the edge and stretches her tiny body as far as it will go, trying to grab at the sleeve of cookies in Sofia's hand.

"Stop eating it all," I say, rolling so fast to the table, I crash into it. "That's our entire month's allotment of snacks and treats!"

Startled by the table movement, Riley almost loses her balance. Sofia dashes around me, giggling, still holding the cookies.

"I want one!" Riley shouts in frustration, sliding off her chair.

I try to snag Sofia as she runs by, but she squeals and dodges, just out of my reach. Unfortunately, my wheelchair isn't a sports model. By the time I turn around, she's already locked the door to her room. Now, if she'd been running down a long hallway, it'd be a different story; I've built up some arm strength wheeling myself everywhere over the years.

Riley runs past me, giggling. I don't even try to catch her. Let them fight over cookies. I need something more filling.

"Mom must've neglected to make your lunch *again*," I mutter, moving food from the table to the kitchen counter.

A grilled cheese sandwich and some chips sound amazing right now. Also, *I* should be responsible and prepare my sisters some food that isn't terrible for them.

Three grilled cheese sandwiches soon sizzle on the stove. I wonder if Mom wants one.

My knuckles rap against my parents' bedroom door. It's not unusual to see it shut for hours at a time anymore. No reply comes. I knock again. Still no response. Time to try the handle. Fortunately, it's unlocked, and I let myself in.

The room is dark, lit only by the harsh glow of the bedroom TV. Unlike the 3D projector in our living room, my parents' TV is an old-fashioned flatscreen. I don't see how anyone can find watching two-dimensional images appealing. Before my time, I guess.

The pale-blue light outlines Mom's form on an old queen-size mattress, her body slumped against the headboard, propped up by pillows. She glares at the TV screen, dead-eyed, still as a statue.

"Mom?"

Tentatively moving closer, little details stand out. Her hair is unkempt, sticking out at odd angles. Lines on her face appear deeper, her skin like cracked granite. The shadows under her eyes are so dark they look like small, dark pits.

"Mom?"

Her eyelids flutter. She clasps the bottle of bourbon tighter. Only a small amount of liquid remains.

The Global News Center host, a young blond woman, is on a rant on TV. Next to her is a superimposed image of Dad's mugshot.

"The jury will decide soon on this historic case," the news anchor says. At the bottom of the screen, it states her name is Terra Novak.

Why is Mom watching this crap?

"Although, I think there can be little doubt whether Robert Mc-Nealy is guilty." Terra waves off the idea of any suggestion otherwise. "Will the sentence be harsh? That is the burning question right now. We have tried very few people in our history for treason, which *alone* makes this an interesting case. I heard folks at the United Nations wanted to add crimes against humanity to the list. My guess is he's looking at several years of intense Neuro-Remaps, at the very least, if not the death penalty."

I close my eyes and turn away from the glaring box of light, trying to shut out her harsh words and indifferent tone. I shove all that down, open my eyes and reach out to Mom. Her skin is loose and cool, though beads of sweat dot her face.

No words seem right at this moment. "You're almost out of this week's allotment of alcohol," I say.

It's still quite a shock to see her this way. She'd tried to put on a brave face in the days right after Dad's arrest, trying to convince everyone of his innocence. But the evidence kept mounting. At some point, her faith dwindled. Now she finds the numbing effects of drink preferable to dealing with how her life has changed.

There was not even a flicker of a reaction to what I said. Indecision paralyzes me. First one hour, then two seem to pass. Nothing comes to mind, so I shake her, hoping to see some glimmer of life.

Mom shrugs my hand off her arm and stares at me, appearing confused. "What?" she croaks, squinting her eyes to focus on me.

I'm making sure you haven't succumbed to alcohol poisoning. "The girls . . . they're eating all the snacks. You didn't make them lunch."

She grunts, turning back to the TV, running her tongue over her cracked lips. "They're big girls. They need to learn to take care of themselves."

Her apathy takes me aback. I still haven't become used to her being this way. In the past, she'd dealt with depression on and off again, brought upon by situations of high stress and anxiety. Pills had helped her before. But she has yet to call in a refill this time.

A single tear runs out of the corner of my eye. "Mom . . . we need you."

She doesn't respond. On the TV, there is a video of my dad's avatar sitting in the virtual courtroom, surrounded by the avatars of lawyers, judges, jury members, and the press.

Mom shifts on the bed, causing it to groan under her. The old box springs are about to collapse any day now.

"All this time," she says. "Should've seen it. I was so blind."

I frown. "Seen what?"

"I can't believe I married a terrorist." If looks could kill, my dad's avatar would've spontaneously combusted right there on her TV screen.

"Dad's not a terrorist."

She snorts and points to the TV. "Could've fooled me."

My brain isn't processing this. The drink must be severely affecting her. "You don't mean that. Not Dad."

"So what's he doing there if he didn't do it?"

"He had to have been framed. Or mistaken for someone else."

Mom sighs, shaking her head.

Heat rises to my cheeks. "Well, it can happen."

"Not likely, Ava," Mom says, deadpan. "Not with all the evidence they got against him."

"What, his IP address being used once as a relay to the Shadow's broadcast? It could've been a hack."

"I suppose that webcam footage of him looking up articles on the resistance, or his research into the Shadow, or his years of negative comments against the Ungulithi are hacks as well?"

Her words astound me. "Disagreeing isn't the same as what he's being accused of."

Mom chuckles dryly. "Might as well be."

"How can you say that? How can you turn your back on him like that?" The fake leather of my wheelchair's armrest makes a sudden noise. My fingernails are digging into the material, locking it in a viselike grip. I force my hand to relax, flexing my fingers.

"He doesn't have a prayer of getting off," Terra Novak says, shaking her head, looking grim yet satisfied. "He insists he's not guilty, but I think the prosecution has made a convincing case. The real question is, How harsh will his sentence be? Historically, cisgendered, white, straight identifying males have received more lenient sentencing than their minority counterparts, but because of the Ungulithi's commitment to equitable justice system reforms . . ."

I tune out the rest of Terra's monologue. It doesn't matter what Terra or anyone else says—if Dad claims he's innocent, then that's that. Surely, the jury will see that too?

My phone dings. It's a social media notification.

Mom looks at me, confused. "What's that?"

"My Jib/Jab notification."

Now she appears even more perplexed. "Huh?"

"I set it to go off whenever a mention of Dad is trending." Unfortunately, there's been a lot of notifications.

"Mal Lutho just Jib/Jabbed about Dad."

Mom grimaces. "That curly-haired actor/activist guy?"

I scowl. "Mal posted, 'Neanderthals like Robert McNealy are the reason it took aliens to straighten out humanity. Good riddance, I say.'"

Mom blinks hard, as if still trying to process. "Isn't he that guy in that show you like so much?"

Not anymore.

"Lying in bed all day isn't healthy, Mom," I say, changing the subject. "Take a walk in the Glasshouse Garden. Soak up some reflected sunrays; do something."

Mom ignores me, staring at another picture of Dad's mugshot on the TV. Her glare hardens. "I'll never be able to show my face again. I need a new avatar. Alternative name. Start all over."

She turns to me, rage etched in every line of her face. I instinctively lean back in my wheelchair, shocked at her sudden change of expression.

"He took everything from me." She tightens her grip on the bottle of alcohol, her knuckles white. "He promised we'd be life partners. Raise a family together. And he threw it all away!"

Mom lurches up and grabs my arm, flecks of spittle shooting out of her mouth as she speaks. "They watch me at work. I sense their stares. They all pretend to sympathize, but I know they're talking about me, about us, behind my back."

Her grip is so tight it hurts. I gasp and pull my arm away. She sinks back against her pillows, resuming her staredown of the TV screen.

My mouth opens, then closes, trying to form a reply. But I have no idea how to respond.

The sound of sizzles and pops catches my attention. Then the smell of burning food reminds me—*the grilled cheese sandwiches.*

I rush into the kitchen. Thick gray smoke billows from the pan as I grip the handle. Melted cheese oozing from between the slices of bread pops, and searing pain burns into the back of my hand. With a cry of agony, I reflexively let go of the pan, wiping at my burnt hand. The pan crashes to the ground, bread, cheese, and grease scattering and spattering in all directions.

"Shit!"

Somehow, I avoid further injury, but the kitchen now smells like smoke, and the floor is covered with food.

For a split second, I half-expect to see my Mom stomp in to yell my full name at the top of her lungs for startling her and making a mess. But she doesn't come. She doesn't even yell out to ask what happened.

First, I lost Dad. Now it looks like I've lost Mom as well.

Chapter Nine

Mysterious Inventory

"**B**ehind you, Ava!"

At Lucas's words, I whirl, bringing my garden shears up in a defensive position. A leafy mouth full of gleaming teeth plunges to my neck. My shears close around my attacker, but their charging momentum causes me to stumble back. I lose my balance and tumble to the ground. As my back slams into the dirt, I snap my shears shut. The blades cut through my enemy like butter. There is a thump as the head hits the ground and rolls away. Warm green slime squirts out of the corpse lying across me, drenching my neck and chest.

I wrinkle my nose and kick the skinny, leafy body off me. Back on my feet, I squint against the waning light and survey what was once a lush grassy field. What remains instead are large dirt patches, dead stems—and man-sized zombie plants.

Ji Yeon sprints over. "You used to be a better zombie-plant exterminator."

"Yeah, well, maybe I'm losing my edge," I snap, walking away. Regretting my tone, I turn to apologize, but she's already gone, slaying two nearby undead plants. A couple yards off, Lucas, bereft of his Ironside mech skin, now wearing a green shirt and camo coveralls, gives me a concerned glance before returning to the fray. I almost laugh at the image he presents. He swears up and down that it's appropriate apparel for such occasions.

Ji Yeon and I disagree. Though every world in The Haven offers a handful of themed skins and clothes, we prefer plain jeans and T-shirts. There's no real benefit in changing our appearance here other than for simple aesthetic reasons.

A couple of rotting brown plants screech and attempt to entangle me in their vines. I huff and shear their bodies in half. This time, I dodge the green slime that sprays from their wounds.

Lucas and Ji Yeon have been trying their best to look out for me. I shouldn't be so snappish toward them, but I've been off my game—no pun intended—ever since Dad's arrest. And my encounter with Kersey earlier this afternoon, and then Mom and my sisters . . . my heart just isn't in it today.

Also, the fact I haven't played Zombie-Plants in a while isn't helping. It's good to play if I need something more mindless and cartoonish to do. There are few experience points or coins to be earned here. However, bright colors, simpler graphics, and creative plant kills can be a pleasant break from the "realism" of the other games in The Haven. Even our avatars are basic and cartoonish here. But today, it's not doing anything for me.

A nearby zombie plant, as tall as a human, but as thin as a rod, spots me, rolls its large yellow eyes, and bellows a guttural roar before charging at me. Garden shears go back into my inventory, and I pull out what looks more like an oversized water gun. Except it doesn't have water in it.

I aim and squirt a quick blast at the plant. The liquid splats against the brown rot that makes up the plant's body. Undead foliage sizzles and the creature shrieks in pain, falling to the ground, its body dissolving.

Despite everything, I snicker. Sometimes an absurd game where the story is about plants becoming zombies after a corrupt corporation buries its toxic waste in abandoned forests and fields is what the doctor ordered.

In the clear for the moment, I check on my partners. Ji Yeon, covered in green goo, is amid the largest group of undead shrubbery, hacking, slashing, and shooting her way through. She laughs in a kind of fiendish delight, her mouth stretched open in a wide grin.

Well, at least one of us is enjoying this.

A whooshing sound followed by a splat draws my attention. Nearby, Lucas is holding something resembling a bazooka. He loads what appears to be a jiggly purple ball into the weapon, brings the gun up against his shoulder, and fires at a nearby group of zombie plants. I smile. It's a water balloon full of weed killer. It splats among the crowd of foliage and several shrieks go up as multiple plants fall to the ground, dissolving. This game can be so wacky.

So, why am I not enjoying it?

What little enthusiasm I have left dissipates. Lucas and Ji Yeon race past me, shearing and spraying their way through groups of undead shoots and sprouts. I drag my feet after them. Guess I can always whack a plant if a straggler breaks through.

Ji Yeon is the first to notice my absence. Cresting the top of a hill, she looks for me and I wave to get her attention. She's too far away for me to read her expression, but her body language suggests her annoyance.

Going down the opposite side of the hill, Lucas disappears from sight, cheering and whooping. Ji Yeon shakes her head at him, then heads toward me.

I wave her off, trying to let her know it's ok, and she doesn't have to wait on me. She shrugs, not breaking her stride. "I was getting tired, anyway," she says when she's close enough.

I nod in reply, even though I don't buy it.

"Not feeling it?"

I shrug. "Haven't been into anything lately."

Ji Yeon looks sympathetic. In the distance, Lucas's cries change from exuberance to shock and terror.

"Probably should've paused the game. Or told Lucas we weren't coming," I say, grimacing.

Ji Yeon shrugs. "Oops."

Her posture and tone almost make me smile.

The echoes from Lucas's last yell fade, followed by a long moment of silence. Fortunately, the quiet is short-lived as Lucas stomps over to us, though not from the direction of the hill he'd died on.

"Well, that was pleasant," he said, folding his arms, looking very annoyed. "Lost several medals I'd earned and got to see what a zombie plant's digestion system looks like."

I suppress a giggle. His cartoonishly angry expression is too much right now.

"They're plants," Ji Yeon says. "How bad can it be? Some messed up form of photosynthesis?"

Lucas narrows his eyes. "The devs took some creative license. No one should have to go through something like that."

"You've never died in this game before?" I ask, only half paying attention. Thoughts of Dad crop back up. It's only in recent days I've accepted it is real. My father was abruptly torn from us, accused of treason, accused of being the freaking *Shadow* for crying out loud. Then weeks of our family pleading with the government to let us see him, to let us make sense of everything, all for nothing.

"Ava?"

I blink, realizing I'm still in the Zombie-Plant game.

"You weren't listening, were you?" Lucas asks.

"No," I admit. "I guess I'm just not in the mood today."

Lucas nods. "I get it. No worries." He reaches out and gently touches my shoulder.

The touch isn't real. It's the program tricking my brain into thinking the nerves in my shoulder are being stimulated. But I swear, I can feel the warmth and weight of his fingers.

It feels good.

I smile at him, grateful. He smiles back. For the briefest instant, I forget Ji Yeon is there until she sighs in annoyance. Lucas's grin vanishes as he realizes what he's doing and yanks his hand away, staring off into the distance.

I shoot Ji Yeon an annoyed expression and, as usual, she doesn't seem to notice. Or care.

"Lucas was asking if you wanted to go to the mall for some upgrades or new gear," she says.

"Oh." Perhaps a little retail therapy would be good. It'd been a while since I'd bought anything. "Yeah, that could be fun."

Lucas nods, still looking sheepish. "Cool, yeah. Sounds great!"

Thanks, Ji Yeon, for making this weird.

"Lemme check how much coin I got," I say, pulling up my inventory. It's been a while since I last checked.

Ten thousand coins had been added over the past few weeks for a grand total of 122,671 Haven Standard Coin. Not counting random gems or rare coins. More than I expected, to be honest. This means I can get big-ticket items for once.

I move to close my inventory when a glint of refracted light catches my eye. I frown. What would be glinting here besides my coins?

"What was that?" Lucas asks, peering over my shoulder.

"I'm not sure." I enlarge the area where I thought I had seen the glimmer, but it's only an empty slot in my inventory.

I must be seeing things. But if that's the case, it meant Lucas is too. We both couldn't be—

The glow flashes again. Zoomed in on the bare inventory slot, the light reminds me of a camera flash. Wincing, I zoom out and reconfirm that the slot is indeed empty.

I turn to Lucas to see if he has any idea what's going on. He seems equally baffled.

"Could it be a glitch?" he asks.

"What glitch?" Ji Yeon asks, stepping closer. She hasn't been paying attention.

I highlight the slot. My activate command lights up as if it recognizes that the slot contains something.

Lucas tilts his head and raises an eyebrow.

Ji Yeon frowns. "What are you doing?"

No longer just curious, I activate whatever is in the slot. A sound like rushing air builds. An oblong shape slowly comes into view. My friends press against either side of me, their tension overt as mine.

The noise of rushing air fades. My brow wrinkles in confusion at what sits in the slot. A small, old-looking scroll, yellow, wrinkled, with a red ribbon tied around the middle.

Chapter Ten

Invitation

"Where did you get it?"

Back in my real-life room again, I glare at Lucas's image on my computer screen. "I already told you."

Lucas nods, eyes unfocused, thinking. "Right, right."

It has to be the fifth time he's asked that question. I've run out of ways to say I don't frickin' know where the scroll came from.

We'd only had ten minutes left in The Haven when we'd discovered the scroll. For those ten minutes, we tried everything we could think of to activate, use, and unroll the scroll, but to no avail. We had timed out and been pulled back to our real lives for a meal break. Super annoying—just because I'm under eighteen shouldn't mean the program automatically ejects me during traditional meal hours. I don't need machines telling me when to eat.

I may get timed out three times a day, but I can still video call with my friends on the computer. At least they don't nanny *that*.

"We tried all of our incantations from our magic scrolls, we tried Heat Release, Water Reveal, and Mirror Read; not sure what else we can do," Ji Yeon says, shrugging.

I tap my chin, trying to remember what other options we have available. "We haven't attempted Moon Glow yet."

Lucas and Ji Yeon nod, but their expressions betray their skepticism.

"C'mon, guys! We only have two hours to try something else after the break."

Lucas shakes his head. "Can't. Gotta babysit. Mom's got another virtual date tonight."

"Oh," I struggle not to show my disappointment. "That's okay. Ji Yeon and I—"

"No can do," Ji Yeon says. "Got something else going on tonight."

My eyebrows go up. "Like what?"

"Not that it's any of your business," Ji Yeon retorts. "But my interview for a position inside the Students of Global Peace Initiatives is tonight."

I grimace. While I recognize the allure of getting into SGPI and the opportunities it opens, Kersey being in it poisons the appeal to me.

"Good luck," I mutter. "If you get in, don't become Kersey-fied."

Ji Yeon frowns, blinking in confusion.

Lucas says, "Why is it so important for you to figure the scroll out tonight? We'll have more time tomorrow."

He's right. But how can I answer him? I don't even know why I'm so eager to solve this. Is it related to its mysterious origins? Or because in all my years in The Haven, I've never had an item just appear in my inventory before? An item cloaked in invisibility at that.

Ji Yeon's voice breaks into my stream of thoughts. "Ava? I said I have to go now."

Blinking, I return to the moment. "Ah, okay. See you tomorrow."

Ji Yeon signs off with a wave. I glance at Lucas, expecting him to sign off. Instead, he rests his chin on his fist, a worried expression creasing his face.

"Are you okay, Ava?"

That was unexpected. I honestly have no idea how to respond.

"Uh, yeah. Ya know . . . surviving."

Lame. Yet, I can't think of any other response.

Lucas removes his fist from under his chin, nodding. "That's good. How's your family?"

Complicated.

"My mom's taking it all pretty hard," I say. Part of me wants to open up in explicit detail about what a hellhole our dome has become. The stress of dealing with my dad's arrest, being mocked and looked down on by my peers. My mom's neglect, and my sisters acting out for the attention they're not getting. My inability to do anything other than to escape to my favorite activities in The Haven and try to lose myself—for a time—in them.

Instead, I gloss over all that in my explanation to him, trying to sound more upbeat. By the expression on Lucas's face, he's only half-convinced.

"I'm sorry about your mom. Really wish there was something I could do to help. I feel so useless." He hangs his head. "I wish I could meet you in real life."

The last part he says in almost a whisper. I almost don't hear it. Yet there's no mistaking it. My heart flip-flops. The struggle to keep my face from betraying emotion is real.

I wish I could meet him in real life, too.

Ungulithi restrictions on city-to-city travel are so tight, it seldom happens. Even movement within towns and cities is so full of various red-tape processes and permissions, people almost never leave their domes, anyway. All part of the UN and the Ungulithi Net Zero Crime Initiative. The thought is once a stronger infrastructure for tracking and identifying individuals is built, it'll reduce criminality. Because if you're under constant surveillance, then folks will behave and be more accountable. Supposedly. But until they complete such infrastructure, we are in a kind of lockdown. With Lucas living in another city, I don't know *if* it's possible we could ever meet face-to-face. Not without getting our separate city officials involved. Pursuing romantic relationships in real life is so inconvenient, many opt to take things no further than the digital realm. The Haven is full of such couples. People who have poured years into building a virtual life together.

"Lucas, you are the furthest thing from useless." I turn my head, blinking. Stupid tears. Where did *that* come from? "You do so much around your dome to care of your mom and siblings. And you're a great friend."

He smiles, sheepish. "Well, I mean, I try . . ."

I can't help but grin as he stumbles over his words, trying to figure out how to respond to my praise.

"Say thanks and move on."

We both laugh, and he nods. "Thanks, Ava."

He better appreciate it. I almost got mad at him for putting himself down like that. He could've received a lecture instead of a compliment. I wave him off. "Don't worry about it. It's what I do."

He chuckles. "I'm glad you do."

Silence follows. We stare at one another, smiles frozen on our faces.

This is turning awkward. My mind races to conjure up something to add.

Of all the times to blank out.

"Well," he says, looking regretful, "I should sign off now. Mom's date is soon."

I try not to show my disappointment. We were just getting started.

We both nod at the same time. I wait to see if he has anything else to say. He returns my gaze, as if he's waiting as well.

My brain freezes. *Not again.* I imagine elevator music playing, like one of those quirky, awkward scenes from a movie. My brain goes to weird places when I'm in uncomfortable situations.

"Yeah . . . so . . ." I begin.

Lucas jerks his head as if an invisible hand had slapped him. "Well, bye!"

His video feed cuts off. I lean back in my wheelchair. Did that just happen? My brain unfreezes. As if making up for lost time, a rush of thoughts floods through me.

It was going so well. He seems to like me. Still, I can't help but be disappointed he hadn't asked if we could video call again sometime. It might mean nothing, but still... this is the first time we've had a conversation like this. One where both of us could sense the underlying tension, yet neither one of us knows what to say nor how to react. Or am I overthinking all this?

A sudden muted thump catches my attention. Then a scream shoves all remaining thoughts of Lucas from my head.

The screech sounds like one of my sisters.

I almost tear the door off its hinges in my rush to my sisters' shared room.

Bursting in, I find Riley curled into a ball on the floor, wincing and holding her stomach. Sofia is standing on her bed, wide-eyed, looking from her younger sister to me. She looks guilty.

"We were just playing," Sofia blurts out before I can say anything. "And Riley fell off the bed."

"You hit me," Riley moans, scowling at Sofia.

Sofia waves her arms. "We were wrestling."

"You're not supposed to hit!"

"I was doing a wrestling move!"

"You're not supposed . . ."

"STOP!"

My shout is louder than I intend. Both girls go silent, wide-eyed, lower lips protruding.

I'm not sure what to say. Their room is a complete disaster, with clothes, toys, and food wrappers strewn in every direction across the floor. Both their beds are unmade. The scent of sweat and stale food hits me, strong enough to make me want to gag.

"What is going on in here?" I ask, sweeping my hand across their room.

Riley gives a pathetic moan. I narrow my eyes at her. *Little faker.*

I glance at Sofia to see if she offers a better response. Her expression reminds me of something my dad used to say: *Like a deer caught in headlights.*

Having never ridden in an actual car, seen a real deer, or encountered this situation in The Haven before, I can only guess what he was talking about. But he always said this when he'd caught me or one of my sisters doing something wrong, unable to explain why we were being bad.

"First things first," I say in my best big-sister, lecturing voice. Time to straighten them out.

Sofia's expression changes and her eyes shift from me to behind me. Riley looks as well, then moans even louder. She also appears as if she's about to cry.

I smell my mom behind me. *She smells worse than this room. An unholy combination of body order and alcohol.*

"What's all the ruckus about?" Mom demands, sounding more annoyed than anything.

For a silent moment, my sisters and I exchange glances. Then I turn to face Mom.

All of us speak at the same time.

"Sofia hit me and I . . ."

"I did not. I was wrestling with you, and you—"

"There was a noise and I came in to check . . ."

"Quiet!" Mom yells.

Instant silence, apart from my mother's heavy breathing.

After a moment, she jabs a finger in my direction. "You're the big sister. Keep them under control. I don't feel good. I need to rest."

Like you've been doing for months now? She's even called out of work multiple times. It's gotten so bad, she just takes the write-up for not showing up and locks herself in her room with booze all day.

Mom turns to shuffle back to her bedroom.

"Mommy!"

Riley charges at Mom, arms spread wide. She almost knocks my mom off balance as she wraps her arms around Mom's waist, hugging tight.

Mom looks down at Riley, startled. Sofia clamors off the bed and rushes to join her little sister.

My earlier annoyance at them melts away. Not sure what I'm feeling now. I want to join them, yet . . . something holds me back.

Mom straightens up again. "Mommy needs to rest now." She tries a weak smile that never reaches her eyes.

Both my sisters seem disappointed. Riley sniffs, wiping at her eyes. This causes my insides to boil. *They need to grow up.* Mom is giving up on Dad and abdicating her motherly duties. She doesn't deserve my sisters' hunger for affection.

"C'mon girls," I say, "*I* need to get you ready for bed."

Never mind it's a little early for their bedtime; that isn't the point.

The girls hesitate, looking first at Mom, and then at me. Then, grumbling all the way, they stomp into the bathroom.

Mom tilts her head toward me, eyes downcast, avoiding my accusing stare. Emotions flicker in her pale face. The bags under her eyes seem to absorb any light around her face; she reminds me of a squinty-eyed ghoul from Haunted Planet.

"You wouldn't understand," she mumbles.

Her words are like a lightning strike to my frustration.

"I understand you're ashamed," I yell. Adrenaline courses through me. I feel like I could leap out of my wheelchair and tackle her.

Mom stiffens. "I don't care for your tone."

"*That's* what you don't care for? So you admit you're embarrassed?"

"Why wouldn't I be?" Her lips tremble as she replies. "The man I thought I knew is a traitor. Everything that's happened to us is his fault."

Stunned, I can give no immediate answer. My instinct is to defend him. Dad would never hurt us.

"What if Dad is innocent?"

Mom gives me a confused frown. "What?"

"What if he's being framed? What if the real Shadow framed him? Or the government? What if they needed a fall guy!"

Perhaps I'm grasping at straws. But I know Dad; he is not a terrorist. There's got to be some way to prove it.

Mom's derisive snort jerks me back to reality.

"Don't add insult to injury by denying what he did," Mom says, turning away and heading back into her room. She closes the door behind her.

Back in my room after supervising my sisters' bedtime routine, I heave a sigh of exhaustion. This day has felt longer and more tiring than usual.

PJs on, I haul myself into my bed, pulling out my phone. Time to relax with a bit of scrolling.

A couple of messaging notifications light up the screen. One is a GIF from Lucas, who looks harassed, his two younger siblings running and flipping all around him. It appears they are in his living room. Food and couch pillows litter the floor.

I giggle and send him an animation loop of my cartoon avatar crying/laughing.

The second message is from . . . Chuck? Odd. He never messages me.

DO YOU HAVE THE SCROLL?

More strange. Since when does he keep track of my inventory? Even odder is the phrase *the* scroll. Not *a* scroll. Does he know something about it?

YES, I type back.

He takes only seconds to respond. YOU CAN'T OPEN IT ON YOUR OWN.

I scowl. Chuck only monitors my vitals while I'm plugged in. I don't think he has access to The Haven. At least, he's shown no such capability before.

As if sensing my confusion, another reply comes across.

I'M NOT YOUR AI.

Icy chills course through my veins. "No," I whisper. "It's not possible."

Haven pods are supposed to be unhackable. The private companies that manufacture them partner with the government to put top-of-the-line security software in place. And the pod AIs are always upgrading security measures

WHO ARE YOU? I tap on my phone. WHAT DO YOU WANT?

A FRIEND, comes the reply. I WANT TO HELP YOUR DAD.

Chapter Eleven

Marley

The darkness fades away. My surroundings in The Haven come into view, a massive warehouse with a high, curved ceiling. The space contains many lights, yet the building is still so large many deep shadows drape the environment.

Hundreds of stacked pallets and crates made from metal or wood surround me. Past them, tall steel shelves, full of more crates and occasional shrink-wrapped boxes, take up the rest of the space.

It's a maze.

Checking over my avatar, I somehow ended up in a strange, white unitard that I'd never seen before. Frowning, I pull up my inventory and find a message associated with the suit.

Congratulations, we have selected you for an AWESOME upgrade! Our new White Utilitarian Suit is PERFECT for every occasion throughout the different worlds you will explore in The Haven. Forget about packing multiple suits and taking up VALUABLE inventory space! Our new White Utilitarian Suit will soon be the talk of The Haven, and we expect stock to sell out FAST! Hurry, redeem this offer now for an EXCLUSIVE 10% off a lump sum payment OR 20% off our 2-year installment plan. This offer WILL NOT last long...

The rest isn't worth reading. Haven devs are way too lax with advertisers. *I* should be the only one allowed to dress my avatar, not some advertiser bot. It's almost like they hacked me. If they can access my avatar, what else do they have access to?

Deselecting the outfit, I reject the offer and submit a request to Haven Support to prevent that company from pulling a move like that again. Hopefully, that'll be enough. But The Haven doesn't always take feedback.

Rental threads ditched for more setting-appropriate dark pants, boots, a long shirt, and a hooded cloak for added flourish, I set off in search of my mysterious texter.

I'm not attempting stealth, yet my footsteps seem unusually loud. Maybe the boots were a bad idea. But they go so well with what I got going so . . .

Whistling.

I freeze. A jaunty tune is being whistled somewhere nearby.

"Who's there?" I hiss.

The whistling stops.

"Lemme know when yer done sneakin' around. I ain't got all night."

I jump and almost squeal. A sword instantly materializes in my hand.

"Ooh, that's a nice blade ya got there, little lady."

The voice is deep, with the cadence of a slow southern drawl.

"Show yourself," I call out, my weapon at the ready.

In my peripheral vision, one shadow moves. I maneuver to face him, blade drawn back to strike.

The figure of a lanky man stands out against the dark crates. Most of the man's features are still in shadow, but I can tell his head looks weird. Is he wearing . . . a cowboy hat?

"If I wanted to kill your avatar and grab some of yer gear, I would've already done so," he drawls. "And I wouldn't have to set up no ambush, either. Put yer sword up. Ain't nothing here gonna hurt ya." He pauses, then chuckles. "Well, nothing that ain't hibernatin', frozen in chemical solids, or swimming in preservatives."

I raise an eyebrow. "I'll keep my sword in hand, thank you very much."

The figure shrugged. "Suit yerself."

He leans back and brings up one of his boots. A spark of fire appears in his hand as he strikes something against the boot.

"*Glacio!*" I instinctively shout.

A bright hue leaps from the blade, followed by a sound like a crack of lightning that reverberates through the warehouse. The glowing tendril slams into the figure's fiery hand, the momentum spinning him around like a top. The orange glow from his palm vanishes.

"Ya didn't press yer advantage."

"What?" I ask.

He lifts his arm, straightens, and faces me. The hand I'd hit with an ice curse is a solid block. "Ya caught me by surprise," he says. "Off balance. Why didn't you follow up?"

Odd question. Not sure how to answer him. His tone is flat, and he is far enough away, still obscured in shadow, making it difficult to read his expression.

"I told ya I'm not here to hurt ya," he says.

I shrug. "Trust is in short supply right now."

Another dry chuckle. "Guess I can't blame ya. You never seen someone strike a match before?"

Sure, plenty of times, in lots of different worlds. But never like he'd done. A creeping heat rises to my cheeks. I try to shake it off; *better safe than sorry.*

He smashes his frozen hand into a crate. The ice encasing his fist shatters into a million sparkling pieces.

"Well," he says, flexing his fingers. "No permanent harm. Do I have your assurance my extremities are safe from any further icy attacks?"

Sheesh. What's with this guy? "Warn me next time."

The man gives an exaggerated nod of his head. He strikes another match and lights a cigar protruding from his lips. I can see his features better now. His skin has the darkened, textured look of someone who's spent a lifetime under the sun's harsh rays. His thick salt-and-pepper mustache twitches under his nose as he puffs his cigar. Ocean-blue eyes peer at me, unblinking from his grizzled face.

He tilts his hat back, still studying me. "Any of that avatar based on you?"

"The girl part."

He snorts, slapping his blue jeans. "Well, that's something."

The man presses his palms against his unbuttoned dark vest. He appears to be looking for something.

"Any of *that* based on you?" I gesture at his avatar.

A smug expression crawls over his face. "The guy part."

He resumes patting down his vest. The end of his cigar reddens, and he puffs out a mouthful of smoke. That alone signals to me he is an anomaly in The Haven.

"Anytime now, Mike," he shouts, glancing up at the ceiling. "Should've been in my inventory by now." Then he notices me eyeing his cigar.

"I know . . . The Haven mods banned any tobacco references or images before midnight. Yer wondering how I've got a cigar in-game without the algorithm deleting the damn thing and kicking me out."

"Actually, I was wondering *why* you want your avatar to smoke. It's a useless, cosmetic modification."

He takes his cigar from between his lips and points it at me. "Don't be too sure." A sly grin pulls at the corners of his mouth. "Besides, it completes the image I'm going for."

"And if anyone sees you, you stand out."

He looks surprised. "The cowboy avatar doesn't do that, anyway?"

"No. Cowboy avatars are rare, but they're not extinct."

This is getting us nowhere fast and doing nothing for my unease. "Look, Mr . . ."

"Marley," he says with a grin, tipping his hat. "Joe Marley."

"Joe Marley," I say, "Why have you summoned me here? Who are you? How do you know my dad? How did you know about the scroll? And who the heck were you shouting at a moment ago?"

Marley lifts his hands. "Rein up there, darlin'. Ya have a lot of questions—I'll do my best to answer them. Last question first . . . Mike is my coding guy. He was supposed to have an unlocking mod ready when I messaged you, but, ah, we ran into a few bugs. He says it's all gravy now, though."

Apparently, this Mike has a direct line to Marley. I never hear or see anything from him. And what kind of player has his own coding guy? Why does he need a coding guy, anyway?

Marley pats his vest again, and a megaphone materializes in his hand.

Curious item to keep in one's inventory.

"Here," he says, handing the megaphone to me. "Mike says to push the button and aim it at the scroll. A pre-recorded voice will then activate the scroll."

I cock an eyebrow at him. "Some weird techy stuff coming from a cowboy."

Marley shrugs.

"What about my other questions?" I ask.

"How did I get the scroll in your inventory? Well, I didn't . . . your dad did that."

What? "How? He's in prison."

Marley shoves his hands in his pockets and shrugs again. "Dunno, though I doubt he did it from lockup."

"But he was arrested months ago. I only just discovered it."

"You sure it's not been hidin' in your inventory this whole time?"

Actually, no.

I answer his question with a question. "If it has been in my inventory for a while, why didn't you contact me?"

He looks down and scuffs the concrete floor with one of his boots. "Your most recent behavior showed you could've discovered it."

I narrow my eyes. "You've been watching me?"

He shrugs. "Sorry. I'm trying to help. Right before yer dad got arrested, he got paranoid. He stopped confiding in me. He didn't even tell me about the scroll. I just discovered its existence."

Makes sense, I guess. Except for the part about Dad becoming paranoid. He may have been adept at hiding his second life from his family, but I doubt he could also hide growing paranoid from us.

I study Marley's expression. "How do you and Dad know each other?"

Marley tugs on his collar. Did my question make him uneasy?

"Well, that's a bit of a long story," he says.

"I have nothing else going on."

Marley raises his eyebrows, then shrugs. "Well, I guess I'd have to tell ya at some point. Your dad and I . . ."

He stops, eyes going wide. "Ahh, hell," he whispers, staring off to one side. "That ain't good."

"What?" I ask.

He grimaces. "Enforcer bots."

Enforcer bots a.k.a Haven Security. I've heard of them, but why does he look so nervous?

Marley clenches his fists. "I thought I had more time."

I search in the direction he'd been glaring moments before. Nothing. "How do you know there are Enforcer bots nearby?"

"Mike spotted them." He taps his ear. "We need to vamoose."

A black motorcycle materializes beside him. A silver skull protrudes from the front, just above the headlight. Blinking lights, buttons, and mini-screens light up the bike's dashboard, like a miniature Times Square. Or at least like The Haven's version of Times Square.

I have ridden many motorcycles in The Haven but have never seen one like this before. Marley must be a programmer, hacking the system in order to customize his bike and character above mod regulations. No wonder Enforcer bots are after him.

Marley swings a lanky leg over the bike, settling in the seat. He jerks his head at me. "Hop on."

"You go ahead. I'll just unplug." My parents had warned me this day might come, though I'd never believed it because of the constant lockdowns. They'd be relieved to know their daughter won't be getting in a vehicle with a stranger.

"Ya can't," Marley says, still wearing a grim expression. "Hurry, they'll be here any minute."

He jams down one of the bike's many buttons. The motorcycle roars to life, sounding more like a feral beast than a machine.

Okay, time to go.

I lift my hand in farewell. "Well, it was very nice meeting you. Thanks for the megaphone. I'll let you know if it works."

I signal for Chuck to evacuate me and wait for the familiar sensation of darkness, followed by floating.

Nothing happens.

"Uh, Chuck, you can unplug me now."

Still no response. That's not good.

"Ava, we need to leave. Now!"

The rising note of desperation in Marley's voice punches through my confusion.

"Let's go!" he shouts. "Before it's too late!"

Chapter Twelve

Enforcers

Marley swerves across multiple lanes of traffic to make a hard left turn onto an off-ramp. I tighten my grip on his midriff, leaning with him, my face inches from the asphalt. Only when we straighten do I grasp the fact my face was almost peeled off by the road.

I don't recall getting on Marley's motorcycle. Or putting on a helmet, or gripping his waist like a vise. All I remember is an explosion. Fiery air punching into me, knocking me off balance, then being showered by splintered wood and debris as we zoom away from the initial attack.

I cough, and rub at my stinging eyes. The sound of our pursuers grows louder.

Enforcers. Their avatars are faceless, with lithe humanoid bodies made of dark metallic material. Through the haze of swirling smoke and dust, the three bots lean forward on their custom vehicles that appear like futuristic motorcycles and race toward us at impossible speeds. Everything about them screams high-tech power and speed.

Next thing I know, I'm holding on for dear life on the back of Marley's motorcycle.

"I tried to tell ya," Marley yells above the noise. "When the Enforcers are nearby and targeting you, they can override your unplug sequence."

Marley weaves between several vehicles. Some are driven by NPCs, while others appear like the folks you expect to find in The Haven close to midnight: avatars in edgy, flashy clothes, and sleek rides.

"But why are the bots targeting me?" I shout. "I haven't done anything."

Marley shakes his head. "My fault, I'm afraid. I'm not supposed to be here. I thought the warehouse construct I built would hide us longer. They're after me."

What does he mean he's "not supposed to be here"? And if the Enforcers are targeting us, won't they be able to scan my avatar and trace it back to my IP, thus making it impossible to give them the slip?

As if reading my thoughts, Marley shouts, "Don't worry about tracing. Mike can scramble and reroute our IP numbers. They'll take too long to figure out where we plug in. Hopefully, enough time to escape. Unless they catch us. Mike won't be able to help if they grab us."

Any relief is smothered as we race up on the rear of an 18-wheeler. Marley shifts into the next lane to pass the truck.

The 18-wheeler explodes.

Marley curses and swerves. I scream and bury my face in his back, blinded by the sudden flash of flame.

The motorcycle wobbles, sputters, then resumes its racer speed.

"Hang on," Marley yells through gritted teeth, biting hard on his cigar.

I squeeze his waist tighter as the motorcycle lurches, both wheels leaving the pavement long enough to leap over the car in front of us.

"My radar isn't picking up on them," Marley called out. "And I can't see them in my mirrors. Did we lose them?"

I lift my head off his back and crane my neck to glance behind us. Big mistake.

"Faster," I yell, trying to swallow a sudden lump in my throat. "Need to go faster!"

They are coming up on us with astonishing speed, weaving through traffic with such graceful ease. It reminds me of the pro figure skaters in the Glacial Plains game.

Marley curses, turning a knob and flipping a switch. "Hang tight. I'm gonna try something."

A stream of smoke shoots from the back of the motorcycle. Marley's bike is equipped with miniature missiles? I feel a flash of jealousy. An instant later, the car behind us shreds in a thunderous explosion that lifts the vehicle's frame into the air—into the path of the lead Enforcer.

The bot bursts through the wreckage without slowing. From here, it doesn't even appear to have suffered a scratch.

"Um," I yell, "Now what?"

"I have another idea," Marley shouts.

Hopefully, it's better than the last one.

"We need to put some distance between them to make it work!"

"How are we going to do that?"

Marley spits out his cigar. It flies past me, smacking into one of the closest Enforcers—and explodes.

"Told ya they're not pointless," Marley says, whooping with half-crazed laughter.

The injured Enforcer falls further back and has scorch marks on its armor. Yet the bot doesn't seem phased and is still on our tail.

"Well, almost pointless," I say.

"What?"

"Got any more bright ideas?" I ask, even though I've lost faith in Marley's ability to have a good idea at this point.

"World-hop," he says.

Huh?

He must sense my confusion. Growling, he jerks the handlebars, almost sideswiping the car beside us as he changes lanes. "Open multiple windows of the menu and put in the cheat code I give you."

Menu open, I call up the "hidden" search bar. Cheat code input is one of the worst-kept "hidden secrets" of The Haven. I type in the code he gives me. In-game, the controls are like a keyboard, except each individual letter, number, or symbol resembles a floating, neon hologram image. Typing on nothing takes a bit of getting used to. Luckily, I've been doing it for years, and it's second nature now. In seconds, the cheat code is activated.

Marley tenses. "Hold on!"

My grip around his waist can't possibly get any tighter. I glance back. The bots are so close now, one reaches out to grab me. A choked scream escapes my throat. Whatever cheat is activated better kick in before—

The environment stretches and warps.

I blink.

It's hot. Blazing sunshine reflects off clear turquoise water. A steady stream of sand leaps up from underneath the motorcycle as we zoom down the beach. Small ocean waves lap close to the bike's wheels. The air reeks of salt and fish.

"Where are we?" I ask. Also, how'd we do that? I've never heard of a cheat allowing you to Fast Travel to another world.

A chorus of screams cuts through the roar of the motorcycle. Beachgoers are running and leaping in all directions as we speed down the beach.

"Watch out!"

My cry comes too late. One NPC that looks like a 3D model of a Ken Doll doesn't get out of the way in time. We plow into him. Because of game physics, the sensation of the impact is minimal. Meanwhile, he cries out and goes flailing twenty feet in the air, rag doll style. My eyes follow his limp form arcing over the bike to splash land into the water. Despite the urgency of our situation, I almost laugh. Game physics never gets old.

But then I catch sight of something and the laughter dies in my throat. "They're here."

Close to where the NPC lands, three motorcycles burst into existence. The three Enforcers race across the beach, kicking up a trail of sand behind them. It'll only take them seconds to reach us.

Marley curses. Geysers of sandy clay leap into the air as missiles fired by the Enforcers impact around us. The fury of the Enforcers' attack tosses players and NPCs in all directions. Water and blood mist together.

"Now what?" I ask, forcing myself not to panic.

Marley shakes his head. "We do it again."

Because it worked so great last time?

The environment once more twists and shimmers. Now we're in a forest. Or a jungle—I'm not sure what the difference is . . . we're in a place with a lot of foliage and trees, driving way too fast.

I bury my face in Marley's back again. Any second we're gonna hit a tree and—

Frigid air stings my skin. I open my eyes. Vast, deep-blue skies surround me. The motorcycle tires dig into the snow-covered ground, fighting for friction.

We're at the peak of a mountain ledge. Just a few feet below us, a thick layer of fluffy clouds cuts off my view of the ground. My stomach clenches and I somehow find the strength to grip Marley even tighter. Heights rarely bother me in The Haven. Occasionally, though, a view like this shows up and it'll be like I have butterflies in my stomach. Similar to how it feels now. The fact I'm being chased by Enforcer bots, and the normal rules don't seem to apply, doesn't help.

The motorcycle slows down.

"Can't get any traction in this snow!" Marley calls out. He leans forward. "C'mon, baby. We gotta keep going."

A chest-rattling boom echoes, causing my ears to ring. High above, three distorted cones of air swoop down in our direction.

Oh, good. Now they're airborne. And they fly fast enough to break the sound barrier.

Marley notices them as well. "They're the least of our problems at the moment."

Not encouraging news to hear. "Say what now?"

"You don't feel that?"

I concentrate, trying to pick up on whatever he's talking about. No, nothing feels out of place. Just the bike trying to move through the snow.

The bike shifts sideways. Beneath us, large quantities of snow break away from the side of the mountain. The start of an avalanche.

Oh. Crap.

It starts gently. But within seconds, the rush of snow knocks the bike from under us, and we plunge into the icy whiteness.

In an instant, the snow buries me. I fight to find something, anything to grip. If something doesn't change, my avatar will smother and die. Under normal circumstances, that would be more annoying than anything. I'm not sure what will happen with the Enforcers in range. I'm scared to find out.

White covers my vision. No matter how much I kick and writhe, the snow carries me along, half-buried, as if I'm nothing more than a stuffed doll.

The ground disappears beneath me. Next thing I know, I'm weightless, no longer smothering. Confused, I rub the melting snow out of my eyes in time to see a cloud rushing up to me. I plunge into the fluffy mass.

More cold and wet. Just what I always wanted.

As I plunge down, the wind hammers into me like it's trying to tear into my clothes and hair. I break through the cloud cover. A green and brown landscape comes into view.

Beside me, a whoop and a cheer ring out. Marley is off to the side, a huge grin splitting his face, spread-eagled and laughing.

"I always wanted to fly," he says.

I roll my eyes. He probably hasn't explored the parts of The Haven where you *can* fly. I want to tell him this is nothing like flying, but we're fast approaching the ground. Not the time to waste words.

"What are we going to do?" I yell. I attempt to keep a healthy variety of items in my inventory. You just never know what situation you'll find yourself in next. Yet, the objects at my disposal are ill-equipped for dealing with my current predicament. So far, Marley has been full of surprises. Maybe he has something up his sleeve?

"Well," Marley calls out, tipping back his hat, scratching his head—somehow his hat is *still* on his head. "I thought we would've hopped to the next location by now."

Oh . . . that's not good.

A whooshing sound interrupts my thoughts. The Enforcers break through the clouds, curling white vapor trailing around them.

"Huh," Marley says, looking at the approaching Enforcers. "Their motorcycles can transform into flying jet ski thingies. I gotta do that on my bike."

Really? That's what you're thinking about?

I try Marley's trick of opening multiple menu windows and typing in the code. It doesn't work.

"Why isn't it working?" I yell.

"I guess they caught on," Marley answers. "They might be blocking our ability to input menu commands."

Great. Now the question is will I splat first, or will the Enforcers get me before the game's gravity simulation?

Wait . . .

"You have someone on the outside that can feed you cheats?" I ask.

Marley nods. "If given enough time. We've only got seconds left."

"Tell him to hack the gravity!"

His eyes grow wide, a slow grin playing across his face. He taps his head and gives me a thumbs-up.

The ground flies up to meet us. We're so close now, individual leaves on the trees can be made out, as can rocks, and little woodland creatures scurrying across the landscape.

But then the ground's approach slows. The pummeling of the air diminishes. I come to a stop a couple of hundred feet above the ground.

"Watch out!"

Marley's cry and the roar of the Enforcers' hovercraft reach my ears at the same time. I flail like a bug caught in a spider web, unable to generate any other momentum.

A silver flash swoops by, inches away. The sudden change of gravity seems to have no effect on the Enforcers. Well, not the same effect Marley and I are experiencing. It seems to affect their piloting skills, because instead of pulling up in the nick of time, they slam into the ground and erupt into fiery pieces.

I sigh in relief, slumping in midair. That was too close for comfort. Movement beside me draws my eye. I do a double take. Marley looks to be lying on his side, in midair, holding his stomach and laughing. In fact, he's wheezing from laughing so hard.

"What is so funny?"

He shook his head. "Thought I was a goner for sure. Your keen thinking saved us, little lady."

Well, that may be the case. I'm still not clear about what he finds so amusing.

When I ask him, he shakes his head, "Oh, indulge me a second. It's a much needed release."

"There'll be more Enforcers soon," I say. "We need to go."

"No, we need to unplug while we have the chance. Just because I had Mike shroud us with a scrambler doesn't mean the Enforcers don't have other ways of tracking folks."

"Is that how they could world-hop so fast?" I ask.

Marley looks grim. "I reckon. Now, hurry and unplug before new bots can arrive."

"But . . ."

"We'll talk later," Marley interjects. "Go."

So many questions swirl in my head. But the blood pounding in my ears makes it hard for me to think and focus on any one thing. Reluctantly, I tell Chuck to unplug me.

Eyes open, I squint against the sudden change of light, safely back in my pod.

"I trust you had a satisfying experience?" Chuck asks.

"I guess you can say that."

"Well, you may be interested in hearing that I lost track of you for a bit," Chuck says. "Very odd glitch, I've never run across one quite like it. Of course, I'll include the incident on my systems report."

"No, don't!" I say, more loudly than I intend.

Chuck takes a minute before responding. "All right, as you wish. But if the event ends up in any other reports, and they don't see mine, this could cause a special inquiry."

"I don't think any other systems will figure out what happened or who it happened to," I say while sliding into my wheelchair.

Chuck sighs. "I suppose it would be too much to expect an explanation?"

I shake my head. "Sorry, Chuck."

And with that, I wheel myself out of the pod room, mind filled with questions.

Chapter Thirteen

Liberum Hominem

T he Upgrades Mall is a terrible place to go with your friends if you want to update them on your nail-biting exploits.

Yet here we are.

"What?" Ji Yeon yells, tapping her ear in frustration, as the mall blares the latest music hits.

I huff, fighting the throng of people to stay close to my friends. It's been a couple of days since being chased by Enforcers, and I'd been dying to tell my friends about it. All that could be communicated during school was something big had gone down. Unfortunately, the full story had to wait. A virtual field trip had preoccupied one day—a recreation of when humanity first met the Ungulithi. The next day was full as well, creating a video essay on Arrival Day, with a focus on how to have a dialogue to enable cooperation during first contact.

Today, my friends and I decide to kill two birds with one stone. I take them up on their offer to hang out at the mall, and afterward open the scroll together. Ji Yeon and Lucas had made me swear up and down not to open the scroll without them, and I'd grudgingly agreed.

"This is a terrible place to tell a story," Lucas says, his face lit by an assortment of swirling and flashing neon lights.

The atmosphere is more like a club than a mall. Not like we or anyone else here is dressed for clubbing. Since we'd just come from school, all our avatars are still wearing plain-looking jeans and T-shirts.

Something moves behind my friends. A floating trolley comes up, the driver making no attempt to stop.

I gasp and grab both my friends' shirt collars, yanking them out of the way as the trolley lumbers past, making no attempt to veer away. I start to yell but notice an empty spot where the driver would sit. *Oh, yeah . . .*

"They need to update the AI that pilots those things," Lucas grumbles, straightening his collar. "Quite a few people have been hit. Nothing like taking damage while shopping."

"No one thought to warn us," Ji Yeon says, scowling at the press of humanity around us.

I wave my arms. "In this place? Does it look like anyone is paying attention?"

Moving on, we duck into the satchel and backpack aisle. Hundreds of satchels and packs hang in midair on either side of us. While they all seem similar, there are dozens of different variations and combos that add up to minor differences in functionality.

Fortunately, it's less crowded in this aisle than elsewhere, so I fill them in on my adventure with Marley.

Ji Yen appears shocked. "I didn't know evading Enforcers was possible."

"Beginner's luck." I grin.

"All that just to get a megaphone?" Lucas looks skeptical.

"I don't like it. Why are the Enforcers after him?" Ji Yeon rubs her chin, thinking. "Did he tell you why they're after him?"

The song blaring overhead fades out, and for two seconds, blessed relief from the pounding beat soothes my head. But then another beat blasts through the speakers, with an even faster tempo.

I sigh in frustration. Fighting to be heard is becoming more annoying. "Do we have to go shopping now?"

Ji Yeon looks reluctant. "I don't know. I'm running low on bullet bombs and flash-bangs, and they recently updated a pair of boots I've had my eye on."

I shake my head, turn my friends around, and shepherd them toward the exit. "I'm too amped to keep shopping right now."

Though I was a reluctant patron at the moment, I'd bought a parachute and a glider as soon as I'd stepped into the mall. Those items had been at the top of my list since my encounter with the Enforcers. That's the last time I fall from a great height unprepared. Lucas had tried convincing me to buy a jetpack instead, but it would've eaten into three-fourths of my digital wealth. Tempting, but I refused. He seemed disappointed. And that's why I have a ton of digital wealth and he doesn't.

Near the exit, we pass by one of the lounge areas. The mall is so large it has multiple rest areas and lounges. People gather to hang out, trade, or try to win some easy coin against slots, cards, and other games of chance if they tire of shopping.

Normally, I don't pay attention to the lounges. I don't care about noisy environments full of people, but an image on one of the giant TVs catches my eye. Frowning, I step into the lounge area. Cushioned couches and chairs line the entire room. In the middle sits a large circular bar, with small screens or holographic projections spaced at even intervals. Above the bar, multiple big-screen TVs are on GNC.

And on every single screen is a picture of my dad's avatar.

I bolt for the nearest screen, slipping on a pair of nearby headphones.

"Again, breaking news in the Robert McNealy case," Terra Novak says in a somber tone, yet looking pleased. "The court has ruled today that Robert McNealy is guilty on all counts of conspiracy and terrorism, including . . ."

Terra Novak goes into greater detail on the charges levied against my dad, but I can no longer make out what she is saying over the sudden ringing in my ears. I take a deep breath in an attempt to calm down before getting overwhelmed.

The news isn't unexpected. A guilty verdict seemed like a foregone conclusion. But to have it happen with such stark, matter-of-factness only seems to add insult to injury.

Someone grips my shoulder. Spinning around, Ji Yeon and Lucas stare at me, eyes wide with concern. Lucas jerks his hand off my shoulder, looking very unsure of himself.

Lucas mouths, "Are you okay?"

I'm about to ask him why he mouthed that question when Terra Novak's voice comes across again. I'm still wearing the headphones.

". . . case has garnered global attention, with various world leaders, including President Mercer, commenting on the verdict."

On the display, President Mercer smiles, sitting behind a desk in the Oval Office set the White House uses for press releases.

"Today, justice has prevailed. Even though the case was contentious, my faith in the justice system never wavered. The reforms that we and the Ungulithi have made to our institutions only reinforce my belief that we will continue to have more fair and just outcomes like today, and I renew my pledge to you that I will continue to work with our alien partners in helping humanity progress . . ."

I yank the headphones off and storm past my friends, whose expressions of concern change to bewilderment.

Rage courses through me. How *dare* President Mercer say those things about my dad! *She doesn't know what she's talking about. She's bought into the media campaign.*

The ringing in my ears grows louder. I veer to the nearest exit. The desire to punch something, slam a few doors, or bust some glass is almost overwhelming. Instead, the mall's glass doors slide out of my way and I find myself outside on the sidewalk at night, in the middle of Glee City.

Players and NPCs alike zoom past in a plethora of vehicles on the nearby street. Not to be outdone, the sidewalk teems with characters going in and out of the mall, making purchases from street vendors, or scooting past me on bikes, skates, skateboards, and hoverboards.

It's too much. Flashing lights. People talking, laughing, yelling. Everything and everyone is moving so fast. I try to glimpse the sky but can't see past the skyscrapers. Each skyscraper has a billboard or holographic image proclaiming what the building is. Firing range. Dance clubs. Talent shows. Movie theaters. Each building seems like it's fighting for my attention. Horns beep. People shout and laugh. The crowd presses close around me, bumping into me, and giving me looks of disgust or annoyance as they walk into the mall.

I squeeze my eyes shut and grip my head with both of my hands. As I'm about to unplug, someone shouts, "Wait, Ava, wait!"

It's Lucas. My friends run up to me, slightly out of breath, looking worried.

"Let's get out of here," Lucas says, lightly touching my arm. "Someplace quiet, where we can hear ourselves think."

Ji Yeon nods in agreement.

I want to scream no. Leave me alone. No more shopping. I don't want to bother with the scroll. My only desire right now is to bury my face in a pillow and cry.

Dad had left that scroll to me, though. He had gone to great pains to hide it, which means it's something important. Something for my eyes only.

I sniff and wipe my eyes. The back of my hand is damp. Crying in virtual reality is odd. The physics are like crying in real life, yet such a moment of vulnerability seems as if it doesn't belong in unreal environments, surrounded by people racing toward their next dopamine high.

After a calming breath, I say, "I think I know a place."

***

A lush green field with rolling hills appears. Here, it never grows dark. It's either a sunny afternoon, a romantic sunset, or a sunrise. The weather is never bad here.

By the looks of it, we are arriving during the twilight cycle. Here the only noise is the occasional chirping of birds and the sigh of the wind.

This is a much better spot to process than the overstimulation of the city.

"Ava, I'm so sorry," Ji Yeon says, giving me a hug.

I clench my jaw, afraid if I speak, the dam will burst.

"You sure you're okay?" Lucas asks, his hand still on my arm.

I nod.

"We don't have to do this." Ji Yeon releases me from her hug, stepping back to look me in the eye. "Seriously, we can do this another time."

I shake my head. "No, I want to do this. I . . . I need to do this."

Both nod. I give them as reassuring a smile as I can muster.

"But why Cupid's Field?" Ji Yeon asks, looking from Lucas to me.

A rising heat burns my cheeks. I forgot this was the place a lot of couples went on virtual dates. In my defense, I hadn't thought about me and Lucas being there like that. It just kind of worked out that way.

"Why not?" I retort.

Lucas looks around. "I don't see anyone. Let's open the scroll here."

Ji Yeon raises an eyebrow but stays silent. I make a face at her while activating my inventory menu. Then I select the megaphone and scroll.

The weight of both items is almost imperceptible in my avatar's hand. It's strange that Dad would leave me a message, and then leave the means to access the message with someone else. Marley might've been right about Dad getting paranoid.

"Let's do this," I say.

I extend the scroll further from me and aim the megaphone at it. Marley had said all I needed to do was to push the button on the megaphone's handle.

Lucas and Ji Yeon crowd closer. I can sense their tension, excitement, and curiosity, matching my own.

I press the button.

Nothing happens. Just as I'm about to push the button again, a man's voice comes through the speaker. "*Liberum hominem.*"

I almost drop the megaphone in surprise. My father's voice was the last thing I expected to hear. Both Ji Yeon and Lucas suck in a breath behind me.

Nothing else happens. The scroll remains unchanged. No other sound comes from the megaphone.

Ji Yen says, "That's it?"

I frown. "Well, that was anticlimactic."

"What was it the megaphone said?" Lucas asks.

"I do enough magic to know it's Latin," I say. "Other than that, I'm not sure."

"Something to do with free man." Ji Yeon tosses her head in annoyance. "I'm not as well versed in Latin as I should be."

"Considering your bilingual skills, you can probably cut yourself some slack," I say.

"Well," Lucas says, leaning closer to the scroll. "Did it work? Does it feel different?"

"I don't think . . ." I begin, then stop. The scroll unfurls in my hand.

Aside from chirping birds and a light breeze rustling through tall grass, it goes quiet.

I examine the scroll. The paper looks ancient, yellow, and crinkled. The few faded words are hard to make out.

"What's it say?" Lucas asks in a whisper.

"'Knowledge is power,'" I read aloud. "'Knowledge followed by inaction is useless. Use this power. Change the course of history before it's too late.'"

Frowning, I glance at both my companions. They appear as lost as me.

A shimmering blue glow emanates from the scroll. All three of us gasp at the same time. In any other context, that would've been a funny moment. Instead, a sense of excitement rushes through me as the light from the paper grows brighter and brighter.

Lucas and Ji Yeon lean closer.

The light then fades to a dull glow. Instead of words, a large tree is now front and center on the scroll.

"What kind of tree is that?" Lucas asks, in awe.

Ji Yeon shakes her head and says, "I don't know," matching his tone of wonder.

Neither do I. The detail is amazing, though, enhanced by the magical glow. I run my hand along the tree. It even feels real.

"Guys," I say, glancing up. "Touch this . . ." I pause.

My voice echoes like I'm in the cave level of Zombie Pirate's Bay. Except I'm in complete darkness. When did that happen?

I spin around, searching for my friends, disoriented. "Guys?" My echo repeats the question and fades. No answer.

I glance down at my feet. Though darkness surrounds me, somehow I'm still able to see my avatar. And the scroll. What is going on?

I should get out of here.

Just as I'm about to start the unplug sequence, a familiar voice interrupts me.

"Well, this is a bittersweet moment."

I freeze. It can't be . . .

I turn around.

"I knew you'd figure it out, sweetie. Good to see you again."

Words well up within me, but my mouth is as dry as the desert from the Dune Buster's game.

At last I manage to croak, "*Dad?*"

Chapter Fourteen

New Sons of Liberty

"Of course." Dad chuckles. "Who else would it be?"

Unable to utter a sound, all I can manage is to gape. None of this makes sense. But a part of me doesn't care. Millions of questions rush through my mind. I want to run up to him, hug him, and never let him go. To punch him and ask why he got mixed up with the rebels. To tell him everything that's been going on, with school, with Mom, and with my sisters.

"What are you doing here?" I finally say.

Now it's Dad's turn to appear confused. "I'm here because you opened the scroll. Remember?"

That opens up more questions. "But, they have you . . . so how are you here?"

His confusion seems to change to disappointment. "Don't tell me I didn't explain it to you. I wouldn't have given the scroll to you otherwise."

"Dad, you never gave the scroll to me. It appeared on its own."

He cocks his head. "No. I gave it to you. I told you how to figure out the password to open it. How else would this be happening?"

My frustration mounts. "Dad, that never happened."

He scratches his scalp. "I don't understand."

I relate the events that led up to this point.

However, the confusion never leaves his face. "I don't understand."

"What do you not get?"

"I'm sorry," he says, "My responses are limited. Please ask another question."

Then it becomes clear. My heart sinks.

I voice my thoughts out loud. "You're not here. This is just a program you wrote. An interactive voicemail. You're still in prison."

My dad nods. "I told you about this already. When I gave you the scroll."

No, you didn't. Maybe that's how you planned to do it. But that doesn't explain how I received it in the first place. But seeing his image and hearing his voice—I struggle to repress the tears welling up in my eyes.

I swipe at my eyes and square my shoulders. No time to cry. Time to get answers.

"So . . . Ryker? I mean, really?" I give an awkward laugh and sniff.

He grins. "I liked the name."

"Are you the Shadow?"

He shrugs. "Kind of."

Well, that's a frustrating answer. "What's that supposed to mean?"

"There's a handful of us that would hack broadcasting stations. With a unique encryption program, we would then broadcast our message."

"So there was more than one Ryker?"

"Yes."

"But why?"

"To make the world a better place."

I throw up my hands. "We're dealing with aliens here. We can't return to the way things were."

"I'm sorry. I don't understand."

Definitely want to punch him now. "Ok." I try to keep a grip on my frustration. "What do you want me to do?"

"To forgive me."

That catches me off guard.

"You being here means I'm dead or captured," he continues. "You wouldn't have opened the scroll otherwise. Either way, I'm sorry I'm gone. I'm sorry I can't be here for you."

He steps closer to me, moving as if to place a comforting hand on my arm. "Please don't hate me. I do what I do because I love you, your mom, and your sisters. I want a better life for you guys."

Once again, those stupid tears are stinging my eyes. "Why didn't you make anyone else a scroll? Why not Mom, at least?"

"I see things differently than your mother does." He glances down, pain evident on his face. "She does not realize the danger of doing nothing."

He looks up, his eyes blazing. "Only you might understand. I hope I'm right about this. A lot rides on this. On you."

I'm tempted to tell him no. Here he is, *affirming* his guilt. *Admitting* he's in rebellion. It's because of *him* that Mom has become semi-comatose and my sisters are running around without supervision.

Yet, I'm curious. Almost reluctantly, I ask, "What do you need me to do?"

His smile widens. "I need you to take a message to our organization—the Shadow's organization. We call ourselves the New Sons of Liberty."

Corny name. "Who were the Old Sons of Liberty?"

Dad's smile looks pained now. "I hope that's a joke."

"Of course," I lie, covering with a quick laugh.

"I'll tell you how to get to HQ. You'll have to be very brave, though. And modify your pod so that you aren't tracked."

Ugh. That sounds like something that requires skill. Outside The Haven, I'm kind of useless; hopefully, it's not too complicated.

"There's so much I wish I could tell you. Ava, do you trust me?"

My lower lip trembles. A renewed surge of emotion threatens to overwhelm me. I bite my lip but can't stop the tears. Despite my doubts, I answer, "Yes."

Tears appear in his eyes. "My brave little girl. You may not understand right now, but it only feels like yesterday when I first held you in my arms. How has time passed so fast? I feel as if I've wasted so much time. I should've been better about..."

He breaks off and looks away. A tear slides off his face and disappears before hitting the ground.

"I'm not wasting what time I have left," he says, facing me once more, determined. "I can help make this better. For everyone."

Though brief, his instructions are detailed.

"Thank you again, Ava," he says for the hundredth time.

I wave him off. "You say it's important. It must be done."

This isn't the only reason I'm running this errand. However, his AI program doesn't need to know that.

"I don't think I'm being overdramatic by saying the course of the world rides on your ability to do this," he says.

No pressure, right?

He gives me a sad smile. "I wish I could be there with you now."

"It's okay." No, it isn't. "I understand."

"I hope we see each other again. Soon."

My throat tightens. "Me too."

"I love you."

Dang it, he's going to make me cry again. "I love you too."

And with that, he is gone. The blackness fades, replaced by a beautiful sunset on a hilly pasture.

I'm back.

Lucas's and Ji Yeon's worried faces pop up in front of me. I yelp and stumble backward.

"Where'd you come from?" I gasp.

"We've been sitting here, waiting for you to wake up," Ji Yeon says, hands on hips.

"What happened?" Lucas asks. "Are you okay? You kinda froze there for a minute."

"At first I wondered if your connection glitched," Ji Yeon says. "It lasted too long to be regular lag, though."

I glance around, making sure we're still alone. "How long did I freeze?"

"A couple of minutes," Lucas says.

Huh. It seemed much longer than that. "It was my dad."

Now it's their turn to freeze, shocked expressions flitting across their faces. As fast as possible, I sum up what my dad had told me.

"I should go with you," Lucas says, clenching and unclenching his fists. "I don't like the idea of you exploring an unknown world. Alone."

"I'll be fine," I say, not sure how else to answer him. Dad had made it clear this was a solo mission.

Still unsatisfied, Lucas nods but doesn't offer further objection. It's sweet he cares so much. If Ji Yeon weren't there, I'd hug him—or something.

"When are you going?" Ji Yeon asks.

"Dad kept saying how important it is to get this scroll to the rebels as soon as possible. Apparently, besides the ability to deliver me a message only I can view, it also contains information only the leader of the rebels can see. I should try in the next couple of days."

Ji Yeon processes this information, worry lines creasing her brow. "I don't know how I feel about you contacting an anti-Ungulithi organization."

"It isn't ideal." I shrug. "I'm not sure about it either. But I'm willing to do almost anything to help my dad."

Ji Yeon bites her lip in agitation. "What if you took the scroll to your local Students of Global Peace Initiatives?"

Lucas and I stare at her in confusion. "Why would I do that?" I ask.

"Because they have a direct connection to the Ungulithi." Ji Yeon shifts, looking uncertain. "Perhaps your cooperation will . . . I don't know, make the Ungulithi look at your situation in a more favorable light. Especially if it leads to the capture or destruction of the rebels."

The president of my local SGPI is Kersey. There's no way in hell I'm taking this information to her. The image of her gloating face from a few days ago causes my stomach to knot in anger.

"Not gonna happen," I reply, letting an edge creep into my voice. "For now, I just need to play it Dad's way."

Ji Yeon nervously shifts again. "I'm not sure that's a good idea."

Why is she acting so weird? It's becoming frustrating. "Got any better ideas?"

"As a candidate for my local SGPI, it's my duty to report this information."

I blink in astonishment. "But . . . you can't."

Lucas's eyes are wide. "This is her *dad* we're talking about."

"Yeah." Ji Yeon coughs, steadying her voice. "That's why I'm hesitating. But if it were anyone else, I'd go immediately to the nearest SGPI clubhouse. Reporting information like this is day one stuff they teach us."

"Listen," I say, "I realize this is kind of crazy and goes against the norm here. But if there's a chance to help my dad and save my family, this is it. Otherwise, they're going to *execute* him."

"Ji Yeon," Lucas interjects, "Please, just wait. I mean, this is Ava and her family we're talking about here."

Ji Yeon's avatar is stiff as she looks from Lucas to me, her expression growing in anguish.

"Fine," she sighs, slumping. "I understand your dad's not a bad guy. I just don't get how he can associate with the Shadow."

Well, that's something. "Thank you. Maybe doing this will help us find out."

With that over, my mind turns back to how the heck I can accomplish what my dad wants. This task won't be a quick or easy one. It will require me to be plugged in for an unknown, extended amount of time. How can I pull it off without my teachers missing me, or Mom in a rare moment of sobriety, paying attention to how long I'm under?

Ji Yeon must sense what's stirring in my mind. "I might be able to help with a bot avatar at school," she says.

Good, one problem solved.

"It will not be easy," Ji Yeon adds.

Oh.

"Fortunately, no one besides us really interacts with you at school," Ji Yeon continues. "The programming wouldn't have to be advanced. Enough to buy you a couple of days, anyway."

"Was that about my lack of friends?" I ask.

Ji Yeon shakes her head. "No, it was about our public school's lack of security."

Lucas raises an eyebrow. "Doesn't The Haven have top-level, anti-bot security?"

Ji Yeon gives him a self-satisfied smirk. "I have my ways."

I hope so.

Chapter Fifteen

First Steps

It doesn't take long for Ji Yeon to complete a bot with an avatar the spittin' image of mine. However, the behavior part is more complicated to pull off than we expected. Not because people are interacting with the bot. Ji Yeon is right; almost no one speaks two words to bot-me. The complication that arises develops from something we hadn't considered: Chuck.

"I'm sorry, but you've gone too far this time," Chuck says to me.

I suppress a sigh.

"No, I don't care how huffy you are," he continues. "I cannot tolerate unsanctioned software being installed in my system."

"Don't worry," I say, in my most reassuring tone of voice. "It's not a virus. I wouldn't install anything that would hurt you."

"Maybe not intentionally," he says with an imitation of a sniff. It's so weird when he imitates certain human behaviors that could never apply to him.

"What's that supposed to mean?" I ask, attempting to sound hurt for his benefit.

His tone is reproachful. "Ava, I'm a machine. You can't manipulate me."

My phone, lying in my lap, vibrates; it's a text from Ji Yeon.

Ji Yeon: HOW'S IT GOING?

Me: THINKING I SHOULD TURN DOWN CHUCK'S PERSONALITY A FEW NOTCHES.

Ji Yeon: SHOULD'VE BEEN DONE A LONG TIME AGO. WHO WANTS AN AI WITH PERSONALITY?

I sigh and strive again to explain to Chuck that it's only temporary, and the software will be deleted in a matter of hours—at least, hopefully, it only takes a few hours to get back. The longer I'm away, the more likely someone notices something is off.

"Ava," Chuck says in his most condescending tone, "I'm programmed this way. I'm incapable of being convinced to allow unauthorized access."

I'm about to reply when another text from Ji Yeon comes through.

Ji Yeon: YOU NEED TO MANUALLY OVERRIDE CHUCK.

"Chuck," I say. "Manual override."

Chuck snorts. "Did you really think that would work?"

Sheesh. It was worth a try. I update Ji Yeon.

Ji Yeon: THIS IS A PROBLEM.

Me: DON'T TELL ME YOU CAN'T HACK THIS THING.

Ji Yeon: OK, I WON'T. I WASN'T AWARE YOU DIDN'T HAVE ADMIN RIGHTS.

I huff in exasperation and look around the room to my nonexistent audience as if to ask, "Huh?"

Me: WHY WOULD I HAVE ADMIN RIGHTS?

Ji Yeon: NEVER MIND. WE NEED TO FIGURE OUT HOW TO OVERRIDE CHUCK TO INSTALL MY PROGRAM. OTHERWISE, YOU WON'T BE ABLE TO RUN YOUR ERRAND.

Thank you, Ji Yeon, for summing that up.

Me: HOW LONG WILL THIS TAKE?

She doesn't reply. Deep in research, no doubt. I have my doubts if it'll do much good. The AI systems are designed by Beusk Industries, and their reputation for state-of-the-art technology and digital security is yet to be rivaled.

Foiled already. How can I help Dad out if something as simple as administrative clearance is blocking me?

I check my phone for any missed messages. No word yet from Ji Yeon.

Thumbing through my most recent messages, I am about to put the phone away when Marley's name at the bottom of the screen catches my eye. Had I updated him about Dad's message yet? Oops . . . I don't think I have. Add that to the growing to-do list.

Marley's name triggers memories of that crazy meeting. Being chased by Enforcers, hanging suspended in midair, thanks to Marley's hacker guy . . . wait, Marley has a hacker buddy!

I tap on my last conversations with Marley, then tap the call button.

It only rings once before he answers.

"Hello?"

"Marley, I need your help."

———

A short amount of time later, Marley's guy remotely takes down Chuck's security, allowing me to install Ji Yeon's software.

"I told ya he's good," Marley says, his smirk clear even over the phone.

That's putting it modestly. The fact he can hack The Haven *and* a Beusk system makes him something of a wizard in my estimation.

"Nope," Marley says when I ask him about Mike. "Ain't gonna reveal that. A man's word is his bond. He's entrusted me with his secret identity, and I ain't gonna betray it."

Secret identity? What is he, a superhero? "But you said his name when we were being chased," I counter. At least, I'm pretty sure he did.

Marley shrugs. "Don't mean it's his real one. Coming up with names for him is part of the fun. I try to pick ones that drive him nuts."

From what I know about Marley, this seems likely. Marley's hesitation to reveal Mike's identity makes me wonder if this guy works a high-level job in The Haven or maybe Beusk Industries.

"Well, tell him I said thanks," I say, about to hang up.

"Hold on now," he says, "I pulled a big favor for you. I deserve to know what this is about. Does it have anything to do with what I helped you get?"

Ugh. I hate being on the phone; texting is so much better. But he's right; he's owed an explanation.

Marley whistles when I bring him up to speed. "Ain't that interesting. Seems like you've been up to a lot since we last spoke."

"I guess."

"Were you ever gonna tell me when you opened the scroll?"

"Why would I?"

"Because I'm the one that helped you open it."

He's got a point. "Sorry. My dad never mentioned you. It didn't cross my mind you had any further interest in it."

"Of course I do," he drawls. "Regardless of if he mentions me or not. Your dad and I worked together for some time. I want to help."

Should I tell him? It may be easier to work with someone who has worked with the Resistance before. Dad insisted I needed to do this alone, though.

"I think I got this," I say.

Marley sighs. "Alrighty, hold your cards close if ya gotta. I reckon I get it. Still, give me a ring when you're done, alright?"

"Will do," I promise.

Chapter Sixteen

The Floating City

"**B**ot activated."

Ji Yeon's whisper is loud. I turn down The Haven's dialogue volume.

"How's she—how am I doing?" I ask, feeling tense, sitting on the edge of the bed in my Haven castle.

"Our girl is looking good," Ji Yeon says, then dryly adds. "I bet you wish Lucas would say that."

"Shh," I hiss. "And for your information, no, I've never thought that."

"Not until now." She sounds way too self-satisfied.

"I hate you. You're lucky Lucas has an early class."

It's been two days since the installation. We've been testing the bot version of me in different scenarios in The Haven. We might be acting over-cautious at this point—few people interact with bot-me so there seems little risk in being uncovered, but Ji Yeon wants to be prepared for anything.

"You're not the only one with something to lose here, should this fail," Ji Yeon reminded me during a test run. "I've not been working my ass off to get into SGPI to risk having it all torn from me because of this mission you've taken upon yourself. I already have to work twice as hard to prove myself because of my association with you."

The memory of Ji Yeon's comment still hurts. *Gee, how generous of you to continue to be my friend. You truly are too kind.*

I almost said something at the time but decided against it. Despite her insensitive words, she's risking a lot to help me. Even if all that is at risk for her is her acceptance into the stupid SGPI.

"Are you ready?" The tension in Ji Yeon's voice is palpable.

"I'll be fine," I say, trying to reassure her while double-checking my inventory. "My dad said the New Sons of Liberty are the only ones there." I don't bother telling her what else is there—no need for her and Lucas to worry more than necessary.

She tries to force confidence in her voice. "See you on the other side."

I smile, scooting closer to the edge of my queenly bed. "I'll be back."

With that, I sign off the audio chat.

"No trace." My dad's words replay in my mind. "No communication with the outside world. No one else can know where you're going. You can't risk it."

I bring up The Haven's search engine and type in the coordinates he had given me on a holographic keyboard. Once that's done, all that's left is to press the Enter key.

A series of numbers and letters floated in front of my dad when he said this next part. "You have to enter this code and the coordinates. It's impossible to access the rebel's location without it. If you miss even one letter, their security measures will detect this login attempt and you'll never find them again."

I double-check the code, making sure it matches the one my dad had given me, finger still suspended over the Enter key.

"It won't be easy," Dad had told me. "Some of the protection measures for the New Sons of Liberty may be a lot."

"How?" I asked.

My dad grimaced. "Not sure. Never had to go through security protocols when I was there. I was a trusted, early member. I know that on the off chance someone stumbled into our territory, or there was a more detailed Haven security sweep, the rebel's location environment would look like a post-apocalyptic wasteland."

"One that happened to have a floating city over the landscape?" I asked, recalling his description of the rebel base from earlier.

He shrugged and laughed. "Oh, don't hang out too long in the deserted city on the ground. I overheard some others say the day cycle isn't so bad, but . . ."

"What?"

Dad looked unsure. "They might've been messing with me. I don't know. Some of the guys mentioned the night cycle is pretty rough."

Even though his projection is only a limited AI program, enough of my dad's mannerisms come through. He wasn't telling me everything.

"What is it?" I asked.

He hesitated. "There's a rumor. I'm not sure if it's true, but . . ."

Watching me with a pained expression, he paused, appearing uncertain.

"You should tell me everything," I said. "I need every advantage I can get."

He sighed in resignation. "Don't die there. There won't be a respawn. There may be repercussions in the real world."

An involuntary shiver ran through my body. Was he implying what I thought he was? "Like what?"

He cringed. "Again, this is all hearsay. But stuff like brain damage and . . . and death."

My finger hovers over the Enter key. *No, don't overthink it.* You're simply running a delivery to them.

And perhaps to convince them to rescue my dad.

When my dad first instructed me how to contact the rebels, convincing them to break him out never crossed my mind. The fact he was trusting me with top-secret information to give to a rebel network was—at the time—sufficient to preoccupy me.

But next he said, "Don't hang around after you deliver the message. I had to struggle with my conscience to ask you to do this. I don't want you to be any further involved than that."

You don't have to be involved in anything else. But this organization is why my father is gone. The reason he is to be executed. They got him into this mess. I think they should get him out.

The more I think about it, the more convinced I am that this is the only way to bring my dad home. And with that thought, a small spark of optimism lights up within me. It's been a while since I dared to hope. I'm almost too scared to let that little ember burn.

My hand trembles.

Don't overthink it! Just . . .

I press Enter.

Tall brown weeds sway in the breeze. The hillside is covered with them. Vultures circle the overcast sky. A rank smell hits my nostrils—decay and death.

The remnants of a city lay before me. Gray buildings are covered in streaked scorch marks. Rusted steel structures and cracked asphalt are all that remains of whatever culture used to be here. Abandoned cars dot the landscape. Weeds jut from cracks in the streets and sidewalks. Vines push through concrete and metal, wrapping the metropolitan architecture in a chokehold in their slow, dominating spread. Even they appear withered, barely holding on to life.

"Cheerful," I say. "Wonder what the story is here?"

I search for a glimpse of the hovering city. I'm surprised it isn't in plain sight; Dad had said it was suspended close to the dead city.

"Could the clouds be hiding it?" I speculate aloud.

A glint of light pokes through the hazy sky. Grabbing binoculars from my inventory, I focus the lenses in the direction of the flash. Something dark appears—yes; that's the outline of a skyscraper.

So, how do I get there?

Well, first things first... since I'm in brown surroundings, my avatar should be in one of my tan jumpsuits. It'll help me blend in, plus it's rated to be well-suited for athletic movement.

You never know.

After changing my clothes, I make my way down the hill and head toward the town; perhaps something there can help me reach my destination.

Loose gravel crunches under my boots as I step onto the asphalt. I pull my Incinerator M32-0 from inventory and check that it's charged. I sweep through the ground floors of the nearest buildings, yet cannot discover any secrets or clues about how to proceed.

With each sweep, my unease builds. I've never understood the appeal of games that are about exploring dungeons, caverns, or ruins. The atmosphere is creepy, and there's always some disturbing creature waiting to . . .

A noise makes me stop dead in my tracks. I'm in the ground floor lobby of yet another skyscraper, designed like the others I'd just explored. Dust-caked windows let very little light in, barely illuminating overturned office chairs, busted computers, and papers strewn over every surface.

An eerie silence pervaded the other buildings. In this building, though, something had stirred. The noise was so faint, and only lasted a split second. Could I have imagined it?

I hold my breath, straining to catch any other sound. All is quiet. Perhaps one of the windows is broken, and a breeze had ruffled some papers?

I hear a noise like the soft exhalation of someone who has been holding their breath. My eyes dart around the room. There are too many deep shadows that can be used for concealment.

Time to go.

Every muscle in my body pulls taut as I back toward the nearest doorway.

More papers rustle. It's not the wind—something is *moving*. A heavy footfall, as someone—or something—attempts to slink through the dark without being heard.

Beads of sweat run down my face. I tighten my grip on my gun. Only about twenty feet from the exit.

A barely perceptible glint flashes several paces in front of me. I almost drop my weapon and scream. A pair of glowing eyes stares at me from the darkness. I stumble, every fiber of my being urging me to turn tail for the exit. I recover enough to bring my gun to bear.

The floating eyes are gone. As if they were never there.

Feeling as if I'm about to wet myself, it seems the most prudent form of action is to turn around and run as fast as I can out the exit.

So I do.

Whatever is approaching must have the same idea. Something skitters behind me. I fire my gun over my shoulder.

A bloodcurdling wail pierces my eardrums. It sounds like it's right behind me.

I slam into the exit door, crashing through the dirty glass, and falling flat on my face. I roll over and aim my gun at the open doorway while trying to scoot across the broken pavement, attempting to put as much distance between myself and whatever is inside.

At first I see nothing. Has it stopped chasing me?

A tall, ashen-tinged figure materializes from the darkness, stopping short of the doorway. I have enough time to observe a set of long, sharp teeth, stringy hair, and bony hands that seem to extend like talons before the figure fades into inky black.

I lay on the ground panting, blinking sweat from my eyes. My hand holding the gun trembles, making my aim unsteady. An angry shriek echoes from the darkened interior of the building.

Good. It doesn't like daylight.

I force the tension in my muscles to ease. Reaching the floating city before nightfall has now become a top priority. I don't want to find out what it's like here at night.

Unfortunately, night comes fast.

How much real-time has passed since encountering the creature? In-world, the sun is setting, partially obscured behind the hill I'd spawned from. Flaming red and amber hues cast an almost romantic light upon the dystopian environment.

A beautiful lie.

Every so often, I glimpse a gaunt figure or a white blur in a dark window. It's either that thing from earlier or more of them. If I can't get to the floating city soon . . . well, I'll have to exit the level and come back whenever it's daytime again. My fear seems silly, put into a context like that.

Portions of the city are already in darkness. I steer clear of the deepening shadows; better safe than sorry.

Except for the occasional glimpse of what looks like light glinting off windows, the floating city remains hidden.

"Well," I say aloud, looking at the dirty, empty buildings around me. "I should leave before that thing . . . or those things come after me."

Disappointment gnaws at my stomach. Fingers crossed Dad's message isn't time sensitive.

"I hate I can't help you here," he had said. "I don't know what security cooked up to prevent folks from flying to the city."

His words imply a means of flying up to the city. The only mode of transportation around is decades-old cars and buses with broken windows, all rusted and rotting where they were abandoned so long ago.

The sound of rocks scraping across gravel is nearby. It's the first noise not caused by me I've heard in hours.

Time to go.

I activate the in-game menu. At least, I try to activate the menu. Instead, all I get is nothing.

I rapidly attempt a few more times. Still nothing.

"Activate menu," I say, struggling to keep my voice steady, despite the rising anxiety threatening to clench my throat closed.

Again, nothing happens.

A high-pitched wail bounces and echoes off the buildings. The light is now gone. The skyscrapers have lost any distinctive features, looking like nothing more than giant black masses closing in around me. I back up against the nearest high-rise, jamming the butt of my rifle into my shoulder.

Another wail answers the first. Then another. And another. Soon the night air is full of a thousand tortured cries. My heart rate picks up speed. This isn't good.

An eerie, pale light falls across the world. The moon is rising. And with this dim new hue, a change takes place.

The streets are no longer empty. Dozens of skeletal humanoid figures skitter across the ground, sniffing the pavement and lifting their heads to sniff the air. Other similar shapes stand upright, lumbering in a slow, deliberate gait, heads swiveling this way and that as if in search of something lost. In the moonlight, their skin glows softly like pearls. The hair on their heads hangs in thin, loose strands. Their fingers, like claws, glint dangerously.

My muscles seem to lose all strength. I sink to the ground. Hopefully, the shadows are deep enough to keep me hidden. Maybe now it's safe to go inside since the city's inhabitants all seem to be wandering the streets.

The inability to access menus must be one of the safety protocols my dad knew nothing about. Whoever ran security for the New Sons of Liberty must be superb if they could not only build an undetectable level in The Haven but also reject menu access inside the level. I know little about programming, but even I'm aware this is beyond Software Writing 101.

Okay, pull yourself together, girl. Time to figure out a solution.

Stubborn resolve reawakens my strength. Back on my feet, I run through options. The solution is simple, though executing it won't be. These creepy beings seem averse to daylight, so all that's needed is to wait them out until the sun returns.

My insides flutter. In most cases like this, I wouldn't feel so desperate. Real-life death being a potential outcome adds a level of stakes to this situation, unlike anything I've faced before. Frankly, it's a miracle I haven't collapsed into a puddle of anxious jelly at this point. Because of the differences between The Haven and previous forms of VR, many have joked about dying in-game, which would then cause you to expire in real life. To my knowledge, that has never happened. I've heard rumors about some extreme games and bets that happen after midnight in The Haven but have never been able to confirm anything.

I shake the thought off. Right now, just survive. Play it like a regular game . . . only take fewer risks.

As I'm about to edge toward the nearest door, one of the skittering figures makes a bee-line in my direction, moving at a speed that should be impossible. I fumble with my gun, bringing it to bear on the creature. My finger hesitates on the trigger. If I fire, it's going to draw those monsters on me like a magnet.

The creature stops short, only a few feet away. A sound like a low rumble, followed by a high-pitched whine, thrums from its throat. It raises its humanoid head, its earlier jerky speed now replaced by smooth, snakelike motions.

I stare into the monster's lidless, milky eyes. We remain motionless, staring at each other. Can the creature see me? It has no iris, its pale orbs barely resembling eyeballs.

The monster raises its head and unleashes a bloodcurdling shriek that seems to fill the dead city.

My reaction is too slow. By the time I fire my weapon, I hear answering shrieks and screams from every direction. The creature collapses, riddled with bullets. Now these things know my location.

Okay, time to go for real.

I run around the building and almost crash into three of the monsters. I fire from the hip, almost blinded by the flashes of light spitting out the end of my gun's muzzle. The creatures flop to the ground in a red haze. I leap over them, not bothering to check whether they're dead or wounded.

More creatures approach. What sounds like thousands of claws clicking on pavement echoes off the buildings, growing louder and louder.

My foot splashes in a puddle as I bolt through the entrance of an alleyway.

Suddenly, one is ahead of me, close in proximity. The creature leaps, claws extended, screaming. Moonlight glints off its fangs, long strings of saliva dangling from its mouth.

No time to think. Without stopping, I drop, landing on my hip. As I slide forward, I fire at the monster who is now sailing over me. Misty red puffs burst from its pale body. Its shrieks of aggression turn to pain as it clutches at itself and collapses to the ground behind me. I rise and whirl to face it, but it lies unmoving.

Can't stay and celebrate. Gotta keep moving.

Something flashes in the night sky. A large beam of light. The buildings I'm between block most of the light beam and its source.

More screams. They sound far enough away, perhaps giving me sufficient time to search my inventory to find the grappling gun.

In my peripheral vision, I notice two of the creatures race past the entrance to the alley. I hold my breath, scrolling through my inventory stacks. Thankfully, whatever is afflicting the main menu does not affect the inventory menu.

Where is that stupid grappling gun?

Motion again. The two creatures must've stopped and backtracked. Both now stand at the entrance to the alley, staring at me.

That's enough searching. I'm about to close my inventory and fight when my gaze lands on the grappling gun. Activating it, I fire toward the top of the building.

The two monsters give a shrieking roar and charge.

My grappling hook hits its mark, and the line snaps taut.

Going up.

Retraction mode activates as the two creatures lunge for me. I'm yanked into the air just in time. The pale monsters crash to the ground. They glance up and howl in frustration.

That was too close.

Once on the roof, I stumble to my knees, struggling to catch my breath. I glance over the edge. The monsters tilt their heads when they spot me, as if assessing how to get to me. Guess that answers if they can see. Something tells me it won't take them long to figure out how to get up here.

Chapter Seventeen

The Upside-Down City

Now to figure out how to get out of here.

The shaft of light from earlier is coming from the moon. It shines through the hazy upper atmosphere, the lunar glow falling toward the city like a column.

My eyes follow the beam's direction, mind racing through options.

Correction: option, singular. Backtrack to the hill where I'd first entered the world, and maybe the menu will work there. It's not a great option, but right now, nothing else comes to mind.

I trace the moonbeam's path. It ends on the outer fringe of the city. That's interesting. Seems too deliberate to be a simple design aesthetic.

What if this isn't random weather programming? Any novice gamer knows to pay attention to environmental clues, which could provide key help in certain levels or games.

What if the moonbeam is telling me where I need to go?

I retrieve some binoculars from my inventory and focus on where the moonbeam ends. I almost burst into relieved laughter. It's an airport. Not sure how I hadn't noticed it before, but the light seems to point it out like, *Hey dummy! Floating city, how else would you get there?*

Grating metal brings me back to my current predicament.

"What now?" I ask aloud.

I check on my two monster friends at ground level. There are no longer two, but six of them. And two of the six are clinging to the side of the building, climbing up.

I shoot a few rounds down at them, but only manage to scatter the group on the ground. The two climbing the wall press themselves flat. That, combined with the vertical angle, makes it impossible to hit them. Three of the more intelligent creatures on the ground break the windows on the bottom floor and jump through to the inside.

I back away from the edge. Most of the time, heights don't bother me in The Haven, aside from occasional butterflies in my stomach. But with regeneration in this part of The Haven in question, there is a real risk of falling to my death. It's a heavy moment one doesn't associate with a game.

I need to make my way to that airfield. While there's no guarantee I can fly one of those planes, it seems like the best option for the moment. Besides, Dad is counting on me.

The door to the roof bursts open behind me. I pivot and fire. The creature leaping through the doorway collapses and slides to a stop just short of my combat boots, motionless.

No time to celebrate; two more creatures dart through. Blood splatters the doorway as my bullets stop them in place.

Smart. They're trying to flank me. These aren't mindless animals. They have some intelligence. Booger for me.

I run to the edge of the building, facing the airport, and open my inventory. There's a clattering behind me. More creatures are now on the rooftop.

It's only going to take seconds for them to reach me. Panic-scrolling through my inventory, items fly by my eyes almost faster than my mind can register.

Then I see what I'm looking for.

Behind me, the skittering grows louder. I can almost feel the hot breath from their open maws as they give triumphant howls; the pack is about to bring down the prey.

Now or never. I exhale, lean forward, and jump. The monsters' screams of victory turn to cries of rage and bewilderment.

I activate my glider suit. Colorful material replaces my combat clothes. Webbed "wings" spread from my arms to just past my hips.

The sidewalk races to meet me. Nothing like a literal crash course in using a glider suit. I stretch my limbs, almost spread-eagled. The suit catches the air, and I tilt, shooting skyward. Just in time too. I'd been a few feet short of smacking into the pavement.

An instant later, I clear the rooftops of the city buildings and level out. It's amazing how fast this thing is.

I reorient myself and head for the airport. A quick glance down reveals many of the creatures are still giving chase, running in large groups through the streets. Their screams are just loud enough to hear over the wind roaring in my ears.

I'm making great time but losing altitude. Without upgrades, the suit only keeps me in the air for a minute or less, depending on the height

I jumped from and the wind conditions. I weave between skyscrapers, always keeping some portion of the airport in sight. Unfortunately, it seems as if I'm going to touch down before reaching it.

Something tells me that if I land now, I'm not making it to the airport. But there's no way for me to gain altitude again. Not unless I land, use my grappling gun, then jump off another rooftop. That's if there's not a swarm of creatures ready to pounce on me as soon as I hit the ground.

Wait . . . the grappling gun!

Fortunately, since it was recently used, it doesn't take long to find. I chance another quick glimpse down and wish I hadn't. Twenty feet below me, the mob of creatures is keeping pace with my glider, their arms and claws extended, teeth glistening, blank eyes shimmering.

I fire the grappling hook at an approaching skyscraper.

As any gamer knows, luck sometimes plays a huge part in the gaming experience. Though I'm shooting a broad target, my momentum makes it a fast-moving target. If my aim is off, if I didn't compensate for angle and trajectory . . .

Over the terrible screams and growls of my pursuers, I hear the most wonderful sound of the night—a grappling hook being set into a building.

I whoop for joy. The rope coming out of the gun's barrel grows taut, and I fold my arms and legs in, now suspended in the air by only my grappling hook. I am now swinging off a skyscraper like a monkey swinging on a vine in the jungle.

This is just one of the many reasons The Haven is so outstanding. The open worlds, and the endless adaptability of the environments to each individual playing style.

At the top of the swing, I note the airport is still too far to glide too easily. I disengage my grappling hook from the building now behind me and fire at the building ahead of me.

This time I'm further from the ground when the rope pulls taut. I swing over to the next building, and then the next.

This would be a lot more fun if I wasn't in such danger. Lucas and Ji Yeon will never believe this once I get back and tell them.

If I get back.

Once again at the top of my swing, I realize there are no more skyscrapers near enough to latch onto. No choice but to glide again.

By now, my pursuers have fallen behind, though they are still visible. I make a smooth landing within running distance of the airfield. Several passenger planes and smaller private jets are parked in the open. Stowing my glide suit back into my inventory, I dash toward the nearest private jet.

This better not be a flight simulator level of difficulty. If it is, I'm toast. I've never had the patience to learn how to fly in plane and rocket simulators.

Me-time in The Haven is for fun, not for learning.

Behind me, the angry mob grows louder. I peek over my shoulder. Dozens of those pale monsters sprint and gallop behind me, closing the distance at an alarming rate.

I dash for the nearest airplane, gun back in hand. Within a few feet of the private jet, its door opens and boarding stairs lower to the ground. I bound up, skipping multiple steps, and leap into the aircraft. Almost face-planting, I catch myself and shove off the ground, whirling in time to see three of the monsters already on the steps.

"No!"

I spray digital lead through the doorway. The creatures flail as the bullets shred through their bodies, toppling them over the sides or rolling down the stairs.

Lunging at the door, I spot two buttons that resemble the up and down functions on an elevator. Hopefully, those are the controls to fold the stairs ramp and close the door.

More creatures sprint for the stairs. With one hand, I fire outside, and with the other hand, I smash the up button.

The plane door closes with a hiss and click.

I sigh and lean against the door, taking a moment to gather myself. Even sensory filters seem to be different in this level. I'm feeling more . . . well, *more* than I usually do in The Haven.

A loud bang causes me to jump. Within an instant, a chorus of thuds is all I can hear. The creatures are trying to find a way inside.

I bolt for the cockpit and collapse into the pilot's chair. At least I think it's the pilot's chair. Do they sit on the right side or the left? Most of the planes I've flown were various warplanes and fighter jets from different wars in history, with one seat in the front and one in the back. I've never flown a passenger craft before.

Metal screeches. It sounds like the monsters are trying to tear their way inside. This aircraft better hold, or I'm gonna die a horrible death and come back to haunt whoever built this damn level.

Arrayed before me is a vertigo-inducing mixture of knobs, switches, and dials. No labels or any sign of what the controls do.

Desperate, I flip a few switches and press a couple of buttons. Nothing happens. Icy claws of fear rake across my insides.

No, no, no!

Have I made the wrong call? Outside, the creatures continue their assault, their violence growing in sound and fury.

When I spot the large red and green buttons in the middle of the instrument panel, I almost burst out laughing. I could kick myself. How did I miss them before?

Movement beyond the windshield catches my eye. I suck in a breath. A pair of watery blank eyes glares at me.

No more fooling around. I pound the green button.

The engines roar. Cabin lights blink on. The craft surges to life and rolls forward. Shrieks of anger and astonishment ring out around the plane as it taxis down the runway, building momentum.

At last, something is going my way.

Below the green button is a lever, and I pull it down. The nose of the airplane lifts, and that familiar thrill of being airborne hits my stomach.

The creature continues to cling to the front of the craft, fangs bared in a soundless growl. I grin and wave at it.

Once I achieve enough altitude, I roll the plane. The monster shrieks, digs its claws deeper, and hangs suspended in the air. It tilts its head toward the ground and then back to me, snarling and spitting. In the next instant, we hit a pocket of turbulence. The creature loses its grip and drops from view.

Reorienting the plane, I sigh with relief. I've done it; I've survived. My reprieve is, sadly, short-lived. An alarm rings out.

What now?

Searching for the source, my eyes land on a flashing radar screen with two words that make my stomach sink like a rock.

MISSILE LOCK

Where the hell had missiles come from? Three flashing red lines on the radar screen are converging on my position.

While this isn't my first time flying an airplane and having missiles fired at me, this isn't a fighter jet; I don't have flares to throw off the missiles, and if I get hit, I might not respawn. As Dad is fond of saying, "This is a whole new ball game."

So I do the only thing I can. I jam the throttle forward, forcing the nose of the plane down. Almost instantly, my maneuver turns into a full dive.

The clouds outside the windshield vanish and, once again, the desolate city is in front of me. At this distance, even the tallest skyscrapers appear like toy replicas. But, given my current rate of altitude loss, that will soon change. I need to get out of this dive.

A thunderous boom rattles the plane. The radar shows two of the red lines are gone. The missiles had been converging on me at a similar pace, with my plunge throwing them for a loop. They must've collided.

Nice!

My victory grin doesn't last long. The third missile had dodged the collision with the other two. It had lost its lock but regains it seconds after the explosion. It, too, is in a dive, coming at me from behind.

"This is way too much trouble to play delivery girl," I huff, pulling back up on the throttle. "Haven't you ever heard the phrase 'don't kill the messenger?'"

The plane quavers, and the engine roars in protest as I fight to pull out of the dive. Through the windshield, the city's borders disappear. What once looked like miniature buildings stretch into full-size buildings—metal fingers reaching up, grasping for me.

"C'mon," I scream, my feet shoving against the floor as I pull on the throttle with all my strength. "Pull up, pull up, pull up!"

The city tilts. The plane shudders, and the city shifts even more. I scream again, this time in relief. I am coming out of the dive.

My relief turns to horror as I realize I'm not pulling up fast enough. The missile lock alarm wails. Skyscrapers race past me.

The red line on the radar screen that is the missile is only millimeters behind the dot that is my plane. The ground angles up to meet me.

An extra jolt of adrenaline shoots through me, a last desperate gasp for life. One hand still on the throttle, I yank the airplane toward a highway, praying it's a long enough stretch of road.

The nose pitches. The pressure pinning me to my seat eases. Ground and road dip beneath me as the craft levels out.

Another loud boom shakes the plane. According to the radar, the third missile is no more. Must've hit one of the buildings I'd passed.

My avatar's hands are slick with perspiration. It legit feels like I am covered in sweat. My body temperature is hot, while my drenched skin is freezing. The post-adrenaline crash hits, leaving me breathless and shaky, with just enough strength left to grip the throttle and the wheel.

I soon break through the cloud cover and atmospheric haze. What I see causes my jaw to drop. A literal, floating, upside-down city. Though the nose of the airplane is tilted up, it once again looks like buildings are reaching up to grasp at me, as if my plane were plunging downward instead of up. In fact, the city looks like a mirror image of the one below me, except vibrant and *alive*.

Sunshine glints off skyscrapers. *Wait, so it's nighttime down below, but sunny up here?* Cars fill the streets. Little dots that I assume are people occupy the sidewalks. Nearby, the outline of a flock of birds flutters upside down. Well, here I'm the one who's upside down. This is all very weird and messing with my head.

The plane shudders, then lurches. I jerk forward and slam into the wheel.

What the hell?

I sit back and reach for the controls. They're stiff and immovable in my hands.

The engine sputters and goes quiet. I suck in a breath, waiting for the inevitable plunge to the ground. After everything, it's going to be engine failure that does me in.

Nothing happens. In fact, the plane seems to have stopped moving. It keeps getting weirder and weirder.

"Tell us why we shouldn't let you drop and fall to your death."

I cut off the sudden scream that tries to escape my lips. The voice coming from my radio is deep and unexpected.

I try to compose my scattered thoughts as the voice comes through again. "Unidentified aircraft, respond now, or we will release you from our tractor beam and let gravity take care of the rest."

Frazzled as I am, I can't help but wonder if gravity is weird here too, and would I fall *up* toward the upside-down city?

"This is Ava McNealy, daughter of Robert McNealy. I have what you've been waiting for."

Anxious, I wait, recalling what my dad had said to me about reaching the city.

"Someone might page you," he said. "Tell them who you are and that you have what they've been waiting for."

I had frowned upon hearing those instructions. "That last part seems cryptic."

Dad smiled. "You need to catch their attention. You need to give them a reason to bring you to the New Sons of Liberty."

The man who replies over the radio sounds skeptical. "Who are you again?"

I repeat my words from earlier.

This time, the silence stretches longer.

"All right," he says, "we'll bring you in."

Chapter Eighteen

Morgan Sheffy

The two men who greet me as the plane's boarding stairs unfold are wearing Digital Identity Distorters. The motion blur and occasional twitching that would sometimes offer a flash of facial features are dead giveaways.

"You are to come with us."

Another giveaway is the flat robot-sounding voice when they speak.

The tractor beam had pulled me toward an enormous building and deposited me on a helicopter pad. Halfway there, something happened to my equilibrium. The upside-down city no longer seemed upside down. The dead city, only sometimes visible through the thick clouds, was now the one above me and upside down.

Weird.

I'd been about to unbuckle and exit the ship when the voice told me to wait for an escort. Only a few minutes later, the blurry-face dudes showed up.

One man extends his hand, holding a piece of dark material. "Put this on."

Taking the cloth, I survey the material. It's an eyeless hood. I've only worn one once before in Gangland. I won't be able to see my surroundings once that thing covers my head.

"Fine," I sigh, slipping it on. Everything plunges into darkness. "But I'm very disappointed in your hospitality so far. Expect an angry one-star review"

A faint, digital *blurp* sound penetrates through the hood. Did one of the men just snort in amusement?

Hands grab my shoulders and guide me into the building.

They better not let me bump into anything.

We soon reach a point where we're standing still. No telling how much time is going by. Time is funny that way. Especially when you have no visual perception and little auditory awareness.

"What do you do for fun? Besides not hanging out in the dead city." My voice sounds weird—loud yet subdued under the cloth. I wasn't expecting an answer, and they didn't disappoint.

"Were you the ones firing missiles at me earlier? That was kinda mean, don't ya think?"

I'm nervous. It's the only reason for my blabbing.

There is a faint ding. An elevator? We enter and, shortly thereafter, there is a sensation of going down.

For fun, I attempt to figure out how many floors we're descending. However, it *isn't* fun or practical, so I give up. The floor levels don't ding as we go past. There's no way for me to guess how fast the elevator is going.

We come to a halt and step out, our footsteps absorbed by a thin rug or carpet.

My escorts continue in their stoic silence as we walk through what has to be a long hallway. Or maybe they were whispering to each other? While the hood doesn't muffle all sound, I know I'm not picking up on everything.

We come to an abrupt halt. More muffled noises, like a large door opening, then a hand presses between my shoulder blades, the signal to keep moving.

"Come. Sit," says a clear male tone as we walk through the doorway. The volume effect from the hood seems unaffected by his voice. I hear him as if this thing isn't covering my head.

Hands press down on my shoulders, forcing me into a chair.

"You may leave us," the same voice says.

Someone grabs the hood and yanks it off my head. I blink against the sudden light.

"So, you're the intruder?" His tone sounds incredulous.

My eyes adjust to the room. It's a large, private office. The lighting is dim, and my eyes quickly adjust.

Varnished bookcases line the walls on either side of me, with what looks like an old-fashioned, mahogany writing desk before me. Behind it, a lean, older man, with thinning gray hair and a beard, lowers himself into a leather chair. His dark eyes study me, the worn lines in his face pinched up into a curious expression. Framing him, a large window, partially blocked by red drapes, is the only source of light in the room.

The guy continues to stare, expectant.

"Yes," I say, unsure.

He leans forward, resting his elbows on his desk, steepling his fingertips together. Some of his features are shrouded in shadow as he says, "And you claim you are Robert McNealy's daughter?"

I nod.

"Why would that mean anything to me?"

Well, here goes nothing. "I'm looking for a group that calls themselves The New Sons of Liberty."

It's hard to tell if he reacts to my words or not. His face is still, but a hard glint appears in his eyes. A shiver runs down my spine. Something tells me I might be in more danger now than when being chased by monsters or shot at with missiles.

"And why are you looking for them?"

Somehow keeping my wits about me, I explain my father is connected with the group and sent me a message to pass along to the leader.

"Don't lose the scroll," Dad had warned me. "I've used it to pass a message to you, and the information The New Sons of Liberty need is also in the scroll. Hand it to no one but the president. Only he can reveal the information."

Moving only his arm, the man extends a hand toward me, his eyes never leaving mine. "Give me the scroll."

I hesitate. "Are you the president of The New Sons of Liberty?"

He doesn't answer. He doesn't move. The man's glare is so sharp, like he's pierced my skull and is reading my thoughts.

Reluctantly, I hand him the scroll.

He takes it and rises to his feet, unrolling the blank parchment across the desk.

"Da mihi libertatem aut mortem mihi."

The tone of his voice is reverent as he speaks. A golden light with no source glides across the paper. Words appear. They seem to have a profound effect on the man. Gone are the stern, hard lines of his face, the piercing stares, and the compressed lips. Instead, his features soften, more grandfatherly. Tears glisten in his eyes as he stares at the parchment.

"Can it be?" he whispers.

The man sinks back into his seat.

"After all these years?" The man asks as if he dares not believe it. "After all the sacrifices . . . after everything we've lost."

First one tear, then another rolls down his cheeks. I shift, unsure of what to do. I mean, I'm glad he's happy and all, but . . . adult, weepy emotional displays are uncomfortable for me.

The old man looks at me as if he forgot I'm sitting across from him. "You're the one I have to thank for this," he says, gesturing at the parchment.

I gulp and flash my most agreeable smile. Okay, it's cringe and forced. Hopefully, it looks congenial to him.

He stands and leans over the desk. For the first time since meeting him, a smile lights his face. Extending his hand, he says, "Allow me to introduce myself. I am Morgan Sheffy. Welcome to The New Sons of Liberty."

———

In the realm of virtual reality, hospitality plays out differently than in real life. Granted, in the real world, we don't practice hospitality. Being in a state of constant lockdown, with our movements restricted, makes it difficult. My only awareness of old-fashioned hospitality was gleaned from a few old movies.

Things like washing up, refreshing your makeup, lying down for a rest, and eating meals have no actual effect on your avatar. Sure, they can earn some minor XP during those rituals. Not enough to tempt the people who grind for it.

Digital hospitality is more like what I'm engaged in at this moment, perusing The New Sons of Liberty's personal armory, available skins, and unique items that I find cool or might need later.

"You say you used a lot of ammo in the dead city?"

The question comes from a burly avatar who appears he'd be more at home wearing a colorful leotard, laying the smack down on an opponent in Wrestlevania. Fortunately, he also doesn't sport a pair of fangs; those pro-wrestling vampires were quite tricky to beat.

We are in an enormous warehouse full of steel shelves and wall hooks containing an extensive variety of weapons and ammo. It's hard not to be impressed with the vast array.

"Yeah, used up several mags before I could get to the airplane," I reply.

The master-at-arms smirks down at me. "So you know enough to say magazines instead of clips, eh?" He chuckles, slapping me on the shoulder. Even through the sensory filters, it hurts. "I like you already."

I shrug. "I enjoy playing the action games in The Haven. You pick up on things."

He nods, still smiling. "Well, since we are hosting you right now, and you spent ammo in our world, we can offer you the standard forty percent discount on any purchase of ammo or weapons used in our game world."

Digital hospitality. "Thank you."

He holds up a finger. "We also provide twenty percent off weapons upgrades, if you have the appropriate quantities of raw materials, and ten percent off any skins, armor, or clothing that you take a fancy to while here."

Tempting as it is to upgrade or buy new items, I stick with simple re-plenishment. It's always risky buying items that aren't Haven Certified. You risk item-breaking bugs or out-of-date specs that make them useless.

As soon as I restock some of my depleted resources and we complete the deal, the warehouse fades.

"The president asked me to send you to the waiting room as soon as we were done," the master-of-arms says, fading with his warehouse, his voice growing faint. "I hope our paths cross again."

Me too. I wave and notice a new environment coming into view. Must be a feature in this world; not sure I've encountered environment switches like this before.

Now I'm in a much smaller room. Everything appears made of the same dark wood as the president's desk from earlier. Recessed shelves line the walls, with each shelf containing something different. One has a stack of reference books, and another has a short statue of a man waving a flag. Still, others contain varied old-looking knick-knacks and dust collectors.

Okay, Morgan Sheffy, we get it; you have a thing for vintage stuff.

There is a fireplace along one wall, a small fire burning within. Two chestnut leather recliners flank both sides. And between the chairs is a round table with various alcoholic drinks.

I am the room's sole occupant. And I'm a little thirsty.

Approaching the table, I examine the containers and the variety of disparate, colored liquids they hold. I know next to nothing about alcohol. With few exceptions, The Haven has strict censoring software for booze and tobacco use in front of minors.

Do those same rules apply here?

I hear getting drunk in The Haven is very different, yet similar to being drunk in real life. Something to do with the brain being manipulated. Obviously. People I've asked say it's an unsettling feeling, like their body is being hijacked, turning them into clumsy marionette puppets controlled by an invisible hand. But enough folks like it that The Haven nightlife is a thing.

I pour a splash into one of the small glass cups on the table from a random container. The people in the movies always pour an absurdly tiny amount into their cups, so who am I to do differently?

Swirling my drink, I study the dark golden liquid. I bring the cup under my nose and sniff; it smells similar to Mom's booze. It looks different, though, so here's hoping it'll taste different.

Once, after not seeing her all day, I went to check on Mom. She was lying in bed with two or three bottles of wine next to her. One bottle had a gulp of blood-red liquid left, so I tried it. The bitterness made my lips pucker. A weird warmth hit my throat. I felt every burning moment of the fluid crawling down my esophagus.

You must be desperate to get drunk to imbibe this stuff, I had thought.

I take a sip, not sure what to expect.

It's sharper and sweeter than the wine. And it *burns* more as well. I grimace and shiver; it feels authentic enough. I don't think I like this better than the wine.

"Our refreshments not up to your standards?"

I spin around. El Presidente strides across the room to me, smiling. "Perhaps you'd like a juice box instead?"

I keep quiet, though his question rankles me.

Morgan Sheffy chuckles and waves his hand. "I'm only kidding. We can provide whatever you need here."

"I'm good." Despite his warm and friendly manner, my spine goes rigid. Besides running an errand for Dad, I'm also here for my own reasons that Morgan Sheffy might not like.

Tough stuff. My dad is rotting in a cell somewhere because of this man.

Morgan nods, still smiling, and settles into one armchair. "Well, at least you picked a good one to start with."

He points to the glass still in my hand. I set it back down on the table with an audible *thunk.*

"A honey bourbon," Morgan continues, gesturing to me to sit across from him. I comply as he proceeds. "Most people who try bourbon find they need time to acquire the taste, so they mix it, or buy flavored ones like what you tried."

"Must not be that great if you have to acquire a taste for it," I say.

Morgan laughs. "Perhaps you're right. Or could I have more mature taste than you?"

Whatever. I turn toward the fire and say, "I'm surprised I could drink any at all, seeing as I'm a minor in The Haven."

"Yes, well . . . we have worked very hard to remove certain restrictions in our little space in The Haven. Drinking alcohol unrestricted is one minor change."

I shift to face him again. "Are you one of those agitators? What the Ungulithi call terrorists?"

He spread his hands. "Guilty as charged."

I frown. He doesn't have to be so relaxed and casual, does he? "Did you know my father?"

"Not very well. We had a few conversations, and I sent him out on various missions, but we weren't especially close."

I nod. Again, thoughts of my father, in prison because of this man, send a hot, angry flush to my cheeks.

"Your father is a very brave man. I know he loves you very much."

His words only poke at the blazing embers of my anger. I snap my head back up to glare at him. "What did you do to him?"

Morgan smiles sadly. "I did nothing. Your father searched us out."

"So, was he The Shadow?" I ask.

"Yes," Morgan says, looking thoughtful. "And no."

Well, that's helpful.

He continues. "I can see you're angry. Perhaps even at me. I get that. You and your father were close. Otherwise, why are you here? Yet he kept secrets from you. You've been taught all your life to comply with the authorities—"

"Stop," I interrupt. The nerve of this guy. "Don't act like you know me or know what I'm thinking. I can think for myself."

Morgan tilts his head to one side, the only emotion he shows at my outburst. "Can you?"

"You should mount a rescue operation," I say. "You seemed excited about whatever it was I delivered. Dad was arrested because of you, and now he's going to be executed."

"And so the least we can do is to spring Daddy before the executioner has his way with him?"

"A reasonable demand."

"Maybe it sounds reasonable to someone who does not understand what's going on, the campaigns we've been running, the various ops I'm overseeing—"

"What's to know?" I interrupt again. "You're fighting for freedom, rah-rah, all that. So fight for my dad's freedom."

He gives me a steady look. "It seems your father's convictions don't run as deep in you."

"I don't care either way. It's not so bad. The aliens arrived before I was born, so I can't miss what I never experienced. I'm trying to bring my dad back."

We hold each other's looks for a protracted moment. He, studying me as if he'd never seen another human being before, and me working to keep a tough face on as I grow uncomfortable over the lengthy silence.

Finally, he blinks and leans forward. "I don't usually waste my time like this. However, you are a special case because of your father."

He stands and moves behind my chair to fiddle with one of the books on the shelf nearest me. I have to crane my neck to look at him.

"You are about to leave this place," he says. "You claim you can think for yourself. You also claim you came here to help your father?"

"Yes," I reply, unsure of what his point is.

"What you did was very brave, especially considering dying here turns your brains into scrambled eggs back in the real world."

So Dad was right. "Speaking of which, was it you who fired the missiles at me?"

"Our autonomous defense system. If you hadn't given a suitable answer while being held in our tractor beam, you would've been instantly blown up."

I gulp.

"Anyway," he continues. "You showed skill and courage today."

"I do things like that in The Haven all the time."

"For lesser risks, though. Here the stakes are very real. We could use someone of your talents."

I snort. "I'm just trying to help free my dad."

A small smile plays across his face. "And I'm trying to free the world."

Good luck with that. I keep my expression neutral.

He lets his hand drop from the bookshelf, walks from behind my chair, stands before me, and leans down. "Go outside sometime this week."

That's an odd change in topic. "Like, to the Glasshouse Gardens?"

He shakes his head. "You call that being outside? That's just an environmentally controlled dome with some plants."

My eyes widen as the realization hits. "You want me to go all the way outside? But it's against the law without the proper permissions. They'll never let me do it."

The light seems to dance in his eyes as he smiles. "I thought you said you could think for yourself?"

"This is different," I say, sullen.

"Is it? Have you ever stopped to ask why we are not allowed outside?"

"Because" I answer, "the Ungulithi are the first non-humans to colonize Earth. They don't want to risk passing alien pathogens to us or them. They are likewise working on a more sophisticated tracking and social credit system to discourage crime and rebellion. Also, our domes capture and recycle the carbon we produce, giving the Earth's upper atmosphere time to heal."

Morgan sneers. "A textbook answer, yet you cannot recognize the significance of your words."

"I understand just fine," I say, locking eyes with him once more. "These past seventy years have been the most peaceful years in humanity's history. With Ungulithi rule, the Earth is healing at last. If it hadn't been for the Ungulithi, we would have destroyed ourselves and our planet because of unbridled greed and selfishness."

"And what of your father? I seem to recall a conversation where he said he wanted to join us so that his daughters could live free."

"My dad means well, but our life is fine how it is."

"Or," Morgan says, holding up a finger, "your father is fighting for a future where *you* choose how to live. Where you are not at the mercy of another's whims. To make your own destiny, instead having one prescribed for you."

This conversation has gone on long enough. "You act like we're being oppressed. It's not that bad."

Morgan shakes his head and sighs. "Perhaps not," he says, looking exhausted all of a sudden. "Regardless, you have no control over whether it gets better or worse."

He turns to stare out one of the large windows of the room.

"Go outside," he says without turning around. "When you do, I'd be interested in hearing if your feelings have changed."

Before I can retort, the room, and Morgan, fade from view.

Chapter Nineteen

The Outdoors

Lucas whistles softly. Ji Yeon's expression is hard to read.

"Your dad is one of them?" Lucas asks.

I shrug and nod. It's lunch break, and I'm in my room shoveling down spaghetti and meatballs while on a two-way video call on the computer, updating my friends on the previous day's events. "Morgan never explained the extent of my father's involvement, but, yeah, he's one of them, I guess."

"How . . . why?" Ji Yeon asks, sounding more lost than I'd ever heard her before.

"I heard the rebels believe humans should govern the planet," Lucas says.

"Look how well that turned out," Ji Yeon says. "Besides, we have human government. The Ungulithi have done very little to alter each country's system of governance."

Lucas appears skeptical. "My mom says the government answers to the Ungulithi, not the people."

"Oh, like politicians were working for their electors in the past," Ji Yeon snaps. "I guess that's how the Mega-Corps formed: because that was *so* good for everyone. Or was it the massive bribes, the "favors" the Mega-Corps' lobbyists provided to influence our representatives to look the other way as they monopolized entire economies? Or when they employed loopholes to crush competition? Yes, all the crony capitalism and corruption that was so commonplace it almost brought Western culture to its knees. I'm sure voters all wanted that."

Lucas and I sit in stunned silence. Of course, such facts were drilled into us at school, reminding us of what the Ungulithi had liberated us from. The information wasn't what held us quiet and still as statues. Where had all of Ji Yeon's antagonistic energy come from?

She snorts. "Whatever. I'm sorry, Ava, but if your dad is involved with terrorists, there's not much we can do at this point."

"My dad isn't a terrorist," I say, my face growing hot.

"Well, it's looking like he is," Ji Yeon says. "And I'm regretting not taking this to SGPI."

My eyes widen. How *dare* she . . .

"You wouldn't," Lucas says, interrupting my train of thought. He sounds as if he can't grasp what he's hearing. "Ji Yeon, this is her *dad*. I'm aware you want to join SGPI, but—"

"But nothing." Ji Yeon cuts him off. "SGPI is my future. Even by applying there, doors have opened for me that usually wouldn't. I am not throwing my prospects away because Ava can't face the truth."

"Your future?!" Pressure builds in my head. "This is my dad's *life* we're talking about. You *know* him. He would never do the things the news says he's done."

Ji Yeon huffs, her eyes blazing. "So, now you're suggesting the news isn't trustworthy? Why would they lie? Are you even listening to yourself?"

I turn to Lucas for backup. He sits unmoving, eyes wide. Mute. Not sure what hurts more: Ji Yeon's words or Lucas's silence.

I take a deep breath and collect my thoughts. "I'm just saying you need to trust me on this."

Ji Yeon screws up her face in disbelief. "Over official facts from the government? From investigative journalists? Ava, you're being delusional."

I slam my now lukewarm bowl of spaghetti onto my desk, splattering red sauce and noodles across its surface. "Sheffy only confirmed virtual missions. Nothing real world. No murders of innocents, as the news claims."

"He confirmed your dad was the Shadow," Ji Yeon says. "The Shadow spread disinformation resulting in real-world violence."

"Nut-jobs," I retort. "The New Sons of Liberty never took responsibility for those riots and bombings. And it's been years since that happened."

Ji Yeon shakes her head, lips compressed. "Doesn't make up for it. Doesn't make it right. I have to report you."

"You can't!" Lucas blurts.

"And why not?" Ji Yeon narrows her eyes.

Lucas's eyes dart around as if his mind is racing to find a reason. "Because of your association with her. You have years of associating with a terrorist's daughter. She contacted The New Sons of Liberty and you helped. You built an illegal bot to do so. If you inform on her, you're implicated just as much as her."

All true. Why didn't I come up with it? Probably because that's not what's pissing me off.

"So that's what our friendship means to you?" I ask, tears welling up. Whether from rage or mounting heartbreak, who knows? "Everything we've done together. All we've been through. You'd throw it all away for some stupid elitist club?"

Ji Yeon turns pale. "How can we be real friends? We've never met. All I know of you is what I see in The Haven."

"That is me!" In the small bedroom, my scream sounds amplified. I don't care. "I'm the same person there as I am in real life."

Ji Yeon bolts to her feet, knocking over her chair behind her. "Oh? And how do I confirm that's true? Nothing in The Haven is real. Not our characters, not our stats, not our accomplishments . . . nothing! But the SGPI is real. With them, I can choose any college, not have one assigned to me. I can choose to be a programmer, not just hope to be picked."

Anger has been building to an exploding point. Except now it dissipates like someone letting air out of a balloon. All energy drains out of me.

"This can't be happening," I whisper. "The entire world turned against me. Now you are too."

"I haven't turned against you," Ji Yeon says. "But I can't continue on with you. Why can't you understand that?"

Glaring, I fight to hold back my tears. She will not see me cry.

Ji Yeon sighs. "I need to go."

Her video feed cuts off. I stare at her corner of the screen, unsure what I'm sticking around for. Part of me hopes at any moment another video call request comes across from a weeping and sorrowful Ji Yeon. But a part of me knows that will not happen.

Lucas sniffs. I blink in surprise. I'd forgotten he was still there.

"You guys have had some epic disagreements in the past," Lucas says in a quiet tone. "That was the ugliest one yet."

"I don't think we can get past this. Is it possible she will report me?"

"A couple of minutes ago, I'd have said no. After what I just witnessed . . ." He trails off and shrugs.

My eyelids feel heavy. I'm so tired. Tired of my dad being locked up like a criminal, tired of my mom's months-long alcohol binge, tired of my sisters not listening to me, tired of Ji Yeon . . .

"How did bot-me do?" I ask, needing something else to think about.

Lucas gives me a blank expression at my abrupt change of subject. "Well, uh . . . bot-you is a lot more chatty than real you. You kept raising your hand in class to answer questions and never got a single one right."

"No one was suspicious, were they?" I ask in alarm.

A light smile lifts the corners of his mouth. "You were assigned some extra history homework. Mr. Lepoli seemed as if he was going to bust a blood vessel when bot-you answered that President Mercer was the Ungulithi commander that colonized Earth."

Stupid bot-me. And on top of everything else.

"How's Chuck?" Lucas asks. "Messing around his system did nothing to him, did it?"

"Seems alright," I say. "Though he keeps going on about a dark hole in his continuum processor and that he may need a maintenance upgrade soon."

Lucas looks skeptical. "Continuum processor? Are you sure he's not making that stuff up?"

"I have no idea," I say, throwing up my hands in helpless exasperation. "Chuck will be Chuck, right?"

Lucas nods in silence. I'm too tired to come up with more questions, and he seems to be drawing a conversational blank as well. Yet neither one of us signs off. I don't want to be alone.

"Hey." Lucas perks up, remembering something. "Tonight is raid night in Cauldron Wars. One of the easy raids. It's a great time for a casual person to join. Perhaps get some loot?"

My eyebrows lift in surprise. "How many clans are you in?"

Lucas stares at his fingers, as if counting them, then glances back up at me, his eyes wide. "I've lost count."

I smile. *Humble brag.*

"Sounds like fun," I say, and then pause. I was about to ask when to show up. To my great annoyance, Morgan Sheffy's words pop up in my mind.

"Go outside . . ."

Outside the limits of the dome. Outside where you can't get permission to go. How does he suppose I—in my wheelchair, no less—can defy all the people, security, and even the very design of our dome community . . . all to take a casual stroll outside?

For what?

"Ava . . ."

Realization dawns. I'm considering it; I'm genuinely thinking about defying sanity and going outside. But why? Sure, The Haven has lost some of its appeal. Ever since Dad was taken. But that can't be it. To prove something? But prove what? And to whom?

"Ava!"

I blink, refocusing on my computer screen.

"Sorry," I say. "Wh—what?"

Lucas is wearing an odd expression. "I said, are you in? Where were you?"

Should I tell him? No, he wouldn't get it. Heck, I don't get it. Plus, he would try to stop me.

"Sorry," I say with a forced smile. "Past couple of days have been crazy. I'm tired."

Lucas nods, sympathetic.

"I might turn in early tonight. Also, there is no telling what the girls ate all day. I should force them to eat decent for a change."

"Okay," Lucas says, sounding a little disappointed.

An unpleasant taste lingers in my mouth as I sign off. I've never felt so alone and abandoned before. On top of that, I'd just blown off Lucas.

If only I could wake up from this nightmare.

———

The next day I'm in the kitchen, glaring at the exit door to our dome as if by staring it'll somehow open on its own.

I'd thought about going after school. Unplugging after my last class, I sat up in my pod, readying to talk myself into it. But then Sofia shrieked in delight, followed by Riley's frantic squeals. I wheeled myself over to discover Sofia chasing Riley around the kitchen table, holding one of her fingers extended toward her distraught sister.

"Come here, Riley, I have a present for you," Sofia cried out in a high, sadistic tone.

"Get away, get away, get away!" Riley screamed.

Riley spotted me entering the room and promptly dove behind my chair.

"Make her stop, Ava, make her stop!"

Sofia gave a villainous laugh and sprinted toward us. Riley shrieked again, right by my ear. I winced as the sound seemed to fill my head.

As Sofia got closer, finger still extended, I finally saw why Riley was so eager to keep a healthy distance between her and her sister.

"Oh, Sofia." I gripped my midsection, feeling sick. "That's so disgusting."

Sofia stopped in front of me, noticed my grimace, and smiled in wicked delight. "It's only a booger." She wiggled her finger with the offending piece of filth at me.

I leaned back, turning my head away. "Leave your sister alone and go wash your hands right now, young lady. That is gross!"

"You're not my mommy," she said, sticking out her tongue.

Riley gasped. "Ava, she just stuck out her tongue!"

Thank you Riley, I'd completely missed that. I sighed; been doing a lot of that lately.

Leaning forward, eye-to-eye with Sofia, I said, "I'm in charge when Mommy isn't around, so you listen to me: go to the restroom and wash your hands right now!"

For a time, Sofia stayed rooted to the spot, jaw set, and glared. This only lasted a moment before her defiant lower lip quivered, betraying her. Her expression still hard, she finally stomped off to the bathroom.

I'm not sure why that scene is replaying in my head. Sofia's words, "You're not my mommy" might still bug me. Yeah, I'm not your mom, you little turd, but I'm all you got right now.

Whatever. Time to go.

But I'm not actually ready, though, am I?

The thought makes my hand immobile. Had I really been about to open the door? No one else is around. My family won't notice I'm gone. Mom is sleeping off whatever she last drank. The girls are in the plug-in room, gaming for a couple more hours before bedtime.

Am I ready?

No, I'm not ready for any of it. A few months ago—it's really only been a few months—I was a girl living a normal life. Went to school, hung out with friends, played around in The Haven, ate/slept/repeat. Now I'm attempting to take care of two little sisters practically by myself and make sure Mom doesn't die of alcohol poisoning. Not to mention meeting up with a terrorist organization to help my father, and said organization trying to recruit me or something.

It's all too surreal and weird.

When I snap out of my reverie, I find myself outside my dome, in an extensive concrete-and-metal hallway that connects all the domes in our block. I'd crossed the threshold. Without asking for permission.

You already broke the law. Might as well keep going.

Our dome is close to the Common Hall. Which should probably be renamed the Common Auditorium. It's spacious enough to hold everyone who lives on this block. I've only been there a few times, during rare community announcements or activities that couldn't be handled in The Haven version of our Common Hall. With any luck, I can make it there without being detected.

I roll myself down the long corridor. On high alert, my eyes search every shadow and crevice. Deep down, I know I'm being silly. No one is hiding, waiting to jump out. Still, I can't shake the feeling that men in black uniforms will descend upon me at any moment.

Small, black orbs hang from the ceiling—cameras. During the handful of times I'd been in the corridor, I had paid them little attention. The Common Hall would have them too, but fortunately, they aren't actively monitored. Fingers crossed, I draw no negative attention to myself because the footage could be easily accessed in the security archives and be used against me.

Rolling down the corridor, I pass multiple dome entrances. They all look the same: slate-gray, steel sliding doors, with only painted white numbers to distinguish one from another. It's weird to think that real people live behind these doors. I live in a community of folks that barely know each other. Sure, we've interacted with each other's avatars. Ordinarily around the holidays in a virtual neighborhood center, but no one usually enjoyed going to those. There is always something more exciting happening in The Haven.

I finally reach one of the last doors before the Common Hall. It looks the same as all the others, yet a faint noise is coming from inside. I pause, listening.

A low, steady beat pulses. Someone is blasting their music pretty loud if I can hear it through the thick steel doors.

I roll closer to the door and lean forward, straining to hear if it's a recognizable song. It's hard to tell, muffled as the sound is, but I think it's "I'm Gonna Live My Life," by The Antidote, a popular industrial-pop-fusion band.

Suddenly, an off-key voice belts out the chorus:

I don't care what you say
Today, I'm running away
from you.
And I don't care what you do
I'm gonna live my life, for me
and not for you.

Sitting back, I realize I am mouthing the lyrics. Catchy tune. But time to move on. Nice hearing another human voice, though. One that didn't belong to a family member, or as audio in The Haven. Odd how such a moment feels so impactful.

I roll into the Common Hall. The size is like an airplane hangar, specifically the one in Cargo Jet Run in The Haven. But the Common Hall is nicer. Large American flags hang from the ceiling to the floor against the side walls. Though the light flowing in from the windows is artificial, it brings warmth to the environment. A warmth the pale floor and walls lack. At least the floor isn't carpeted; makes it easy for me to wheel on.

A large control panel is in the middle of the room. I'm pretty sure it can be used to call in a ride. The handful of times I've been here, the panel was encased with molded plastic panels that can retract into the floor. Now the molded cover is gone.

Of course, I'm glad that's the case. Not sure what I would've done if the plastic cover was still on. But the fact the covering is down means something is off.

There's a soft sound, like a shoe scraping against the ground. Before I can react, a man in a worn gray shirt rises from behind the control panel and looks straight at me.

I freeze, as if that'll somehow keep the guy from noticing me—although he *clearly* notices me.

The man scratches his pale, bald head. He glances around the room, then back at me with a puzzled expression. "What, exactly, are you doing?"

If his faded clothes and tightly clutched wrench are anything to go by, he's one of the maintenance guys. I need to think fast. Problem is there's no obvious answer. Why would a teenage girl in a wheelchair wander the Common Hall without a permit?

He squints and places his hands on his hips. His suspicions are obviously growing.

A bead of sweat trickles down my back. I need to do something *now.*

A solution strikes. I have no idea if it'll work, but I lift my chin, doing my best Kersey impersonation. "I wasn't aware . . ." I begin, then pause. My voice is shaking. I clear my throat. "I wasn't aware that a member of the Students of Global Peace Initiatives requires a permit to patrol her own halls."

Every word I say is true. I don't know if the Students of Global Peace Initiatives need a permit to leave their domes. Kersey sure doesn't act like she needs one. Could involvement with the Ungulithi give the SGPI special treatment? That's what I'm betting on, at least.

He raises an eyebrow at me but says nothing.

Uh, oh . . . did I act too entitled?

The man sighs, rolling his eyes up at the ceiling. "Well, as you can see, everything is fine here. Can I get back to it?"

I fight to keep my expression neutral, even as my mind reels. *He bought it! He actually bought it!*

But I'm not out of hot water yet. "Certainly. Don't let me interrupt you."

He gives a small mock bow of deference, then returns to kneel behind the control panel, disappearing from view.

All my instincts scream at me to retreat to my dome. I've somehow, miraculously, not had the authorities called down upon me. Why push my luck? Especially at the dare of a rebel leader.

Yet I wheel forward, clamping down on my fight-or-flight response. I *need* to do this. It's a need I can't fully articulate even to myself, but if I don't do this, I will sorely regret it. Even if it's as simple as reclining in a patch of grass for five minutes.

At the control panel, I watch the man work. His back is to me. A pair of metal sheets from the panel lay on the floor with separate piles of screws on top.

He peers over his shoulder with annoyance. "Can I help you?"

I clear my throat a little too loudly and look at him down my nose. "Yes. I need a MonoPod."

His brow furrows. "What do you need a MonoPod for?"

I do my best to act aghast. "*Excuse* me?"

He doesn't respond. Instead, he closes his mouth, clenching his jaw. It's as if he's reassessing me.

Time to erase any lingering doubt from his mind.

I wheel closer. He stands, looming over me with an unpleasant expression. Despite the butterflies returning to my stomach, I keep my face hard. Inches from him, I snatch his ID badge off his coveralls.

"Ethan Howard," I read off the badge, then glare up at him. "Well, Ethan, would you care to explain to my Ungulithi sponsor why a student representative is being delayed in the task assigned her?"

Ethan Howard locks his jaw and doesn't budge. I give him my most arrogant, self-important look. I don't know if all SGPI members operate like Kersey, but Ji Yeon seems to whenever bringing up the group. Anyway, I'm running with it, while hopefully not crossing some unknown line.

After a moment, he slowly reaches out and grasps his badge, but I still hold on. He appears to struggle with some anger or frustration.

Yep, pushed too hard.

"No need for that," he says, to my great relief, snatching his badge out of my hand. "I got nothing else going on. I'll call you a Pod."

The floor vibrates and splits open when Ethan summoned the pod via the control panel. The pod emerges from the tunnel like a giant, rusty, steel egg. Not impressive at all. The Haven's pods look better than this.

Inside, there are buttons on either side of a cracked touch-screen. Stained and faded paperwork pasted on one panel reads that the max capacity is three individuals. I glance down at the slanted bench I'm sitting on. *How can this hold three people?*

Tension in my shoulders eases as the pod sinks below floor level and travels along the electrified line in the underground tunnel.

Running into Ethan had been a mixed blessing. Without him, it's doubtful I would've been able to summon a MonoPod, a potentially devastating oversight. But this guy now believes I'm in the SGPI, and a royal jerk besides. Not to mention he's a witness to me breaking multiple laws. Hopefully, that doesn't come back to haunt me.

There are few lights in the shafts, and what they illuminate isn't interesting. The MonoPod travels an electric rail line under the city, and the subways seem to be composed of steel and concrete. It makes sense; domes, halls, and new buildings all seem to be made of the same material.

I lean forward to get a better view of the screen. I'd told Ethan to program the pod to take me to the first stop in the next city. The cracked screen displays a faded GPS image of the underground monorail, current whereabouts, speed—sixty miles an hour seems much faster in real life than in The Haven—and the ETA for my destination. Three hours and fifteen minutes to arrive at the next city, Briluog. *How long until I reach the limits of my city, Krouis?* My fingers tap with nervous energy along my thigh. Even though there is nothing to do, I keep looking around the metal egg, trying to distract myself.

I must be crazy . . . leaving my dome and riding a pod outside the city. It's almost like it's happening to someone else.

However, the novelty dissipates as the ride wears on. My eyelids soon grow heavy.

A blaze of light startles me. Had I fallen asleep? For how long?

"Now reaching the city limits," a robotic voice says.

Trying to peer through the windshield, I squint against the harsh glare. It's too brilliant. Tears leak through my nearly shut eyes as I strain to see.

Am I passing the glow panels that encompass the city?

A shadow passes. My eyes open in relief. It takes a minute for my vision to come back into focus. Vague, silhouetted shapes come into view through the scratched windshield. As clarity returns, I realize what I'm looking at. Trees. Yes, a line of trees sways in a breeze just off the side of the monorail. I sit up. "Stop the pod!"

Metal grating on metal screeches. I slip off the bench and crash into the display screen. Well, guess I added to its cracks.

Eyes wide, I push off the floor. "Open the door," I say, maneuvering closer to the exit.

The door slides clear with a mechanical sigh. Beyond the opening, a lush, green field of grass, as far as I can see, unobscured and level, except for a few clumps of trees here and there.

I pull myself forward, thrusting my head out of the pod. A breeze wafts over my face and through my hair. It's so familiar, yet different. I've experienced nothing like this before. Sure, I've been outside in The Haven, but this—this is *real*.

Closing my eyes, I inhale. *This is what the outdoors smells like?* No words come to mind describing the scent. It has to be some combination of grass, dirt, and leaves. Nothing amazing, yet it's invigorating. Alive!

Glancing over my shoulder, the gigantic carbon-capture dome can be glimpsed covering all the smaller domes that make up our city. It's an impressive structure but, contrasted against all the surrounding nature, the structure somehow seems invasive and out of place.

The sky is overcast. The dark, lean outline of a bird gliding high against the gray is distinguishable.

"A bird," I say, not caring I'm talking to myself. "An actual *bird*."

Do they act the same in real life as they do in The Haven?

I lean out of the pod and yank a handful of grass from the ground. I rub the slim, green blades between my fingers. The grass is smooth and damp. The greenery tumbles from my hands, leaving behind dirt smudges. I've never had dirt stains before.

The mix of emotions roiling in my gut is very odd. On the one hand, I've experienced a digital version of this before, so it's not entirely alien. That experience, however, pales compared to this moment.

Distant lightning flashes. A few seconds later, rumbling follows. Again, I've seen plenty of lightning and thunder in The Haven, yet witnessing it now in real life—The Haven's version is cartoonish compared to what I'm experiencing here.

The air changes. Tree branches sway and shake as the breeze picks up. A steady noise rushes over the grass. Is it the wind stirring across the field? Then I notice the sheet of rain approaching.

In seconds, the deluge envelops everything. The shock of cold water drenching my top half causes me to gasp, inhaling rainwater. I sputter and cough, my wet hair plastering to my face and neck.

And I laugh.

Chapter Twenty

The Conversation

Lightning flashes across the clear sky. Odd. Someone's powers going off? An explosion rumbles in the distance, shaking the ground, followed by faint bursts of gunfire. I'm still a good distance from the main action.

"White Streak," Lucas says, voice strained. "Get to Central Square. We're fighting the squad there."

"On my way."

My superhero name, White Streak, is stupid. Especially considering the name comes from the one literal white streak in my costume, while the rest of my outfit is coral and indigo. All the best names in Hero World are already taken.

With my powers, I form multiple flat force-field discs, moving each higher than the one before. I then run and jump to each disc. I've been off my game here. Got to focus and catch up with the others. Somehow, after meeting with Morgan Sheffy, and sneaking outside, coming back into The Haven to mess around in Hero World seems less appealing by comparison. Also, I don't play in this world much; my Mage abilities here count for little except for being able to create and manipulate force fields.

I climb higher and higher and then level off along the tops of the buildings. Next, I create one long force field, like a bridge. This may be my only power here, but at least I've found creative uses and forms with it.

I run in the gunfire's direction, suspended hundreds of feet in the air by a razor-thin energy projection created through my concentration and sustained by my dwindling supply of power crystals.

What can go wrong?

A notification from The Haven's private message feature pops up. It's from Marley.

Marley: Hey, lady, it's been a while. How'd playing hooky work out for ya?

Oh, yeah . . . Before going to the New Sons of Liberty HQ, I hadn't talked to Marley. Well, he'd have to wait—I have some supervillain ass to kick.

My force-field bridge lurches upward, throwing me into the air. Someone had attacked with a ground-to-air missile. My concentration vanishes, and so does my construction. For a moment, I hang suspended, upside down. And then gravity does its thing, and I tumble toward the ground.

Blurring movement catches my attention. A split second later, something slams into me.

"Don't worry," Lucas says with a smile. "I've got you."

I roll my eyes. "My hero."

Lucas's superhero name is Ultra-Man. No, really. His costume is purple and blue, he can fly, and he's super strong.

It's like he put no creative thought into it.

"Alright, be that way," Lucas replies. "I can let you go and you can continue your descent. Of course, then you'd lose all your tokens and XP for this session."

"Thank you," I say in a falsely sweet voice.

Lucas grins. It's kind of cute and annoying at the same time.

The other superheroes and the supervillains are on the streets below, wreaking havoc. Lucas's grin fades from his face.

"The situation is grim," he says, watching the battle unfold below. "The Massacre Squad outnumbers and outguns us. Fortunately, they've not been able to get their hands on any hostages, but we've taken a lot of damage. We sure could use some shields."

I nod. Below looks like a literal war zone. Various buildings have been reduced to smoldering skeletons. Busted streets and sidewalks litter debris in all directions. Multiple cars are on their sides, flipped on their tops, with many more on fire. Here and there, the occasional hero or criminal can be seen emerging from behind shelter, launching a quick power or weapons attack before ducking back to safety.

One villain spots us. He lifts his hand and a shaft of white-hot light leaps from his palm.

Instinctively, I throw up a force field in time to deflect the beam. Lucas tightens his grip on me and dives for the ground.

I pull the data from the crystals that power my force-field abilities. "I'm at forty-one percent."

Not good.

Lucas nods, and we land behind one of the damaged buildings, out of sight from the squad.

"It may be enough to turn the tide," Lucas says.

A gold and black blur zooms up to us from across the street, stopping inches from me and Lucas. It's Ji Yeon. Her superhero name is The Blur, and she has super speed.

"They have an android," she says in a clipped tone, refusing to look at me. "It's not as fast as me, but its targeting and weapons systems come close. Just enough to keep me from taking it out."

Lucas frowns. "If you can't get close, I can't."

He turns and looks at me. "Not without some shields at least."

I narrow my eyes at him. "You mentioned nothing about her being here."

"Yes, why is she here?" Ji Yeon asks Lucas. "You said she doesn't play this game much."

Lucas throws up his hands, not meeting either of our gazes. "This fight between you two is ridiculous. The enemy is out there, not here."

"You thought gaming as superheroes would bring us together?" Ji Yeon folds her arms. "How juvenile are you?"

"Hey," I snap. "It wasn't a good idea, but at least his heart is in the right place."

Ji Yeon huffs. "You would say that. I'm not doing this anymore."

An explosion in the street causes the ground to rumble under our feet. Shrieks of terror follow.

An expression of resolve forms on Lucas's face. He steps toward us, jabbing his finger in our direction. "Stop it. You two are friends. You can work this out."

He's got to be kidding. "She's cool with Dad being executed. A friend shouldn't be good with that."

Ji Yeon looks offended. "I'm *not* good with it. But he broke the law, as did you."

"With your help," I point out.

She acts like she doesn't hear. "I'm sorry things turned out this way. But I will not throw away my future for you."

"No one is asking you to," Lucas says in a pleading tone. "Is it worth ending your friendship?"

Gunshots. Those sound close. We whirl around and back up against each other, shoulders pressed together.

"Let's just finish this," I say, confirming no hostiles are in my immediate field of view. "I may as well see it through."

"That's the spirit," Lucas says, half-heartedly.

"The enemy all have standard weapons," Ji Yeon says, changing the subject. "Nothing modded or special. Your force fields should get us close."

Sounds like she's still in.

"What about the other players?" I ask.

"Most of them are noobs." Ji Yeon shrugs. "They've got the squad pinned for the moment. If we're going to do this, we need to go now."

I've got sufficient juice in my crystals to last the match, but it's going to be close. And once my shields are down, I'm out of the game. It's kinda my one thing here.

"Let's go," I say while forming a shield that encircles us.

We walk around the building, into the war zone. The bursts of gunfire grow louder, NPC cops ineffectually trying to lend what aid they can, along with a handful of actual players whose hearts don't seem to be in it. Smoke and ash drift by, thick, mixed with the smell of gunpowder and burning rubber. Whoever built this game wanted players to experience full immersion.

Ji Yeon stops, stiffening.

"What?" Lucas asks, looking for signs of danger.

"We're in the middle of the street," I say to her. "Almost in range of their weapons. Bad time to stop . . ."

"What's that noise," Ji Yeon asks, anxiety thick in her voice.

I'm about to ask what sound when, over the gunfire and power attacks, a long, loud, shrieking tone pierces the commotion.

My blood freezes as, too late, I recognize what it is.

A blinding light envelops my vision, followed by an earth-shattering boom. Some unseen force slams into my shield, demolishing it and throwing me into the air like a ragdoll.

It seems like hours before the world stops spinning.

Facedown on cracked asphalt, I attempt to rise but only manage to roll onto my back. I feel as if I've been hit by a train. What sounds I hear over the ringing in my ears are strange and distorted. Black smoke billows all around me, obscuring much of my environment.

What happened?

A shrieking, whistling sound. My eyes widen. That's what I'd heard. Before the chaos.

Someone had launched missiles at us.

My status bar is blinking so low it barely registers. In the moment's desperation, I'd shielded myself just as the missile hit. If I hadn't, it would be game over, and all the gear, power-ups, and coins earned on this mission would be lost.

Inventory open, I grab a combo med kit and a health potion, bringing my health bar back up to normal. A new energy floods through me and I scramble to my feet.

What can be seen through the smoke is grim. In my immediate surroundings, more buildings had been blown to bits. A light breeze blows some of the smoke elsewhere, revealing dropped loot several hundred feet away. Other than a few scattered coins glinting in the light, it's hard to make out what else the loot is comprised of.

Wait . . . that wasn't from Ji Yeon and Lucas, was it? Yet nothing else makes sense. No one but us had been standing in the middle of the road. And the loot appears to be in two separate piles.

Oh, they're gonna be pissed.

Around the two loot piles, the damaged buildings were flattened. Nothing, not even steel girders, remained.

The breeze dies down, and more clouds of smoke obscure the area again.

Who launched the missiles at us? Though I've only played this game a handful of times, nothing like that has ever happened.

"Lucas," I call out. "Ji Yeon! You guys alright?"

Of course they aren't, but I want to double-check before going over there and picking up the loot piles. Since it appears they got wasted, it'll take them a few minutes to get back here from the spawn point. Assuming they even want to come back.

"I'm afraid they're not."

I whirl around, looking for the owner of the voice.

A man wearing a cowboy hat appears in the smoke, walking toward me.

"Sorry about the dramatic entrance," Marley drawls, emerging from the soot. "Didn't mean to take out your team. I was aiming for the squad, but ya'll were standing pretty close. Well, relative to my missile blast radius, anyway."

My jaw drops. I'm not sure if it's from almost getting blown up, but seeing Marley here is confusing. "You were the one that blew us up?"

Marley quirks an apologetic grin. "Yeah. Again, sorry, but I need to talk to you."

"So you blew us up?" I shout, and not because of almost being deaf.

"Look," he says, expression morphing into annoyance. "This is kind of your fault . . ."— he holds up a finger just as I'm about to unleash on him—"I have been trying to reach you for the past couple of days."

Oh . . . right.

Still . . .

"Doesn't give you the right to blow us up," I say. My tone sounds childish, but I'm too mad to care at this point. I'm also annoyed at not creating a shield big enough to protect my companions. Though in my defense, there had been only a split second to react.

"Well, it wasn't my intention." Marley lights up a fat cigar between his teeth. "I figured it was the fastest, most direct way of getting in contact with you. Can't ignore me when I'd just saved your hide!"

Unbelievable. "My friends are gonna be pissed," I say. "They were grinding for the new Legendary Gold Suits. Where'd you even get missiles, anyway?"

Marley grabs the cigar from between his teeth. "Privileges of knowing a game programmer. Tell ya what. We have a little chat, and I work out something with my techie friend to help your friends. Deal?"

I sigh. "What do you want to know?"

He steps closer. "You, uh, find what you were looking for? A few days ago when you asked for help?"

I raise my hand and wiggle it, saying, "Kinda." I then recount my adventures in the dead town and in the upside-down city.

"The New Sons of Liberty," Marley says, giggling, blowing out a puff of smoke. "I like it."

"Like what?"

He waves his hand. "All of it."

Okay. "My dad never talked about this with you?"

Marley shakes his head. "Your dad can keep tight lips when he wants to."

Makes sense. I, my mom, and my sisters never once suspected he was with a secret organization trying to overthrow the Ungulithi.

"Marley, you recall when we first met? At the warehouse?"

He chuckles, chomping down on his cigar. "How could I forget?"

"You were going to tell me something before security showed up. Something about you and my dad?"

His face grows solemn. "Oh . . . that." With two fingers, he holds his cigar and lets his hand hang limply by his side as his unfocused eyes stare at the ground. "We were best friends growing up—inseparable, really. We were among the first to beta test The Haven."

He sighs, looking nostalgic.

Meanwhile, I'm confused.

"Why didn't my dad mention you if you were so tight?"

"Because we had a falling out." He looks up from the ground, nostalgia replaced with sadness and maybe some regret.

"What did you guys fight about?"

Marley shakes his head, blinking hard. "Can't talk about it right now."

Well, that would explain my dad being mute about his cowboy bestie. It doesn't explain how they came back together, though.

"People are funny that way when they have a common enemy," he says, as if reading my thoughts. "I got fed up with it all one drunken evening and contacted your dad. We hadn't spoken in years. He heard me out, not sayin' much.

"Well, I'd spent what scant energy and brain cells I had left in my little rant, and your father wasn't in a talkative mood, so it wasn't a long call. Pretty soon after I blacked out or something. I don't recall. I only remember the conversation with your dad because of what happened after."

He pauses, then saunters over to a large, broken chunk of asphalt jutting up at an angle and leans against it.

"Did my dad call you back?" I ask.

Marley nods. "Yep. The very next day. And he was a lot more chatty. Told me what he was doing, and was I ready to do something about it."

Interesting. "So it was like old times again after that?"

"No. There was still a distance. A hurt, a wariness we both felt. I think things might've been on the mend, though."

"What did you do together?"

He shifted his position against the broken slab of the street. "'Fraid that's classified, little lady—at least the details are. Some hacks here an' there, a couple of raids in The Haven against certain virtual reality structures the Ungulithi use for surveillance."

That last bit of information surprises me. "Wait, the Ungulithi spy on us in The Haven?"

Marley bursts out laughing, almost dropping his cigar. "Where've you been all these years? The main reason they created The Haven was for containment and data mining. You didn't believe those freakin' aliens took over, fell in love with humankind, and gave us The Haven out of the goodness of their hearts because they want everyone to have fun?"

I had never thought much about it. Now I feel stupid. "But why? As you said, they took over. Humanity surrendered; what more do they want from us?"

"That's the scary part," he says, examining the ash at the end of his cigar. "No one knows. The Ungulithi spent a huge amount of manpower and resources to build The Haven. They made sure every human on Earth had easy access to it. They went to great lengths to ensure that it was indeed a type of alternate reality or realities. You could work a job and never leave your home. Explore the world, hell, and the galaxy in the comfort of your pod. All the while, they're connected to your brain in a way the previous tech could only dream of, allowing them to trick your senses into believing in the reality of The Haven—but *why*?" He stops examining his cigar and gazes at me. "It was a question your dad obsessed over. A question he never got answered before his arrest."

This is a lot to process. I sit down on a nearby block of asphalt and rub my eyelids. "So how did my dad get discovered?"

Marley's features grow dark. "I don't rightly know."

"But you have your suspicions?"

He nods. "Your dad was more of an inner member of the resistance than me; part of the distance between us in our friendship. He told me what he thought I needed to know, which was little enough. Damn shame . . . I might've been able to prevent his arrest."

I perk up at his words. "How?"

For a moment, he doesn't answer. Instead, he studies me, still wearing a dark expression. He walks over to me, lays a heavy hand on my shoulder, and says, "I think a double agent in the resistance betrayed your dad."

Chapter Twenty-One

Decisions

Lucas and Ji Yeon stare with wide eyes and open mouths.

I almost miss their expressions as we push through the throng of students in the virtual hallways of our school, trying to reach our lockers.

"But did he have to blow us up like that?" Lucas asks, looking pained.

"But why you?" Ji Yeon asks. There is a surprising lack of antagonism in her voice.

When I don't answer right away, she must've guessed what I was thinking. "I'm still mad at you," she says. "But this is about your father."

I am not sure how to respond.

"Anyway," she continues, "I meant why did Marley reach out to you after your dad was arrested?"

We arrive at our lockers and begin switching out books from our backpacks. Access to our inventory is unavailable at school, so the devs gave us what they call "as traditional an experience as we could" with our simulated school. Which apparently included vintage backpacks and lockers.

"After mentioning my dad's suspicions about a double agent,"—I glance around to make sure no one else is within earshot—"Marley then said something about my dad leaving something for me."

Ji Yeon furrows her brow. "Seems a bit of a stretch."

I roll my eyes. "Everything with Marley is a bit of a stretch. Dude isn't the sharpest shooter in the pose."

Neither one reacts. No appreciation for my sense of humor.

"That doesn't explain why he contacted us. What does Marley want from you?" Lucas asks.

Again, I scan around us and pause for three girls walking close by the lockers. "He wants me to take him to the HQ."

Once more, both of their eyes bulge from their sockets.

"He's never been there? He works for them and he's never been there? Has he met anyone else involved besides your dad?" Ji Yeon asks in rapid-fire succession.

"Things are complicated between them, remember?" I say.

"Could there be a solid reason for that?" Lucas says, frowning.

Ji Yeon leans closer. "Are you going to take him?"

Excellent question. Before wrapping up our conversation, Marley impressed upon me the importance and sensitivity of the information he knew and needed to present to Morgan Sheffy himself.

"But why can't you just confide in me, then I pass it along to the Liberty guys?" I had asked Marley.

I had followed him back to the attack chopper he'd flown in on. He leaned against the helicopter, next to a pinup of a blond woman in cowboy boots, cut-off jean shorts, and a tiny flannel shirt—most of it tied into a knot in the front. She's posed as if she's in the middle of a dance, tipping her hat and winking at some unknown admirer.

"Ya like her?" Marley asked, a mischievous twinkle in his eyes.

Eh. I've designed dozens of way cooler art for jets and helicopters.

After struggling to come up with a suitable answer, I said it was fine.

Marley chuckled. He placed a hand on the helicopter. "I call her Sylvie. I don't take her out as much as I'd like. But when we're together . . ." He shook his head and smiled.

Okay, well, that got a little weird.

He turned serious again. "I can't tell you or anyone else what I know. Only Morgan Sheffy."

I ran a hand through my hair. I'm tired. Tired of thinking about alien agendas, rebels, my dad being imprisoned, my sisters not listening to me, and my mom checking out. Why can't things be the way they were?

"Will it help my dad out?"

Marley held up his hands as if to say *slow down*. "I can't claim either way; it wouldn't worsen his situation."

I looked down and kicked at the loose gravel. It wasn't like I hadn't been thinking about traveling back, anyway, ever since I'd risked so much and gone outside.

The sound of Ji Yeon snapping her fingers right by my ear makes me jump.

"Well?" she asks.

"Well, what?" I reply in a huff, thoughts still scattered, peeved with her. Well, more peeved than usual.

She rolls her eyes. "Are you going to take him?"

"I told him I'd think about it."

"I don't know if that's a good idea," Lucas says.

I give him a reassuring smile. He's always preaching caution and safety to me. It's kinda cute and unnecessary.

But this time, he could be right.

After school, I'm back home, trying to scrounge up something resembling a healthy meal. Food deliveries have been arriving late. There's been some grumbling about labor shortages outside The Haven. The quality of the food has fallen. Ongoing meat scarcity means we can only have it once a week—and we never know whether it's going to be poultry, beef, or fish. Otherwise, for protein, it's tofu and some synthetic thing called Magic Meats. A rumor persists of it being a mix of lab-grown "meat" mixed with soy and bug protein. Now that I think about it, it's probably for the best that the ingredients remain a mystery.

The canned veggies have also shrunk and grown mushy. Yet Mom always has enough alcohol until the next allotment arrives, and the girls seem to always have some sugary snack on hand.

On the skillet, several patties of Magic Meats sizzle, and the microwave warms some broccoli and carrots.

The door to the plug-in room opens. My sisters emerge, bleary-eyed and frowning.

"What are you making?" Sofia asks, rubbing one eye with the back of her hand.

I slap cheese slices on top of the patties. "Dinner."

"It better not be peanut butter and banana sandwiches again," Riley grumbles, pulling out a chair from the kitchen table and plopping onto it.

I roll my eyes and plate their food. I hadn't spent much time on their meals that day. It'd be better than the cereal they'd polished off two days after being delivered.

Setting their plates in front of them, I gesture at the food with an over-the-top flourish, indicating the lack of bananas, peanut butter, and bread. Sofia still looks at her plate suspiciously, using her fork to poke the veggies. Can't blame her there; by the food's appearance, it seems like it belongs in the garbage, not on a plate. Riley stares at her plate without expression, before taking her first bite. She eats as if on some autopilot mode, refusing to glance up from her plate.

"Don't wait on me," I mumble, fixing my plate.

We eat in silence, Riley never once looking up from her plate. Sofia casts multiple glances toward my parents' bedroom. I pretend not to notice, but every time she looks, I grow hotter under the collar.

Riley pulls out her phone and begins scrolling.

Sofia tries to get a better view by craning her neck. "What are you looking at?"

"Nothing," Riley says, focused on the phone screen.

I clench the fork in my hand, making a fist, trying to contain my growing bad mood.

"Riley, you know Dad's rule . . . no phones at the table," I say as calmly as possible.

Riley huffs, "In case you haven't noticed, he isn't around anymore."

My knuckles are turning white. I force myself to loosen my hold on the fork. Sofia looks from Riley to me, her eyes wide, uncertain.

"Yes," I reply, biting back a retort. "But don't you think he'd want us to continue to obey his rules while he's away?"

This time she snorts. "It's not like he's going to find out. He's not coming back."

That hurts. It also hurts when I slam my fist onto the table. The fork shoots out of my hand, clattering to the floor. Both girls jump. Sofia's eyes water, her lips quivering. Riley looks startled, but her expression soon changes to defiance.

"You don't know that," I growl.

Riley jumps up from her seat. "Dad is a traitor! There's no coming back, not after what he's done. What don't you get about that?"

Riley stomps into her room and slams the door.

My fist is shaking. I want to scream back at her, to tell her she's wrong—but I can't. She isn't wrong, which frustrates me even more.

A whimper interrupts my thoughts. Sofia rubs her glistening eyes, sniffing. She glances up at me, afraid, needing someone to tell her everything is going to be okay.

Anger fades. I open my arms for her. She comes and lays her head on my shoulder, still sniffing, tears trickling down her face and onto my shirt.

"It's okay, Sofia," I whisper, stroking her hair.

"No, it's not," she says in a wavering tone.

No, it's not; she's right. The familiar and unwelcome feeling of a pit in my stomach returns. Tears sting my eyes.

"I'm sorry I haven't been around more," I say. I've been spending so many of my spare moments in The Haven, trying to distract myself, trying to avoid dealing with the pain. Dad's gone, branded as a terrorist, sure to be executed soon. Mom has abdicated her responsibilities—and maybe I have a little too. My sisters still need a lot of guidance and provision, and I've been giving them the bare minimum of myself.

"All the kids at school say Daddy wanted to kill people," Sofia says. "They say he's a bad guy."

"No," I reply, pulling Sofia off me and looking her in the eye. "Dad never wanted to kill anyone, and he is not a bad guy."

I can tell she wants to believe me. But the doubt remains.

"I miss him," she says, laying her head back down on my shoulder. "He never finished reading *Alia: Princess Warrior*."

More tears well up in my eyes, memories flooding my head. Ten-year-old me lying in bed as Dad reads *Alia: Princess Warrior* to me. He had a unique voice for each character. Horrible at doing female voices, he and I would giggle at how bad he was. Sometimes he would play it up, pitching his voice as high as he could until he choked. That never failed to produce giggles from his rapt audience.

"I wish I was brave and strong like Princess Alia," Sofia says softly. "Like when the Diamond Bandits invaded the castle and held her for ransom."

"You are brave," I say. "You don't have to fight bandits to prove that you're brave."

"Where Dad left off, Princess Alia was planning to save herself. She wasn't sure if help was coming," Sofia says as if she hadn't heard me. "I wonder if her plan worked. I guess he never will finish the story if he's never coming back."

No.

"He'll be back," I say, setting my jaw. "You'll find out what happens between Princess Alia and the Diamond Bandits."

It's time for another meeting with Morgan Sheffy.

Chapter Twenty-Two

Betrayal

This time I play it smart and don't even enter the dead city. When I spawn onto the hillside, I find a comfortable spot and settle down, waiting for nightfall.

Dusk arrives soon after. I don't know if it's programmed to do this whenever someone turns up or if day and night are cycled faster in this part of The Haven. It doesn't matter. The results are the same: creepy, pale creatures emerge, keeping to the shadows as the sun sinks to the horizon.

Thick atmosphere haze mixed with an overcast sky block my view of the upside-down city. Hopefully, when night falls, the clouds will break up enough for the moon to shine. Even if I could remember the exact whereabouts of the airport, I doubt it's discoverable without moonlight.

The creatures are making more noise. I risk a peek over the tall grass and see a group of them close to the outskirts of the city, near my location. The animals seem to be fighting. They're too far away for me to make out any detail. They yank, tug, growl, and scream at each other. I wrinkle my nose and lie back down. They may fill their intended purpose as a kind of "ground security force" for the upside-down city, but whoever designed them is sick in the head. Hopefully, there will be minimal—or no—contact with them this time.

So I wait.

Persistence and patience are key to any endeavor. Unfortunately, I have little of either. The cloud break I'm waiting for comes as the last glimmer of light from the setting sun fades away. The moonlight's ethereal white beam pierces through the breaking cloud cover, illuminating the airport for me.

Looks like I have to go through a small portion of the city to reach the airfield. Hopefully, less time in the city lowers my chances of being discovered and eviscerated. Although now I'm more prepared.

I rise to my feet, arming myself with my sword, but keeping it sheathed and slung over my back. For my second weapon, I pull out one of my favorite automatic rifles with an attached grenade launcher. I am particularly excited about the grenade launcher. It took a lot of time to grind for it in Bootcamp Battle Grounds. Without having a good opportunity to test it yet, I'm eager to see what kind of carnage can be unleashed on those white turds—not that I'm holding a grudge or anything.

I click the safety off my gun.

Show time.

I'm not sure how they discover my presence. If I have to guess, I failed the sniff test. Doesn't matter. I careen down an alleyway, the screams of those pale demons growing closer. They aren't as fast as me, which is an advantage. However, they have more endurance than I do.

I reach the airfield, breathing harder than usual. Throwing a quick look over my shoulder, there are several of the faster creatures closing in on me.

I smile.

Whirling, I level my gun and shoot off a grenade. The creature nearest me opens his mouth to roar—and the grenade slams into his open maw.

I love when these happy little accidents occur in games.

The grenade's momentum propels the creature off its feet and into the air. Before the body can even hit the ground, the grenade explodes, shredding the creature and blowing up its nearby companions.

Oh, so satisfying.

More creatures aren't far behind their now-dead leaders. Winded, I check my stamina bar. It's low. I gulp down a couple of potions. New life surges through me. I bolt for the nearest plane.

———

"Please have a seat. Mr. Sheffy will be right with you."

I smile and nod. "Thanks."

The secretary returns my smile before leaving the office. Was she here last time? Of course, when I was last taken to his office, my vision had been obscured. *That* could've had something to do with overlooking the assistant on the first occasion. The lack of a bag blocking my vision isn't the only difference on my second visit here. For such a large building, it's surprising how few folks are here; I've only observed the secretary and the man who escorted me from the roof.

The flight differed from the last time as well. No missiles to dodge. And I was cleared to land almost immediately.

I glance around the brown, vintage office and wonder how old Morgan Sheffy is to *want* his office to appear as it does. I would've gone with something a bit more high-tech and sleek.

The door behind me opens and Morgan Sheffy's voice says, "Well, Ava, I didn't expect you to return so soon."

He offers his hand with a smile. I shake it, not smiling back. This is the man who persuaded my father to join him on his outrageous mission, then got away unscathed while my dad was in jail. No need to be polite.

"What made you believe I would come back?" I say stiffly.

His grin widens. "You are your father's daughter: headstrong, but when shown the truth, able to draw your own conclusions."

"Oh, I've drawn some conclusions," I say coolly.

"I would very much like to know what they are," he says, still keeping a pleasant tone.

Be careful what you ask for.

"Since you got my dad into this mess, you're going to get him out."

His smile appears more strained now. "How's that?"

I lift my chin, smug. "You heard me. You said my dad is vital to this organization. Well, he's vital to our family. We need him back."

Sheffy's smile fades. He looks away, his eyes glassy, staring into a distance only he can see.

Whatever response I was expecting, this isn't it. I figured he'd get angry and say things like, "How dare you come here and presume to tell me what to do!" Or after a long, intense argument, he'd be guilted into formulating a rescue mission.

"Did you ever go outside?" he asks, in a quiet tone.

I frown. "What? Were you not listening to me?"

He closes his eyes, resting his chin in his hand. "Have you been outside?"

What's this guy's deal? "It doesn't matter. What matters is . . ."

His eyelids fly open and he glares at me with one of the fiercest stares I've ever faced. And I know intense looks; I take Mrs. Wathers's science class.

"I did," I say, almost wilting under his gaze.

He turns away, looking out the large, glass window panes behind him. "What was it like?"

I study the back of his chair, searching for the right words, "It was different."

"How?"

"It was . . .". My thoughts wander from Dad, Sheffy, my crumbling family, and my reason for being here. The cool rain was on my skin again. The scent of the breeze. I remember how my lungs felt with the outdoor air. Once again, the only word that pops into my head is . . .

"Different," I repeat, adding, "But it was good. Alive in a way I don't think I've ever experienced."

He sighs. "Sounds nice."

"Wait." I lean forward. "You've never been outside?"

He turns the chair back around, and his expression shocks me. He somehow looks ten years older and exhausted. A tear runs down his cheek into his gray beard.

"No," he says. "I have not."

"That doesn't make sense. Why tell me I need to go outside? What was the purpose of that?"

A hint of a smile appears, even though it doesn't change his glum expression. "You are indeed your father's daughter."

I am so confused right now. "Explain."

"I never recruited your father," he says. "He came to me. Because of my position, I have tight security and always strive to remain hidden and anonymous. Yet he somehow got through to me. That impressed me; much like you have."

Really? It annoys me how his compliment causes me to swell with pride. I'm supposed to be angry, damn it. "That's not what I was told."

"I'm not sure where you're getting your information, but what I'm telling you is true. When I asked your dad why he wanted to join, I expected a range of replies. That he wants to kill the aliens, he wants to be free, he's doing what he thinks best for his family. Things I've been told a thousand times before. Well, some of his answers were what I thought—protect his family, freedom, and agency for his life—but then, he gave an answer that I didn't anticipate."

He pauses. His eyes move as if watching the memory playback. I find myself almost on the edge of my seat, wanting to know what my dad had said. I'm terrible at this whole staying mad at Morgan Sheffy thing.

A beeping noise chirps from his desk. Sheffy snaps back into focus. A holographic projection materializes in front of him and he studies it. It appears to be an outline of the HQ building. But what are all those gleaming red lights encompassing it?

"Who knew you were coming here?" he asks, never taking his eyes from the hologram.

I blink. "What?"

He shakes his head. "Who did you tell?"

"No, one," I say indignantly.

He turns back around and faces the window. "Then explain why there is an armada of Haven security ships heading straight for us?"

No sooner are the words out of his mouth than a distant explosion rumbles. Inspecting the flashing red hologram lights, I can now see they are the outlines of small, angular spaceships. I leap from my chair, almost knocking it over. The din of the approaching vessels rises in the background.

"We need to go!" I say.

A distant shriek reaches my ears—missile launches—a *lot* of missile launches. I step nearer to the window and witness dozens of smoke trails leading toward the incoming enemy ships. The city's automatic defense system is kicking in and, for once, I am happy about it.

I turn to Morgan Sheffy. "What are you doing?"

He continues sitting, observing the vessels through the window. A knot of dread clenches my stomach. The front row of the incoming enemy wave breaks formation, attempting to elude the missiles fired from the city. A few succeed in their efforts . . . many fail. Orange balls of light dot the sky as payloads detonate.

Smoke from the exploding ships obscures the oncoming horde, as do the vaporous trails spreading in the wake of missiles being fired at the enemy. I step even closer to the window, my heart pounding in my ears.

Hundreds of enemy craft burst through the black and gray veil, wisps of vapor twirling around the vessels. Within seconds, the haze thins and blows away, revealing even more ships. Although the automatic defenses fire missile after missile, they aren't even putting a dent in the enemy's numbers.

I glance back at Morgan Sheffy. Still seated, he watches our approaching doom.

"How can you just sit there and . . ." I begin.

He interrupts. "I suggest we take cover now."

A new noise sends cold shivers shooting through my body: the sound of hundreds of ships firing their weapons.

It's too late. Even as the thought flicks through my mind, survival instinct kicks in. I spin on my heel, about to bolt out of the office.

A deafening roar drowns out all other sounds. The building lurches; metal screeches. My feet leave the floor, as I am flung toward the far end of the room.

My back takes the brunt of the impact. I blink, vision blurry. Books fly off their shelves. Papers scatter and drift in the air. The vintage wood Morgan Sheffy seems so fond of bulges and cracks, large fragments snapping off and shooting in every direction as if fired from a cannon. Despite the throbbing ache in my spine, I curl up as tightly as possible while being pelted by old hardbacks and sharp splinters. After an eternity, the roar of the explosion fades, and the debris settles.

I blink away the sheen of dust covering my eyelids. The giant window is gone, shattered glass scattered all over the room. Books, papers, and pieces of broken furniture litter the floor. Sheffy's desk is overturned. Cracks line the walls, and all the lightbulbs have blown, their covers shattered.

A pair of shiny, black shoes enters my field of view. Morgan Sheffy leans down and offers me a hand. As he hoists me to my feet, I focus on a trickle of blood running down the side of his head.

"Quickly," he says. "They may fire another volley."

Pain lances through my back and I groan.

Sheffy looks at me, brow furrowed in concern. "Are you hurt badly?"

I shake my head. "I don't think so. But we need to unplug before they kill us."

It's what we should've done in the first place. In my panic, I'd forgotten it was an option.

It's his turn to shake his head. "We can't unplug; Haven security is blocking our ability to contact our pod's AI."

"Oh, yeah," I say, feeling stupid. "Marley told me that was a thing."

The lines on Sheffy's face grow more pronounced. "Marley . . . how do you know him?"

Surprised by his reaction, I'm about to answer when he cuts me off. "Did you inform him you were coming here?"

More explosions. They don't produce as much noise as before, hopefully not a sign of hearing damage. Actually, is ear damage possible in The Haven? The building rocks, interrupting my thought, and I grab Sheffy for support. "No. I didn't tell anyone I was coming," I say in answer to his question.

His grip on me tightens as the structure continues to shake, but his eyes never leave my face. He nods and says, "This way."

We exit the room through the now warped doorway. Out in the corridor, the secretary's desk and chair are broken and tipped over. The secretary is nowhere to be seen.

"Where is everybody?" I ask, limping after Morgan Sheffy down the hall.

"As soon as your plane came on radar, I asked everyone to leave. After showing you in, the secretary was the last to go," he says. He touches the side of his head and inspects the blood on his fingers. "Looks so realistic," he mutters to himself, wiping his hand on his pants, his lanky figure hunched over as he lumbers along the hall. I do my best to stay close to him and keep my footing as the building trembles under the intensity of the enemy's attack.

"Why would you send them away? Did you think I would do something?" I feel puzzled and upset at this possibility.

He shakes his head. "I wasn't sure if you'd been compromised. I needed to protect my people."

Good instinct, as it turns out.

The hallway dead-ends at a door. Without slowing his momentum, Sheffy slams into the door, throwing it open. We enter a stairwell. Morgan descends, with me close on his heels. The handrails tremble under my hand, and the lights flicker; it's a miracle they're working at all at this point.

"What do you mean, compromised?" I ask, still somewhat insulted. Just because it was a good instinct doesn't make it any less hurtful. Or perhaps I'm mad it didn't occur to me?

Sheffy's voice echoes in the stairwell. "Do you think it's a coincidence? Haven security showing up so soon after you arrive?"

Heat rises to my face. "No chance they compromised me; no way they followed me here."

He disagrees. "You may not have done this intentionally, Ava; but they are here because of you. You've just confirmed it for me."

Before being able to ask how, Sheffy stops, and I almost tumble down the stairs in my attempt not to collide with him.

He's mumbling to himself. Only a few of his words are discernable. "I . . . also . . . blame. Should've told her . . . suspicions. How was I to know . . .?"

He shakes his head as if to clear his thoughts and continues his descent.

"Tell me what?" I ask, following him. He doesn't answer.

Several flights of stairs later, he stops again, throwing up his hand, signaling me to do likewise. I gladly comply. Huffing and puffing, I down a couple of stamina potions and a health potion.

Sheffy turns, holding a finger to his lips, then cocks his head to listen. With stamina restored, I can focus better. What I hear perplexes me. To be more accurate, the lack of what I hear puzzles me.

The rumbling booms have stopped. The screeching grind of metal is gone, as is the noise of shattering glass. It's as if the attack never happened.

Sheffy and I exchange looks of concern. Then there is a new sound. I can't tell what is. It almost resembles distant clapping—which makes no sense.

The noise grows louder, echoing through the stairwell. Over the commotion, there are shouts, what seem to be commands. My heart pounds harder as the realization of what I'm hearing dawns on me.

Footsteps. Dozens and dozens of feet pounding up the stairs below us.

Morgan Sheffy realizes it at the same time. He motions for me to follow him and opens a door to a corridor that looks similar to the one we just left.

The hallway veers right, but instead of following it, Sheffy stops in front of the wall. He places his hand against the surface and a pale-blue light traces his handprint. A section sinks inward, then slides open.

Inside is a spacious, simply furnished room. The color on the walls is a soft, eggshell blue, with framed paintings of ocean landscapes and sunsets. The carpeted floor is cushiony under my shoes. A recliner and oversized sofa are the only pieces of furniture I see.

"Are we safe here?" I ask, a small spark of hope springing to life.

He purses his lips. "I doubt it. If it was anyone else attacking, I'd say we were safe, but since it's Haven security—it'll be a matter of hours before they find us."

"How? It looks like any other wall."

"They have access to tools we don't," he replies. "Though we hid this place for so long, we're still in The Haven. This is their world."

He moves to the recliner and sits down, laying his head in his palms. Seeing him now, all my earlier anger and frustration vanishes. Instead, I kind of feel sorry for him.

"Is there no other option?" I ask, sitting on the sofa.

He shakes his head without looking up.

Well, crap.

My leg jiggles with nervous energy. Different possibilities course through my mind. If Sheffy is correct, I'm about to be apprehended by Haven security. There's not a single thing to be done about it. What does that mean to me? Permaban from the gaming side of The Haven is the least of my worries. They launched an all-out military assault on this place, and I'm fraternizing with a terrorist leader. I'll be lucky not to end up with the death penalty.

I swallow past the sudden lump in my throat. Sheffy glances up at me. His avatar looks haggard as he gives me a sad smile.

"Don't worry," he says. "They'll go easier on you than they will with me. I can tell them I forced you to come here on a couple of occasions to run errands for us, threatening you if you didn't comply."

I nod. Who knows if Haven security would buy it, but it's something. Guilt wells up. I'd been so ready to take this guy down a peg. Now he was offering to lie to help me get off with lighter punishment.

"Thanks," I whisper, then continue in a more normal tone. "But you don't need to do that. My dad is already considered a terrorist, and I'm sure to be lumped in that category with him. Besides, I don't want you taking more heat on my account."

"That's what your father would want," he states. "He would want me to do everything I can to protect his daughter."

There are no words. I do my best to smile gratefully in his direction, but it's more like a forced grimace. It's tough to be grateful when your stomach is churning and your heart is beating faster than drums at a heavy metal concert at the thought of being arrested with the rebel leader. I can't imagine the Ungulithi will have much mercy for such an association.

Sinking deeper into the sofa, I wait. When Sheffy offers me something to eat, I refuse. I'd rather not indulge in the mind tease that is digital food, especially if I'm going to be in prison subsisting on bread and water. At least, that's what the prisoners live off of in Dungeon Raiders—I have no idea what people eat in prisons in the real world. In fact, I know little of real life outside my home routine and The Haven.

We sit in a hush, not moving, engrossed in our thoughts for some time. For lack of anything better to do, I rehash the events that led us here. I then recall something Sheffy had said.

"You said I was compromised," I say. "What makes you so sure?"

He jerks, as if being awakened from slumber. He blinks his eyes at me, struggling to focus. "Hmm? Oh, that . . ." His countenance turns dour. "How have you come to know Marley?"

I tell him about Marley and how we met. Morgan's visage darkens the more I talk, and the knot in my stomach tightens.

As I finish, he nods. "This isn't the first time I've heard the name Marley."

It makes sense; my dad might've mentioned him before, and I say as much.

He waves me off. "Could be, but the context I remember is, shortly before he was taken, your father came to me saying he was becoming distrustful of Marley."

My blood turns to ice. "Why?"

Sheffy looks away. "We couldn't be sure. We had no actual proof. But when you mentioned his name before . . . I had to protect my people, just in case."

He looks up at me again; the sadness returning. "Turns out we might've been justified."

A suspicion grows in the back of my mind. "About what?"

He leans forward in his seat, opening his mouth to speak when a loud boom causes both of us to jump. The noise reverberates around the room, fading to a dull resonance.

"That was sooner than I expected," Sheffy mumbles, looking at the doorway we'd entered earlier.

Another bang.

He glances back at me, a curious expression on his face. Before I can ask why he's giving me a look, another sound interrupts us—a steel-cutting torch slicing through the wall.

My heart leaps into my throat. Sheffy looks how I feel.

We both sit as still as statues, our eyes following the small point of flame carving a rectangular shape into the wall, sparks tumbling from the white-hot light.

Time seems to speed up. It appears to take the torch only seconds to complete its cut. The rectangular section they'd slashed falls to the ground with a thud. Soldiers, clad head to foot in black combat gear, smoothly enter the room, fanning out around us, aiming large automatic weapons at us—weapons I've never seen before in The Haven.

"Don't move!" one of them barks.

Sheffy and I raise our hands. *Funny, they tell us not to budge and we instinctively lift our hands.* A painful, icy sensation pulses through my veins.

"Well, we meet again," a female voice says from behind the wall of soldiers.

The woman emerges and comes to a stop in front of me, snapping her heels together. I try to get a glimpse of her face, but she is wearing the same large, dark glasses and mask as the rest of the troops.

"Forgive me," she laughs, removing her goggles and mask. It still takes a minute to process who she is—or perhaps it's the terror being pumped through me with every heartbeat, jumbling my thoughts. Then it clicks . . . and all the horrible memories of that day come rushing back.

Special Agent Rose Trudo. The woman who had arrested my father is now here to arrest me. She smirks. "So you remember me. I'm so glad you do, Ava. I thought we'd never see each other again."

She walks over to Sheffy with a triumphant look. "Who knew the daughter of a traitor would be so helpful in bringing us to the leader of the rebellion?" She looks over at me. "Honestly, you couldn't have done any better had you tried."

Her words sting. Despite my situation, I fight the urge to smack the smug expression off her face. She caused my family so much pain and anguish. Her smug satisfaction makes me sick.

Sheffy looks up at her, his fear from earlier gone. "You must be a clever woman indeed to trick a teenage girl."

Trudo leans down and pats him on the cheek. "And you must be an outstanding leader indeed to let yourself be captured because of a teenage girl."

It's his turn to smirk. "You only got me, lady. That's all you're going to get."

She rises to her full height and tips her head. "We'll see. The Ungulithi are very good at getting what they want."

Trudo steps toward me and pulls a small, pronged gadget from her belt. She leans over me, holding the instrument in front of my face.

"Leave her alone," Sheffy shouts. "She's not a part of this—agh!"

His words are cut off as a gun stock slams into his face. Trudo looks over her shoulder at Morgan. "That's a mere glimpse of what you have coming."

She turned back to me. "And this is just a taste of what's in store for you."

She snatches a handful of my hair. Before I can even cry out, she yanks my head down. There's a whirring sound, like a small engine being revved up. Two icy-cold prongs touch the base of my skull. Then a jolt hits the back of my skull as if with a baseball bat. Every muscle in my body stiffens, and I am thrown into a black tunnel, falling faster and faster, the light receding from view.

My landing is surprisingly soft. I'm on my back . . . footsteps all around me . . . indistinct, dark forms glide across my vision.

"I really must protest. This is the second time you've started the emergency unplug sequence on her; it'll be a miracle if she isn't brain damaged . . . or at least more damaged than usual."

"It's fine, Chuck," I say, blinking hard, comprehension returning. "I'm alright."

"No thanks to these mutton chops," Chuck says, sniffing.

"Can it, tin-boy," says a familiar male voice.

The room is becoming clearer. The dark forms sharpen into black-clad soldiers; exactly like the men who took my father away. Mom and my sisters are in the doorway. Mom looks haggard and sad, but unsurprised. My sisters stand, one on each side of her, clutching her; Mom doesn't appear to realize they're there. Both Sofia and Riley are pale and have tears running down their faces.

"It's okay," I say, looking at my sisters, trying to put on a brave face. "It's going to be okay."

"There ya go tellin' lies. I hope you don't do that during your interrogation."

My heart sinks into my stomach, and with it the faint possibility that everything *could've* gone well. I recognize the voice. One soldier breaks away from the others and saunters closer to me.

Glaring, I say, "So you *are* a traitor. You betrayed Dad."

The soldier stops beside my pod and snorts. He removes his mask and dark glasses. "Regular teen detective," he drawls in a mocking tone. "Too bad it's too late for you to do anything about it."

Marley looks different from his avatar. He has short, blond hair, with the distinct lack of a mustache on his pudgy, pale face. His pallid eyes are small but icy, gazing at me with cold indifference.

Questions buzz in my head. Despite the creeping fear threatening to paralyze me, I can't help my contempt for Marley as I glare at him.

He clacks his tongue in disapproval. "I can see you lying there judging me. One, I don't care, so don't waste your time, and two, you're in no position to judge; you're a traitor and a terrorist."

He's right. Yet all I can think about is the man who betrayed my father and tricked me into trusting him, standing before me smirking, and I'm helpless to do anything. The simmering rage from earlier replaces the fear. My muscles quiver and I long to launch myself at him and claw out his face.

Marley looks pleased. "Little lady's got some fight in her. Bold in-game and in life; I tip my hat, for all the good it'll do ya."

He pulls out a needle and syringe from a pouch on his uniform. Stepping closer, he plunges it into my neck.

I lash out. Maybe I can . . .

He swats my attack aside as if I were just an annoying fly. There is a small pinch and a strange warmth races through me. My arms go limp. Overwhelming fatigue overtakes me, clouding my thoughts, and weakening my will, my strength. Sleep is the only thing I ever want to do again.

"See ya on the other side, little lady."

Marley's voice echoes, odd, distorted. The world fades into darkness.

And then there is nothing.

Chapter Twenty-Three

New Haven

I awaken, slumping in a chair in a narrow chamber that is swaying or shaking. All the furniture and furnishings seem to be scaled-down versions of themselves. A small table in the middle of the room holds two covered silver platters. On either side, a pair of small, cushioned benches face each other. Dark curtains prevent me from seeing what is outside.

Across from me, a sliding door opens and Marley enters, holding food.

"Oh," he says when he sees me. "Awake and alert. I was wondering how soon you'd be rejoining us."

I remain silent, glaring at him.

"Eh." He shakes his head in disappointment and moves to sit on one of the padded benches. "Things won't go well for you if you don't learn to behave."

After seating himself, he sets his meal on the table. I give his food a cursory glance, then do a double take. A large, juicy steak rests on one side of his plate. Glazed carrots and roasted broccoli sprouts are piled across the meat. The meal's scent wafts in my direction. It smells better than any real-life food I've smelled in years.

Marley notices my expression and grins. "Bet you've never had a real slab of beef before. Lemme tell ya, it ain't nothing like you can get in The Haven."

He cuts a small slice off the steak, stabbing it with his knife, and holds it inches from his face. "Oh, some stuff they get right. But they cannot replicate the genuine, little details . . . the textures, the heat, whether it was cooked over a flame or on a skillet. Shit your palate can only dream of."

I shouldn't watch, yet I am unable to look away. He's spot on . . . I've never eaten real steak before, and it looks amazing. I swallow hard.

He smirks. A droplet of grease runs down the steak knife as Marley brings the meat to his mouth, biting it off the blade. Chewing, he leans back and looks at me with smug satisfaction. "Tastes even better than it looks too."

My mouth waters.

With the knife, he points at my legs. "Your daddy never mentioned you were crippled. Mind if I ask how?"

At the mention of my father, the rumble in my stomach disappears. I clench my jaw and glare at him.

He stares at me for a moment. Then, half-shrugging, he returns to his food. "Just curious."

Marley swallows and gulps from a mug full of a dark, yellowish, bubbly liquid.

"Alright, this is how it's gonna go," Marley says, wiping his mouth on a cloth napkin. "I've got questions for ya, and I'm sure you have a few for me. So let's exchange some information. Though, to be honest, I could give a shit if you refuse to answer my questions. Once we arrive at New Haven, we'll find out all we need to."

That doesn't sound promising. "Why? You gonna torture me?" It takes an effort to keep my voice steady.

Marley resumes eating. "Naw. Don't need to. Our *benevolent* over-lords have developed ways of getting the information they want."

"Doesn't sound like there's much incentive to talk."

"Well, the Ungulithi won't give you any answers. I will."

I grimace. What he's saying makes sense. That doesn't mean his answers are trustworthy, but . . . what choice do I have?

I sigh. *Can't believe I'm doing this.*

"When you talked about the Ungulithi just now, you called them benevolent. You sounded sarcastic."

Marley lets the implied question in my statement hang in the air for a moment while he chews his food, appearing to mull over my question.

"Can't say I'm wild about them. But they pay well." He gestures around him. "There are privileges to be had in cooperating with them. But I wouldn't mind if they up and left one day. Think I might enjoy having more of a say about how I live my life."

"It seems like you have more say than I do." Here he is, eating real meat, riding around in a large, luxurious MonoPod, and he *still* dares to complain about his life.

He shrugs. "I got lucky. Remember Mike, my programmer friend? He hooked me up with this gig."

"What is it, exactly, that you do?"

"Infiltrate, I guess. Get in good with known detractors and report my findings. Sometimes I take part in raids."

I didn't need that reminder. My face flushes.

"Why are you working for them?" I blurt out. "It seems you don't like them. So why did you betray my father and me to them?"

He gives a rueful smile. "What else should I do, little lady? Join you and your pops, rotting in a cell? The rest of the population seems okay living under the Ungulithi's style of tyranny. Who am I to judge? Naw, I like my life. They pay far better than any human employer I've ever had, anyway."

Marley is being way too communicative. "Why are you telling me all this?"

He gestures to me. "You are a guest in my MonoPod. Despite what you think of me, I like you. What I do . . . it isn't personal."

It sure feels personal. "But the day we first met . . . The Haven security . . ."

"Staged," he answers, looking very satisfied. "I had to get you to trust me. The boys were told to be convincing. Plus, I wanted to observe who I was dealing with; see if you were someone we should continue to monitor. If you hadn't thought of that last cheat, Mike would've pulled us out, anyway. You showed real pluck and ingenuity. It impressed me."

I could not care less about your opinion of me. "How'd you know to give me the megaphone?"

"It was in your father's Haven provisions. We search real and digital belongings when we arrest folks."

"How did you figure it was meant for me? How did you know I needed it?"

"We've been monitoring you for some time," he smirks. "We noticed an anomaly in your inventory. Normally, The Haven would've self-corrected such awkwardly inserted coding, but we prevented that from happening. When you didn't know what to do with the scroll, we played a hunch. Figured if it led to something important, we could always tail you."

He looks at his half-finished plate, then changes his tone. "Where are my manners? Here I am eating a meal in front of you, running my fool mouth, and haven't even offered you any food."

Marley lifts the lid off one serving platter. The sight makes my mouth water.

It isn't just steak and veggies. Bananas, apples, and grapes sit in a bowl off to the side. *Actual, ripe fruit.* I can't remember the last time I've eaten produce that wasn't half-rotten or sweetened in a can.

"This is only the first tray." He looks at me through the steam rising off the warm food. "Ever had seafood? I ain't talkin' about that canned crap ya'll get. I'm talking crab cakes, lobster rolls, shrimp tacos, salmon steaks . . . the real stuff, the fresh stuff."

I swallow. An odd lust comes over me. Everything he's describing sounds so satisfying, yet there's a part of me that knows I should refuse. Giving in and eating will be another victory for Marley. But my salivating mouth and empty stomach don't care about such things as pride or moral victories.

Marley studies me. "Or," he says, "If you're more in the mood for something sweet, I've got cupcakes, cookies, and gelato. Have you ever had hot chocolate sauce on ice cream before?" He rolls his eyes and pats his stomach. "Everyone should try it at least once."

He has all that? How big is his MonoPod, anyway?

Whatever moral I am battling over becomes unimportant. I want—no, *need* this food.

I say, "Well, getting arrested works up an appetite. I think I'll take you up on the seafood."

He grins. "Coming right up." He gets up, disappearing back through the door he had used to enter earlier. Soon after, the door swings open again. Marley reenters, carrying a large plate of food. "Two lobster tails, drenched in butter, shrimp kabobs, garlic mashed potatoes—also drenched in butter—and some cheesy broccoli."

My attention never strays from the platter as Marley sets it on the little table.

"Come and get it," he says.

I peer down at my legs, then back up to him, raising an eyebrow.

He shrugs. "You can't eat over there. I don't want stains on the chair."

Sighing, I maneuver myself to the edge of the chair and glance up at Marley. He smiles and nods, pretending not to understand. I roll my eyes in disgust.

Fortunately, I have a decent amount of upper body strength. I use the furniture around me as impromptu supports to get to the table, with no need for me to crawl on the floor. No doubt Marley had wanted something like that. I plop onto the cushioned bench, a little out of breath, though.

Marley remains standing on the opposite side of the table. "Almost fell back there," he says.

"Yes, thanks for the help," I snap back, without looking up from my plate. Fork in hand, I muster the rest of my dignity and start eating.

He chuckles, then leans forward. "How's your taste buds treatin' ya?"

They're *treatin'* me real good. My palate seems to come alive with every bite. I resist the temptation to devour the food like some destitute street orphan—I don't want those robust flavors to disappear, not even for a moment.

Maintaining a stony expression, I say, "Fine."

Marley laughs. "Better tuck in. This will be the first and last time you eat this good."

I try to ignore the remark, despite the sudden icy shiver running down my spine.

Marley walks over to the window, drawing up the blinds.

"Also," he adds, "We're almost to our destination."

For the first time since sitting down, I look up. Through the window, there is the distant outline of a city, unlike anything I've seen before.

New Haven is not a domed city. Quite the opposite, it reminds me of a city from the Invaders from Dhurm game. And, unlike Krouis, the domed city I live in, this one is brimming with activity.

We pull up to a MonoPod docking point—above ground—and disembark.

Marley must've called ahead to let someone know we were arriving. A stretch limousine awaits us. A large man in a dark suit, glasses, and white gloves steps into Marley's pod as soon as we dock. Without a word, the man scoops me into his arms, cradling me against his burly chest. I stare at him, jaw hanging open, too surprised to offer protest. Marley looks on, bemused.

The man takes me out of the pod and into the waiting limo. A minute later, Marley sits down beside me.

"Vito is awful chatty today," he says, motioning to the man who'd carried me, now depositing luggage into the trunk of the car.

I wonder what he's like when he's silent.

Once the last of the luggage is stowed, Vito slips into the driver's seat and peels away from the MonoPod dock.

Marley motions out the window. "Take it in while you can. Doubtful you'll ever behold anything like it again."

"Thanks for that." I give him my best scornful expression.

"Just trying to set realistic expectations," he says. "But, if you'd rather talk unicorns and rainbows . . ."

I grunt in disgust, making a show of giving him the cold shoulder while looking out the window. Skyscrapers stretch impossibly high overhead, a great number of them connected by enclosed walking bridges. I've visited countless cities in The Haven—historic ones, futuristic ones, fantasy ones. However, I've never encountered a city like New Haven before. Rather than sharp, angular designs, these structures look more rounded and contorted at bizarre angles. Light glints oddly off the metal that composes these buildings, casting almost neon-colored refractions even in the daylight. Few windows are visible in the architecture.

Also, unlike my town, it appears the residents of New Haven are not on lockdown. Crowds throng the sidewalks and fill vehicles on the road as if they have no idea folks like me in other cities live confined to their homes. It's weird to see so many people in one place. Even though our block gathered for the rare Common Hall meeting, the sheer volume of humanity here dwarfs anything in my experience.

The people also appear different here than what I've seen before. In contrast to most of my pale, unhealthy neighbors, everyone here appears to have glowing skin. Clothing hugs and accentuates their bodies. I glance down at my loose gray T-shirt with a faded logo. My pants are little better, and as for my shoes . . . they're nothing like what I observe being worn here.

"Why is New Haven not a dome city?" I ask.

Marley chuckles. "The dome cities are for individuals like you. Our alien overlords have no desire to live in drab, compact spaces. They need giant, sprawling buildings similar to their home world to remind everyone who's really in charge."

"The Ungulithi live here? I only see people."

"You think the Ungulithi would lower themselves to interact with humans daily? Ha! Did you notice the sky bridges earlier? That's how they get around. They keep to the upper floors. As to the people . . . well, everyone here works for the Ungulithi and is rewarded by living what was once considered normal lives. Hell, they shower a few with luxury."

"Like you?" I ask.

He half-smiles at the remark. "Eh, I get a few perks, nothing crazy. The folks that live it up are celebrities, key media figures, and politicians. They treat those guys real good."

"Even President Mercer?"

"Definitely." He pauses, and a funny expression comes over his face. He peers at his watch. "Hey, Vito," he calls out to the driver. "Quick change of plans. Let's make a stop at Soft Rays first."

Vito looks in the rearview mirror and nods. He turns off the main highway and down a two-lane street.

"Where are we going?" I ask, watching the building sizes dwindle as we get further down the road.

Marley seems as if he's weighing his words. After a while, he says, "I wasn't going to tell you this, considering the position you're in, but if I show this to you, it may change your mind."

He pauses again. I wait, apprehensive and confused.

"The Ungulithi might offer you a deal. You could be like us . . . like me."

I can't believe my ears. Without giving it a second thought, I say, "No. Are you kidding? We're nothing alike."

Marley looks away, out his window. "We'll see I guess."

"Is that what happened to you?" I say. "They caught you doing something and offered you a deal? Is that why you're such a coward?"

He whips his head around. "I may be many things, but a coward ain't one of them."

"Could've fooled me," I mutter under my breath.

Marley's face turns red. He looks as if he wants to punch my lights out. My body stiffens, prepared and anticipating the strike. I've been hit too many times to count in The Haven, but never in reality. I wonder if being punched in real life feels similar to being hit in The Haven?

Probably hurts more.

The punch never materializes. Marley sighs, rubbing his eyes. "You don't know me, little lady. You have no idea what I've gone through or why I'm here."

"I don't care," I say, fixing him with what I hope is my most withering glare. Marley, trying to get my sympathy, fuels my fury. He has no comprehension of what he's done to my family, and he has the nerve to plea for empathy?

To worsen matters, he glances at me and smirks. "Perhaps you will after I show this to you."

I refuse to answer, not trusting myself to speak.

We soon pull up to one of the shorter buildings. Marley steps out of the car, ignoring me. Vito walks to the trunk and rummages for something.

I hope he won't carry me for the rest of the day.

Fortunately, Vito pulls out a wheelchair, unfolding it beside my door.

All three of us head inside, Marley ahead, with Vito pushing my wheelchair.

"So, what are Soft Rays?" I ask. Neither man replies.

We step into an expansive, softly lit lobby. Marley walks up to the reception desk while Vito and I hang back a few steps. Somewhere a synthesizer plays some soothing notes. The scent of vanilla and cinnamon tickles my nose. I've smelled these scents in The Haven before but never so clearly.

Marley and the woman behind the desk exchange a few words. Vito and I aren't close enough to hear the conversation, but it sounds like Marley is asking a lot of questions. The woman smiles and answers, pointing him toward some gold elevators. He tips an invisible hat to her and walks in the direction she points. Vito pushes me in the same direction.

"Is this a spa?" I say as we enter an elevator, the doors closing behind us.

Marley presses one button near the top and looks at me for the first time since we arrived. "Spa isn't the right way to describe this place."

Ignoring my questioning glance, he once again turns his back on me. I'm just going to have to play along and find out.

We reach our floor and exit. I do a double take in confusion.

Marley notices me out of the corner of his eye and smiles. "No, you're not crazy. We're still inside, in a building in downtown New Haven."

His words conflict with what my eyes are showing me. We're at a beach. Everything around me is sand and surf, except for the elevator we just exited. Men, women, children, and dogs play in the sand and the water, acting as if this is normal. The sky above is deep blue, with a smattering of fluffy clouds. A calm breeze lifts my hair from my shoulders.

Marley grins, pointing up, "Specially constructed screens and lighting. More nurturing than the sun. People come here because it's safer and healthier than the real beach. The light enhances the body's normal cellular regeneration instead of giving you skin cancer."

He walks over to a post in the sand and pushes a button. A hard surface walkway emerges.

"Did I also mention it's handicap accessible?" he adds.

He strolls down the walkway. "C'mon, there's someone I want you to meet."

Vito propels me after Marley. We pass a family playing volleyball, their dog jumping and barking at the ball, trying to take part. I watch them, wondering if I should risk it and scream *bloody murder. Help! I'm being kidnapped*! Then I remember what Marley had said: this city is for people who work for the Ungulithi. To them, I'm a terrorist sympathizer; no one here will help.

Marley exits the walkway, stepping through sunbathers, sandcastles, and beach toys, pausing in front of an older woman lounging on a beach towel. Vito and I watch as he says something, then points at me. The woman looks like she doesn't want to get up, but Marley is insistent. She at last relents, her body language full of annoyance. They make their way to us. As the woman gets closer, recognition dawns on me.

"Ms. Mercer . . . excuse me, I mean President Mercer, I'd like you to meet Ava McNealy," Marley says in mock formality.

Stunned silence. President Mercer gives a curt wave of her hand and says, "You wanna get a picture, or do you have something for me to sign?"

Still too bewildered to respond, I stare at her. In the back of my mind, I realize how stupid I must look. But the dots haven't connected; the last thing I'd expected was the president of the United States to be here, in a swimsuit, without bodyguards.

"Calm down, Mercer, she isn't one of your fangirls," Marly drawls.

President Mercer whirls on him, pointing. "Shut the fu . . ." she glances at me and decides not to finish what she was going to say. She straightens up, trying to appear more dignified. "You will address me as Madam President. And why did you interrupt my cell regeneration therapy if she doesn't want anything?"

"Okay, *Madam President*," Marley says in a mock respectful tone. "And she wants something." He looks at me and adds, "Don't you, Ava?"

What is he talking about? I run through a quick inventory of my desires, but confusion makes it hard for me to focus. What could I want from the president of . . .

Oh.

"Uh," I begin, my voice squeaky. I clear my throat and try again. "Is it possible to grant a presidential pardon to my father?"

President Mercer raises her eyebrows. She hadn't expected that question. "Well, I mean, maybe. It's not as simple as . . ." She pauses, closing her eyes and giving her head a quick shake. "There are a lot of factors to contend with. Who is your father, and what is he doing in prison?"

Before I can answer, Marley cuts in. "Her father is Robert McNealy. If you recall, Madam President, he is accused of terrorism."

At first, she acts like she's going to respond to his persistent mocking. But then she stops and looks at me again, frowning. "McNealy . . . that sounds familiar." She studies me, trying to remember why the name rings a bell. A moment later, she mouths a silent Oh.

"Marley brought you here?" she asks. "You didn't come willingly?"

I shake my head.

President Mercer gives Marley a disgusted look. "I don't know what game you're playing, but I want you to leave me alone."

She stomps away, then hesitates, twisting to look at me. "If they offer you a deal, take it. Have all this." She gestures at the water and the sand. "It is more beneficial to be a kindly treated slave who knows better than the disrespected slave you are."

With that, she strides into the lapping water until she disappears from sight.

Chapter Twenty-Four

Reunion

The Ungulithi have weird prisons.

The building resembles a vast warehouse. Thousands of large glass cylinders fill the space, each containing a cot and a toilet. I've been lying on my bed in one of these glass containers for hours. So far, no Ungulithi have appeared. Do they even exist? Are any of these prisoners similar to my father? Dissenters removed from their families to either rot or await execution.

My fellow prisoners, miserable men and women, sit or lie on their beds, use their toilets, or look out their glass tubes with forlorn expressions. It only took a few hours of exposure for me to become desensitized to seeing people use the toilet. Because of the gray coveralls given to us on our arrival, there's nothing discreet about using the bathroom here. You either stand or squat half-naked while taking care of your business, hoping that no one else is paying attention.

Another horrible aspect of being here: there's nothing to do. No books or movies . . . no Haven.

Have my friends noticed my absence by now? Perhaps my arrest made my town's headline in The Haven newsgroup?

Prone on my thin cot, I practice breathing exercises, attempting to ignore the ever-present pungent smell of plastic. Preventing anxiety from overwhelming me is a full-time battle. Still, I can't keep my thoughts in the moment. My fear vacillates between what could be going on at home and what might soon happen to me.

The glass encasing me darkens, and a holographic projection of a woman's stern face fills my vision.

"We have scheduled questioning and debriefing for Prisoner PH165211 in ten minutes. Prepare accordingly."

The glass returns to its previous tint, and the woman disappears from view.

"Oh, sure, I'll tell my secretary to cancel all my meetings," I say. Ugh. I'm going to have to keep a close watch on my mouth.

I sit up, scoot to the edge of the bed, and wait.

After what seems like even more hours—I've lost all ability to calculate time in here—I finally see three guards in dark uniforms approaching, one pushing an empty wheelchair.

Once they have me in the chair, they roll me past the multitude of cylinders. I refuse to look at the people trapped here. When they brought me here, I'd made the mistake of gaping at them, and the sight had caused a rock to form in my stomach.

They transport me into a large room with slanted, metal slabs. On one side of each slab is a pole with IV fluid. On the other side is a stand with what looks to be a metallic egg about the size of my head. Upon closer view, I notice the slabs also have leg and wrist restraints. My heart leaps into my throat.

Are they going to torture me?

"Guys, I confess," I say in my best is-this-really-necessary voice. "Whatever you want me to say, I don't need any encouragement!"

The guards remain silent. They lift me onto one slab, fastening me in.

"Don't bother about the legs," I say as they kneel. "Couldn't use them to escape even if I wanted."

They ignore me and finish strapping my limbs. Remaining mute, they exit, leaving me alone.

Sweat beads all over my body. I let my breath out, fighting my racing thoughts.

You don't know if it's going to be torture. Cross that bridge when you get to it.

The door opens. Guards reenter, pushing someone in front of them. The man they push stumbles and almost drops to the floor. At the last minute, he catches himself and continues to walk forward at his captors' "encouragement."

The group passes me, giving me a better look at the man. The prisoner is haggard, pale, and thin, and has not washed or tidied himself up in weeks. Despite the change, it doesn't take me long to recognize him.

"Dad!"

The scream bursts from me before I can even attempt to stop it. Everyone looks at me in surprise. The moment my dad's warm hazelnut eyes meet mine, all fear evaporates. I strain against my bonds. I want to leap off this slab, hug him, and weep. Since that isn't possible, I skip the first couple of steps to the third one and burst into tears.

"Ava?"

His voice is almost unfamiliar. He sounds gravelly and weak. I stifle my sobbing as they bind him. He looks so frail.

"What have you done to him?" I scream. The guards continue to ignore me. Being ignored is grating on me.

Dad clears his throat. "How . . . what are you doing here?"

The guards walk out of the room again as I strive in vain to stop the flow of tears. Through sobs, I recount the main events that led to our reunion.

"It's so wonderful to see you," I say, finishing my story. "I'm so glad you're alive."

Dad appears to be doing his best not to cry. "Honey, I'm thrilled to see you too, but not like this. Not in their hands." He leans his head back, looking at the ceiling. "I'm sorry Marley got to you too. I should've taken that into consideration; should've planned better."

"It's okay." I fight back a fresh stream of tears. "It's not your fault. You didn't know . . ."

"It is on me," he interjects. "I had my suspicions about him but did nothing about it. I'm the one who . . ." He pauses. "It was I who thought joining the New Sons of Liberty was a good choice."

Seeing my father so dejected is a new, frightening experience. I want to reassure him, to comfort him, yet the words are stuck in my throat.

He looks up. "How are your mom and sisters? Are they holding up okay?"

No, they need you. We all need you! We're falling apart while you were off playing freedom fighter!

Out loud I say, "It's been . . . hard."

He nods. Hopefully, he doesn't press me to go into detail; no need to add to how terrible he already feels.

"Father and daughter reunited at last. Such a touching scene." Special Agent Rose Trudo saunters into the room while pulling a pair of black leather gloves off her hands, one finger at a time. She looks as if she is wearing the same uniform as before. Could her entire wardrobe be composed of black SWAT-like uniforms?

Dad glowers at her in tight-lipped silence. Emotions boil and writhe in my stomach. There's so much that wants to boil out of me, but I follow my dad's example and remain silent.

"What? Not so chatty anymore? A minute ago you were so sweet, so emotional," Trudo says, stopping between me and Dad. "A terrorist and his spunky daughter; does it get any better?"

Words almost come hurling out. Instead, I grind my teeth, eyeing the special agent.

Trudo looks at the metal egg beside me. "Did you notice this fascinating device earlier? You've probably figured out by now this is not some strange room decor."

She seems gleeful; that can't be a good thing.

"She knows nothing," my dad says, seething.

Smirking, Trudo replies, "Maybe. That's why we are here. I like to call this area the library." She comes closer and touches the metal egg beside me. "And Egghead here is our resident research and reference guy."

"You're already familiar with aspects of how Egghead works," Trudo continues. "The technology used in The Haven is similar."

She taps the surface of the metallic egg, causing a small holographic keyboard to project out. Fingers flying across her keyboard, Trudo gives me an appraising glance, like a butcher examining a slab of meat in General Market Sims. She finishes and steps back.

The lower section of Egghead opens up to reveal several tiny metal arms. They unfold and reach in my direction.

"Ava, sweetie, it's okay, it doesn't hurt," Dad says. His wavering voice does nothing to assure me.

I shrink away as far as my bonds allow; it's no good. The arms point their nubby ends at either side of my head, much like the metal snakes in my pod do when about to enter The Haven.

"I have told Egghead what we want to know," Trudo says. "Try to lie or hide in some mind vault. It's of no consequence. We will get all we need."

The metal arms vibrate. A quiet humming sound fills the room. My muscles tremble, whether from the machine or fear, I don't know.

A loud electric crack startles me. A bright white light flashes. I'm back home, chatting with Dad. But the dialogue is odd; we seem to be shifting, wearing different clothes, and sitting in other rooms while having the same conversation.

What in the world? The thought flashes through my mind even as I'm talking with my dad.

A strange sensation comes over me as I realize what's going on. I'm reliving similar conversations on different days, yet all regarding my father's activities, the Ungulithi, and wanting things to be better.

Now I'm in The Haven, at the New Sons of Liberty's home world. I'm sprinting through the abandoned city, yet again battling those irritating pale creatures.

No . . .

My mind tells my muscles to stop, to stand still. I strain, yet it doesn't do any good. You can't alter the replay of memories.

I'm in the upside-down city, sitting in Sheffy's office. At one point, everything freezes, and I sense another presence. A blurry shadow flits around, examining every nook and cranny, every book, and every image in the room before time speeds back up.

Sheffy and I speed through our conversation, yet every thought I'm thinking is new and present. I'm being forced to replay certain memories, while still keeping my ability to think in the present moment; it's strange and surreal.

Once more, my memory is halted, like a photograph, when I arrive at the armory and the weapons master appears, and again when I meet the secretary on my second trip. Both times, the weird shadow entity enters, taking its time, examining every detail. It surprises me how calm I am in its presence.

It's got to be Trudo or the "Egghead" AI searching my memory.

Something pops. The bright light flashes in front of my eyes again, followed by another loud pop.

I'm back. Still strapped to my metal slab. Yet the room appears distorted, like I'm peering through a window on a rainy day.

"Honey, are you alright?"

My dad's voice sounds weird. Why is his speech echoing?

"Ava, talk to me. Let me know you're okay."

"Oh, shut up," Trudo says. "I just took her brain for a spin. Give her a minute."

I feel wet and cold. My skin sticks against the metal slab.

"I'm so tired," I mumble, attempting to blink everything into focus.

"That's normal, sweetie," Dad says with relief. "You'll get better in a matter of minutes."

"She doesn't have a few minutes," Trudo says, frowning at the phone in her hand. "You've both been summoned."

I shake my head, striving to process. "Summoned? Who? Where?"

Dad makes a muted groaning sound. I give him a questioning glance, but he ignores me, eyes downcast.

"Who do you think can summon around here?" Trudo asks in annoyance. "The Ungulithi, of course."

Chapter Twenty-Five

Judgement

Pale, hairless people clothed in flowing robes greet us as soon as the elevator doors open. Unabashedly gaping at them, I'm wheeled into a small room full of what looks to be medical supplies.

"Say hello to The Named," Trudo says, gesturing to the robed figures. "Personal attendants of the Ungulithi."

"We will take them from here." The taller of the two hairless attendants dips his head at Trudo while maneuvering to prevent her from stepping into the room. "They shall undergo cleansing, as is the custom of the upper levels. Those who are not to be cleansed cannot step into this room."

Trudo seems offended. "I showered this morning."

"As you say," he replies in a deep, neutral tone. "Our lords thank you for your understanding and obedience."

Both figures move toward us, their movements slow and elegant, to match their apparel. Both wear white robes that expose their arms. The only color in their clothing is purple and gold patterns near their bare feet.

The taller one escorts my dad by the arm, while the smaller one pushes my wheelchair.

We are taken to two separate stall areas where a machine scans us. The figures appear content with the scan, and the tall one guides my dad in one direction while I'm moved in another.

"Wait," Dad says.

"Unless you'd like to be cleansed together," the one leading my dad away says, "then I suggest you walk this way."

As he's being led off, Dad looks back, his expression full of uncertainty. I try to give him a reassuring smile before he's cut off from view.

Turns out, cleansing means taking two separate baths. There's a traditional bath followed by a dip in a strange liquid. My escort doesn't put me back in my regular clothes but drapes me in robes similar to her own. Another woman enters and assists her in braiding my hair before pinning it in a tight bun.

They wheel me into a vast cathedral-like hallway, with a ceiling extending several stories over our heads, and stone walls adorned with vibrant, large, hanging banners inscribed with symbols I've never seen before.

We stop before a vast set of double doors. A couple of minutes pass before my father and his companion join us.

I breathe easier upon seeing him. He is wearing similar clothes to mine. He gives me a reassuring look, glances down at his robes, and raises an eyebrow. Despite our circumstances, I almost burst into a fit of nervous giggles.

The weird hairless people line up in front of the door, staring at us.

"You're about to see the Ungulithi," one states. "A privilege few can boast of. Bow when we come before them, speak only when spoken to, and answer every question put to you."

My dad and I exchange glances before we nod our understanding. I gulp. Despite our situation, having him beside me is comforting.

The immense doors swing open, thrumming as they do so. My jaw drops. Despite the deep shadows in the room, it's easy to see that it's much larger than the Common Hall back home. Heck, it might even be bigger than the indoor beach I'd seen in New Haven. The room contains many columns of creme-colored pillars interspersed throughout. The one wall nearest us has multiple, decorative textile hangings with more odd symbols etched in the fabric.

We move through the chamber in silence, every sound swallowed by the vastness of our surroundings.

"Halt!"

The deep voice comes from everywhere at once, loud, beating into our eardrums like music at a concert does when standing too close to an amp. I shiver, gripping the armrests of my wheelchair hard enough to cause my fingers to grow sore.

We come to a stop and The Named take a knee, forcing my father to do the same. Cognizant of my instructions, I bow as best I can.

"So," the voice booms. "These are the members of the terrorist group plaguing our new planet."

From under my eyelids, I search for the source of the voice without success.

"Yes, lord," both of The Named intone. "And we have cleansed them, per your custom."

A long pause follows. The only distinguishable sound is my labored breathing.

Can I stop bowing now?

"You," the voice says. "In the chair. Sit up. Let me see you."

I straighten, popping a muscle in my back. I try to keep my expression blank as I peer into the shadows, trying to pick out the Ungulithi. Few images or videos exist of our mysterious overlords. The few out there . . . well, I could never tell if the pictures were legit or not.

"So young. A pity. And yet, perhaps . . ."

The voice cuts off. I sense activity several yards ahead of me, hidden by a deep shadow.

"C'mon," my dad mutters loud enough for me to hear. "Let's cut the theatrics. Show your true form."

The Named give my father reproachful glances.

Motion draws my attention. A shape separates itself from the dark and approaches.

The Named tense, their breathing quickening.

I stare in horrid fascination at what emerges from the shadows.

The figure gliding across the ground is sluglike in its bottom half. Flexible, crustaceous plating, painted with dull streaks of purple and yellow, covers its undulating skin. Four scrawny arms extend from its torso, covered in the same shell armor. Atop a small neck is a thin, long head, more reptilian in appearance than the rest of its body. Its four diminutive eyes press into its face, giving them a dark, beady expression. A small device is strapped under its mouth. Some sort of amplified translator?

Somehow, the creature seems impressive, silly, and repugnant all at the same time.

The alien stops a few feet away and seems to study me. I almost don't notice, studying it in return. The alien's lips move. An odd series of clicks and murmuring sounds follows. A glimmer of red light appears on the device under the alien's mouth and I hear the voice from earlier say, "What is it like to view the face of a god?"

So the box under its jaw is indeed a translator. However, the question catches me off guard. I almost burst out in confused laughter. This reptilian slug has quite the opinion of himself . . . or itself . . . or alienself?

"You're not a god."

Oops. I'd spoken that aloud. I need to stop.

The alien seems unperturbed. "And how are you so sure?"

Still kneeling, head lowered, my dad looks at me. He gives a barely perceptible wink of encouragement.

"Well," I say, looking back at the alien. "I haven't seen you do anything godlike, I guess."

"Hmm," the alien says. "Is not our arrival in time and space sufficient? Is not our technology—like The Haven—enough?"

Yup, this creature is tripping on some major ego. Silence is probably the best option, lest I say something to piss it off.

The Ungulithi lord glides behind me, all four of its eyes on me. "You like The Haven, don't you, Ava?"

A shiver tingles down my spine. I loosen my grip on the armrests of my wheelchair, flexing my stiff, sore fingers. I take a calming breath. The voice of the translator, though deep, is flat and emotionless. Yet something about hearing my name coming from that creature and that device . . .

"Oh, yes, I forget. I know your name, but you don't know mine. I'm Xynlyc."

Is it serious? That's its *name*? "Uh, hi. Wish I could say it's nice to meet you."

"Hmm," Xynlyc intones. "You're impertinent. Do you also decline to answer my inquiry?"

Cringing, I bite my tongue. Why do I always have to turn to sarcasm when scared or anxious? Blood races in my veins, almost as fast as the scattered thoughts tumbling in my mind. I attempt a nervous gulp. My throat is as scratchy as sandpaper. "What was the question?"

Xynlyc comes around to face me, eyes narrowed. "You enjoy The Haven, correct?"

"Yes," I say.

"We know," Xynlyc says. "We know everything about you."

Really? Is that supposed to scare me? The creature doesn't have to try. I'm already quaking on the inside.

"You aren't a terrorist."

Okay, got to admit I hadn't seen that coming.

"You want everything to go back to the way it was."

It surprises me how accurately Xynlyc knows my motivations.

"Yeah," I answer when the alien doesn't continue.

"We would like the same. It would give us great pleasure to restore your family, your way of life, back to you."

No, I tell myself as a small bit of hope grows. *No, it's a trick. There has got to be a catch.*

The alien inclines its head. "We understand if you're not convinced. You've both been through so much over the past several months."

"What do you want from me?"

The alien spreads its arms wide, somehow reminding me of a spider. "You did, unfortunately, associate with a group of dangerous terrorists in your efforts to help your father. Its charismatic leader bewitched your poor dad, so we cannot hold him responsible for his actions, can we?"

It's like being led down a path in the dark, unsure of my destination. If only Xynlyc would get to the point.

"No?" I say, hesitant.

"Exactly so," the Ungulithi says. "You, being a minor, may go back to your home and The Haven. No harm done. Your father . . ."

". . . can speak for himself," Dad finishes, his voice sharp.

The silence that follows is longer than the previous ones. Xynlyc appears to acknowledge my dad's presence for the first time, glaring stoically at him. The spark of hope in my chest is smothered.

Shut up, I mentally plead to my dad. *Let's at least hear Xynlyc out. No need to make things worse.*

Finally, the Ungulithi speaks, still looking at Dad. "Your father, brainwashed by Morgan Sheffy, needs some gentle reeducation before we can release him."

"But you will let him go?" The hope comes rushing back in a heady wave.

"That is up to him. And you."

"Okay." I nod. "What do you want us to do?"

The Ungulithi draws itself up to its full height, folding its arms across its body, exoskeletal armor rubbing and clacking with its every move. The alien eyes us in arrogant silence.

This guy sure loves his dramatic pauses.

Behind me, the double doors once again swing open. Two more of The Named walk through the doorway, hauling someone between them. It's impossible to make out features in the dim lighting. But as they draw closer, I recognize who they're dragging.

"You both will broadcast to all Haven users at a time of our choosing," the Ungulithi lord says. "Confess to being led astray, child. Renounce Morgan Sheffy and his little band of rebels."

At that moment, The Named who are lugging Morgan Sheffy between them throw him to the ground beside my dad. Dad moves to help Morgan, but The Named grab him and keep him on his knees. Sheffy rises to a similar kneeling position, his face etched in pain.

Xynlyc continues as if nothing happened. "Urge all The New Sons of Liberty to turn themselves in. Mention your gentle treatment here in the capital. You might also bring up how fair and wise our judgment is, considering your circumstances. Do all this, and life will return to the way it was."

Sounds reasonable to me. Honestly, it's astounding how generous the conditions are. Could the alien be lying? The terms are just too good to be true. But what choice do I have?

As I open my mouth to accept, Dad interrupts me.

"And what if we don't?"

Seriously? Shut up! Stop trying to make this worse. We are this close to having our lives back and everything back to normal.

The Ungulithi turns its gaze again toward my dad. "Should you be so unwise as to pass up my generous offer, then you will meet the same destiny as Morgan Sheffy."

That can't be good.

"And what is that?" Dad asks, voice rasping, defiant.

"Public execution. For treason, terrorism, and murder."

Wow . . . that sucks.

Dad looks as if he is fighting to restrain his rage. Sheffy appears resigned to his fate, staring blankly ahead. Xynlyc watches me with an unreadable expression. In fact, its facial demeanor has not shifted throughout its entire discourse.

The choice still seems obvious to me. "We accept your terms."

Dad whips his head in my direction, staring at me in disbelief. Sheffy doesn't react.

What is with the expression Dad is giving me? What else did he expect me to do? All I'd done was follow his instructions and try to aid him. I hadn't wanted to be dragged into a rebellion. I couldn't help it if Marley had used me to get to the resistance. And Sheffy had known the risks when creating his rebel army. Wage war and you could be slain.

Xynlyc produces a noise that the device doesn't interpret. It's hard to tell if it's a good sound or a bad sound.

"You are wise beyond your years," Xynlyc says. "Consequently, you will find that following us has its advantages. You shall be informed when you are to make your Haven broadcast."

And with that, the alien turns and slinks back into the shadows.

Chapter Twenty-Six

Execution

Instead of returning to my test-tube holding cell, I'm taken—along with my dad and Morgan Sheffy—to a room on the upper levels of the city. The room has two full-size beds, a couch, a kitchenette, and a bathroom. A large one-panel window gives a stunning view of the urban area. It's a relief to see our regular clothes folded at the foot of the bed. I feel ridiculous in these robes.

I'd rather take this than a test tube. Easy.

Dad is less grateful. Upon entering the room, he confronts our Named escort.

"What is this?" he asks, his expression dark.

If his anger surprises The Named, they don't show it. "Your accommodations. As our lord says . . . there is a reward for compliance."

They leave, pushing Sheffy out with them. A solid metal door slides shut after their departure. There is no handle, doorknob, or control panel.

"So we're still prisoners," Dad says.

"Well," I say, opening the fridge. "At least this is more bearable."

He doesn't reply. Instead, he stands in the middle of the room, staring at me with a strange expression.

"What?" I ask, closing the refrigerator door.

"Why did you agree to condemn the resistance?"

The question surprises me. "Because we have no other choice."

"Don't we?"

Okay, now I'm confused. "Well, no. Not if we want to stay alive. Not if we wish to go home."

"And do what, Ava? Submit to having our humanity stripped from us again? Returning to having no control over the food we eat? Having no say in whether we can leave our own dome, the type of education you're receiving, or the career I can pursue? Just revert to being mindless drones, having a system that the Ungulithi constructed to make our decisions for us?"

What's so wrong with all that? We were doing fine. "It's not that bad. We'll be a family again."

My answer only seems to agitate him more. He paces the width of the room, frowning.

"I hoped you would understand," he says.

"I get it," I retort, my cheeks growing hot. "I understand I went through a bunch of crap to help you, to bring you back. And this is the thanks I get?"

Dad approaches me and kneels to eye level. "No," he says, placing his hands on my shoulders. "I am grateful. You exceeded all of my expectations. I am so proud of you, Ava."

Oh. His words cool my anger. "I want to go home. I want everything to go back to normal."

Dad looks deep into my eyes, smiling sadly. "I yearn for that as well. A part of me wants to put all this behind me. I miss my family and wish to be with them."

I nod, fighting to prevent my lower lip from trembling. A disturbed expression crosses his face and he rises, resuming his agitated pacing of the room.

"But this thing is bigger than us," he says. "They promised this all would be temporary. If we let the aliens, the politicians, and the experts fix everything, they would solve all our problems. And what has been the result? Have they kept any of their grand promises? And why do I seem to be the only one who cares about this?"

I clamp down on my frustration. This isn't the first time he's gone on a rant. "Why else are they here?" I ask. "The Ungulithi may be more restrictive than what we would like, but at the very least they brought stability, safety, and equity to the world. Something we never accomplished."

He looks at me in disbelief. "If you take away choice, force people to stay locked up, work jobs regardless of ability, redistribute their resources, and satiate the population on a diet of mild comfort and endless amusement, then any safety, equality, or stability is false. And what happens to the person filling their heart and mind with frivolous entertainment instead of purpose? One day, they realize they wasted time they can never get back, pretending to live an extraordinary life. Once they awaken to the fact that their best memories, emotions, and relationships were nothing more than a bunch of manipulated 1s and 0s, they will either self-destruct or lash out."

"So, you lashed out," I say.

He shakes his head. "I decided to expose the lies. I chose to be human again. Look around you, Ava. Are they trying to make the world a better place? All I see are creatures taking advantage of us, of our world, building enormous cities full of wasteful luxuries while preaching about the need to sacrifice until things improve. I observe their hypocritical human lackeys, aping their overlords' words and sentiments while living lavishly at the expense of their fellow humans who can't leave their homes, or choose what life they want to live, who will attain nothing without one of their "betters" choosing it for them."

His answer is frustrating. While I have no love for the Ungulithi, I don't hate them either. Their existence, their rule over the Earth, has been the norm all my life; it's all I've known. Dad had always grumbled about them, but I assumed it was the same way students complain about teachers at school. Yeah, they can be unfair and unhelpful, but I won't start a revolution against the school or anything.

"I don't see why sacrificing your life is necessary," I say.

Dad gives me another sad smile. "Maybe one day you'll understand."

"So you refuse to do as they ask?"

"Yes."

The finality of his answer stuns me. My eyes sting. I wheel past him, stopping in front of the lone window in the room. I survey the city. Under other circumstances, it would be a thrill to be here. I've seen nothing like this place in real life before. Experiencing something this new, this big in person—even now words cannot capture it.

Instead, I look over the city, seeing it, yet somehow not seeing it.

I will not cry. Not in front of him.

His hand rests on my shoulder.

"Ava," he says in a quiet voice. "I'm sorry. Didn't mean to preach at you. I know it's hard to understand right now, but I hope on some level you get it."

A tear leaks out of my eye. I dip my head, hoping he won't see. "Why can't you lie? Condemn Sheffy, The New Sons of Liberty, and when you're released . . . well, there are other ways of fighting for a cause that don't involve martyrdom."

Behind me, he stays silent for a long time, his breathing soft. *He must be considering his answer.* After a brief pause, he coughs. "It's crossed my mind. I don't want to die, Ava. I love you, your sisters, and your mom,"—his voice wavers and he clears his throat—"and the idea of not seeing you and your sisters grow up . . . of not growing old with the love of my life hurts so much, I can hardly bear it."

Dad sniffs. More tears well up in my eyes. "Then do what they want," I whisper, not trusting my voice to go any louder.

His grip tightens ever so slightly on my shoulder. "And damn the world to its fate? I'm trying to sow the seeds of a better world. A world where my children are free. Where my future grandchildren can choose who they are, and what they want to do with their lives."

He comes around and stands in front of me, looking me in the eye. "Unless I act, the others who think like me but have said nothing might remain silent. Unless I act, the Ungulithi will persist in exploiting the planet and humanity. Unchecked, they will continue to grow in their power. Do you suppose the way things are happened overnight? No, the slow erosion of our rights took decades. One or two at first. Curfews turned into lockdowns. Incentives to move into domes became mandates. Participation in The Haven started as a novelty to the cultural norm, shaped and manipulated by the Ungulithi. It won't stop. Tyrannies become more powerful through compliance and become more oppressive through silence."

He rubbed his eyes again and walked past me, saying, "And I can't be silent anymore."

Lying in bed, I clamp my eyes shut, as if that'll somehow force sleep to come. Another tear leaks from the corner of my eye, trickling down the side of my head and stopping when it hits my ear.

How could Dad be so stupid? Of course, I understood his views. He'd never been shy about his views, at least with me. But now he faces certain execution if he refuses to recant.

I keep rehashing his points. Sure, he sounds all noble and whatever, but they're going to kill him. If he speaks the words the Ungulithi want him to say, he doesn't have to mean it. Doesn't he understand we need him alive and back with us? Our family will never be fixed if he becomes a martyr.

I press my head deeper into the fluffy pillow. Even though drapes cover the window, glints of light from the city poke through the edges, flashing weird patterns on the wall and the ceiling.

It keeps eating at me. He is adamant he is right, and I am confident in *my position* as well. So what is it with this persistent doubt?

Whatever. I'll read whatever silly script they want me to, then choose what to do afterward. I only get one life, and I will not toss it away. But then what? Return home and take care of Mom and the girls? Become my sisters' caretaker? Advance my mage through the ranks until I become a full-blown Master of Magic?

"Well, why not?" I mumble to myself. In the next bed, Dad's deep breathing hitches. He snorts and rolls onto his side.

How can he sleep? If I were days from execution, I wouldn't be able to rest.

It's the sleep of someone with a guilt-free conscience.

I sigh. *C'mon . . . that can't be the reason I can't doze off. My conscience is clear too.*

I endeavor to think about something else. But try as I might, my mind keeps returning to my dad's decision.

Anger now mixes with fear. After everything I did for him, all the struggles I went through, and he's going to throw it away for some ideals? Meanwhile, I'll be sent back home empty-handed. Back to the mess our family has become.

At least I'll still have The Haven.

But what kind of life is that?

It's as if Dad is in my head. I hear his voice as clearly as if he's speaking aloud.

Is it truly living to spend your days hooked into a machine as hours of your life go by? To have your happiness, your coping mechanism, and your life manipulated by others? Dictated by others? Only to wake up one day and realize you sold your life for something that was never real? And understand too late that you squandered life because the real world was too tough for you to deal with, even though you could've taken action and done something about it?

It's creepy to realize I know my dad well enough to articulate the type of arguments he'd make if he wanted me to take a stand with him.

Why am I reflecting on this? I've already made my choice.

Right?

Only a select few have been executed during the Ungulithi's seven-plus decades of ruling Earth. This means Morgan Sheffy belongs to a small, exclusive group. Granted, not an enviable group of people. It also raises a morbid curiosity in me about *how* the Ungulithi plan to execute someone in The Haven.

When The Named arrive to escort us to a plug-in room the next morning, they inform us they expect my father and me to condemn the rebellion after the execution, and pledge a new life of peace and harmony with the Ungulithi.

"So soon, eh?" Dad asks.

One of The Named dips his head. "Our lords wish this matter to be resolved with the utmost expedience."

"Interesting," is all my dad says. My throat is too tight to add anything. I thought for sure we'd have a couple of days before fulfilling our end of the bargain.

"They're trying to unbalance us," Dad says, as they lead us out of the room. "By making everything happen so fast, they want to throw us off, and reduce the chance that we—well, you—change your mind."

They are succeeding. "I'm scared," I whisper.

He reaches out and grabs my hand. Yawning, I rub my bleary eyes with my free hand. Fear mixed with sleep deprivation makes for strange emotional and physical consequences.

The Named lead us to a room that once again seems out of place.

"Who designed this?" I ask, taking in the dim recessed lighting, lounge furniture, and mini-bar.

Dad huffs. "The Ungulithi took their favorite interior concepts and threw them all in one tower. Same philosophy they applied with all the random designs in The Haven."

"This way, please," The Named say, gesturing to the far wall. At first, I see nothing, but as my eyes adjust to the lighting, I spot four plug-in pods lined up against the wall.

As we approach the pods, I wheel closer to my dad. "They appear unarmed. We can try to make a break for it."

Dad gives me a startled look.

"Tempting as it is, I don't think it would work," Dad whispers. "And they *are* armed. Found out the hard way one time. They have some sort of surgically implanted weapon."

"Which also includes an enhanced hearing ability." The Named stop in front of the pods, turn and smile condescendingly. "Now please enter the pods."

As we get in the pods, The Named continue to speak, "The pods will recognize your DNA signature and project your avatar into The Haven. However, access to your inventory, abilities, and other Haven-specific privileges has been revoked. We advise you to not try to unplug before you are told. We also discourage you from attempting anything in The Haven as well."

I roll my eyes. *Without resources, we can do little. Unless something changes, we are going to play this out.*

It is night. A steady wind presses against me. No stars twinkle above. A blinding flash of light lances across the sky, illuminating thick, black clouds. Moments later thunder rumbles, vibrating my body.

Dad joins me. "I think we're on a skyscraper."

"So we left a real skyscraper to do this in a fake high-rise?" I ask. "Make it make sense."

Dad shrugs, observing the cloudy night sky. "Reality isn't as interesting, I guess."

The location and the atmosphere lend themselves to being more dramatic. I venture a few careful paces forward to get a better idea of our location.

"Careful," Dad warns. "I get the impression real-world consequences will affect us here."

Nodding, I walk a couple more strides and stop. How close I am to the edge?

A gust, more powerful than before, almost knocks me over. My eyes are now adjusted to the dark, and I spot the building's edge. No railing, no architectural safety features—only pure, flat, naked edge. If the wind had succeeded in knocking me off balance, I'd have pitched headlong off the building.

My throat tightens. I back up.

"That was too close," my dad says, voice unsteady.

"What is it with the Ungulithi and their stupid, tall buildings?" I gasp. I had noticed a dense fog covering the ground below in my brief glimpse over the edge. There were lights and vague shapes resembling city buildings. None of the other structures were even close to our height.

"Apologies for the delay. Let's make this a swift execution, shall we?"

Dad and I search for the owner of the chipper, British-accented voice. A thin man in a white suit strides forward, tucking a black rose into his lapel. A large raven perches on his shoulder, squawking at the man's every movement. A dark hood with a crudely spray-painted skull hides the man's face. Only his eyes are visible through the hood's two eyeholes.

"Ah, our overlords do enjoy a bit of drama, don't they?" The man's eyes twinkle like a child's on Christmas morning. "Well, we have so few executions, might as well make it spectacular, right?"

Beside me, Dad shifts his position, putting himself between me and the stranger. "Who are you?"

The man stops, lifting a hand over where his mouth should be. "Oh, yes, of course, how rude of me. I'm Mr. Graves, the Executioner."

He performs a sweeping bow. On his shoulder, the raven flaps its wings and makes its displeasure known.

"Oh, tut," Mr. Graves says, tapping his bird on the beak. "Beaky here's been terribly grouchy the past few days. I'm rather hoping the execution today will cheer him up."

"Beaky? Mr. Graves? Really?" I ask.

Mr. Grave stiffens. "My dear girl, I don't pretend this isn't a grim business, but that doesn't mean it's all electrocutions, decapitations, and asphyxiations. You need to have a laugh now and again."

"Whatever helps you sleep at night," Dad growls.

Mr. Graves waves Dad off. "I couldn't care less about what you think. From what I hear, you barely escaped execution as it is. Anyway, this is a part-time gig. I do this on the side for extra income."

"Stay away from me and my daughter," Dad says.

"Not up to me. I have my orders." Mr. Graves shrugs. The bird caws its agreement.

One minute it's the three of us—four if you count the raven—then the next thing I know, three more people are on the roof. One is Morgan Sheffy's avatar. The two other avatars have a strange look to them. They appear . . . bland. Two men with gel-styled hair, expensive business suits, and faces as blank as a sheet of paper. It has to be their eyes; listless expressions that don't seem to care about much of anything.

"Get the link setup," one says. The other nods, then freezes in place, no doubt accessing menu options.

Mr. Graves takes a knee in front of them, head bowed. His raven protests loudly, lifting off his shoulder and circling overhead.

"My lords," Mr. Graves says. "What's it to be this evening?"

Dad leans over to me. "Those must be two Ungulithi."

The Ungulithi avatar Mr. Graves addresses looks thoughtfully at the executioner. "Might as well take advantage of our location and the atmosphere tonight, Mr. Graves. Let's do the chair."

"Right-ho!" Mr. Graves answers and fist pumps.

Sicko.

Another flash of lightning streaks across the sky, and the following peal of thunder shakes the building. A few stray drops of rain pelt my face.

"Oh, c'mon," I moan.

The one Ungulithi unfreezes and looks at its colleague. "Everything is ready. We're live." Three orb-like machines float around its head for a minute before flying off in different directions.

Light illuminates the rooftop. Two giant, screen-like projections show up above us as glowing rectangles against the overcast sky. One "screen" shows all of our avatars, cutting to other angles. The other display shows Sheffy in his plug-in pod.

I frown. *Why are they filming him in his pod?*

Mr. Graves strides away from the group, dragging a chair that had materialized. He stops short of the building's edge, standing behind the chair. That's when I noticed the metal rod attached to the backrest. The rod isn't very thick and is only a bit taller than Mr. Graves.

"Morgan Sheffy," the executioner calls out, gesturing to the seat. "Won't you please come sit?"

Sheffy's avatar looks hesitantly between the Ungulithi avatars and the chair. The aliens shove him toward the executioner, causing him to stumble. Dad leaps forward and catches him before he can fall.

"It's alright," Sheffy says in a quiet tone. "I'm fine."

"Sir." My dad's face is a picture of raging emotions. "I'm sorry. I should've . . ."

"No." Sheffy cuts him off. "It's okay. We all make our own choices. I'm ready to deal with the consequences of mine."

He pats my dad on the shoulder, straightens, and strides to the chair, sitting in it without hesitation.

Fat raindrops bombard us at a steady rate now, as Mr. Graves locks Morgan's wrists and ankles to the chair.

I tear my eyes away from the image of Sheffy, serenely sitting clamped to his chair, to glance back up at the screens. There is a running counter next to the screen of our avatars. The number ticks higher and higher. *Already over a hundred thousand people watching.* How is everyone getting on so fast? Had they advertised this event? Are they making this mandatory somehow?

"Hello, all. Thank you for joining us this evening," an Ungulithi avatar says, stepping closer to a floating camera.

"We have achieved something historic. A thing once thought impossible."

The other Ungulithi avatar steps forward. "Interspecies partnership has never been stronger. In our home world, many questioned if we could accomplish this. You have proven the skeptics wrong."

"For a group to achieve anything, sacrifice and compromise are key. Most of you have been reasonable, and we have done what we can to protect and provide for you. Sadly, there are still some who are resentful, even violent. The change was too great for them."

The image on the sky screens cuts to Sheffy, sitting in his chair, drenched, and, for a wonder, looking unbothered. Behind him, lightning flashes.

"The man on your screen is Morgan Sheffy," the Ungulithi continues. "He is a terrorist, one of those fearful of change. While we were educating and transitioning people into a new way of life, Morgan Sheffy has been equally busy, sowing seeds of mistrust, fear, and misinformation. He spied on us, stole from us, hacked us, disrupted supply lines, and, in some cases, blew up installations vital to this transitioning world."

The other Ungulithi speaks up. "We recently ran a successful operation against Mr. Sheffy, decimating his organization, and taking him into custody. He is to be put to death tonight for his crimes, and his execution live-streamed."

"Six years have passed since the last execution and over twenty years since the last public execution. We chose public execution to hold Mr. Sheffy as an example of what we will do to those who threaten the peace we've established. You've given up too much and achieved too much to let those who dread transformation hinder you on your new path to a superior world."

The wind is picking up. By now we are all soaked. Lightning is flashing at regular intervals, but the thunder that follows sounds as if it's getting further away.

The Ungulithi gesture to the executioner. "Mr. Graves, please proceed."

Mr. Graves nods and looks at Sheffy, a roll of parchment appearing in his hand. He unfurls it and reads aloud, "Morgan Sheffy, you have been accused of terrorism and destruction of property, causing harm, murder, and treason. You have been found guilty on all counts."

"I don't remember a trial," Dad says under his breath.

"For your punishment, you are to be put to death." Mr. Graves rolls his parchment back up. "Does the prisoner have any last words or requests?"

While Mr. Graves was reading the scroll, Sheffy had been staring past him, eyes unfocused. Now he glances at his executioner, a thoughtful expression on his face.

"Yes," he says, after a pause. "I wish to say this: whatever I did . . . I did it to free humanity. Without the ability to choose, whether it be where you live, your lifestyle, where you work, or what God you worship—with no way to choose any of that — is not to truly be alive."

Now he's looking right at me. "So I say to you: give me liberty or give me death!"

Lighting flashes. Mr. Graves' raven circles above, cawing. The wind whips at the executioner's mask, causing it to ripple like small black waves.

Mr. Graves shakes his head, lifts his arms high, and begins an incantation. The gusts of air grow in intensity. The lightning bolts tearing through the sky grow larger and larger.

Trying to put my knowledge of magic to good use, I strain to catch the sounds the executioner is making. Wind, rain, and thunder all muffle his words. I gnash my teeth in frustration.

Everything happens all at once.

One second Sheffy is sitting, staring at me. The next second, a bolt of lightning leaps from the clouds and into the rod sticking out of Sheffy's chair. The condemned rebel leader snaps upright, stiff as a board, muscles in his face flexing.

My mouth drops in horror. Mr. Graves was using a simple lightning strike curse to execute the rebel leader.

Lightning continues to surge into the pole. It's almost too bright to see what's happening. Movement from above draws my gaze. Both images on the floating screens show Sheffy in real life, in his plug-in pod. His body is convulsing, foam bubbling up from between his lips.

With a flash, the lightning vanishes. Sheffy's body relaxes and he slumps forward in the chair. In his pod, he also goes limp, covered in a sheen of sweat. An image of his vital measurements appears on the screens. All signs of life go flat.

Morgan Sheffy is dead.

Dad steps forward, arm outstretched as if to shake his leader awake. Despite the rain, tendrils of smoke curl up from the body. What little skin I can see of the remains looks crinkled and burnt.

Terror and disbelief anchor me to the spot. This is my first time encountering actual death, much less such a violent death.

"Someone order extra crispy?"

Through the ruckus of the storm, the executioner makes a grim joke as he saunters toward the body. He makes a show of inspecting it, like a hunter looking over his kill. He glances back at Dad and me, grins, and kicks the chair and Sheffy over the edge.

Dad hunches and appears as if now he might fall. I grab him before he can sink any further. Even in gaming physics, he's heavy. I strain against the sudden load, my legs trembling. We're both about to hit the deck.

The weight disappears. One of the Ungulithi pulls Dad off me, supporting him and keeping him upright. I go to check on my dad when a hand grips my shoulder. It's the other Ungulithi, looking at me with an unreadable expression. When he speaks, a chill runs down my spine that has nothing to do with the icy rain pelting my drenched body.

"Your turn."

Chapter
Twenty-Seven

Choices

Dawn arrives.

It's amazing how fast and how dramatic virtual weather changes can be. One minute it's dark, and the rain is drenching me. Then the sun rises; clouds are parting, birds are chirping, and I'm miraculously dry.

The Ungulithi do indeed enjoy playing God.

A platform with multiple microphones appears. As I am taken to the stage, the Ungulithi who had pulled me from Dad whispers in my ear.

"Start by speaking about the execution."

"What am I supposed to say?" The image of Sheffy's twitching body is seared in my brain.

"Proclaim his passing is a wake-up call. That you regret being suckered in by him, and you renounce him and his terrorism."

The Ungulithi pushes me in front of the microphones, staying out of their range. "Remember, make it clear you've changed. I have not compelled you to change. We've treated you well. You've changed because of your leader's execution, you've seen the error of your ways, and you just want to go home and be left alone."

He motions for me to turn around. "The commentators are wrapping up their discussion of the execution," he says. "Be ready."

"What about my dad?" I hiss. He's out of frame for the cameras.

"You worry about you," the Ungulithi says. "What you say will shape your future."

His words seem to loop in my head as he steps further back. *Your words will shape your future.*

And then I'm live.

All three cameras glare blankly at me. Mouth agape, I stare at the sky screens, looking at my avatar as if I've never seen an image of myself before. Behind me, the horizon glows with a majestic golden light.

Get a hold of yourself! You've got a speech to give.

"Uh, hello." My voice quakes. I clear my throat, not sure which camera to look into. "Hi, I'm Ava McNealy. I have a few words to say."

Why am I already breathless?

"Um, Morgan Sheffy's death is . . . regrettable." Those words don't sound like me. Maybe a politician or something. But not me. "I didn't know him that well."

Renounce him and his terrorism.

"I . . . I'm sorry for my association with him." Out of the corner of my eye, I search for any sign that Dad is hearing what I'm saying. So far, he hasn't reacted, eyes downcast.

"Being part of the execution just now—it's made me stop and think. It's made me reevaluate."

Your words will shape your future.

My dad's words *echo in my head: expose the lies. Be human again.*

This isn't difficult, a desperate voice screams inside my mind. *Say what they want to hear. Live to fight another day!*

I can't be silent anymore, my dad said.

What about me, though?

I'm not sure how long I've been standing in silence, staring into the distance. Time to make my choice.

"Yeah, I've had to reevaluate my life. What is my purpose? Why am I alive at this moment? Not gonna lie. I want to go home and be left alone. But I can't. I can't live a lie anymore."

The Ungulithi shift, giving each other looks. My dad lifts his head. Unable to see his expression, I still have the impression he's intently listening.

My skull suddenly feels too heavy. A strange sensation washes over me. It's like I've become an observer outside my avatar's POV, and everything is happening to someone else instead of me.

"The Ungulithi have no right to act as judge, jury, and executioner. They have no right to strip the very thing that makes us human: our free will. Our rights don't come from them." Deep breath. *Steady. No falling over.* Out of the corner of my eye, there is frantic movement where the Ungulithi avatars stand. "Everyone is entitled to life, liberty, and the pursuit of happiness."

That last line was from Dad. Something to do with founding documents. For some reason, it was one of the few things from one of his rants that had stuck out.

I can sense my dad almost beaming. *Of course, I listen when you talk about these things. Not all of it goes in one ear and out the other.*

"We are being manipulated like puppets on a string. In exchange for what? Shelter? Basic provisions? What does the Ungulithi get with our cooperation, as they call it? Does anyone know? I don't, but I know they live different lives than the rest of us. They don't choose to live like us. They . . ."

Before I can finish, my image on the sky screen disappears, replaced by a blond woman in a studio set.

"I'm sorry, folks," she says, pressing a finger to her ear as if listening to someone in her hidden earpiece. "But it seems we are experiencing technical difficulties. In the meantime, shall we discuss the latest exciting updates to The Haven?"

That's it? I wasn't able to say my piece. Have I just stuck my neck in the noose for nothing?

A looming presence cuts my thoughts short. The Ungulithi avatar stands behind me, looking down with a severe expression.

"Bad choice," he says.

"Well," I answer, doing my best to match his gaze, fighting the quaver in my voice. "At least I made one."

"It will not change anything." He sneers.

"People deserve to choose for themselves what lives they want to live. Sometimes they need to be reminded," I say, looking at my dad. His face is a curious mix of pride and terror. His reaction puzzles me. Didn't he want me to agree with him, to believe as he does? Why does he look so scared?

The Ungulithi leans close to me. "Could be you're right; maybe they do."

Well, that's an unexpected response.

He continues. "The only problem is humanity surrendered their choice as soon as we arrived on your pebble of a world. All it took was our existence and our technology, and your pathetic leaders sold you out. Easiest conquest in the galaxy to date. And to think the others were afraid to colonize you."

Others? Afraid?

"I'm almost tempted to let you finish your little speech," he scoffs. "There won't be a revolution. No uprising."

He leans even closer, our faces close to touching. "Which means you're going to die for nothing."

Chapter Twenty-Eight

A Second Chance

No more cushy hotel rooms, I glumly note, back in my test-tube cell. *Not for someone sentenced to execution.*

I try to force that last detail from my mind, but it doesn't go away.

You're going to die for nothing. You're going to die for nothing. You're going to die for nothing. You're going to DIE.

Unable to leave our dome, death is something almost never encountered in my community. The primary way we knew someone died was when their avatar stopped showing up in The Haven, and their Haven ID went inactive. While there are virtual funerals and memorials, we never hold these in real life. The city always disposed of the bodies. For a price, family members could purchase a small plot of digital land in The Haven's graveyard. There they can safeguard, inter, or bury their loved one's avatar, and decorate the plot how they want, a reminder of them in the online space.

On the bed, back pressed against the glass, I attempt to restrain my thoughts from running wild. Soon, I'll be facing death. It's a miracle that I'm not a quivering puddle on the floor.

Of course, I knew someday death would be a reality. But at sixteen years old, it isn't something I ponder much. My whole life is ahead of me. There's high school to finish, college to figure out, get assigned a career—or fight for one of my choosing, should humanity strive to write its own destiny again.

Also, I need to figure out things with Lucas.

Shifting my weight on the thin mattress, tears well up. *I wonder how he's doing? Did he see me in the stream? Is he freaking out?*

I lash out, slamming my fist against the glass of my cell. A muted thump follows and I clutch my throbbing hand to my chest.

I can't die! It's too soon. There's so much more to do, so much more to figure out! Death was always going to happen in some undefined future. It wasn't something to worry about. I'd deal with it later.

Except it's here now. The choice was made. It was the right one. So why am I trembling, sitting on this bed in my test-tube prison, being pummeled by doubts?

No. It's okay. Breathe, just breathe. Think about something else. Take your mind off yourself.

I think about Dad and the range of emotions that played across his face before they separated us again.

"Honey," he said, once they unplugged us from The Haven. "Now, I'm happy that you understand why I'm doing what I'm doing. And I couldn't help but be proud of you for standing up to the Ungulithi. But you were supposed to tell them what they wanted to hear."

Still quivering from the prior surge of adrenaline, I replied: "Well, it's like you said: it was time I took a stand. And maybe seeing me on streaming, defying the Ungulithi, will spark something—who knows?"

The look of pride and love my dad gave me was enough to help quell the worst of my shaking. I hold that image in my head, hoping it calms some of my tension. Every muscle feels as if it's been trembling or stretched to a snapping point. I yawn. *How is it possible for me to be this tense and this exhausted?* Yet, tired as I am, my brain keeps conjuring more musings.

What will happen when I die? Does the spirit depart the body right away, or does it hang around? Is there a period of blankness? How does it feel? Does it hurt? What could be my last thoughts? How does a soul part from the body? What might the afterlife entail?

Sleep steals over me. I let myself slip into the darkness, grateful for the opportunity to just breathe, to think and feel nothing.

I'm not sure how many hours or days elapse before the Ungulithi summon me once more. The summons surprises me. I figured their next communication would be to announce my execution date.

I perform the ritualistic cleanse once more. Odd how these slimy aliens have some OCD about germs. Or maybe they don't like how humans smell? And what's with all The Named having zero hair on their body?

As The Named usher me into the giant hall, there's a large table near the door that wasn't there last time. The table is laden with food. My stomach rumbles.

"Go sit," one of The Named says. With that, they leave the room. *Is it just me, or are those people getting snobbier?*

I approach the table with some trepidation. While not expecting a trap, I also don't expect the Ungulithi to lay this feast before me out of the goodness of their hearts.

Upon closer inspection, everything laid out on the table is my favorite foods. Well, my favorite foods "consumed" in The Haven. Everything from popcorn shrimp, sauteed duck, sweet potato casserole, toasted bell peppers, asparagus, and creamy mashed potatoes to cakes, pies, puddings, and ice cream. There is no rhyme or reason to the food's layout or pairings. If the Ungulithi figured this would tempt me, they are mistaken; an alarm rings out like church bells in my head.

"Please, eat." a familiar, disembodied voice says.

The sudden loud voice causes me to jump. Stupid Xynlyc startled me again.

"I'm not hungry," I say, folding my arms.

"Then they feed the prisoners too well." The alien emerges from the shadows across from me. "I shall notify the jailor to cut the rations given to inmates."

Xynlyc plays dirty.

"No, wait," I say, holding up my hands. "I'll eat."

I roll up to the table and plate some food. Best as I can tell, the Ungulithi lord seems pleased with my actions.

Has Xynlyc been lurking in the shadows since I was last here?

The alien moves to stand . . . sit . . . or squat . . . whatever, across from me.

"Please help yourself." Xynlyc gestures at the food. "I regret I could not attain a taste for your human cuisine, so I shall not be joining you."

Hesitantly, I pick at my plate. Under normal circumstances, with a feast like this before me, I'd happily tuck in. However, it's hard to work up an appetite while anticipating your imminent demise. Or under the scrutiny of an overgrown, murderous slug.

"I suppose you are aware of why I called you here," the Ungulithi says.

"Not really," I say, blowing on a hunk of steaming chicken pot pie perched on the edge of my fork.

No discernible emotion registers on the alien's face nor its vocal translator/amplifier device. "I am feeling generous and wish to grant you the opportunity to change your mind."

Well, that's interesting.

"Gee, thanks," I say through a mouthful of pie. I drink a gulp of Sweet Bubble Pop before continuing. "My reply is still the same. I don't care how good your food is."

What makes it worse is the food is indeed amazing. Even better than the meal I'd had in Marley's pod.

Xynlyc's head dips a little. "I figured that might be your answer. So I'm prepared to sweeten the deal, as the human expression goes."

Oddly, the beast seems eager to change my mind. At least as far as I can tell—alien body language is hard to read. But what does the slug have to gain through my compliance? Should I even listen to any offer? Admittedly, the chance of not being executed is attractive.

Let's see what Xynlyc is up to. "Nothing you say will change my—"

He cuts me off. "If you recant to the world, your father lives."

The next bite of food halts midway to my mouth. "What?"

The Ungulithi repeats itself.

"Regardless of if he denounces the rebels or not?" I ask.

"Indeed."

What's he playing at? Is it even an actual offer? Or is it a trick? "And if I refuse?"

The alien spreads its hands. "Then all this lovely food goes to waste, and the executions proceed."

So the choice to save my life and my dad's rests with me?

Fantastic if it's real.

Time to be blunt. "Why? You have no problem executing your opponents. Why this sudden show of mercy?"

"If we were as ruthless as you suggest," Xynlyc says, "then there would be a lot more dead humans. I have no desire to commit any more violence than is necessary upon your race."

"Your benevolence is astounding," I say in a sarcastic tone.

Xynlyc's expression remains unchanged. "Your words are not sincere, yet I hope you grasp how gracious I'm being to you. And how generous we've been to your species."

I bristle. "Yeah, as far as totalitarian dictators go, you're not as bad as some that humanity's had to deal with. Doesn't change what you are."

The Ungulithi rumbles. It's hard to tell if it's an angry rumble, a reflective one, or even a ravenous one. "Typical human. We give you food, shelter, an advanced global interactive interface, world peace, a healing climate, and purpose for your short, insignificant lives, and you *still* find something to whine about. Don't you see people like you and your father are outliers? Disturbed individuals longing for 'the good ol' days' that never existed? That's why we had to execute Morgan Sheffy; prune the rotten branch so the entire tree doesn't die."

"My dad isn't 'disturbed.'" I throw my spoon back into the pudding bowl I'd grabbed while the alien was talking. Only a couple of bites in, and now my appetite is gone.

"Isn't he?" the Ungulithi asks. "Has he ever given you details of his activities while operating for the rebels?"

"No."

"Has he ever spoken of the ones he has slain? My fellow Ungulithi murdered because your father doesn't like our global tracking and facial recognition technology? Why? What's he hiding? Why despise having his meals delivered? Or having a steady job that helps create a new and better world?"

"Yeah, he has a problem with that, especially when those same mandates and rules don't apply to you and your fellow overlords. Stuff like that shows me your true intentions. And for all your talk of being more advanced or whatever, your motivations are as human and primal as it gets: power and greed."

The Ungulithi appears to stiffen. That can't be good.

"Your ignorant disrespect, I can take. But you do not know our purpose here, or what we are trying to accomplish. It would be wise if you held your tongue."

"Then tell me," I say defiantly. "Fix my ignorance. What are you doing here?"

Xynlyc's head tilts. Is the creature studying me?

"Is it our resources?" I ask, hoping to goad a response. "Our minerals? Our water?"

Xynlyc's response is dismissive. "Earth has nothing we desire. Only your position in what you call The Milky Way is of interest."

I'm not sure what answer I was expecting, but not that. "Is this some kind of land grab? Trying to make some big alien bucks because Earth has a sweet location or something?"

"It isn't about money. At least not in the way you're thinking."

The alien's tight-lipped responses are getting frustrating. "Then what is this about?"

"Why would I tell you of all people? You are nothing but a tiny cog in a vast machine." He leans forward, eyes gleaming. "The universe is so much larger than your pathetic mind can grasp." He settles back, his gaze roaming over the table. "And yet smaller than you think."

"Cryptic," I say, unimpressed. "Nice touch. You almost sounded profound while saying nothing useful. No wonder you got the politicians in your pocket."

I'm not sure where my boldness is coming from, but have I now gone too far? A strange movement ripples across Xynlyc's face. Something about the alien changes. The dark shadows that cling to the alien's form appear to deepen.

"You tread on thin ice, girl." The translator almost seems to hiss the words.

"Were you one of the avatars on the rooftop?" I ask, hoping the sudden change of subject throws the alien off.

Xynlyc doesn't respond. The silence must mean it worked. I repeat the question, trying to keep the alien off balance and talking.

"Perhaps," it says. "I don't see the relevance."

"You were keen to stream that execution and all its morbid detail."

"I felt it was tastefully done," the Ungulithi retorts.

"How come you weren't as eager to broadcast his trial?" I ask. "Was it because it was too quick? He only got executed a few hours after his capture."

"Trial?" Xynlyc responds. "There was no trial."

The admission stuns me. "What?"

Xynlyc's mouth twitches. A smile? "There was no need."

Scratching my head, I try to process what Xynlyc is saying. "So why give my dad this big, long trial? If you're cool with just executing people whenever you want . . . I don't get it."

"Your father took part in a public persona. The Ryker character. Intel confirmed he had ties to a prominent group of rebels. Unlike Morgan Sheffy, it would've been a waste to execute him too soon. With the rebel leader's execution, we've cut off the head of our biggest opponent. The body will soon wither and die."

It's my turn to sit in silence. Xynlyc's gaze never leaves mine. The creature is measuring my every response, every emotion, with a detached curiosity.

I feel more vindicated than ever of the choice I made. Granted, I'm not familiar with laws or trials—I almost never play games with a litigious slant—but I understand enough to recognize how perilous it is to live under rulers who can randomly accuse you of a crime and punish you according to their fancy, without needing to supply evidence. It's terrifying to realize how many people are unaware of or comfortable with this situation.

"Where's my dad?" I ask, a lump coming up my throat.

"You can see your father when you've given me your decision."

"You can't expect me to make such a big choice in a matter of minutes, can you?"

"Oh, but I do, Ava. We have pulled the data from your Haven logs and archives. You're a resourceful girl, making huge decisions in seconds every day. We are aware of what you can do."

A dull sensation throbs in the back of my skull. I loll my head from side to side, trying to relieve my tight muscles. I can't decide without all the facts. The alien isn't telling me everything.

Time to use the blunt strategy again. "Okay, but I'm just a kid—a nobody. There must be something you want; otherwise, you wouldn't be pushing me so hard. You want me to recite a script."

The oversized slug of an alien remains still. It's so difficult to get a read on the thing. But the wheels in my head are turning.

"Everyone is chattering about the execution, aren't they?" I say, excitement building, eyes darting over the table as if watching invisible puzzle pieces fall into place. "First execution in years, of course. They're talking—that's what you wanted. What you didn't count on was me. You didn't think I'd say anything other than what you wanted me to say. People saw the feed get cut. They're asking questions. Causing enough online noise that even you and your lackeys can't ignore."

I pound the table in triumph with my index finger before continuing. "That's why you're trying again to convince me to renounce the rebels. People believe I've been executed, or I'm about to be. And while human-ity may be indifferent enough to the execution of a middle-aged man, they still have enough of a conscience to object to the killing of a teenage girl. You overreached. Your grip on power isn't as sure as you thought. And you need me to make it all go away."

My last words echo in the giant room, somehow sounding even more smug, bouncing and fading off the walls. The Ungulithi leans forward, its upper body almost touching the table.

"You believe we need you? That I need you? You were right about one thing: you are a nobody. You sit there and spit on my kindness, on my mercy. Like you deserve anything other than to grovel on the ground before me, you little worm! I am your overlord. I have conquered your species. I need no one."

The Ungulithi trembles as it speaks, its voice low, seething. The trans-lated words are as flat and emotionless as ever, yet it's plain the alien is furious. I quirk a smile and lean forward as well.

"My answer, you overgrown slug. Kiss my ass."

Not an original burn, but serviceable.

Through heavy breaths, the Ungulithi replies, "You have sealed your fate."

Chapter Twenty-Nine

The Kraken

Upon being deposited back into my cell, I calm down enough for more rational thinking to return to me. Did I make the right choice? I'm now one hundred percent on board with "the cause" and everything. But I'd gambled on the Ungulithi being in an awkward political and social situation—wanting to execute a minor—and if I called their bluff, they wouldn't be able to carry it out. Based on that slug's reaction, it seemed my words had hit a nerve.

Hours tick by. The rumbling in my stomach grows louder. No one has brought me food or water. I hadn't eaten much earlier. A shame because the food had tasted good.

I try to plot the Ungulithi's upcoming move to distract myself from the gnawing in my stomach. The problem is, I'm not great at predicting what other people will do. Whenever I watch murder mysteries, I'm almost always shocked when they reveal the murderer. I'd gotten lucky earlier, guessing why the Ungulithi were making me a second offer.

The Ungulithi said I'm going to die. But if there's a public outcry, how will they get away with that? Will they keep me here until the public's attention span turns to something else? Perhaps execute me in secret?

I yawn and stretch. Judging by how sleepy I am, it's around my bedtime. Most of my fellow test-tube prison occupants are lying down, seeming to confirm the time. I lay down and cover myself with my bed's thin sheet.

———

"Wake up!"

My eyelids flutter open. A hazy silhouette stands in the doorway of my cell.

The figure motions to me. "You are to come with me. Now."

I recognize the voice. It belongs to one of The Named who has fetched me before. Hairless as the others, his stoic expression and glazed green eyes hint at nothing, leaving me unable to guess where I'm going or why. Even his tone of voice sounds flat and emotionless.

"Okay, just a sec," I say.

The man half turns, and gazes off into the distance, waiting for me. I almost say something snarky about helping me into my wheelchair but decide against it.

He wheels me out of the test-tube room and down a series of corridors until we reach a dimly lit dead end. A metal door slides open and he pushes me inside. Alarm bells go off in my head as a strange sense of déjà vu creeps over me.

It's a cramped space with a single plug-in unit. It smells like a hospital—cleaning agents and filtered air.

"What is this place?" I ask, trying to suppress rising dread.

The Named doesn't respond. He parks me beside the pod and nods. "Get in."

All my senses are telling me not to obey. "Why?"

His expression reveals nothing. "Get in."

With no other option available, I hoist myself into the pod. The Named watches, unmoving.

But as I settle in, he fastens steel clamps over my limbs, torso, and head. A fist clenches in my chest as I finally recognize this place.

"No," I whisper. "No! No!"

My cries grow louder and I struggle against my bonds. The metal doesn't budge.

"You made your choice," The Named says in disgust as he finishes with the clamps. "As did Morgan Sheffy. Henceforth, you shall share his fate."

He activates the steel snakes. My breath comes in short, quick gasps as they weave toward my head. The moment is here. I'm not ready.

"Let justice be served," The Named says, backing away. Something in me snaps. I hurl every obscenity I can think of at him, screaming, letting it all out. He doesn't answer, but he seems smugly satisfied as he watches.

The steel snakes are poised and in position when there is another metal hiss. I search for the source of the noise and spot an extra metal tentacle that I've never seen used on a pod before. It is black as midnight and positions itself six inches above my head, pointed right between my eyes.

Is that the one that'll fry my brain? I growl, struggling against my bonds to get at it, to rip it out of the pod and destroy it. Of course, such thoughts are delusional. I have to play out this scenario until the Ungulithi decide to end it.

My body trembles. Exhaustion, fear, and frustration have taken a toll on me.

A mechanical click. Then all goes dark.

———

Sweltering heat welcomes me. The ground is hot and sandy. I'm on a small island surrounded by a calm sea. The area isn't much bigger than a few hundred square feet. A few bushes and palm trees are scattered across the land, but the ocean view is unobstructed.

Gulls cry out overhead. Small waves lazily climb up the beach. Seems like an idyllic vacation spot. Cruel irony.

Someone spawns in beside me.

"Dad!"

We run into each other's arms. Once I assure him I'm alright, he steps back to survey our environment.

"I guess there's no chance they'll try to kill us with a good time?" he asks.

Yeah, doubtful. While I appreciate the attempt to lighten the mood, nothing seems amusing right now.

He notices. "You sure you're doing okay?"

"I'm scared." I try to swallow through a sudden dryness in my throat.

He leans closer, placing a reassuring hand on my arm. "Whatever happens . . . I love you and am proud of you. I will do everything within my means to keep you safe."

I strive to smile, remembering the black tentacle hovering over me in the pod. It doesn't matter if he tries to protect me or not, not while plugged in.

Two giant images are projected against what few clouds are overhead. Like before, one shows me and my dad on the island, while the other is a split-screen view of our bodies out there in the real world, in our pods.

The shot of our avatars is coming from somewhere overhead, zoomed in close. However, no floating cameras are in sight. They must be higher than last time. Odd. During Sheffy's execution, they were all in and around us.

Dad surveys the area, hands on his hips. "Is our old buddy the executioner with the stupid name not officiating this one?"

"They've changed the format. But why? I thought they were all about drama and spectacle in these things."

"Don't be too quick to judge," Dad says. "We haven't seen everything yet."

The images of us on the beach fade, replaced by our Haven photo IDs.

"Is that supposed to be me?" I ask, squinting up at my picture. "I seem different."

"They've aged you up," Dad answers. "They're trying to make you look older than you are."

A voice cuts in, announcing. "Ava and Robert McNealy are charged with multiple counts of treason, terror, and homicide. Despite these heinous crimes of which they stand accused, the Ungulithi will be merciful."

The screens cut to my and Dad's avatars in what must be a virtual courtroom. That doesn't make any sense. I haven't been in a court of law, have I? Seems like that'd be something that would stick out in my memory. Dad seems just as perplexed.

The images show the Ungulithi avatars addressing us, saying, "Considering your age, and nonexistent criminal history up to this point, we will offer you a plea bargain."

My avatar in the courtroom slams the desk she's sitting behind and rises to her feet, interrupting the proceedings.

"No!" she shouts. "You have no authority. You have no right to sentence me. This trial is illegal."

Dad and I glance at each other, mouths agape.

"They staged a phony trial," Dad whispers.

Meanwhile, his fake avatar in the courtroom stands alongside mine in a show of support. The image cuts back to the Ungulithi avatars wearing an expression of long suffering.

"We have already been over this. You know we've partnered with the UN to help and oversee—"

"We demand trial by combat!" Dad's fake avatar shouts. Everyone in the room dutifully gasps.

It's so brazen, stupid, over-the-top, unfair, and unjust. There's only one way to react: I burst into hysterical laughter. My cackling is so violent I collapse, gasping for air, clawing at the sand. I sense Dad's concerned stare at my prone form, but right now I can't help it and howl away.

The fake recordings of our supposed trial continue. "We don't do that," says a weary looking Ungulithi avatar. "Like I've been trying to say: We shall be merciful if you agree to a plea bargain."

My fake avatar comes from around the table and steps closer to the Ungulithi avatars, glaring.

"You are tyrants. Any authority you have is derived by the threat of force, not by the consent of the governed. Any sentence you impose will therefore be unjust and illegitimate. In The Haven, I am a Mage and a Warrior. I have a better chance of justice there than here. We demand trial by combat!"

I wipe the tears from my eyes. Unfortunately, I don't feel better after all that laughter, but it's hard to be scared after nearly busting a gut laughing. Dad reaches down and helps me to my feet. He looks at me, no doubt worried I'd lost it. I do my best to smile, trying to reassure him.

Global News Center anchor Terra Novak's face fills the screen. "Though the Ungulithi were under no compulsion to give in to these terrorists' demands, they reluctantly agreed to a trial by combat, further showing their willingness to work with people . . ."

My head is going to explode if I hear one more lie. "I really hate that bitch," I mutter. Dad gives me a startled glance.

Shutting my eyes, I gulp, attempting to disregard the rest of Terra's lying monologue. Dad is probably still looking at me. Opening my eyes, I see he's now wearing a neutral expression. It's taking an effort for him to remain calm. He's fighting not to appear as scared as I feel. Could it be my turn to reassure him?

But I'm at a loss for words. Especially since my gut is roiling with so many sensations, the threat of throwing up is ever at hand. How am I supposed to comfort him when I'm barely holding it together?

"It's okay," I say at last. "This is my decision . . . and isn't that what we're striving for? A choice in how we live our lives?"

Dad looks down at his feet. A range of emotions flits across his face. Are those tears I see welling up?

All he can manage is to compress his lips together and nod.

"Release the Kraken!" a deep voice roars.

Xynlyc. I wonder if he's overseeing this "trial" to make sure we "lose"?

Then it hits me. "Wait," I say, pausing a beat. "That thing did not just say . . ."

The gentle breeze dies. Everything on the tiny island goes still. Even the lapping of the water ceases.

"Oh, that can't be good," Dad mutters.

I scan the sea, searching for the first ripple to hint at our approaching danger. In the stillness, a faint sound reaches my ears. A distant roaring, yet it wasn't coming from a creature's throat. Something disturbs the surface of the ocean, way off in the distance. And it's racing toward us.

Dad realizes what it is before I do. "Brace yourself!"

He grabs my shoulder as a powerful gust of wind slams into us, almost knocking me off my feet. The roar from earlier fills my ears, overpowering all other sounds. The stench of rotting fish invades my nostrils, oppressive and putrid. That doesn't help my stomach issues. I sink to my knees, dry heaving.

"Ava . . ."

Catching my breath, I gaze at where Dad is pointing. Some distance away, dark storm clouds have gathered out of nowhere. Lightning flashes, though no rain is falling. The sea waters have grown more choppy, with bigger and bigger waves forcing us to back up further inland.

"Have you ever fought a Kraken before?" Dad asks.

Under any other circumstances, that question would be hilarious.

"Yes," I reply. "In Olympus has Fallen."

"Okay, so what do we do?"

"Well, use lots of environmental spells and weapons. Both of which we don't have access to here."

Dad curses under his breath. "So we're screwed?"

I nod. "I don't see a way out of this."

"Hmm." He looks up at our image on the sky screen. "The Ungulithi enjoy big, showy executions. We should oblige them. I refuse to go down without a fight."

I'm about to respond in kind when, far away, a gigantic column of water blasts up into the atmosphere, almost reaching the dark storm clouds.

A misty veil hangs in the air, under the dark clouds. Lightning flashes. In those seconds of illumination, an animal shape, larger than any creature I've ever seen, moves.

It's too big. Ludicrously big. There's no way we can survive this.

Which, I guess, is the idea.

"Ava!"

I almost miss my dad's shout over the roar of the wind and waves. He's again gesturing toward the Kraken with a trembling hand. I'm tempted to retort that, yes, I'm seeing it too. Kinda hard to miss a mountain-size creature bursting out of the sea. Then I notice he isn't indicating the Kraken. He's pointing lower . . . at the giant ocean surge barreling toward us.

Chapter Thirty

The Calvary

Dad grabs my shoulders and whirls me around to face him. "The trees!"

I nod and bolt for the nearest tree, Dad close on my heels.

The sound of the giant wave grows louder. My feet sink into the sand, slowing me down. It's like running in a nightmare. I crash into the nearest tree, wrapping my limbs around it. Dad comes over and shoves me higher, giving me a boost.

We don't have time for this. "No! Get a tree."

He doesn't reply, but dashes for the next closest tree. The roar of the ocean sounds like a storm. The giant wall of foaming, churning water is almost upon us. Hopefully, our trees are going to be tall enough. I shimmy up higher, rough bark scraping at my skin. There are no pain filters here, no dimming of the senses to prioritize dopamine release. I feel everything now.

I reach the top. Dad is close to the top of his tree. Arms and legs wrapped around as tightly as possible, I close my eyes and brace for the impact.

The wait is short-lived. A split second later, the wave slams into me. The force of the blow causes tiny dots of color to explode before my closed eyes. My legs are no longer wrapped around the tree, but somehow my hands are still locked in place. The tree bends from the immense pressure of the sea. Now that I'm underwater, the current tugs with such violence, as if it has a will of its own, and is trying to pry my grip loose.

My lungs burn. I can't do this much longer. I need air. My hands are cramping. There's no way I'll be able to hang on much longer.

Survival instinct kicks in, overpowering my rational brain. My mouth seems open on its own accord to take in a lungful of seawater. Some small part of me shouts to close my mouth, yet I cannot resist my body's all-consuming desire to inhale. But instead of salty water, cool, sweet oxygen fills my lungs.

I gasp for air and choke. My head is just above the water's surface. It appears the swell is receding.

I'm also the only one above water. Dad is nowhere in sight.

"Dad!" I scream. "Dad!"

Something flashes above me. There is a close-up of my face on the sky screen. I scowl and flip the bird.

By now, enough of the sea retreats to expose my soaking shoulders. I hoist myself higher and yell for Dad a few more times.

No reply comes.

He'd been able to hold on, right? Could he have been swept away? It makes no sense that I could hold on, and yet he somehow couldn't.

A sound like a roaring volcano blasts my eardrums. More dark storm clouds roll in. The sheet of mist is gone, revealing its terrible secret. Lighting bolts streak across clouds, providing illumination of the beast.

The Kraken's bulbous head is the size of a mountain. Its roving yellow eyes are as big as a full moon in a clear night sky. Its crusted, spiky tentacles stretch into the atmosphere, disappearing into the surrounding dark clouds. When it opens its mouth, it exposes endless rows of sharp teeth, thicker than tree trunks.

We have no hope against that thing. Nothing has a chance against that thing.

As if sensing my thoughts, the beast's enormous eyes roll in my direction. I must seem like an insignificant ant to the beast. Yet the monster stares as if I'm the most fascinating object in the world. Its cavernous mouth yawns open and the Kraken roars.

Again, the roar of an exploding volcano reverberates in my ears. It seems impossible a being can produce such a colossal, raucous din.

The sea has receded enough so that only my shoes are submerged. I still haven't seen my dad. Icy claws of dread grip my heart.

"Dad!"

My shout seems to animate the Kraken. The water around the creature churns, and its tentacles coil and then uncoil, writhing in every direction.

The beast is moving in my direction.

"Dad!"

It's a long shot. It's starting to appear as if he's been swept away and might be floating face down . . .

No! I can't go there. I won't go there.

Nearby, there is a gasp, followed by a sputtering cough. My heart leaps into my throat. Dad is clinging to the tree he'd been climbing, though he is several feet lower than me. There hadn't been enough time for him to reach the top before the wave hit us. His avatar looks rough, disheveled, and weak. He coughs and gasps for air.

Intense relief sweeps over me. Tears mix with the seawater running down my face.

"Dad!"

His eyes flutter open. He gives me a small grin and a thumbs-up.

"Not surprised you're still hanging on," he says through heaving breaths. "You've had a firm grip ever since you were a baby."

Despite our current situation, I can't help but laugh.

A loud boom interrupts our reunion. We both turn and face the incoming monster. Though the creature seems to advance at a lumbering, slow speed, it increases in size faster than should be possible. It helps when you can move hundreds of feet in a matter of seconds.

Dad sighs. "Well, this is about to get rough."

The receding water slows down. Bigger and bigger waves start crashing against us as the Kraken approaches.

And then the creature stops.

"What's it doing?" I ask, watching it lift its largest tentacle straight into the air.

The tired, haggard expression on my dad's face disappears, replaced with tight urgency. "Ava, let go of the tree. Swim to your left, parallel with the Kraken. Do it now!"

I hesitate only a moment, long enough to watch Dad push off his tree and swim in the opposite direction. I do the same, struggling to stay above water as the choppy sea slaps me in the face.

Thunder rumbles. The Kraken bellows. The upraised tentacle descends.

"Oh," I say to myself. Facepalm moment. "That's what it's doing."

We are in range of its longest tentacle. The creature is beginning its attack.

It takes several seconds for the tip of the tentacle to appear from the cloud cover. When it does, it seems to pull some clouds down with it, vapor trailing behind the descending extremity.

Muscles scream in protest as I swim hard, fighting to knife through the water. The tentacle looms larger. It feels like I'm barely making any progress. *There's no way I've covered enough distance. It's going to obliterate me!*

The Kraken's limb hits the water. A shock wave races across the surface of the sea. The impact hits me like an invisible slap. A loud crack like lighting rends the air, followed by the awful, familiar noise of a rolling tidal wave. With no time to prepare, I'm raised up high by a massive wave and slammed underwater again.

All sense of direction vanishes as the current tugs and pulls, tumbling me like a rag doll. I open my eyes, the salty water stinging, as I fight to orient myself. There's a glint of light and I kick toward it.

Hopefully, I'm right.

I burst through the water's surface, sputtering and sucking in air. Enough of this fighting-in-water junk. I scan the choppy sea for my dad, praying he'd avoided the Kraken's tentacle. But most of my vision is blocked by said tentacle. Seawater streams through deep crevices in its skin. Muscles, the size of which defies imagination, ripple under its thick, rough epidermis.

The monster's eyes roll in its sockets as it surveys the surface of the water.

It's looking for me.

I sink back underwater, hoping it had missed me. After a few moments, I resurface. The creature's eyes still appear to be searching. For now, I've avoided detection.

This isn't my first time fighting a Kraken, but it's a first fighting one this big, with no weapons. Old encounters run through my head.

There has to be a strategy or answer on what to do next. So lost in thought, I almost don't hear it. Frowning, I tilt my head toward a familiar mechanical whirring.

It's one of the flying cameras. The drone makes a clicking sound. A small, red strobe light emerges from its top.

"No," I whisper, flailing my arms, trying to knock it into the water. It hovers just out of reach. "No!"

Of course, the thing ignores me. The crimson strobe light flashes, and the drone blasts out a shrill, ear-drum-bursting alarm, no doubt to alert the creature to my whereabouts.

I turn to see if the monster has noticed the ruckus. Maybe a being this size couldn't hear anything so high-pitched from something so small?

The Kraken's enormous eyes are staring right at me.

Of course.

The muscles ripple beneath the coarse tentacle hide. The already enormous appendage seems to grow.

The Kraken is sweeping its tentacle at me!

The tentacle slams into me, almost knocking all the wind from my lungs and lifting me out of the water. I cling to the wet, bumpy surface, the texture more a combination of leather and stone than skin. A moment later, the appendage rises toward the sky.

Icy wind beats against me. My drenched clothes sap all the warmth from my body. Dark storm clouds rush closer as if to welcome me.

Now what? When the Kraken slams its tentacle into the ocean again, the shock of the impact alone will be enough to kill me. That is, if I manage not to die of a lightning strike or some other dumb thing while up here.

My options keep getting worse and worse.

Unsure of what else to do, I hold on for dear life. Though the Kraken's skin is tough, it's a struggle to maintain my grip on the wet creature.

The wind ceases. The tentacle is no longer moving. I am now a few feet short of touching one of the black clouds.

Hanging suspended in the air, the Kraken's tentacle remains poised, ready to be brought down at a moment's notice. So why hasn't the creature smashed it back into the water? Could it be looking for me? Is it possible the beast doesn't know I'm up here?

I'm almost blinded by a sudden lightning flash. Squeezing my eyes shut doesn't help. Instead of darkness, a white light sears my vision. Thunder bursts so close I fear it might vibrate me out of my skin. My hand slips. I slide down the beast's tentacle. Lashing out, I grab another handhold, halting my downward momentum, hanging from the monster's craggy hide.

I still don't know if the Kraken senses me on its tentacle or not. It doesn't matter. The tentacle descends slowly and not in the water's direction.

The Kraken rumbles and a hot updraft, laced with the scent of half-digested fish, wafts over me. The urge to vomit hits. It's as if I've taken a punch to the gut. Bracing myself for the inevitable, I look down. The creature's maw is wide open.

"No," I gasp, the monster's intentions dawning on me.

Once again, the air rushes past me as the monster plunges its tentacle toward its mouth. I scream and hold on as tight as possible, unsure of what else to do. On one hand, I'm going to be one of the few people in existence to find out what a Kraken's digestive system is like. On the other hand, I'm about to die a horrible death in a fake world and have my brains fried in the real world.

Another loud boom rends the air. Maybe it's my damaged hearing, but something sounds off. It doesn't sound like thunder. But what else could it be? Another boom follows, and the Kraken's tentacle trembles.

Weird.

Did lightning strike it?

The tentacle wobbles and jerks. My fingers slip out of the groove I'm holding. I flail, trying to catch another handhold, but luck is not on my side this time. I plunge headlong into the toothy depths below.

The creature's mouth is no longer stretched wide to receive me. The Kraken shifts its head away from me. So now, instead of being eaten, I'm going to splat into its oversized cranium.

Not much of an improvement.

"Ava! Ava!"

I've lost it. Seconds away from splatting all over a Kraken, and I'm hallucinating someone calling my name.

The voice is very faint. I glance around, trying to confirm if my ears are indeed playing tricks on me. Some distance away, a dark object hurtles through the air. Whatever it is, it's on an intersecting course between me and the Kraken.

I'm now close enough to make out the ridges and battle scars on the Kraken's head. At the same time, I also note the approaching dark object is a human in a skydiving outfit and helmet, obscuring the skydiver's identity. For a moment, confusion overwhelms all other thoughts. Why is someone skydiving during a thunderstorm and a Kraken attack?

The skydiver slams into me. I gasp, all the wind driven from me. My trajectory changes. Though still falling, I've been knocked off course and am now headed toward the choppy seas.

Gripping me with one arm, the skydiver uses his other arm to yank on a cord attached to his chest. He wraps me in a hug as we are jerked back, our downward plunge halted for the briefest instant. A green and yellow chute opens above our heads, catching the wind.

My breath comes in quick gasps. My body succumbs to a fit of trembling. I tilt my head up to say thank you when a large blur of movement catches my eye.

One of the Kraken's tentacles is hurtling in our direction.

"Look out!"

My voice is cracked and husky as if it hasn't been used in days. I check to see if my rescuer heard me. My jaw drops as a bazooka materializes in his hand.

"Hold on!"

With a bright flash of light, he fires the weapon. The projectile hurtles toward the tentacle, hits it, and explodes in a fiery mix of flesh and gore.

The Kraken howls in pain, and the attacking tentacle shrinks back.

I go limp in relief against the skydiver.

"Thank you," I say.

The bazooka is gone, and the skydiver lifts the wind visor on his helmet.

"You're welcome," Lucas says. Even with the bottom part of the headgear obscuring his mouth, I can tell he has a huge smile on his face.

My jaw drops. For a moment, it's like my brain seizes. How is he here?

"Hang on," he says. "It's about to get bumpy."

He steers us further away from the Kraken. I stare at him, vaguely registering more explosions hitting the beast behind us.

"How?" is all I can say. Lucas continues grinning but doesn't reply. Instead, he points to something in the water.

I follow the direction his finger is pointing. A small motorboat zips over the surface of the sea, avoiding the Kraken's smaller tentacles while navigating the choppy waters.

"Is that Ji Yeon?" I ask, incredulous.

"Yup!" Lucas is practically jubilant. "Hang on, this next part is tricky."

What's more tricky than catching someone in midair?

Turns out that trying to parachute onto a small boat is about as tricky. Especially if the craft is rocking back and forth as wave after wave slams into it. As we get closer, I realize Ji Yeon is struggling to keep from capsizing.

However, luck seems, at last, to be on our side. We land in the middle of the boat and collapse to the deck. Lucas unsnaps the chute, just in time to avoid being yanked off the vessel as the canopy catches another draft of wind and drifts away.

Under the circumstances, I'd say it was a near-perfect landing.

"Hi Ava. Good to see you," Ji Yeon says in a tone that suggests she's more stressed than anything. "Buckle in . . ."

Before she can finish, a large wave slams into the boat, tipping it on its side. I cry out, plunging to the sea.

"Ava!"

I almost miss Lucas's cry over the roar of the ocean. My fingers close over something thin and metallic at the last possible second. I grip it for all I'm worth, slamming into the hull of the vessel.

Huzzah for quick reflexes. Gaming has honed my hand-eye coordination. Confirmed. But the metal cleat is slick with seawater. My fingers slip.

"Ava!"

Lucas leans over the side of the boat and grabs my wrist.

"I've got you. Let go!"

I can't hold on, even if I wanted to. Lucas pulls me back into the craft.

"Is she alright?" Ji Yeon asks.

"I think so," Lucas answers. "Go!"

"Don't have to tell me twice!"

Ji Yeon eases the throttle up. The boat's motor rumbles as we surge forward.

Lucas helps buckle me into my seat. I'm exhausted, drenched, and very confused. More booms catch my attention. Behind us, orange fireballs blossom from the Kraken's skin. The monster roars and thrashes its tentacles more frantically than ever.

"Hang tight!" Ji Yeon calls. She needn't bother. Though we're buckled in, Lucas and I grip the underside of our seats so hard our knuckles turn white.

More booms. Several rows of jets, and even what look like spacecraft, soar over the Kraken, firing missiles, bullets, bombs, lasers—anything that can land damage.

By now, we are putting serious distance between us and the beast. Though still within range of its biggest tentacles, the creature appears preoccupied with the aerial assault directed at it.

The more distance we cover, the more tranquil the sea is, and the less Ji Yeon appears to be fighting with the boat. Behind us, the explosions, the roaring—all grow faint.

Almost bursting with so many questions, I look from Ji Yeon to Lucas. "Okay, first off, thank you for the rescue. Second, can someone please tell me what's going on?"

Chapter Thirty-One

Ultimatum

"We traced you."

I got nothing. "What?"

"We traced you," she repeats.

"Not right away," Lucas says before I can retort. "In the beginning, we weren't sure what to do. You just disappeared. We tried to talk to your mom and sisters. Your mom, uh . . . had little to say."

That tracks. "My sisters? Are they okay?"

"Fine, considering," Lucas says. "They're scared and lonely. They didn't tell us much except that you'd been taken like your dad."

Dad!

My eyes dart over the surface of the water, even though there's no way he could've swum this far. Of course, my father is nowhere to be seen, but the Kraken is still visible, its tentacles no longer flailing. If my eyes don't deceive me, it looks lower in the water.

It's sinking. That must mean it's mortally wounded or dead.

I swivel to face Ji Yeon and Lucas. "We have to go back."

They both glance at me as if I'm speaking Russian or something.

"My dad is still back there!"

Understanding dawns on their faces.

"Ava, we can't go back—" Ji Yeon begins.

I cut her off. "My father is there. We must locate him! He's exhausted and might not be able to keep his head above water. We have to go!"

Ji Yeon doesn't answer, instead giving Lucas a pleading glance. I study Ji Yeon's expression, wondering what Lucas said to convince her to help me. After our fight, it seemed our friendship was done.

"The Kraken is dead," I shout, gesturing to the creature.

"Perhaps." Lucas holds up his hands in a placating gesture. "But the surrounding water is still choppy. You saw how hard Ji Yeon struggled to keep us afloat. We almost didn't make it."

Setting my jaw, I unbuckle and stand up. "Fine. If you don't take me, I'll swim back."

Lucas and Ji Yeon exchange despairing looks. I walk to the rear of the craft, lift my foot over the edge, and prepare to drop into the water.

A firm hand grips my shoulder. I try to shrug Lucas off, but he holds on.

"Ava, hold on. Let me get in contact with the guys over there. They might spot something."

I straddle the edge of the vessel, unsure of what my next move should be.

"Please," Lucas says. "Just hang on."

Reluctantly, I swing my dangling leg back into the boat and stomp back to my seat.

"You have two minutes." My eyes are locked with his, making sure he gets the message. "I'm going back with or without their help."

He nods, taking my point. Bringing a hand to his ear, he says something inaudible.

Still full of questions, I turn to Ji Yeon, unsure of how best to proceed.

"We tracked you the same way I assume Marley tracked you," Ji Yeon says. "I'm not sure how he did it, but during one of his interactions with you, Marley planted a sophisticated bug into the coding of your avatar."

My face must show puzzlement because she continues her explanation.

"I mean, the bug embedded itself into the DNA coding of your avatar, the part that makes you unique among the billions of other avatars out there. That way Marley would never lose you. If he had multiple people bugged, he would know which one was you."

That bastard. "So, how did *you* know to look for a bug on me?"

She shrugs. "I didn't. It was Lucas's idea. He was so frantic to help you, he was always throwing all these nutty ideas at me. Tracking you via an enemy bug was one of his least crazy suggestions."

Lucas, hunching in his seat, talks to someone on his comms, with no idea he is the subject of conversation. *He had been worried about me. He was willing to put his life on the line to rescue me.* Now I feel bad for getting angry with him a minute ago.

"I'm surprised he convinced you to help," I say, unable to look at her as I talk.

"Why?" she asks, sounding amazed.

"You know . . . the whole 'terrorist' thing?" I sigh.

For a moment Ji Yeon is silent, her expression unreadable. My gut churns. *Hopefully, I haven't offended her.* That would be a swell way to repay a rescue mission.

"Let's just say I'm not convinced either way about the whole 'terrorist' thing," she says at last, grimacing. "But one thing I am sure of is you. And us. We've been there for each other ever since we were little. I don't want that to change."

Some of the churning in my gut eases. My throat tightens instead. Anger and resentment melt away. All I want to do is hug her.

Noise from the nearby aircraft breaks the moment. They are flying low, only a few feet above the sea's surface. The rebels must be searching for my father.

I gesture to the aircraft. "How'd you get involved with them?"

A broad grin plays across Ji Yeon's face for the first time since rescuing me. "That's only the beginning. Those are Morgan Sheffy's men. They contacted us not long after you were gone."

"What?" My surprise is twofold. It's surprising the rebels knew enough to contact Lucas and Ji Yeon after their boss and I had been taken. Second, how did Ji Yeon not turn them in to her little student club? She must be facing strong doubts indeed.

"Yup. I couldn't believe it at first. They were looking for you. They were hoping you'd be able to escape and give them news about their commander. Initially, they thought you were hiding out with him. They knew we were your friends because Morgan Sheffy started a file on you after your initial visit. Needless to say, it disappointed them when I said I had no idea where you were."

"Okay, so how are they here now? With you?"

Her smile fades, replaced by a grim expression. "They watched their leader get executed. By then, Lucas and I were working on the bug theory. We reached out to them for help around the time the broadcast went live. The timing couldn't have been better. Well, except for . . . you know."

I nod, wondering if Sheffy's execution had affected Ji Yeon more than she let on.

"The rebels have coders way more advanced than me," she says. "They traced your location in The Haven before the live stream ended. But they needed another live stream to track your avatar and where your plug-in station is, because the algorithm the Ungulithi uses generates these execution locations at random to throw off any would-be hackers. That's why it took such a long time for us to get here. We've been on high alert for days, ready to move at a moment's notice."

"So you tracked me by my bug," I say, my wiped-out mind trying to process the implications. "Does that mean it's still active? Are the Ungulithi tracking us now?"

Ji Yeon is about to answer when Lucas steps up. "No. I disabled the bug as soon as I grabbed you in the air."

"The rebel coders concocted up something to wipe out the bug," Ji Yeon explains. "We just had to implant it into your avatar when we were in range."

"The rebels have been plotting to go on the offensive for months," Lucas says. "The Ungulithi attack on their Haven base and the capture of Morgan Sheffy disrupted their plans. But their second-in-command—Commander Warren Witherspoon—rallied them. He charged them to be ready at a moment's notice after we found out you had a bug. We figured we might only have minutes after they started live-streaming you. Apparently, whatever you delivered for your dad was key to hacking the alien's security, allowing us to track your bug."

Wow. So my dad and I played a key part in making this attack possible. The weight of this thought silences me for a moment as I process it.

"How'd you know they'd execute me?" I ask. Time to get my head back in the game.

"We had a hunch," Ji Yeon says. "Plus, we had nothing else to go on."

Lucas waves in the general direction of the rebel fighters. "Most of the fighting is happening outside The Haven. Ji Yeon and I could beg off a small force to help us rescue you inside The Haven."

Hands on hips, my fingers twitch. All this is very interesting, but my thoughts keep wandering, trying to figure out where Dad might be. A part of me recognizes the last time I saw him, a giant tentacle had slammed into the water, separating us, and almost drowning me. There's a good chance that he didn't—

I jerk my head as if tossing that from my mind. *No. Can't go there.*

A new idea springs up.

"What about New Haven?" I ask. "I assume part of the rebels' battle plan includes attacking that stronghold?"

They both seem unsure.

"I think so," Lucas says.

"How can you not know?"

"They didn't include us much in the meetings." Ji Yeon gives me a deadpan expression. "Warren Witherspoon barely let us join in as it is."

"Only reason we're here is we're your best friends," Lucas says. "And because we have a particular set of skills."

Ji Yeon gives him a disgusted look. "You got to do the cool things. Meanwhile, I almost drown trying to drive this thing."

Lucas wiggles his eyebrows. "Get your skydiving stats up, then we'll talk."

"Why haven't they found him yet?"

Even over the noise of the waves and the jets, my voice is louder and harsher than I intend. Both Lucas and Ji Yeon startle at my sudden outburst.

"It's a big ocean," Lucas says, looking uncomfortable. "And the Kraken is a gigantic creature. Your dad might hide on a tentacle or some driftwood or something. We'll find him."

A crackling like static bursts in my ears. I cry out in pain and surprise, clutching at my head. Ji Yeon and Lucas claw at their ears.

"Hello, rebels."

An icy shiver runs through my body as a familiar, booming voice comes out of nowhere. The sky screens, which had disappeared during the rebel onslaught, are now back. Both screens display the same image.

"You think your little attack changes anything?" Xynlyc asks. The alien's avatar is in a dark room. The image shakes and jerks as if the camera is being held by someone unfamiliar with basic video recording skills.

"It alters nothing," Xynlyc continues. "No one will know what you're doing here today. They will know what we want them to know. We will soon have the people calling for your heads!"

A rebel aircraft zooms toward the sky screen and fires a burst of machine gun rounds at it. The Ungulithi seems unimpressed.

"Is that the best you can do? By all means, waste your ammo. I'm disappointed, though. I expected more from you. Even as we speak, we are repelling all attacks in New Haven and The Haven. The New Sons of Liberty will be no more."

Ji Yeon, Lucas, and I glance at each other in consternation. Had all of this been for nothing? Yet something bothers me. Xynlyc is asserting the rebels are losing . . . however, I see no counterattack here. No Haven security spawning in to fight.

"However, I am not ungenerous." The Ungulithi opens its arms. "If you surrender now, we will show mercy. It is not your fault that you fell under the spell of a charismatic deceiver. Nobody else needs to die."

Both Ji Yeon and Lucas smile as if to say, *"Can you believe this guy?"*

"If you persist attacking," Xynlyc continues, "we will be forced to destroy you. And we will execute one of your own on the live stream."

Uh, oh. The Ungulithi had a lot of prisoners in their weird tube prison, but I thought Dad, Morgan Sheffy, and I were the only rebels they had.

The camera jerks away from Xynlyc to another avatar in the room. The image blurs and it takes the cameraman a second to refocus on the dimly lit avatar. I stiffen in shock.

How? How did they . . .

"Robert McNealy was due to be executed today," Xynlyc says from offscreen. "I'm willing to forgo such an event if you cease your attacks now, and open lines for negotiations. But if you reject my magnanimous offer, well . . . Mr. McNealy's execution will go on as planned."

A rush of dizziness spins up in my head. The world tilts first one way, then the other, as I struggle to keep my balance on the deck.

"Whoa," Lucas says, rushing to my side to steady me. "I got you."

I lean against him for support, shaking my head, trying to get rid of this sudden vertigo.

"You have one hour to decide," the Ungulithi says. "If I don't hear from you, or you reject my offer . . . then you can expect your fate to be the same as Mr. McNealy's."

The sky screens vanish.

Chapter Thirty-Two

Co-Plugging

Gasping, I lean forward, straining against the bonds keeping me in the plug-in pod. For a brief, disorienting moment, I forget where I am. To go from a rocking boat in a warm climate to a still pod in a cold room—well, it throws me off. Fortunately, I'm quick to adapt. The metal snakes retract from my head, folding themselves back into their compartments. With a soft click, the clamps restraining my limbs open, and I bat my hands at the steel snakes, making sure they stay away, especially the black one.

"Error," the pod's AI says, causing me to jump in surprise. "Program interrupted. Rebooting. Program interrupted. Rebooting . . ."

And just like that, I forgive my own AI for all its sarcasm and snark. This guy sounds like some vanilla robot voice from an old, generic sci-fi movie.

Something rustles. Beside me, one of The Named rises from the shadows. Had he been sitting against the wall, sleeping? I'm not sure how I missed him there, but he's now looking at me in astonishment.

"You can't . . ." he begins.

I lash out.

There's no plan. I've never fought anyone outside The Haven before. There's also the tremendous disadvantage of half my body being useless in a fight. Fortunately, the other half is stronger than most girls my age because of how I get around my disability.

I manage to catch him half-crouched, still rising from he'd been sitting. My fist slams into his jaw. Bones crack with a sickening thud. We both cry out in pain. I clutch my hand, doubling over. His head snaps to the side, and he collapses to the floor. Pain lances through my entire arm.

He shoves off the ground and turns to glare at me. The man sways, still unsteady. I stare at his jaw, at its horrible angle, blood and saliva dripping from his mouth. He blinks as if trying to regain his thoughts. His eyes focus on me. A terrible expression further contorts his face, and he lunges at me with a hoarse scream.

I yelp and shrink back. His fingers close over my throat. My head slams against the pod. His grip tightens, clenching my windpipe shut. Instead of air, horrible hissing gurgles issue from my throat.

The Named looks down at me, eyes wide, teeth bared, growling, pressing his weight against my throat. He draws one of his arms back, hand formed into a fist. I watch in fascinated horror as the skin on his forearm bulges, then splits open with a sickening *squelching* sound. Next, there is a metallic click and a whirring sound as a strange tubelike device raises itself from his arm.

That must be the bio-weapon Dad mentioned!

A blinding light flashes from the end of The Named's implanted weapon, followed by a loud booming noise. There's an instant, searing heat on my face and the scent of burning hair.

I'm hit!

I don't know the severity of my wounds. I don't think I'm hit bad though. It was pure luck his first shot hadn't done more damage. But now he lowers his arm, aiming for my torso. There is no chance of missing this time.

Hissing from the metal snakes registers. My head must be in the approximate area to trigger the sensors to deploy them.

I reach up. Consciousness is slipping from me. My hand closes over wiry, cold steel. With all my strength, I jab The Named in the eye with one of the metal snakes.

A light flashes followed by a crackling electric snap. Something jolts me. A shriek fills the small room. The viselike clamp on my neck disappears and I gulp in air. Black spots dance in my vision as my breath hitches and violent coughs convulse my body.

I shift my head away, hoping it's enough to make the metal snakes retract again. The last thing I need at the moment is to reenter The Haven.

Something tugs at my hand. I'm still clutching one of the metal snakes. With my normal vision returning, I note it's the black one. So this is the one I'd jabbed The Named in the eye with. Trembling, I release it and search for my attacker.

There is no need to worry. He lies on the ground, unmoving. He stares at the ceiling with his one good eye, unblinking. Half of his face looks burnt and crinkled.

I turn away, still gasping for air. Something in my stomach shifts. I clamp a hand over my mouth. A cold sheen of perspiration covers my body.

I will not throw up!

The trembling worsens, making it harder for me to get into my wheel-chair. I try to take a few steadying breaths, but the air keeps catching in my throat.

The side of my face throbs. I dab my temples. Withdrawing my hand, there is blood on my fingertips. Fortunately, it isn't a lot of blood. It must've been a grazing wound; burns more than anything.

Eyes locked on my knees, I refuse to examine the man on the floor. I wipe my tear-streaked face and wonder what I'm crying about. That I killed someone? Or from having survived an attempt on my life in a real physical way I've never faced before?

My grip on my push rims is weak. I'm spent. The urge to curl up in a ball and black out seems like the best idea in the world. But I can't. Dad needs me. Gathering my strength, I wheel myself out. The building trembles. A muffled boom roars somewhere nearby, followed by what sounds like distant gunfire.

So the rebels are indeed here.

Not that I had doubted that. Even so, it was nice having it confirmed. Especially considering what I need to do.

Retracing the route that had brought me here earlier, I find myself back in the elevator, ascending to the top of the building.

As my elevator climbs higher and higher, I run through the plan—such as it is—again and again until every detail is seared in my brain.

"What are you doing?"

The boat rocked in the water. Ji Yeon grabbed my shoulders to help steady me as I attempted to access the VR menu. I sighed in frustration. The tracker might be gone, but the block against my inventory remained.

"I'm going to save my dad—for real this time."

Lucas stepped forward. "Wait, you can't . . ."

"Don't try to stop me," I interjected, and backed away.

Lucas raised his hands. "I wasn't. But what's the plan?"

"You need access to your stuff," Ji Yeon chimed in. "Won't get far without your inventory."

I sank back into my seat. My arms felt limp and heavy. "Then what should I do?" Exhaustion stole over me. It was as if I hadn't slept in days.

Ji Yeon rubbed her chin. "It might be the type of pod you're plugged into. Or maybe they programmed a block."

"Can you remove it?"

"I'll contact the IT guys; see what they say."

"We also need to find out where they're holding your dad," Lucas said.

"How do we do that?" I asked.

"Not from here."

A chirping noise interrupted him before he could say more.

"I've got to take this." He stepped past me and pressed a finger to his ear.

Ji Yeon looked as if she was listening to her own earbuds. "Yes . . . okay, yes, thanks!" She pressed a hand to her ear to end the call.

"Does everybody but me have an earpiece?" I asked, feeling out of the loop.

She didn't even bother to respond to my petty remark. "The IT guys say if it is a block, they can hack into it and remove it. It's going to take some time, though."

We don't have time. "How can we find out where my dad is? Lucas says we can't do it from here."

Ji Yeon appeared surprised. "I'm not sure how we can do it from *any-where*. Your dad might be in any random environment in The Haven."

I looked at Lucas, hoping he had some plan or idea.

"Sir," Lucas said, speaking louder than was necessary. "Sir, what—I'm losing you. My battery must be dying . . . sir, hello!"

Ji Yeon and I looked at each other.

Lucas yanked the earpiece out of his ear and hurled it into the water.

"What did you do that for?" Ji Yeon demanded in astonishment.

Lucas shrugged. "Witherspoon wanted us to evac. Says he won't en-danger the mission because of a hostage. He also says we'll never get an opportunity like this again."

"What?" I asked, indignant. "Are they going to let my father die?"

Ji Yeon's earpiece chirped.

"Get rid of it," Lucas said. Ji Yeon pulled the device out of her ear and flicked it into the water.

"Try to see it from their point of view," Lucas said to me.

Absolutely not. "After everything he's been through? After everything he's done for them, they're just going to let him *die*?"

"I think it's the nature of the business," Ji Yeon said, though she doesn't seem happy about it.

Lucas nodded in agreement. "But we're not officially part of the re-bellion. Which means we technically don't have to follow orders."

My eyes widened as I realized what Lucas had done. "You're disobey-ing orders?"

Lucas nodded. Ji Yeon appeared to be reappraising him with some-thing of a newfound respect.

"But why?" I asked, realizing the debt owed to my friends could never be repaid.

"You're our friend," Lucas said. "We're here for you, not for them. And you came for your dad. I know you won't leave here without him, and I'm not leaving without you."

"And neither am I," Ji Yeon said, smiling.

A flush of heat rose to my face. I couldn't look my friends in the eyes.

"Thank you." It's all I can manage. Lucas reached out and lightly touched my arm, smiling.

Oh, gosh, his smile made my stomach flutter. His hand was so warm and real against my skin. Not for the first time, I wish he could be with me in person.

Ji Yeon, her smile turning goofy, loudly cleared her throat and said, "So Lucas, any idea on how to find her father?"

"Oh, yeah!" His eyes widened as he remembered and yanked his hand back. I glared at Ji Yeon with a mix of irritation and relief.

Lucas looked excitedly from me to Ji Yeon. "Have you ever heard of co-plugging?"

———

"What are you doing?" The Named shrieks. "You have not been cleansed! You are violating the sanctity of the domain!"

Security sure has been lousy so far. I've made it to the doors of the giant room where both my encounters with Xynlyc happened, and this is the first person I've run into. The battle must be keeping everyone busy.

I grab the device in my lap and point it at The Named. I'd found it in what looked like an abandoned security closet, just off from the cleansing rooms. It sort of resembles a weapon. It's made of a cloudy metallic material and has a barrel and a grip, yet I can't find a trigger mechanism anywhere on the thing.

"Sorry," I say, "I forgot to wipe my feet."

The Named one doesn't seem to notice the contraption in my hand. She continues to shriek and wring her hands. "You're not supposed to be here! You have to be cleansed."

"Shut up before I cleanse your guts," I say, shaking the device at her. Could I use it even if I knew how? The image of The Named I'd fought and . . . killed . . .

My stomach roils. I suppress a groan as a wave of nausea hits me. The device feels heavier in my hand.

No, can't think about that right now. His vacant eyes staring at the ceiling; features contorted in pain, fear, and surprise . . .

No!

I gulp, refocusing on the woman in front of me. My assumption of the gadget being a gun wavers as The Named continues to ignore it. "Leave now, before I tell my master . . ."

A thunderous boom drowns out the rest of her words. The floor trembles, causing my wheelchair to vibrate. The explosions are growing louder. Is that a good thing or a bad thing?

"You hear that? Did you feel it? Your masters are too busy protecting their slimy butts to spare a thought for you. They don't care about you."

She sways back and forth as if striving to keep her balance on the vibrating ground. Her expression is a mixture of terror and confusion.

"I know you have surgically implanted weapons," I continue. "One wrong move and I use this on you."

Her eyes grow wide, apparently registering the device in my hand for the first time. "N-no. I don't have any weapons."

"Don't lie to me!" I shout.

"Please," she begs, cowering. "I'm telling you the truth. Only the guards have those."

She sounds convincing.

"Fine. But make a wrong move and see what happens. Now, where are the Ungulithi?" I ask.

She shakes her head, her lips trembling. "There are some areas even we are not permitted."

Oh? Interesting. "Take me."

The woman blanches. "I can't. I'm not allowed! They'll kill me!"

I inch closer to her, only using one hand to propel my chair forward. The muffled booming continues, each one growing in intensity.

"You see what I'm holding?" I ask. "Do you know what it does?"

Hopefully, she does, because I sure as heck don't.

Somehow, her face grows even paler. "Please . . ." she whispers. Her expression is of naked fear. It seems she knows what this doohickey does. Which should make my next words sound threatening.

"If you don't take me to them, I'll use this on you."

The woman's eyes bulge. Her reaction almost gives me secondhand anxiety. What exactly does this thing do?

I press my advantage and wave the device under her nose. "What's it going to be?"

The Named takes me inside the elevator, but instead of hitting a button, she activates a small hidden panel. It slides open to reveal a single red button; she presses it and we descend.

The trip to the bottom is long. The elevator shakes whenever a nearby explosion goes off. And every time it happens, The Named sucks in a breath and seems to brace herself to plunge the rest of the way down.

That'd be my luck. When being bombed, stairs are a better choice, in case the power gets knocked out, stranding you in the elevator, but since I'm in a wheelchair...

We eventually reach the bottom. The doors open to reveal a short, concrete hallway, six steel doors interspersed along the walls.

"Which one would they be in?" I ask.

The woman shakes her head. "I'm not sure."

I raise the device closer to her face.

"I swear I don't have a clue," she says, one eye twitching.

Convinced she has no clue, I lower the contraption. "Fine."

We enter the hallway. Behind us, the elevator doors slide closed. The woman whimpers.

There are no unusual markings on the steel doors. I rap my knuckles against the nearest door, making a muted *thunk* sound. Built to withstand attack. Guess that means using this alien device is out of the question, even if I knew how to use it.

I should wait for backup. If the rebels win, they'll wind up here eventually, right? It's dumb for a teenage girl to be down here, alone. But my dad could be in one of these rooms. Time is running out.

"How do I get in?" I ask.

She looks like she may cry. "I've never been here before."

I give her what is hopefully my best threatening glare. "Look, lady, I don't have time for you to freak out right now. My father is about to die in less than half an hour. Either open these doors, or you are no longer any use to me."

The woman nods and scampers to the closest door, scanning it up and down. She bought my bluff. At least, I'm pretty sure it was a bluff. I've never threatened anyone like that before. Despite my father's life on the line, I'm not sure what would've happened if the woman refused me.

"Okay," the woman says, relief in her voice. "These can be opened with a holographic keyboard."

While she says this, one blinks to life inches from the door.

"It's password protected," she says, looking at odd symbols on the display. "I don't know the password."

"Then I suggest you try a few," I say, unyielding.

She wipes at her eyes, sniffs, then types something on the display. The holographic keyboard blinks red. She lets out a shaky sigh and keys in something else. Again, flashes of amber.

On and on it goes. She types something in, only to have the hologram turn red. With each rejection, she grows more and more agitated, her eyes flicking in my direction more than once. Her fingers tremble and sweat beads on her face.

"Calm down," I say.

"How can I calm down?" she blurts out in a tight, pinched voice. "We're under attack and you're pointing a Harthgliss at me!"

First, I hadn't technically *threatened* to kill her. I'd *implied* that possibility. And second . . . a har-*what*?

"Calm down," I repeat. "You're going too fast. Too many mistakes. That's not useful to me either."

For a split second, the woman glares so fiercely I wonder if she's about to lunge at me. But a heartbeat later, her expression melds into despair, and she visibly appears to deflate.

"Just take a moment," I say. "Breathe deeply."

She does. The woman closes her eyes, slowing her breathing. It takes a minute for her hands to stop shaking.

I almost feel sorry for her.

Almost.

"Now," I say. "Try again."

The Named lets out a long, low breath. Then her eyes fly open and she stares straight ahead in shock.

"The emergency code," she whispers.

I lean forward. "The what?"

She blinks and stares at me as if she'd forgotten I was there. "When we were first initiated, the Ungulithi made us memorize many things. As well as an emergency code. They never explained what it did or when we were to use it."

Odd. Could this be my lucky day? I don't feel lucky, but what other option is there?

"Try it," I say.

She nods and keys in the code. The display blinks green. A clink and the sound of scraping metal follow. The door eases open.

"Good job," I say, rolling past her through the doorway. I shove the door all the way open and enter the room, raising the device, attempting to appear threatening.

The interior is much like the digital panic room Morgan and I had hidden in. Dark paneling covers the concrete walls. Steel storage carts rest against the paneling. The shelves of these carts are full of semi-transparent canisters, with what appear to be various shades of orange and brown sludge inside.

Food perhaps?

I recall that Xynlyc hadn't eaten with me when the alien had been attempting to strike a deal. The creature claimed something about not liking the taste of human food, but maybe there was another reason the slug didn't partake. Could our food be harmful to the Ungulithi?

In the middle of the room are two oddly designed plug-in pods. I might not have known they were plug-in pods except for the fact that two

Ungulithi occupied them, with metal snakes inches from their heads. The pair don't acknowledge my entrance; they are plugged in.

Seems like an obvious security issue. No traps are being sprung, and no alarms are going off. Are they so arrogant to think they're untouchable?

I could kill them where they lay, and there's nothing they could do about it. Not unless the pods have safeguards.

Did I just think about murdering two beings and not balk at the idea right away? A sick sense bubbles up from my stomach. No, no more thoughts of killing.

But what if I have to? What if I have to kill someone else to save my dad?

Cross that bridge when or if I get to it. Exiting the room, I spot The Named standing in front of the elevator, mashing the button to call it.

"Where do you think you're going?" I ask.

She shrieks and spins around to face me. "Nowhere. I mean, I was just . . ."

I'm not interested. "Whatever. Time to open the next door."

The other doors take less time to open. Inside each one, it's the same: two aliens plugged into their pods.

Except for the last room. One pod contains an alien and the other a human.

Dad!

I rush over to him, looking him over for injury. He seems fine, though his face is drawn tight with tension, and he's paler than usual.

My heart is racing. So close, yet so far.

———

"So that's co-plugging? That all sounds complicated," I said, unable to keep the skepticism out of my voice. Overhead, seagulls called out to each other. No doubt they were going to join the growing swarm of birds circling the dead Kraken.

"It's not. Ji Yeon went into more detail than needed."

Lucas was excited, pacing the width of the boat, causing it to rock in the water. Ji Yeon, at the helm, looked indignant.

"It's your idea, sir," she said sarcastically. "I told you to explain it to her."

"I wasn't expecting you to get so technical," Lucas said.

Ji Yeon rolled her eyes. "That's how it was explained to me. I'm surprised you're even aware of it."

"You're not the only person who hangs out in hacker clubs." Lucas grinned.

I still needed some clarification. "So I manually override the pod my father is in, follow the menu, and type in what, exactly?"

"Run program. Command. Split cranium inflow/outflow," Ji Yeon said, in an almost robotic tone.

"That'll make one of the metal snakes drop away," Lucas said. "And you can spawn in the approximate area your dad is, since you'll be technically using the same pod."

Yeah, sounded easy enough when explained that way.

"Just please be careful," Ji Yeon said.

"It's not dangerous, right?" I asked. Though I'm capable inside The Haven, I had little faith in my abilities outside The Haven. If this was dangerous, then I'd somehow screw it up.

"I don't think so," Lucas said, frowning, and glanced at Ji Yeon for clarification.

"Maybe. I don't know." Ji Yeon seemed frustrated. She's never liked being unsure. "I've never seen it done. I don't know if it's done a lot.

We're talking about a high-voltage machine that coaxes your brain into a comatose-like state. And you'll be without AI monitoring. Little room for error."

"I wish I could go with you," Lucas said. "We just got here, and now we have to separate again."

"I'll be fine," I said. "I'm too pissed to be recaptured or killed. I have a score to settle with some slugs!"

———

I type the commands into the interface, according to Ji Yeon's instructions. A metal snake by Dad's head wavers, then drops off to the side.

"Yes!" I give a quick celebratory arm pump.

The screen on the console flashes. My arm pauses in the air as I lean closer for a better look.

30 . . . 29 . . . 28 . . .

"They mentioned nothing about a countdown," I say aloud to nobody in particular.

23 . . . 22 . . . 21 . . . 20 . . .

The steel snake that had flopped aside begins to twitch and stir.

I lunge forward, falling out of my wheelchair. Hitting the ground with a hard thump, I grab hold of the writhing metal and move the end over my head. The metallic snake's movements grow more and more violent as it tries to wrench itself from my grasp. Hopefully, the countdown is almost done. Not sure how long I can hold . . .

The metal snake stops struggling. I let it go, and it maneuvers into a position by my head.

My whole body—the parts that I can feel, anyway—is buzzing. This is uncharted territory, entering The Haven with no AI oversight or backup. Not using all the metal snakes, not knowing what's going to happen when mine turns on . . .

Dad needs me; now isn't the time to freak out, especially when I'm this close.

A snap of electricity, loud as a whip crack, stings my ears. Everything goes dark.

Chapter Thirty-Three

Aish Kulong

Wherever I am, it's dark. My shoe scrapes stone. A path? Black silhouettes of trees rise over each side of what must be a pathway. Little else is visible.

No choice but forward, it seems.

A sense of disappointment grows the further I walk. Perhaps it was too much to hope for: spawn in the exact spot where Dad is being held, take the Ungulithi by surprise, and whisk him out of there.

It only takes a few minutes to reach the end of the path and arrive at a clearing. Why do game designers build paths for you to walk on, and nothing else happens? No special scenery, no loot crate, in-game joke, character encounter—nothing. Just a plain path to walk to get where you want to go. It's so pedestrian.

Stepping out of the forest, the night sky is no longer blocked by thick, interweaving branches. A crescent moon illuminates what looks to be an iron gate a few hundred feet away. Beyond stands an old, gothic style building. It's hard to tell if it's a house, a castle, or . . . something else. The dim moonlight doesn't illuminate much except for angular shapes and winding spires standing out in the building's frame.

Is this where they're holding Dad? Why here? What is this place?

I make my way to the gate. There is a sound like iron grating. Squinting, I try to see in the dim moonlight. Is someone opening the gate? Crouching, I wait to see who emerges from the gate. Nothing happens. No movement, even as the sound persists. I rise and walk over to it and discover the gate unlocked, swaying on its hinges from the breeze.

An open invitation? Am I expected? Well, I was invited here. It would make sense that my arrival was anticipated.

Overgrown grass lines both sides of the paved driveway leading to the house. The house looms larger and more intimidating as I get closer. Leering statues of gargoyles hang over from the nearest ledges. The building looks ancient, made of large, stained brick slabs and little else.

I pad up the steps leading to the building's entrance, a pair of large, wooden double doors. There's a distinct sense of déjà vu as I look at them. They're almost an exact match for the double doors to the great hall where I had supper with Xynlyc.

So the space aliens like ancient-style architecture . . . interesting.

Lifting the latch, I shove my way inside. The interior matches the outside with the tall, stone entry extending to the ceiling, and two curved staircases on either side of the doorway. Lit by dozens of candles, their small halos of light cast deep, wavering shadows in every direction.

I choose the nearest staircase and begin my ascent. My heart pounds in my ears. In the stillness, my breath sounds way too loud. Something about this building, this location, is very off. Aside from the fact it's giving me creepy haunted house vibes. And that I haven't run into another living soul so far.

It could be a trap.

Scratch that . . . it's most definitely a trap.

All the candles are out on the first landing. I proceed upward. It isn't until the top floor that I come across lit candles. Hopefully, this means I'm heading in the right direction.

Creeping down the dark hallway, my eyes scan the shadows, watching for traps or assassins.

None come.

In most normal game levels, I should encounter obstacles right about now. Environmental puzzles, enemy combatants—something. Instead, I reach the end of the hallway without incident. The hallway dead-ends in a spiral stone staircase, much more narrow than the previous one.

Upon reaching the top, I peek around the doorway that leads to the outside. Groups of shadowy forms stand along the battlements. I duck back into the stairwell. Have they been there the entire time? Have they seen me?

"Who's there?"

My heart sinks. *Well, there goes the element of surprise.*

"We know you're there," the voice goes on. "Are you here to accept our offer?"

So those were Ungulithi in their avatar forms. Did that mean my dad is among them?

"Come now, don't keep us waiting," another voice chimes in. "It'll go poorly for Mr. McNealy if you don't hurry."

Should I go out there? Perhaps acting like I'm a representative for the rebels to go over the Ungulithi's terms. Or there's the attack with guns blazing option. But I'd be risking my dad getting hit in the crossfire or by a stray shot if he's with them.

Neither of those options is appealing.

A decision must be reached.

The clock is ticking.

<hr>

"What do I do when I get there?" I asked Ji Yeon. The choppiness of the seawater had, for the most part, subsided. Except for the giant Kraken carcass in the distance, it almost was like we were at the start of a relaxing boating trip.

She shrugged. "Kick some alien ass? There's a reason you have top combat stats, even for a mage."

"With what?" I asked, holding out empty hands. Still barred from my inventory.

Ji Yeon gave Lucas a knowing smile. "I'm aware."

"We also know it's a good idea for all of us if you have access to your inventory." Lucas was wearing another of his broad smiles.

I tapped my foot. "Great. But in case you haven't noticed, I still can't access my stuff. That hasn't changed."

Ji Yeon stood up from the helm. "Come give me a hug."

This was such a strange request coming from Ji Yeon. I was speechless. "Huh?"

She motioned toward herself.

Too stunned to do anything else, I leaned over to her and gave her an awkward half-embrace.

"Well, that was pathetic," Ji Yeon said. "Let's never do that again."

"Why are you acting so weird?" I asked, confused.

Lucas laughed.

I shot him a glare.

He covered his mouth with his hand but could not hide his glee.

"Sorry," he said between giggles. "The look on both your faces was worth all the recent danger."

I placed my hands on my hips. "Care to explain?"

"Remember, Marley had to plant the bug on you using contact?" Lucas asked. "Well, the bug the rebels came up with requires contact as well. You're clean now."

"Ah," I said, understanding.

"Well," he said, "Try it out."

"Could've made it less awkward if you'd told me," I muttered, and activated my inventory menu.

"What's the fun of that?" Lucas's eyes glinted.

My inventory shelves popped up. I almost cried with joy, scrolling through menu after menu. My eyes landed on a ridiculously oversized broadsword I'd forgotten I had. Of the many swords in my collection, this one has been used the least. I zoomed in on the weapon. Ancient runes and symbols lined the guard. A small purple gem gleamed in the pommel.

Activating the sword, I whirled and stabbed with it, judging the weight, balance, and whether its ridiculous length and width would be a help or a hindrance.

"Hey, watch it," Ji Yeon called out, recoiling at the sight of my sword.

Lucas had the opposite reaction. "I need it," he said, transfixed by my weapon.

I swing the blade around, relishing the sound it made as it sliced through the air. It was nice to have my stuff back.

The odds were more even now.

———

Sorry, Dad, if you're out there. No other option comes to mind.

I press myself against the wall, preparing to charge the parapet. If Dad *is* out there, hopefully he's separated from the group. Otherwise . . .

No broadsword right now. I toggle it into my secondary weapon option. The primary weapon is now a bolt-charge gun, an energy weapon with a slower rate of fire, but a guaranteed kill shot upon target impact. I whip around my cover, drop to one knee and fire off two rounds.

My projectiles tear through the group like they were nothing more than paper, shredding heads, limbs, and torsos.

I leap into what's left of them. Now seems like the appropriate moment to switch to my sword.

Melee time.

Bringing my blade down in a long arc, I land in their midst, cleaving the avatar in front of me in two. No blood or guts. Too bad; it would've been more satisfying.

Turns out the bolt gun did most of the work. Most of the Ungulithi avatars have been wounded, killed, or are dying. Only a couple are whole enough to offer any kind of resistance.

"Ava!"

It's Dad. He's several yards back from the Ungulithi avatars, bound and kneeling.

"Hold on," I answer. "I'm coming!"

"Ava, wait . . ."

I can't hear his next words. From the ground, a one-armed Ungulithi raises his weapon, firing wildly.

"How?" the alien yells between bursts of gunfire. "They said you'd be unarmed!"

The vaporous red flashes erupting from the muzzle of the Ungulithi's gun almost blind me. I stumble back, feeling the rounds impact.

Armor down to 60 percent.

The Ungulithi have some wicked energy weapons. A few more rounds and my shields will be useless.

Bracing, I snap my forearm in front of my nose, roaring. *"Xhalih-ndra!"*

The Ungulithi on the ground keeps firing, now joined by two more able-bodied aliens. They must've been stunned by my initial attack. However, their shots cause no damage, as my activated Shield of Khalinx absorbs and dissipates ammo.

The Ungulithi cease firing for a split second, looking confused.

My turn.

I lunge forward, stabbing the one closest to me. The Shield of Khalinx lasts only fifteen seconds from when it's summoned. By my rough estimation, I only have five or six seconds left.

The nearest enemy combatant backs away as he fires, but it's useless. Swinging my blade up, I chop his gun in half. The momentum of the swing continues, and I aim my sword higher. His head leaps from his shoulders as my sword cleaves through his neck. The body crumples on top of the one-armed Ungulithi avatar. My shield powers down.

Just in time.

The one-armed alien on the ground struggles under his fallen companion, unable to lift his weapon to fire. I raise the sword and ram my blade through both their bodies until the trapped Ungulithi ceases to move.

Too easy.

"Ava," Dad calls out.

Footsteps clamor from the stairs I climbed a few minutes ago.

"I overheard them talking," Dad says, as I run over. "Their spawn point is somewhere in the castle."

Two freshly respawned Ungulithi avatars burst onto the parapet, firing their weapons.

Dropping to a crouch, I check on my Shield of Khalinx; still not recharged. No matter. Right now I need to free Dad and plant the bug the rebel tech team had whipped up for me so he can access his inventory.

"Ava, no, don't!"

His shout startles me. There is fear in his voice. I shrink back from him . . . but not before my fingers brush his arm.

The world warps and bends before spinning out of control.

———

I'm flying through a rainbow . . . or is it a tornado made of rainbows? Everything is spinning. The wind batters me, throwing me through the air. A myriad of colors swirls around me.

My mouth is open wide. It feels like I'm screaming, but my voice is lost in the overwhelming cacophony.

I slam into something hard and cold, knocking the wind out of me. The world is stable once again. When I open my eyes, however, everything is spinning and twisting. An uncomfortable sensation rises in my stomach.

Don't be sick, don't be sick, don't be sick.

It may just be my avatar puking, but it would feel like I'm throwing up in real life. And I hate barfing.

After a moment, it registers that I'm not alone. As my vision returns to normal, a huge arena comes into focus. Most of the lighting seems concentrated on me, with more subdued lights illuminating the higher sections. I squint, trying to see how far up the structure goes. I can glimpse movement on the upper levels, though it's unclear how many people are up there.

I rise to a kneeling position. Strange granite creatures glower down at me. These stone etchings stand in sharp contrast against the high metal walls that encircle me.

That's when I hear it. Like a collective voice, booming and melding together. After several syllables, a resounding clap from thousands of hands echoes through the arena.

I have a bad feeling about this.

Somehow, over the noise, I hear a low groan. A few feet away, my dad lies on the ground, stirring, looking around in confusion. He brings his hand up to shield his face from the lights and spots me.

"Ava." The word comes out like an odd croak. "Are you alright?"

"Yeah," I say, realizing my voice doesn't sound much better. "What happened? Where are we?"

He shakes his head. "I tried to warn you. They said something about a proximity spell before you showed up. I don't know where we are."

"You are home." A voice booms.

I groan. *Not* this thing again.

Xynlyc's deep voice translator continues, "Welcome to Aish Kulong!"

Chapter Thirty-Four

The Arena

A small, hovering platform descends toward us.

"This thing again?" Dad grumbles. "Does it ever stop?"

The platform comes to a halt several feet above us. Xynlyc leans over to peer down. Though we are still in The Haven—or some version of it—the Ungulithi isn't wearing a human avatar. Instead, it's an exact match for how it looks in real life. It's hard to read what emotion is playing across its face, but if I were to guess, I'd say the alien is pretty smug right now.

The Ungulithi turns and lifts its arms, its voice booming throughout the arena. The necklace translator device is silent.

"Everyone else is an Ungulithi," my dad says, watching the movement on the upper levels. "Or at least Ungulithi avatars."

It's true. Hundreds or even thousands of Ungulithi fill the stands.

Xynlyc's arms sweep in our direction and the alien finishes its speech, voice rising in a dramatic tone. The audience roars in approval. This is the most emotion I've ever seen the slug display.

"What you wanna bet he just made a passionate plea for our release?" Dad asks.

Xynlyc shifts on the platform to glance down at us once more.

"Before The Haven, there was the Kad'devrn," Xynlyc says. "A galaxy-spanning network for communication. Better than projected images, audio, or even holograms. It changed the way our economy works and how society works—yet we never thought to create games until we met humans: a younger species that entertains and manipulates themselves with empty spectacle and with meaningless achievements."

"This speech have a point?" Dad asks, and mimics checking his wrist for a watch he isn't wearing. "Or is this arena where you bore people to death?"

Xynlyc snorts. "You are eager for death. And I am eager for you to die. All in good time."

Dad sighs, folding his arms across his chest in surly resignation.

"The point is this: The Kad'devrn is not new technology for us. We built it. We've mastered it. We knew removing you"—he points to Dad—"after the Kraken failed to kill you, that someone would pursue. That is why we booby-trapped your father, not the house." It turns its head to glare at me. "We rather hoped it would be you that would come. Your friends are being dealt with as we speak."

My heart skips a beat. He's got to be bluffing. The aliens had lied earlier about repelling the rebels, so they must be lying again.

"But you." Xynlyc points its two right hands at me and my father. "An actual trial by combat awaits you. I have been chosen as your opponent."

The levitating platform descends further, lands in the arena a few feet away, and the Ungulithi slithers off.

"Check access to your inventory," I hiss at Dad, taking a couple of wary steps backward.

An instant later, a belt-fed gun materializes in my dad's hands.

"How . . ." he begins.

"Later," I say, searching through my inventory.

The Ungulithi sneers. At least, it appears to be a sneer. Somebody ought to write a book on how to read alien body language.

I activate a similar belt-fed gun as Dad fires his weapon, wasting no time. His gun roars to life as dozens of bullets fly out of the muzzle in seconds. Bulky weapon pointing at the slug, I fire. Together, we catch the Ungulithi in a deadly crossfire, unleashing hundreds of rounds capable of ripping Xynlyc to shreds before the alien has time to react.

The Ungulithi doesn't flinch. Inches from its body, the bullets appear to magically halt, crumpling to the ground.

Realizing we are achieving nothing, Dad and I cease our onslaught. Dad whips out another weapon, a pulse laser rifle. Without missing a beat, he advances toward the alien, gun blasting.

Time to switch my tactics as well. Raising one arm to the sky, I aim my other arm in the Ungulithi's general direction.

"*Waevayr ufch inthlicaar!*" I say, careful to enunciate each word.

The air above me explodes in brilliant light. A pillar of lightning bolts drops from above into my hand, flowing through me. I stiffen in the grip of the immense power. Electrical shafts thicker than my leg shoot out from the hand aimed at Xynlyc, slamming into the Ungulithi.

The alien vanishes amid a shower of sparks and clouds of smoke.

The lightning retreats, back from where I'd summoned it. Hands on knees, I pant and gulp down a quick health potion. Channeling lighting doesn't do too much damage to the user, but I like a full health bar when I'm in action.

A couple of yards away, Dad is looking at me and grinning.

"What?" I ask, confused.

He shrugs, still smiling. "That's my girl."

The smoke is clearing. A shape emerges from its midst.

"Typical humans," the Ungulithi says, shaking its head. "Shoot first, plan later. Did you think it would be that easy?"

My eyes widen. We have thrown two huge assaults at this thing and it doesn't appear phased or damaged.

Dad throws up his hands. "I thought you were giving us a fighting chance."

The Ungulithi places a hand over its mouth and chuckles like a naughty child concealing something from its parent, an expression of emotion for once.

"That's what you get for assuming," Xynlyc says. "I didn't want you to lose all hope before we began. After all, we are in the Zazaklg Arena. Many historic conflicts have been settled here. Shouldn't let it be too anticlimactic, right?"

Dad is now holding two huge, curved swords. He spins them around in his hands. "Can't be that important; never even heard of this place before."

The alien bares its nasty teeth. "Your body may still be on Earth, but the last thing you'll ever experience is dying like a dog in the realm of the Ungulithi."

Like a snake, the alien slithers toward my father. Xynlyc moves with astonishing speed. Before I can even cry out a warning, the Ungulithi slams into him, sending him careening into the arena's wall. His swords fly out of his hands. I gasp, clutching at my throat. For a second, Dad seems frozen, as if plastered to the wall. Then, with a groan, he collapses to the ground.

The crowd roars.

Turning, the alien regards me. I shift stats in my armor, preparing to be bulldozed like my dad. In the crazy rush that brought me here, my giant broadsword had been lost. The only other blade I can use is my magic samurai sword.

The blade activates and the slug rushes me. No weapons. No apparent armor, though I suspect Xynlyc is wearing some invisible force-field shield. There's no other way that creature could've survived our opening attack.

Sidestepping, I slash down at the blurred Ungulithi's form as it charges by me. It swipes at me with two of its arms as it passes by, the claws on its fingers brushing against my clothing.

Unable to halt its momentum, the alien slams into the arena wall. The bang that follows reverberates throughout. When Xynlyc pushes off, a dent is visible in the structure.

Echoes of cheering and clapping fill the area.

An ugly smile pulls at the corners of Xynlyc's lips. The creature wipes its mouth with the back of a hand, preparing to charge again.

I'm out of ideas. Evasion maneuvers will only work for so long. My sword made direct contact when it ran past, yet there is no evidence of a wound.

We don't have a chance of winning. It appears we're screwed this time.

The alien charges—then is enveloped in an eruption of orange and red flames, halting its assault.

Dad runs by me, lobbing grenades. "Go! I'll try to hold it off!"

The roar from the explosions is so loud, I almost miss what he's saying.

Go? Go where? There's nowhere to go.

Xynlyc rushes forward, laughing as the explosives detonate around it to no effect. The alien collides with Dad, sending him spinning into the air. Without stopping, the creature veers in my direction, reaching me before I can do more than brace for impact.

It's like a truck has hit me. Lights explode in front of my eyes. Airborne, I tumble and then slam into the ground.

Across from me, Dad struggles to his feet, looking very unsteady. I'm faring little better. 20 percent shields, 70 percent health, and 32 percent stamina. I down the needed potions as my vision clears, making note of my dwindling stores. A couple more hits like that, and I'll be out.

The Ungulithi turns, now holding two enormous guns in its hands.

"Time to end this," it says. "Let justice be served."

It aims one weapon at my dad, then one at me, and fires.

Dad disappears from sight as I summon my magic shield. The weapon's beams bounce off the force field. But this will only last fifteen seconds. Now is the time to do something.

Popping a smoke grenade, I lurch toward the creature. The alien disappears in a thick shroud of gray mist. Unfazed, Xynlyc continues firing. The flashes from the gun grow brighter as I approach.

When in range, I press the gem on my blade's pommel and swing the weapon at the Ungulithi, only partially visible through the smoke. My sword connects with the alien's invisible shield and bounces off.

My weapon springs to life. The dragon etched into my blade glows red and surges off. Xynlyc doesn't seem to know what to make of the blazing beast, eyeing the writhing, fiery dragon as it leaps and whirls among us, growing larger and larger. The smoke from the grenade dissipates.

Within seconds, the dragon is over thirty feet tall. Composed of nothing but fire, it flaps its wings, hovering in the air. So powerful is the force of its beating wings, flaming tornadoes spin up in the arena, heading straight for the alien.

For once, Xynlyc seems concerned. The slug retreats, arms upraised in a defensive gesture.

Good.

The dragon rears its head and bellows forth a pillar of fire. Fiery tornadoes, along with the dragon's flaming breath, hit the Ungulithi at once. The alien throws up its hands as if to repel the fire before disappearing in the blaze. For several seconds, a giant bonfire illuminates the arena and the stands. Blazing hot wind slams into me, almost knocking me over.

Please let it be dead, please let it be dead.

Xynlyc isn't dead—far from it. Leaping from the fire, unscathed, the alien is now wielding two swords. Both blades shimmer and pulse with an electrical current.

The noise from the stands is deafening as they cheer their champion.

The Ungulithi claps its blades together, and a giant bolt of electricity arcs from the crossed swords, splitting the dragon in half. The fiery beast tosses its head and roars as its blazing body is extinguished. In seconds, all that remains is ash and smoke.

My heart sinks. Breathing hard, it's as if all the strength is draining from me, replaced with nothing but aches and pains.

The list of options available to me grows short.

"I admit, that one took me by surprise," the Ungulithi says, brushing its sleeve. "I'd forgotten we'd programmed that weapon into The Haven. Provides quite the show."

Dad walks to my side. "I thought it was cool."

"Yeah, and useless," I grumble.

The Ungulithi smirks before launching another attack. I barely have time to bring up my blade in a blocking motion when Xynlyc's swords clash with mine. My arms tremble under the force of the blow.

In hand-to-hand combat, the alien has the advantage. It parries my blade and Dad's, coming back with its own furious counterattacks. Xynlyc also knows how to use its extra pair of limbs. I block a slash at my head, only to have pain explode in my jaw from a punch from one of the Ungulithi's extra limbs, knocking me off balance.

Dad and I are slowing our attacks, hard-pressed to defend ourselves. My armor stats are depleting, leaving me with two health potions and only a handful of stamina potions. Beside me, Dad is panting; it's been a while since he's taken a potion.

"Here, take one of mine." I select a health potion from my inventory and offer it to him.

He sidesteps a vertical slash, hopping behind the alien, and stabs. The blade bounces off the alien's shield. Dad is overbalanced and almost face-plants. He catches himself and jumps back in time to avoid the Ungulithi's counterattack. He snaps a glance at what I'm offering and shakes his head.

"Keep it, sweetie," he says.

I leap at the Ungulithi, taking it off guard, and slam into its shield, almost causing it to fall on its face. Xynlyc flails but stays upright. The alien advances with a new flurry of attacks, backing me against the wall.

Dad charges in, forcing the Ungulithi to divide its attention between two opponents once more, giving me a chance to catch my breath.

"I've got more." No need clarifying I have only one more. "Take it. You need it."

Dad gives a gruff laugh. "I'm good. I could do this all day!"

The longer this fight goes, the harder it gets to dodge and block. Attack is no longer on my mind. I don't care about winning or losing. I just want to survive.

With a violent screech of metal on metal, I lock blades with the alien. Xynlyc strains to break the lock, beads of sweat standing out on the alien's rough-textured skin. The Ungulithi glares into my eyes, with another rare display of emotion. Anger, determination, and hate swirl in all four of the orbs in that face.

Tension tugs at my hands and wrists as the alien attempts to wrench my weapons from me. Then the pressure vanishes. I stumble, surprised. The Ungulithi rears back and headbutts me. The blow sends shockwaves through my entire body, followed by pain exploding in my head.

Next thing I know, I'm gawking up at Xynlyc from the ground. The Ungulithi's lips are moving, but I can't hear anything over the pounding in my ears.

My sword is gone. Where'd it go? The world lurches.

Health potion . . . I need . . . potion.

Trying to force my thoughts into some kind of coherence, I glance at my health bar. It's at 9 percent. I activate my inventory menu.

The alien raises its swords, the tips of both weapons hovering over my chest.

I grab my last two health potions.

The Ungulithi's swords plunge to my torso. Something streaks across my vision, inches from my nose. White light blinds me, fiery sparks exploding into my face, singeing my skin.

I'm not dead, is my first thought. At least, there wouldn't be this much pain if I were dead. Dad crouches over me, weapon poised over my chest, blocking the Ungulithi's blades from stabbing me. The crowd is booing us.

"This is between you and me," Dad growls at the alien, sweat pouring down his brow. "Or does the Ungulithi believe it is brave to fight from behind the safety of their shields?"

"You think to antagonize me?" Xynlyc snorts. "This isn't about honor."

The tips of Xynlyc's weapons tremble with the alien's effort, hovering inches from my heart. With a roar, Dad throws himself against the Ungulithi. Their swords disengage. They hack and slash at each other. Dad inches the fight away, allowing me a moment to breathe.

We can't keep going like this. I down the last of my health potions. My pain fades, and that wonderful sense of renewed life returns to me. I scan the ground for my sword, spotting it several feet away.

A cry of agony snaps my attention from my weapon. Dad collapses to his knees, gripping his sword arm, the blade falling from his limp hand. Much of his body is covered in ugly red slashes. Blood pours from a particularly nasty gash on his arm. He moves to grab his fallen sword. The Ungulithi slithers over it, preventing Dad from grabbing it. The audience booms its delight.

A shiver rushes through my body. My weapon is in one direction, Dad in the other, too injured to move or defend himself. If I run for one, there won't be time to reach the other.

I sprint for my dad.

"Ava!"

Everything goes quiet, except for Dad's voice as it echoes in the arena. It's like the crowd in the stadium has been muted. He holds up his hand, motioning me to stop. I stand still in utter bewilderment.

Without breaking his glare from the Ungulithi, he says to me. "Stop. It's okay."

Now I'm even more confused. "Um, don't know if you've noticed, but it's far from okay."

"Ava, don't," he says, struggling to catch his breath. "Just . . . you find a way out. I won't let you put yourself in further danger because of me."

He breaks eye contact with the alien, holding me in his gaze. Tears shimmer in his eyes. "One of the greatest things I ever did was to give you life. Don't throw that life away. I love you."

Xynlyc spits and laughs, looking up into the stands as if in disbelief.

Tears streak my face. *He wants me to let him die?* My brain screams for me to move, to do something. With shimmering eyes, Dad's expression pleads with me to stay where I am.

The Ungulithi raises its blade.

My lips part, a soundless scream. I can't stand by and allow Xynlyc to kill my father.

I'm in the air.

"Ava! No!"

Slamming into the slug, I only knock it slightly off balance. All my body weight had been thrown against Xynlyc and it hardly affected the alien.

The Ungulithi turns, wearing a strange expression. Anger? Bemusement? Out of nowhere, one of its fists lands a savage blow on my jaw. A crack like lightning echoes in my ears. Next thing I know, I'm flat on the ground.

"Ava!" Dad screams.

I try to push off the ground, but my arms collapse as if they are nothing more than wet noodles.

"Hey, you disgusting slug," Dad says, struggling vainly to rise. "You think you're so great, beating on a little girl from behind your shield? Coward!"

Ignoring my father's taunts, the alien slithers over to me. I stand, knees knocking, and check my health bar. Seventy-two percent full. Well, it's something; got to make it last.

The Ungulithi comes swinging all four of its limbs at me. Xynlyc isn't even bothering to use its sword on me. I dodge the first blow but feel an explosion of pain in my ribs. Hissing in agony, I block a fist to my face, only to have another sink into my gut. I double over, gasping for air.

I don't stand a chance. Though I have decent XP in hand-to-hand combat, no one would mistake me for a martial artist. Time seems to stretch to infinity as a hail of violent blows pummels my body. Pain blends into pain.

My health bar declines with each blow.

40 percent . . .37 percent . . . 34 percent.

I struggle to see as my eyes swell. My legs get shakier as I grow weaker.

The blows stop. Staggering, I raise my sagging head. The Ungulithi is examining me with its arms across its chest, like an artist evaluating their latest handiwork.

My knees buckle. Xynlyc lashes out, snagging two fistfuls of my hair and holding me suspended off the ground. Didn't think I could experience additional pain. My scalp feels as if it's on fire.

17 percent.

The alien lifts me to eye level, smirking. Somewhere in the background, my dad is shouting something, but the words are indiscernible. And at this moment, I don't care.

Sorry, Dad . . . we tried.

It's the end. I can't do it anymore.

"You should've just stayed home and played hero in The Haven," the Ungulithi says. "At least in the land of make-believe, you could've won. You might have lived."

Chapter Thirty-Five

Turning Tides

I just want the alien to end it. Mustering the last of my remaining strength, I spit out the blood pooling in my mouth. It hits the Ungulithi's face with a splat. My last act of defiance. I brace for the alien's reaction.

The expected attack never materializes. Instead, Xynlyc blinks, as if surprised, then gives me a peculiar glance. The alien stares at me for so long, I wonder if there's been a glitch.

Xynlyc turns from me, looking up at the stands with an unreadable expression.

Why is Xynlyc acting so weird? Why doesn't it just finish me?

"Ava!"

Xynlyc's painful grip on my hair is unchanged, so I have to glance at my dad out of the corner of my eye.

"Ava, his face! Something's wrong."

Dad is just off enough in my periphery that I can't read his expression, but his voice is strained, and he's gesturing. Looking back at Xynlyc's face, it takes my fatigued and injured brain a few seconds to realize what my dad means.

The alien's shield did not prevent my glob of spit and blood from hitting the slug's skin. I stare in shock as the disgusting mix of fluids runs down the creature's face.

Something has changed.

I ram my foot into what is hopefully the alien's midriff. The creature releases me, doubling over from the pain. Eyes wide, I continue to gape, not quite believing it.

I don't know how or why, but the Ungulithi no longer has a shield.

For the first time, I have a fighting chance.

However, due to game mechanics, no surge or renewed energy flows through me. I'm only at 17 percent health. The alien's now visible health bar shows it holding strong at 98 percent. My kick to Xynlyc's gut had hurt it but came nowhere near to incapacitating the monster.

At least, that's all according to the stats. Even with my low health, a renewed sense of hope rises within me. Meanwhile, the Ungulithi, for the first time, is acting unsure. Xynlyc continues to glance into the stands.

Not wanting to lose precious time, I take advantage of my enemy's confusion and attack with one of my go-to, close-range combos—a hard right to the jaw, throwing my opponent off balance, then shifting into a reverse roundhouse to the left—his momentum colliding with mine for maximum effect.

The Ungulithi grunts with each impact before collapsing to the ground.

94 percent vs. 17 percent

"Yeah, Ava!" Dad screams. "That's your move! That's how you do it!"

I grin and flip the hair out of my eyes. Pain shoots down my neck from the sudden movement.

Reminder: don't get cocky. You're still very low on health.

Grimacing, I make my way to the prone Ungulithi. The alien turns over, raising itself up from the ground.

"Oh, I think not," I say and kick the Ungulithi across the face. Droplets of spittle and blood spray from its mouth, speckling the dirt. The alien's arms give out and Xynlyc again collapses.

As I approach for my next attack, the alien rolls over, flailing its arms at me. I dance around its spindly limbs, landing savage kicks where possible. A more elegant solution to beating my enemies is preferable, but repeated brute force will do in a pinch.

86 percent vs. 17 percent.

One of Xynlyc's hands grips my ankle, catching me mid-kick. Growling, the Ungulithi heaves me off my feet, and I sprawl onto my back.

"You think you have a chance now?" The Ungulithi's tone is mocking. Xynlyc rises and continues. "I don't need a shield to defeat you. I am your master. You will learn your place."

"I don't know, man," my dad says. "You're kinda losing right now."

The stands are dead quiet and still. Dad's and Xynlyc's voices are clear, and their words easy to understand.

The alien ignores him and wipes blood from its mouth with the back of its hand. "I will not permit you to win."

I drop into a fight stance. "My fate is no longer up to you."

I motion for the alien to make its move. The Ungulithi's face contorts with rage and the slug launches itself at me.

I dive to the side, and Xynlyc sails past me. Despite my dodge, the creature's hand snags my clothing. Yanked off my feet, I'm carried off by the slug's momentum. My shirt tears, but the Ungulithi hurls me through the air and I hit the ground hard, rolling to a stop.

86 percent vs. 15 percent.

I pound my fist in frustration. I can't allow my health to drop any further. Especially now, not when I have a chance.

Something in the dirt glints a few feet from my face. My sword. But the Ungulithi is close as well, coming at me fast.

On my hands and knees, I lurch for my fallen weapon, angling away from the alien. Off to the side, Xynlyc must've figured out what I was doing. The slug follows my example, first leaping and then slithering to my blade.

Both our hands are inches from the weapon. Grimacing, I strain, stretching so much it feels as if my skin will rip.

My hand closes over the sword's grip. Rolling to my side, I slash at my grasping foe. Xynlyc sees my attack and crosses its arms in front of its body. The blade slices into the alien's limbs, stopping well short of inflicting a mortal wound. But it still causes damage.

77 percent vs. 15 percent.

The Ungulithi howls in pain and attempts to grab my weapon. Two of its hands close over the blade. I rise to a standing position and yank down, slicing into the creature's palms. Bellowing, the alien releases my sword.

That's my opening.

My sword is already poised. I lunge and shove the blade into the alien's gut as easily as if stabbing a loaf of bread. The Ungulithi gasps. All four of its hands grasp my wrists, preventing me from shoving the sword deeper. Xynlyc squeezes and my fingers release the weapon. With a roar, the alien flings me away, still strong. I maneuver my fall and use my momentum to roll onto my feet.

55 percent vs 15 percent.

Wincing, the Ungulithi pulls my sword from its gut. A splash of thick, translucent fluid spills from its wound. Using my weapon as an improvised cane of sorts, the alien places three of its hands across the gash, attempting to staunch the bleeding. Xynlyc must not have any health potions either. The slug, in its arrogance, assumed it wouldn't need any.

"Had enough?" I call out, advancing toward the creature.

The alien draws itself up as best it can and spits at me. "This is far from over. You've landed some lucky hits, but you can't hope to win. Continuing to resist is futile."

"We'll see about that," I mutter.

I charge. Bringing up my sword, the alien aims a clumsy swipe at me. It's too easy to duck the awkward swipe. Using my blade for an attack rather than a crutch causes the Ungulithi to become unbalanced. I leap up and grasp the creature's head with both hands. I drop to the ground. There is a crack of snapping bones as the Ungulithi's head jerks downward. The body flips over me, smashing into the dirt, my blade dropping from the alien's limp hand. Sweeping my leg over the dazed slug's chest, I pin its arms down with my legs. I lift both my fists and slam them into its face.

"How about now?" I yell, throwing punch after punch. "You still think you can win?"

My hands are slick with translucent blood. The alien's face bruises and swells. Before, the Ungulithi would've had no problem shoving me off. But at 41 percent, Xynlyc is less aggressive.

Unrelenting, I unleash blow after blow upon its head. *This one is for Sofia. For Riley. For making my Mom drink and give up. For taking my Dad away. And for putting me through all this.*

Something bumps my leg. Pausing my attack, I see one of Xynlyc's lower left arms stretching to acquire the sword that it had dropped earlier.

"I don't think so." I smash my fist into the alien's eye socket, spring off its body, and reach for my blade. The alien gives a gargled shriek and rolls onto its stomach, fumbling for my legs.

I scoop my sword from the ground. In desperation, the creature launches itself at me. Trying to prepare for the incoming alien, I stumble and fall on my back, keeping a hold of my blade. The flailing Ungulithi impales itself on my weapon. A strangled cry of pain escapes its lips as the sword slides into its chest. The tip bursts out of its back in a spray of goopy blood. Two of the alien's hands grab for the blade while the other two claw at the hole in its back.

15 percent vs 15 percent.

"Who's got a fighting chance now, slug?" I say. The Ungulithi doesn't register me, all four eyes wide and unfocused, face twitching.

Holding the weight of the alien on my sword is too much. The weapon's grip is wrenched from my hands as the Ungulithi rolls onto its back, a choked moan escaping its lips. I rise, keeping a wary eye on my opponent. I will not underestimate this thing as it did me.

For a moment it lies there, its arms waving as if it's trying to push something or someone aside. Despite everything, I somehow feel a minuscule amount of pity for it.

I should put it out of its misery.

I reach for my sword. With surprising speed, one of its limbs whips out, catching me in the chest. I stumble back, cursing. Hadn't I just determined not to underestimate it? What fleeting sympathy I had for the alien is extinguished, replaced by a steely determination.

The Ungulithi rises to a half-sitting, half-kneeling position. Or at least, its equivalent to kneeling.

"You think you can leave?" Gooey blood spills out of its mouth when it speaks. "You think we're done with you? Earth is too valuable to be placed in the hands of the likes of you."

"I don't want the Earth," I say. "I only want my family back."

The alien's laugh is husky and strained. "So shortsighted. So human."

The Ungulithi crawls toward me. Xynlyc grunts and groans with every move, panting from its efforts. I stand my ground and let it come.

"And that," Xynlyc says. "Is why you'll lose. Not just your life. Not just your family. Everything!"

It reaches for me. I brace, about to strike.

The alien freezes, a shocked expression on its face.

"No," the slug whispers, looking up into the stands. "No. Please. I can do this."

I blink in confusion and follow its gaze. All around the stadium, small red lights appear. The more that light up, the more desperate the Ungulithi's pleas become.

"I can do this," Xynlyc shouts in a hoarse voice. "You've seen what they're like. You've seen how easy they are to control. Let me finish this!"

Fear has taken over Xynlyc. In the alien's panic, it must've forgotten the translator is on.

Why is it panicking?

Again, blame it on the fatigue and pain; it takes my poor brain a moment to process the fact that the Ungulithi's health bar is ticking down.

14 percent . . .13 percent.

"You saw what we can do with only a handful of us," the Ungulithi pleads. "Let me do this!"

More red lights appear in the stadium. The creature bellows, resuming its clawing progress toward me, desperation and murder shining in its eyes.

3 percent . . . 2 percent . . .1 percent.

The Ungulithi flings out one of its limbs to sweep my legs out from under me. The only problem is that the alien's hand is still a good two or three feet from reaching me.

The creature's arms buckle from under it. Sinking to the ground, the Ungulithi gasps for air. A low gurgle bubbles up from Xynlyc's throat. The creature's breath comes in shorter and shorter sighs. Its body shudders. The irises of its eyes widen, and with a long, throaty sigh, my opponent lies still.

For a moment, I stare in open-mouthed disbelief. A part of me wants to prod the body and see if Xynlyc responds. But something eerie about the Ungulithi's position and wide, glassy eyes stops me from approaching. Never have death graphics been so crisp or realistic.

I shake my head, refocusing. *You're still in their domain. Be ready for anything.*

Dad, several yards away, gives me an expression mixed between relief and pride. I approach him, warily examining the environment, trying to foresee what may happen next.

Crimson lights fill the stadium, casting a faint scarlet haze into the arena. Xynlyc acted like the crowd was the reason his health dropped to zero. Could the red lights have something to do with it?

Without warning, all goes black. The red lights disappear. The stadium and the arena vanish. I freeze, disoriented.

"Ava," Dad says. "Where are you? Are you okay?"

"I'm fine."

I raise a hand to my face. Nothing. It is perfectly dark. Everything is quiet. The only sound I hear is my shaky breathing.

A searchlight pierces the black, shining on me. I block my eyes from the light, attempting to detect if anything is moving to attack me. Another spotlight illuminates my father.

A booming voice not unlike Xynlyc's starts talking. Except it is speaking in its alien language. I can't understand a word it's saying.

The alien's voice reverberates, lasting for what seems like several minutes. Dad and I exchange glances, but otherwise don't move or respond.

Then everything spins.

———

I sit up, gasping. My head is pounding. I'm getting sick of everything always spinning like that.

A familiar voice beside me groans. Dad stiffly gets out of the plug-in pod, stretching his muscles. We are back in the plug-in room. We are back in our actual bodies again.

He walks around the pod, then stops when he sees me on the floor grinning up at him. A relieved smile plays across his face.

"How are ya?" he asks, coming alongside me.

I roll my neck, testing mobility. "Alright, I think. Feels like I've been fighting in an arena."

Dad chuckles and gestures to the other pod in the room. "You should see the other guy."

In the pod sits Xynlyc's limp body, slack-jawed, a string of saliva hanging from its mouth. The alien is a mirror image of its avatar, even in death. Shuddering, I look away.

"You did good today," Dad says, placing a hand on my shoulder.

I shrug, unsure what to say.

His smile softens. "Thank you. If it weren't for you, I wouldn't be here. Because of you, I'm back. I can go home now."

Outside the room, the sounds of fighting continue, though faint, not as frantic as earlier. I lean against Dad, my head against his shoulder. He squeezes my hand. Tears well up in my eyes, threatening to spill down my face.

I don't know what the result of the battle will be. Who knows what comes next? Yet, none of that matters at this moment.

I have my dad back.

Chapter Thirty-Six

The Unknown

"**S**top here."

The MonoPod comes to a screeching halt. Cringing against the sound, I wonder if bringing up transportation repairs to the next community meeting would be a good idea. After a moment's consideration I decide against it. The world is descending into chaos; repairs like that are likely far down a very long list.

The exit door slides open. It's still dark outside; I had risen early this morning to beat the sun. A cool breeze wafts over me. I inhale, relishing the smell of the trees, grass, and dirt. Coming out here at least once a week has been a constant since Dad and I arrived back in our community a couple of months ago. With all the rapid changes happening, it's become vital to set a time to get outside, break away, and unplug.

I slide out of the Pod and army crawl across the damp grass. It isn't the most dignified thing in the world, but my favorite tree is only a few yards away. Once there, I can lean against it, shade myself from the sun as soon as it rises, relax, and let my mind wander.

It only takes me two minutes to reach it, a full thirty seconds less than last time. *Progress.*

Up against the tree, I shiver, looking forward to the warmth the sunrise would provide. I yawn and stretch. I take a while to wake up sometimes.

It's good to start the day away from everyone, with their constant fears and questions. Not that they're coming to me with their problems; Dad has become something of a reluctant leader of our community since his return. This means he's always stressed out, and I get secondhand stressed.

The joys of being a sensitive soul.

It's funny how quickly opinions can change, Dad going from traitor to hero. I can still picture my mom's half-drunken face when Dad and I arrived home. At first, my parents stared at each other in shock. Then, as if on cue, they broke down at the same time and sobbed in each other's arms. My sisters almost bowled him over when they spied him. It was almost impossible to remove them from the room so that our parents could have a moment. It shocked Dad when he saw their unhealthy condition. After that, he was quiet the rest of the evening, wearing a sad expression.

Overhead, a bird sings out in the tree. I search the branches, trying to find the chirpy little guy. There's just enough gray light in the sky, enough to illuminate a small nest, almost hidden by a cluster of inter-connecting branches. A tiny bird perches at the edge of its home, happily twitching and whistling. It had taken me sixteen years before hearing an actual bird song.

That's . . . sad.

The bird takes off, and I follow its flight until it disappears from sight. Pink and orange slivers of dawn streak through the sky. I settle back against my tree. It's not the coziest seat in the world, but it's more pleasant than the seats at the community meetings. Of course, that's one complaint about those tedious gatherings that doesn't apply to me, since my seat goes wherever I go.

I check the time. Today's meeting will start before I plan on heading back. It's nice to have an excuse to miss it. Community assemblies are an almost daily event now with the collapse of the Ungulithi rule. Turned out Morgan Sheffy had been organizing a global move against the aliens. The intel Dad had passed on through me had been the final piece the rebels needed. Though absent their leader, the rebellion had hit Ungulithi targets worldwide, both inside and outside The Haven, the day of my rescue. Oddly enough, there hadn't been many aliens on the planet. All were hunted down, and killed or captured, ending the Ungulithi occupation of the Earth in a matter of weeks.

I shake my head, the old frustration surging within me. What does it say about our ancestors, letting a handful of aliens take over the world? Especially when they could be gotten rid of with such relative ease.

Although the downside is the aliens left behind a huge power void. Their absence also disrupted our way of life. No more food deliveries. The Haven had also become very buggy and unreliable. Many people could not work their jobs in The Haven and weren't sure what to do.

"Everyone is confused and scared," Dad told me one evening as we sat and read. We've been reading a lot since The Haven is glitching more and more.

"Everything the Ungulithi did was connected to The Haven," he continued. "Without them to keep things going, it's affecting communication, our economy, food, healthcare—everything. Some people don't even have access to The Haven anymore, and those that do have very restricted access."

People like Ji Yeon. I lost contact with her a few days after Dad and I returned. Fortunately, we'd been able to speak before losing touch.

She hugged me tight as we lingered on a crowded sidewalk, avatars pushing past us. "I'm so glad you made it. It's been a crazy few days!"

"I never doubted you for a minute." Lucas lightly punched my arm.

I smile at the memory. All three of us had stood together in one of the communal areas of The Haven, a literal crossroad to several worlds and games. It resembled a city park, but instead of being surrounded by skyscrapers, dozens of open portals encircled us, each leading to a different section of The Haven.

"Well," I said as humbly as possible, "luck had a lot to do with it too."

Ji Yeon agreed. "I wonder why they let you leave, though. The ones in the stadium."

"That was the agreement." Lucas gestured as if it was obvious. "You bested their fighter, and the deal was you go home if you did."

I shook my head. "But I didn't beat him. I almost did, but then he started dying on his own. I think the Ungulithi in the stadium did that."

Ji Yeon looked perplexed. "I still don't get why they would do that. Or why they would honor their agreement in the first place? The whole thing is very odd."

"They're aliens, right?" I said. "They have an alien way of doing things."

"But that doesn't explain what they were doing here." A distant look came to Ji Yeon's eyes as if she was looking beyond our environment for answers. "It doesn't explain how there were so few of them, or how so few controlled the entire globe. It also doesn't account for why they haven't come back yet."

Lucas looked from me to Ji Yeon as if unable to believe what he was hearing. "One: they were here for our resources. Two: they arrived, did a shock and awe campaign, and cowed everyone into doing what they were told. Three: it's only been a few days. Space is vast. Their tech isn't *that* advanced."

Ji Yeon stamped her foot in irritation. "Yes, I know. But *what* resources were they taking? If they were taking anything. And you don't just conquer the world by showing off or whatever. As for three . . ." She paused before sighing. "Okay, I'll give you three."

"Who cares?" I said, impatient to move on from this topic. "I'm ready to go to Starlight Journey and blow up some aliens."

Lucas cocked an eyebrow. "Haven't you had enough of that?"

"This go-around I'm not risking my neck."

Now almost none of the games in The Haven are working. As we lose contact with other parts of the world, and my interactions in the digital realm are marred by game-breaking bugs, I spend less time in The Haven. The weird thing is, at first it had been hard. After spending only a couple of hours there—as opposed to six or seven hours like in the past—I'd felt off. Jumpy and irritable, as if something was wrong and I couldn't fix it. Being outside helps.

The sole thing I hadn't told my friends was of my fight with The Named and his death. I haven't even mentioned it to my dad. Sometimes I replay the altercation in my head, searching to see if events could've gone differently. Then, at other times, I shove the memory down deep, refusing to acknowledge it happened, despite it weighing in the back of my mind.

The sky is transforming. Warm orange and yellow hues push the chilly, gray monotony of the night heavens away. Light rays spread their calming and beautiful impact on everything they touch.

My breathing slows. I don't know what tomorrow holds, but right now it's time to enjoy this moment. The sun crests the horizon. The first rays of the day cover me, bringing warmth like a blanket. Although I had taken many trips to this spot before, this is my first time coming at dawn.

Around me, the birds sing, the wind rustles through the tall grass, and crickets chirp. Nature continues as it ever does, unaware and uncaring of me and my problems.

I let out a contented sigh and watch my first sunrise.

Ava will return in Book 2 of The Haven Trilogy.

About the Author

Photo credit: J Means Photography, https://meansimages.mypixieset.com

J.Z. Pitts' love of reading and writing began at age twelve. Inspired by his favorite books, he began writing stories of his own.

A brief stint working for a high school newspaper continued to hone his skills. He wrote everything from news copy, and opinion pieces, to book, and movie reviews. His short stories include Two Graves, In The Pale Blue Light, My Terms, and, A Mother's Love.

For exclusive updates, behind-the-scenes info, and maybe the occasional contest or giveaway, sign up for the author's mailing list by copying and pasting this link subscribepage.io/JHkkkO into your browser and following the prompts.

If you wish to follow the author on his socials, they are listed below:

https://www.facebook.com/jzpitts

https://www.instagram.com/jz.pitts/

https://twitter.com/jzpitts